*For my children, Zadie, Ben, Luke,*
*and my grandchildren, Rhia, Georgie, Kit, Harv.*

*And in memory of my dear grandparents,*
*Uncle T and Aunt Ida,*
*both of whom I still miss every single day.*

# The Day I Fell Off My Island

## Yvonne Bailey-Smith

Myriad Editions
An imprint of New Internationalist Publications
The Old Music Hall, 106–108 Cowley Rd,
Oxford OX41JE
www.myriadeditions.com

First published in 2021 by Myriad Editions
This Myriad paperback published in 2021
First printing
1 3 5 7 9 10 8 6 4 2

A CIP catalogue record for this book
is available from the British Library

ISBN (paperback): 978-1-8383860-4-7
ISBN (ebook): 978-1-912408-96-2

Designed and typeset in Adobe Caslon Pro
by Studio 26, www.insidestudio26.com

Printed and bound in Great Britain
by Clays Ltd, Elcograf S.p.A

# Part One

# Chapter 1

I finally learnt to ride a bicycle on my twenty-first birthday. It was an ambition I'd held from the age of thirteen, when I watched in awe and with a sense of envy as my teenage half-brothers, shirts open, rode their bicycles fast and fearlessly along the chalky roads surrounding my father's village. I admired their freedom and was determined to experience that feeling for myself. The time came when, tired of being just a spectator, I persuaded Errol, one of the more amenable of my half-brothers, to give me a turn. He was quick to hand over his bike. He then watched with a bemused expression as I made several attempts to climb on to the very tall machine. The bicycle was old and temperamental and my attempts to make it move soon sent me crashing into a clump of stinging nettles. When I looked up, a crowd of village boys had gathered. Most were howling with laughter, except one very tall, black-skinned boy, who seemed intent on seeing what I was wearing under my skirt, which had hiked itself way too far above my knees. My shame was complete.

Yet now, when I hop effortlessly on to my bicycle, I wonder why it took me so long to learn what turned out to be such a simple skill. Then I remind myself of the saying 'nothing happens before its time.'

. . .

My life began on a typically hot day in August 1955, on the Caribbean island of Jamaica, where I was born to one Violet Pearl James. Violet was thirteen-and-a-half years old when Miss Melba – mother to sixteen, grandmother to many more, and the unofficial midwife of the entire district – delivered her own daughter of her first child. In time she would deliver my mother of a further three children: a girl named Patricia, and two boys, Clifton and Sonny. It was my Grandma Melba who told me the story of my birth, although she hadn't been able to recall the exact date. However, she was certain that I was born on a Sunday and that my birth was registered some weeks later by her son Cleveland. My Uncle Cleveland was known for his love of the strong white rum produced on the island. Grandma Melba used to say, 'When him tek de rum, it mek him behave like a fool-fool man.' And, according to her, it was because he was drunk that he managed to lose the scrap of paper on which my name had been written, which is how I came to be registered with the name Erna, instead of *Irma*.

Cleveland had staggered back to the house and handed Grandma Melba the long strip of off-white paper with its columns completed in black ink in the most stylish handwriting.

'I beg you read out everyting it seh on de certificate,' Grandma urged him.

To my Grandma, words on paper were just a jumble of confusion. She had never entered a schoolhouse and, as far as she was concerned, she learnt everything she needed to learn from 'de fullness of de good Lord's book,' which she would say was 'a forever learning someting.' Her Bible learning came from her infrequent visits to the village church, and, as soon as I was old enough to read, from me. Otherwise, she felt proud of what she knew. She had learnt plenty about the land, how to look after my grandfather, their children and grandchildren, and how to help young women birth their babies safely. And now her daughter had left her to look after her baby while she went to work for a couple that lived in another village many miles away.

Grandma Melba nodded along as Cleveland read from the birth certificate:

'Date of birth, Twenty-six of August 1955.'

'Is dat a Sunday?'

'Yes, Miss Melba, it's a Sunday.'

'Good! Me glad si yuh get dat right, at least, because a Sunday de chile born.'

Cleveland continued, 'Mother's name: Violet Pearl James. Father's name... Dem just put a line through this box, Miss Melba. You didn't tell me a name to give dem.'

If he'd hoped that Grandma Melba would tell him who the father of his sister's child was, her silence left him unenlightened.

'Place of birth, Rose Hill District.'

Cleveland had taken his time to get to my name, as Grandma Melba later told me: 'Mi could tell him figet someting, but because of de rum inside him, him nuh did know what him figet!'

'Child's name... Erna Annette Mullings.'

'Erna? What kind a name dat? Nuh, *Irma* Annette Mullings mi did tell yuh seh de chile name should be! Yuh see how de rum a mash up yuh head, Cleveland? Yuh better pray to God fi help yuh before yuh dead!'

But Grandma knew there was no changing the name. She had registered enough babies to know that once a name was recorded in that great big book that was it. So, Erna I became.

# Chapter 2

Fewer than a hundred people lived in my village and nearly all of them were related to my grandparents in some way. There were brothers and sisters, others related by marriage, and cousins several times removed. Many were old or middle-aged, but there were still plenty of children back then. Later on, it was as if the Pied Piper had arrived one day and persuaded an entire generation of young women and men to leave the village and follow him to a land of no return.

There were around thirty houses scattered over several acres of land, all brightly painted in an array of greens, oranges and sea blues. Many of them were set off with flowerbeds edged with whitewashed stones. As a child, I thought our house was huge – it had four similarly proportioned rooms – and I believed it to be one of the prettiest in the village. The floor of my grandparents' room was tiled in red-and-white Spanish tiles, a legacy of the Spanish colonisation of the island in the sixteenth century. The rest of the house, including the room I shared with my sister and two brothers, had floorboards made from cedar wood. One of my jobs was to apply copious amounts of Cardinal polish to the floors on a daily basis, which kept them gleaming like mirrors. There were wide gaps between the boards in our room, which made it easy for all manner of small creatures to crawl in. I often saw large scorpions, tails curled over their backs, hovering in corners, or many-legged centipedes making their way to some hiding place. Most nights I laid in bed and watched as sugar lizards raced each other up and down the walls and across the ceiling.

The third room, which was called the 'Hall', had multiple uses. It housed an etched-glass cabinet decorated with flowers. Inside were dozens of pretty glasses, china plates, bowls, cups and saucers. There was a black case with blue velvet lining containing a cutlery set with creamy bone handles. On the underside of the box, it said *Made in Sheffield*.

When I asked Grandma where Sheffield was, she sucked her teeth and waved me away. 'Cho, chile, dat is a question fi yuh Grandfada. Yuh well know seh me nuh school good. Anyway,' she continued, 'de tings belong to yuh mada. She did seh she a collect tings for har bottom drawer, but mi nuh know wah she did mean by dat and, as yuh can si, de tings dem still deya a ram up de place.'

The Hall was where my grandparents sometimes met with visitors. On Sundays we would all eat around the table there. It was also the room where visiting relatives slept on a double bed, the mattress of which remained encased in thick see-through plastic. I never understood how it was possible for anyone to sleep well on that bed.

The mattress of the iron-framed bed I shared with my brothers and sister had more broken coils than it had intact ones and all three of them wet the bed on a nightly basis. This meant that finding a spot to sleep on that was neither wet nor sharp was almost impossible. Sometimes, I would escape from our urine-soaked bed and creep into the Hall, where I'd climb on to the big high mattress, but it wouldn't be long before I'd wake to the smell of heated plastic, covered in sweat. In the end, I usually decided that I'd rather put up with the smell of urine and the broken springs.

The fourth room, which was used as a kitchen, had been added later. It had a concrete floor and, like the other three rooms, a door that led outside. The single window was covered over with wire mesh, preventing insects from entering at night. A two-burner paraffin stove took pride of place, and next to it a long, waist-high concrete shelf, which allowed the dish washing to be done standing up, rather than having to bend down to a bowl on the floor. There was another long shelf for the pots, pans and enamel plates, bowls and mugs. Fresh vegetables and fruit were kept in large baskets on the floor, and a wooden cupboard contained dried foods and everything else that was needed. The kitchen door was always kept open when my grandparents were cooking. This helped to dissipate the intense heat that would quickly build up inside, but also allowed the cooking aromas to escape the room. The smells that emanated often attracted my Great-Uncle Dummy – just before the meal was ready, he'd appear, sit himself down on the jutting foundation wall and wait. That was the way Great-Uncle Dummy fed himself most days; when he wasn't waiting outside our kitchen he was guaranteed to be found waiting outside some other relative's kitchen. His saving grace was that he usually brought freshly picked coconuts with him – his way of contributing to the meal – and often did odd jobs around the place after he'd been fed.

Growing up in our big house, we children knew we were lucky. For one thing, our grandparents really loved us, unlike our friend Marva and her little brother, Henry. Their grandmother, Miss Rose, didn't talk much but she delighted in beating them. Grandma Melba, on the other hand, was a gentle soul. She even had special names for each one of us. Mine was 'pretty gal'.

'Pretty gal, come over here and sit wit yuh old grandmada a while,' Grandma Melba would call out to me. 'But mi beg yuh, nuh touch mi foot bottom!' I loved tickling the bottom of her feet – the slightest touch would send her into fits of hysterical laughter. But, because I didn't know when to stop, her laughter would often turn to tears, and then crossness. 'Chile! Stop now!' she would cry. And when I didn't stop she would try whatever flattery came into her head in an attempt to stop me. 'Erna, yuh pretty so and yuh big eyes dem jus full of questions,' she told me one day, through her laughter and tears. When that didn't get me to stop, she added crossly, 'Erna! Yuh face shape jus like one a dem blow-up balloon!' Later that day I stared at myself in a piece of broken mirror I found lying in the yard, but I could find neither the question in my eyes, nor the balloon shape of my face. But Grandma Melba was very wise, so I decided that if that was what she saw in my face, then that must be what was there.

Patricia was given the slightly unfortunate name of 'dry head', because it didn't matter what oils or potions Grandma rubbed into her scalp, her hair refused to grow more than a few inches. But she came in for extra praise from both our grandparents because she would do all sorts of things that the rest of us children weren't interested in. She enjoyed helping around the home, and would sit over a basin of clothes and try to wash them – even though she was this really small, skinny child. There was only one problem with Patricia: she was stubborn. She never came when called, but always some time later, when she'd appear with the most innocent of faces.

'Yuh did call mi, Grandma Melba? Mi nevah did hear yuh!'

Beating her made little difference, so after a while Grandma Melba decided to accept it. 'A wah wi fi do, Sippa,' she told Grandpa, 'a soh de pickney stay. It nuh like she nuh hear what yuh tell har fi do! She jus do it when a ready she ready.'

Our little brothers were given that slightly elevated status that little boys all over the world are given. Clifton was a handsome fellow who was (so we were told) the spitting image of our mother, apart from his knock-knees. He was very keen on his appearance, especially his hair, and he'd often beg Grandpa Sippa to cut it. Long before it was fashionable for boys to have different looks, Clifton would insist on having his hair styled with a little tufty bit on the top of his head and the sides cut very short. He was also the clown of the family, not because he was funny or told jokes, but because of the way he reacted to things. He had this habit of suddenly repeating something he'd heard days before and then he'd do this loud belly laugh, while rocking back and forth. One day, when he was sitting beside me on the verandah while I plaited my hair, he noticed the tiny hairs that had started to sprout under my arms.

'Lard, Erna,' he exclaimed, 'a beard a grow under yuh arm dem!'

Days later, when the three eldest of us were returning home carrying bundles of brushwood, there was a crash and Patricia and I turned to see firewood scattered all over the ground and, in the middle of it, Clifton crying with laughter.

'Lard, a beard Erna a grow under fi har arms! Huh, huh, huh!'

When he'd calmed down a little, we helped him put the bundle back together and lift it back on to his head. After that, whenever we heard him chuckling behind us, Patricia shouted out, 'If you drop it again, Clifton, we a lef yuh, and Grandma Melba ago beat yuh backfoot!'

Finally, there was little Sonny. Sonny was not his real name, but my grandparents had renamed him because he was the last of our mother's children that Grandma Melba had delivered. Whenever Sonny was in reach, Grandma would pass her hands gently over his smooth little head and declare, 'Yuh is all our children, but dis one is our little Sonny.'

His head was always smooth – Grandpa Sippa would scrape it clean with his cut-throat razor and then polish it with some of Grandma's home-made coconut oil. Sonny never complained because he had never seen himself with hair. To add to his comical appearance, he had chubby cheeks and a little round belly that popped out like he was a tiny man who'd been drinking too much beer. His navel didn't look right either. It sat on top of his belly like a second little belly, and when you pushed it flat it would bounce back as though it had tiny springs inside. Grandma Melba said it was air, but none of us understood what she meant. The first thing Grandma would do when she saw him in the morning was pull at his cheeks and rub his head, and Grandpa Sippa would greet him in the evening with even more head rubbing.

# Chapter 3

Despite her bird-like size, Grandma Melba had managed to give birth to sixteen children, including three pairs of twins – though the twins had all died shortly after their birth. Her greatest loves were her grandchildren, her Bible, Grandpa Sippa and tending to her animals. She suffered from frequent headaches and was sensitive to any touch to her head, which meant she rarely combed her mass of matted greying hair and tended to keep it covered with a thick black net. But she had the gentlest of faces that was always ready to break into a smile. Her slanted eyes were golden brown and her skin was a deep black, which I loved because it was exactly the same colour as mine. In fact, we were the two blackest people in the village, something that I was teased about throughout my childhood.

It was hard to be in Grandma Melba's company without feeling happy. When she wasn't smiling, she could be heard laughing, or loudly singing her favourite old spiritual, 'We Shall Overcome'. She had learnt the tune and words from a radio on the other side of the deep gully that separated us from the neighbouring village. The words that the breeze failed to bring she would make up herself.

One day, as I sat shelling corn with Grandma Melba and her younger sister, Miss Eula, I listened intently to my great-aunt speaking in a hushed voice about what she described as 'woman's trial'.

'Is so tings go here on de island,' she said. 'When baby dem want fi born, nutting kyaan stop dem! Dem nuh gwaan wait for doctor to come all de way from town. Woman ave to be strong and be dem own doctor and deal wit whatever de good Lord trow at dem.'

'Amen to dat!' Grandma Melba responded. 'Our mada help us born our children and a we hafi help our daughta dem born deres. A soh it go, sis!'

'We still is blessed,' Miss Eula continued. 'De good Lord bless me wid two pickney. An yuh know seh, Carmen she dead five minutes after she born and mi only left with Aaron. But mi still ave much to be tankful for! Im bless me with six pickney of him own, soh what mi nuh have innah children, mi mek up in grand pickney dem.'

Great-Aunt Eula changed the subject when she noticed how hard I was listening. I'd decided that I was never going to have any babies of any kind, ever, but I was still curious as to how my Grandma had managed to find sixteen. Yet, when I tried to broach the subject, they avoided answering me directly.

'Calm, Erna!' Great-Aunt Eula said, when I asked again. 'Fi yuh grandmada is de calmest sumady in de whole place.'

Grandma Melba gave her sister a slightly disapproving look. I well knew that whenever us children crossed the invisible line that we didn't always know was there, Grandma Melba would be anything but calm – something she always reminded us of with the same refrain: 'Oonoo pickney know seh me is not a woman quick fi angry.' Then her smile would disappear to be replaced by a frown, which we knew meant trouble.

Grandma's smile did its disappearing trick one afternoon when I'd returned from an errand to Mass Baldwin's provision shop, where I'd been buying salted mackerel. I made several mistakes that afternoon: first, I took the foolish decision to

13

spend Grandma Melba's change – a shiny thruppenny bit – on three dozen mint balls, all of which I devoured in record time. Then, I took a brief rest before first plucking out, and then eating, the eyes of the salted mackerel. Finally, I opened up the mackerel and picked away at its tasty salty flesh.

When I got home, Grandma was sitting quietly on the verandah in her favourite old wicker chair. A snake length of rolled tobacco laid in a coil in her work basket, alongside her cutting board and knife. The large silky tobacco leaf spread across her thigh signalled she was about to begin her cigar making. I handed her the fish, carefully rewrapped in the greaseproof paper, having no idea just how much of it I'd eaten.

Grandma took the parcel and placed it in the palm of her right hand. Elbow bent, she moved her hand up and down a couple of times. She had a unique ability to judge the precise weight of an item – be it a yam, or a half-devoured salted mackerel. I was about to be rumbled. I wanted to run, but decided that standing very still and waiting was perhaps a better option. My best hope was that Grandma would not burden herself with my little misdemeanour.

She placed the mackerel on a nearby tin plate, then said, 'Pickney gal, mek mi ave mi change.'

'Mass Baldwin nuh give me no change, Grandma Melba.'

I felt a trickle of pee seep into my panties. It felt like it wanted to be a gush, but Grandma had told me that I'd only ever wet myself once – and that was when I was three years old and had seen a great big green tobacco bugaboo with its horrible feelers doing a slow crawl up my dress towards my chest – so I squeezed my legs together and prayed that my face gave nothing away.

'Pickney gal,' Grandma Melba said again, 'mi a go ask yuh one more time fi mi change and, while yuh a sort out de answer fi dat, yuh kyan find de answer for wat appen to de mackerel at de same time.'

'But, Grandma Melba, it nuh lie mi a tell! Mass Baldwin nevah give me no change and a soh de mackerel did stay!'

I'd forgotten that she hadn't even looked at the mackerel.

'So, tell mi, chile, is how de mackerel did stay?'

'Me nuh know, Grandma, a so it did come wrap up, and, and!'

'Stop, pickney! Stop right now wit yuh foolishness because yuh a mek mi blood pressure rise. Mi want you fi go down a gully an pick one switch and carry it fi me.'

Relieved to be out of Grandma's presence, I dashed off to the gully with a plan. Once there, I broke off the thickest piece of wood I could find on the switch tree. I calculated that there was no way Grandma was going to beat me with some great big piece of wood, and, anyway, she wasn't the beating type. However, when I returned with my stick, I quickly spotted half a dozen of the slimmest, bendiest switches lying beside Grandma's right foot. She ignored the piece of wood I tried to hand her and carried on rolling the cigar she was making. I stood and watched as she deftly rolled the perfect cigar shape, cut it in one swift movement to the right length, and sealed the end with her home-made paste.

'Mi kyan go now, Grandma Melba? Mi ave fi feed de chicken dem before it get dark.'

'Den is what yuh a wait for, chile?'

I skipped away, hoping that Grandma Melba was no longer angry with me. Grandma was still rolling her cigars when I returned to let her know that I'd fed the chickens. The orange sun hovered above the horizon; soon it would make its sudden descent and plunge the island into darkness. I saw that the giant wooden mortar, used for pounding cassava and dried corn, had been dragged into the centre of the yard, but the pestle was nowhere to be seen. Lying next to the mortar were Grandma's bendy switches, which had been tied together to make one big, supple switch. She rose from her wicker chair and walked slowly towards me.

'Mi glad seh you come back innah good time,' she said, as she took me by the hand and led me over to the mortar.

My eyes searched again for the pestle, but it definitely wasn't there, and I realised, with rising dread, that the mortar wasn't going be used for its usual job. Grandma's grip on my hand tightened as she bent to pick up the switch. Then she placed the fingers of my right hand at full stretch on the mortar's edge and brought the switch down with a swish! But, just as quickly, I removed my hand before she could make contact. She made two more attempts before, exasperated, she clamped my hand firmly on the mortar and brought the switch down three times, swish, swish, swish! Then she swapped to my left hand.

The sting from each strike drew a guttural scream from me. 'Ow, ow, mi a beg yuh, Grandma Melba, please, mi beg yuh!' I cried. 'Mi won't do it again! Mi a beg yuh!'

Grandma threw the switch down just as I was thinking that one more strike and all my fingers would surely be cut in half. It felt as though my hands were on fire and the burning sensation crept up all the way to my head. It was hard to look at Grandma Melba after that, I was feeling so vexed because she'd never hurt me like that before, but when I did sneak a sideways glance, I saw that she looked almost as tired and vexed as I was. She lifted her apron and used it to wipe away the beads of sweat that had gathered on her brow, before walking slowly back to her seat.

Once settled, she called me over and covered my fingers with slices of aloe vera and then wrapped my hands in gauze. The cool of the aloe felt good.

'Erna,' Grandma spoke quietly, 'mi did have to beat yuh. Yuh know seh, it nuh something mi do without reason, but a fi mi duty to teach yuh. Mi nuh want yuh fi grow fi be a liar and a tief! Yuh go an lie down now, chile, till de food ready. Yuh Grandfada a go come home soon a look for im dinner.'

. . .

Evening time was when Grandpa Sippa was mostly at home. This made his presence special, not just for Grandma, but for us children, too. People in the village regarded Grandpa Sippa as a gentleman, and the general consensus was that he was a good husband to Grandma Melba and a good grandfather to his grandchildren. Grandpa would always talk to Grandma in a nice, soft manner. Whatever she asked him to do, he did it, and he always kept his promises. He wasn't a big drinker, like some of the men in the village, but at the end of each day he would measure out a gill of white rum and drink it down in one single swig. Once quenched, Grandpa Sippa would sit down and peruse passages from his King James Bible, while Grandma and us children prepared dinner. On Sundays he took over all the cooking. Grandpa Sippa was a better cook than Grandma, not that anyone would dare to express such a view out loud. His red peas soup with salted pork was delicious and always generously flavoured with Scotch bonnet peppers. Sometimes, when Grandpa washed out the salt from the pork before cooking it, he'd miss a few of the fat little maggots that feasted on the meat, no matter how salty it was, so it wasn't unusual to find a few well-cooked maggots floating on top of our soup. But Grandpa would dismiss any complaints by telling us, 'Rememba, what nuh kill, fatten!'

Grandpa Sippa was as tall as Grandma was short. And although he was a proper grown-up, he still bore the nickname 'Leanside'. The widely held belief was that it was his great height that caused his body to lean slightly to one side. His crumpled brown face housed the softest of eyes in which I never once saw even a flicker of anger. In fact, I never knew my grandfather to lose his temper over anything. He had a preference for long-sleeved shirts, whatever the weather, even when working on the land, and his skin, when it was revealed, was a pale brown that contrasted strongly with Grandma's ebony tone. Occasionally, after his evening wash way down by the old tank, Grandpa would walk back to the house wearing just his faded long-johns and old merino vest. That's when you'd see how pale his over-long arms were. They were paler than his face and hands by far. It was years after we grew up that we found out from the family tree – compiled by a family member over a twenty-year period – that Grandpa Sippa looked the way he did because his grandfather was a Scottish slave owner. The tell-tale signs were also there in his short-cropped hair, which laid on his head in tiny straight strands, and in his eyes, which resembled the dull grey of sky preparing for rain.

I never heard the story of how my grandparents came to be married, but I knew that Grandpa was born in the village of Falkirk, a village several miles away from our own. His mother, who was known as 'Queen Mother James', was rumoured to have had more children than any other woman on the island – twenty-three in total – and the records showed that she died when she was one hundred and eight years old. Apparently, Grandpa's Sippa's father died from exhaustion. The family tree also revealed that Grandma and Grandpa were second cousins.

Since he was eighteen years old, Grandpa Sippa had regularly visited Cuba – the story went that, for that first trip, he and his younger brother Basil built their own boat and sailed it the ninety miles from our island all the way to Cuba; as a child, I had no idea how improbable that was, but it was never disputed by anyone in our village. Following the birth of his first six children, Grandpa Sippa travelled to Cuba again. After some three years away, he returned from this final trip and discovered that Grandma Melba had somehow given birth to two extra babies, a girl and a boy. The babies each had different surnames, neither of which were my grandparents'. Grandpa Sippa must have truly loved Grandma because, despite this turn of events, the marriage continued without interruption and a further eight children were born, all carrying my grandfather's surname.

After my grandmother, Grandpa Sippa's next biggest love was for his land. He grew a variety of vegetables – from root staples, like yams, cassava and sweet potatoes, to corn and various types of peas and beans – as well as herbs and spices. There was an abundance of fruit trees all over his land too. One of our jobs as children was to climb the trees to pick and collect the fruit, as each variety ripened. It was a responsibility we revelled in, particularly in mango season. Then there were his fields of tobacco, which he grew for Grandma to make her famous Cuban cigars – at her most productive, she could make up to five hundred cigars in a week.

The two of them were always up at the crack of dawn, awakened by the incessant crowing of Percy, our proud rooster. 'De noise dat fowl mek coulda wake up de dead,' Grandma often joked. Percy had a habit of keeping up his racket until everyone in the village was awake. Then he'd stop as quickly as he'd begun.

Grandma Melba's mornings started in the kitchen. Her first task of the day was to prepare Grandpa Sippa his Thermos of strong hot coffee. Then he'd take the cigar she'd rolled especially for him and set off to get started on whatever work was needed. At some point he'd be joined by Alfredo and Garfield, the two young village men who worked with him to do the digging, planting, lifting and moving that was required that day. Before getting started on breakfast preparation, which was the only meal that Grandma Melba was adept at cooking, she would gather us children for our daily dose of peeled bitter aloe, followed by a small tin mug of sweetened cerasee tea – although no amount of sugar was ever able to disguise its bitter taste. She was passionate about our health and she believed the aloe vera plant and the cerasee bush could rid us of any ailment and prevent others from developing. She would then set about making a breakfast of salted codfish and ackee. If ackee was out of season, Grandma would cook Grandpa's preferred breakfast of callaloo and salted mackerel. Breakfast was always accompanied by a combination of root vegetables, fried dumplings and cassava flatbread, which we called bammy. Grandma always cooked our breakfast with love and she would sit and watch as we ate, listening to us murmuring constant sounds of enjoyment.

'Mi see oonoo lick yuh finger clean again,' she would say. She liked nothing better than to see us lick every last bit of taste from our fingers and then mop our plate clean with a piece of bammy.

If we weren't in school, we would head off with Grandma to bring Grandpa his breakfast, and then, while Grandma returned to make her cigars, we'd help Grandpa work the land. He trusted us with razor-sharp machetes and hoes, which were taller than we were, and we often worked alongside him and his workmen to clear the land in preparation for the new season. Our grandparents prided themselves on growing or making just about everything we needed – Grandma even made our own cooking and hair oil from coconuts.

But our daily life was far from all work. Once we'd completed our chores, we were free to play to our hearts' content. We ran impromptu races and climbed trees, daring each other to climb the highest and thinnest of branches. We created swings from slimy vines and made skipping ropes from sisal. We played hopscotch, Punchinello, dandy shandy, jacks, and a marble game called chinking. And Patricia and I developed our own small business, making spinning tops and toy cars out of scraps of wood and discarded tin cans. There were no restrictions on our play, and we took equal pleasure in creating grass dolls one day and then playing cricket the next, alongside all the village boys. Any child who could hold a bat and throw a ball halfway accurately was allowed to join the team. On the last Saturday of each month, we'd join our grandfather and the young men who gathered from across the district to play village cricket, unless a professional match was being played on the island on the same day – then, the village games were suspended and everyone would head to the district cricket pitch to listen to the big match being relayed over a radio hooked up to loudspeakers.

In our village no one owned a radio, so sometimes we joined the other village children and entertained ourselves by singing songs that were meant for funerals, because they were tuneful and full of nice words. We argued and play-fought and sometimes had real fights, drawing a crowd eager to take sides. Someone would give themself the role of referee, while everyone else jumped around giving advice to the fighters on where to land a good punch: 'Go on, Erna, punch him innah im big mout now, man!'

In the evening we'd gather in our yard under the massive breadfruit tree to listen to Grandpa Sippa tell duppy and Anancy stories. These were the only times that Grandpa got involved with us children at a playful level, and we listened, captivated.

'Duppies,' Grandpa explained, 'are long-dead humans who are said to return from their graves during the hours of night in order to right a wrong, or to torment a wicked person. The dead can return in any form. Human, animal, and even birds.'

Grandpa told us that one of the scariest duppies was known as the Rolling Calf – a cow that had the ability to turn itself into any animal. It never actually attacked anyone, but anyone who had the misfortune of encountering it would definitely end up in the madhouse. I often begged Grandpa Sippa to tell us one of the Rolling Calf stories as we gathered with other village children under the breadfruit tree. Grandpa would start every story as tradition demanded with a call and response.

'Mi seh crick! Yuh seh crack!' he'd say.

'Crick!' he'd shout, and 'Crack!' we'd respond.

'Once upon a time, a man was walking in de street one night when him met up wit a Rolling Calf. It was a duppy with fire

21

and flames coming outta him eyes. But de man didn't know it was a duppy, so him ask him for a light. De duppy started grinning im teeth at de man. De man get frighten and start to run. But when im reach de other end of de road, de Rolling Calf was right dere again. "So we meet again," said the duppy, and de poor man him fall down dead wit fright.'

Grandpa Sippa would tell two or three stories each night, embellishing them each time one of us children would ask, 'So a what de duppy do next, Grandpa?' He would always finish the last story the same way he started the first, with a 'mi seh crick, an yuh seh crack!' And with that we knew the evening had ended and it was time for bed. 'You children, memba yuh have school innah de morning,' Grandpa would say, as we scurried off.

# Chapter 4

Rose Hill School was a two-roomed Victorian structure that sat at the top of a rocky outcrop opposite the Anglican church. It seemed a strange place to build a school, or a church for that matter, given that there was plenty of empty land at the bottom of the hill, but I suppose that God and education deserve the highest elevation.

The daily walk to school was a seven-mile round trip, if you took the main road. The alternative, shorter route featured a series of rocky dirt tracks lined with overgrown vegetation that took you directly through neighbours' yards. Invariably, this meant that any child who chose to use the shortcut ran the risk of being bitten by snarling, ill-tempered dogs. Thus, dirt track walking was often accompanied by a chorus of 'Hold yuh dog, mi a beg yuh, hold yuh dog!' in the hope that the owner, or someone who knew the dog, would be nearby to save us.

Once the school came into view on its perch high on the hill, I had to decide whether to divert to the main road, or scramble up the steep rocks which would take a good fifteen minutes off my journey. My greatest fear was arriving late, because even with the best of excuses lateness was not tolerated.

The headmaster, Teacher Palmer, was a stern man. He had the kind of face that looked as though it had never broken into a smile. He ran Rose Hill school like a military camp. Every rule had to be followed, no matter how obviously pointless, and he meted out punishment at every opportunity with his infamous leather strap – which he affectionately named 'Staffos the Killer'. I sometimes noticed what looked to be glints of pleasure in Teacher Palmer's face when he used Staffos to beat the boys on their bare backsides. To us girls, he'd give no less than six mighty whacks straight on to the palms of our hands. I suspected that he would have liked to beat our backsides as well, but then he would have had to do so through our clothing, and it appeared that his preference was to hear the lash of Staffos directly on bare skin.

With no village clock or even a watch to guide me, I learned how to use the position of the sun to estimate the time. On rainy or cloudy days, it was a green silver-backed leaf plucked from a particular tree that I used to predict the time. I would throw the leaf into the air and, if it landed green side up, I was good for time; silver side up meant lateness!

Teacher Palmer often took up a position at the top of the hill, where he could see every child as we clambered up the rocky path. He would then direct us into separate lines: the 'registration and inspection' line for those who were early; the 'inspection and beating' line for latecomers.

By the time I turned nine, I was expected to get myself organised for school *and* help Grandma get the boys ready, before walking them twenty minutes out of my way to Miss Lucy's basic school. (Strangely, on school days Patricia would get herself up, dressed and out of the house in record time.) Sometimes, the extra chore caused me to be late for school and, on such occasions, rather than face Teacher Palmer and Staffos I would spend the day hiding in the nearby woods, where I'd read and re-read the story of *David Copperfield*. At the end of the school day, I would return home pretending to have been at school all day. The trick was either to avoid the other children or to make up an elaborate lie to avoid being caught out.

But, one day, it was my third time late in a week and there was no question of hiding out in the woods three times in a row. For sure the news of my absence from school would get back to my village; there was always a loudmouth who might spill the beans. When I arrived, Teacher Palmer was already part way through his morning talk, which always came across as more of a fervent sermon. As I approached, I could hear his booming preacher denunciations from outside the two-roomed school building. There was only one entrance for late comers: the door nearest Teacher Palmer's lectern. I snuck in and tried to merge my body into the space held by another girl, but Teacher's eagle eyes spotted me instantly. He darted me a look which left little doubt of my punishment to come.

'So, Erna, yuh mek it to school again today! Mi sure seh Teacher Palmer was happy to see yuh, man!' said Tony, at our first break. Tony was my friend Dorcas's brother, so, like Dorcas, was a cousin several times removed. He was always in trouble with Teacher Palmer for looking scruffy – even first thing on a Monday morning, his uniform looked like he'd slept in it all night.

Cousin or not, I didn't really take Tony seriously. He was a boy and he didn't have half the chores that I had to complete before setting out for school, so getting to school on time was never a problem for him.

'Lef me, man, unless yuh want mi fi buss yuh backfoot again,' I said in response to his sarcastic remark.

Tony had always had too much to say about things that were none of his business. I'd beaten him in two fights the previous week after he'd stolen a penny from Patricia, which she had saved specially to buy sweets. I'd sent him home with his khaki uniform ripped up in several places. When he told his mother, Miss Clara, what had happened, she gave him another hiding for letting a girl beat him up. Then I fought him again when he commented on my buck teeth.

I was late that third morning running because I'd chosen to use the short cut, despite the risks. As I made my way through the village, accompanied by the growls and barking of dogs, I heard the most terrifying screams. At first, I thought it was Mass Calvin beating his wife, Miss Gina, again, but then I remembered that Miss Gina had run away from the district after one beating too many – apparently Mass Calvin had hit his wife with a chair leg, busting her head open. She'd sent a message from the hospital telling him to take care of their daughter, because she wasn't coming back. I soon realised that the screams had to be coming from their daughter, Delphine, another of my cousins, at least three times removed. She hadn't been seen at school or out and about in the village for several months. Questions about what had become of her had died down when a rumour spread that she'd run away to live with her mother. But now I was worried that Mass Calvin had turned his angry self on his daughter and was trying to bust her head open too.

'A dead mi a go dead! Dis a too much pain! Lard a dead mi a go dead!' It was clearly Delphine that I could hear shouting. 'Murder woe! Murder woe!' she wailed, 'Mi kyaan tek no more a de pain, Miss Melba!'

She must have come back to the village without anyone knowing.

'Mi know it hard fi yuh, chile, but yuh kyan do it,' I heard Grandma Melba reply, 'yuh hafi persevere. Yuh nuh ave choice now! Mi nuh know who did dis ting to yuh, but God willing everyting wi come right. Yuh jus push hard when mi tell yuh.'

Grandma had left the house very early that morning, telling Grandpa that she had some business to attend to, and now she was at Delphine's house – so clearly it wasn't Mass Calvin beating Delphine, it was my Grandma Melba helping her with… I didn't know what. I waited for a while at the end

26

of the path listening to Delphine's screams get louder and more anguished. Sometimes it sounded like she was having trouble breathing, then she would let out a loud groan and go silent for a while. Suddenly, Delphine started screaming again, 'Miss Melba, yuh might as well kill mi now! Mi prefer fi dead. Mi nuh waan fi do dis!'

I silently prayed that whatever was happening to Delphine never happened to me, and I also prayed really hard that my Grandma wouldn't listen to her and kill her. I lost a lot of time standing at the bottom of Delphine's yard and by the time I finally got to school I was tired and upset and ready for a fight. Tony didn't help himself by getting on the wrong side of me that morning; I hardly even noticed the six licks that I had to endure from Staffos. On my way back through the village that afternoon, I noticed Grandma Melba sitting on the verandah of Delphine's house. There was total quiet. Grandma's head was slumped on to her chest and I could see that she was more tired than usual. I approached on tiptoes, but somehow she heard me and lifted her head with a start.

'A weh yuh creep up pon mi like dat fa, child?'

I realised she'd been catching up on some much-needed sleep.

'Yuh hereso all day, Grandma Melba?' I asked.

'Since marning!' she replied. 'Mi whole day dun yasso.' Grandma lifted herself with some effort from the old wicker chair. 'Come wit mi, Erna. Mi waan fi show yuh de kind a trouble yuh mus keep yuhself fram.'

She led me by the hand into a room lit by a Tilley lamp hanging from the ceiling on a hook. Delphine was sitting propped upright on a wooden bed holding the smallest baby I'd ever seen. She was much fatter than the last time I'd seen her. On her previously flat twelve-year-old chest she now had two enormous woman-sized breasts. The baby's tiny mouth was clamped firmly to a nipple.

'Where yuh get a baby from?' I asked her.

'From the bogeyman,' she responded.

'Is your baby?' I asked.

'Yes, a my baby. His name is Leslie.'

'Where yuh did see de bogeyman and why him give yuh baby?'

Suddenly Grandma Melba, who'd left me alone with Delphine and baby Leslie, bellowed from the verandah, 'Erna! Stop wit yuh dyam foolish question dem. Yuh nuh see de pickney dead a tiredness?'

The news had got to school the following day, long before I arrived. 'Delphine ave baby! De bogeyman give it to har!' someone shouted, as soon as I stepped into the school yard.

Teacher Palmer's lesson that morning went like this: 'I want all you childen to open your ears and listen! Especially you girl children. I must warn you, the devil work in mysterious ways. When you put your mind to your learning,' he beseeched, 'you will not find time to go romping with the devil.'

Delphine didn't return to school. Her mother wasn't around and her grandmother was too frail to help her. Instead, she remained at home and in between taking care of Leslie she worked on the family's smallholding. When Leslie grew to a size where other children were comfortable to hold him, I would stop by Delphine's house and play with him.

Just under a year after Leslie was born, I was making my way to school one Monday morning through the village when I heard Delphine weeping from inside the same room where she'd given birth. This time there was no screaming, just a deep, dull wailing. I'd left my grandmother at home, so I was sure that Delphine wasn't having another baby. I walked on slowly to school full of contemplation and dread. On my way back that afternoon I discovered Grandma in Delphine's yard, along with a bunch of neighbours. Everyone had black bands around their wrists and some of the women were wearing black headscarves. I knew immediately that someone had died, but who?

This time, it was my Grandma who called me over.

'De baby bwoy dead,' Grandma Melba said in a voice thick with emotion. 'Who know why de good Lord bring dese kind a trial pon sumady so young?'

Delphine could be heard loudly sobbing inside. I had no idea what I could say to her, so I remained outside with Grandma. It turned out that little Leslie had developed a terrible fever during the night and died before anyone could get him to a doctor.

'De poor ting nevah had a chance!' said one of the mourners.

I felt overcome with sadness for Delphine. At the age of only thirteen she'd experienced the birth and death of her child. I was a whole three years younger than her but I was acutely aware of the profound nature of what had happened and I couldn't get the knowledge of baby Leslie's death out of my head. I'd only stopped to play with him a day earlier. His little round belly had vibrated with laughter as he watched my old wooden peg spin out of control and dig itself into the caked earth. I wasn't sure why this had made him laugh so much, but it hadn't mattered. It was lovely just to see his funny little face all scrunched up with enjoyment. Delphine had come over and sat down alongside her son, clearly enjoying watching him having fun. And now he was gone.

The next morning, Teacher Palmer's weekly inspection of our uniform and overall presentation was due. My heart felt ready to break for both little Leslie and Delphine, but I doubted that even the story of Delphine's dead baby would have softened Teacher in any way. We all hated these inspections, because we knew that most of us would be called out on something. Teacher Palmer walked down the line, missing out the children whose presentation immediately met his approval. He came to a stop directly in front of me, and with his wooden ruler he carefully lifted the collar of my white blouse. He used the ruler to move apart the pleats of my pinafore, checking that each one was properly ironed into place. Then he whipped out a pencil from his breast pocket and poked it roughly through my plaits. I had head lice at the time and I prayed hard that he wouldn't spot one of the horrid little creatures streaking across my partings. But it was my lucky day, not one single louse revealed itself, and cousin Petra, who was one of Grandma Melba's nieces, had made a great job of my hair that morning, so when Teacher Palmer pushed his pencil into the three large plaits, it ran smoothly through. The boys' inspections included checking that their hair was cut regulation short, partings were in the right place, and their khaki shirts and shorts were clean and stiffly pressed. My brother Clifton, who had now joined us at Rose Hill, had his hair with a high-top and shaved sides, yet somehow managed to pass Teacher Palmer's inspection. Perhaps it was because – as I secretly believed – Teacher Palmer liked Clifton's style as much as the neatness of the cut; for anyone else, such breaches would have surely incurred his wrath.

After inspections were complete, Teacher Palmer surprised us all with one of his sermons.

'Children,' he bellowed from his platform, 'this morning, I would like us all to come together and join hands. I want us to pray for the innocent soul of little Leslie Belton. Leslie was only one year old when the good Lord decided to take him away from the sins of this world. It may seem to some that his life was too short, or that his death was untimely, but we know different. The Lord does not make mistakes. But we are not all equipped to deal with the Lord's decisions. We are lowly sinners! Today, oh Lord, we bow our heads in prayer and we pray, oh Lord, for his young mother, Delphine, a formerly diligent and respected student of this school. We know, oh Lord Jesus, that baby Leslie

30

is without sin and so is due to take his place by your father's feet in Heaven with the angels. Amen! Glory be to God!'

'Amen,' we all echoed.

Within a week of little Leslie's funeral, things were back to normal. Mass Calvin decided to send Delphine to stay with a relative in town who promised to get her a job as a housekeeper, and back at school talk of Leslie's death quietened down. It was obvious that the whole episode of his birth and sudden death was something the rest of us, the girls in particular, struggled to comprehend, and certainly nothing Teacher Palmer had said in his sermon helped. Nevertheless, I couldn't avoid the daunting possibility that some of these strange mysteries of life and death would also be visited upon me one day. It was girls and women whose stomachs grew full with babies. How, I wondered, did these babies get into their stomachs? And what exactly did my grandma do to help the babies get out again? And, as for death, everything about it seemed so frightening and final – was it just night-time when death stole folks away? I had so many questions, but didn't know where to find the answers to these mysteries.

# Chapter 5

The Pentecostal church in my village stood in stark contrast to the Anglican church, which was across the road from Rose Hill School and was the most beautiful building to be in, and to sing in. The Pentecostal church had no walls, just a zinc roof that was held up by wooden poles. The seats were makeshift and were never sufficient for the mass of people who would turn up from neighbouring villages on Sunday mornings. The congregation consisted mainly of older women, and the pastor, who was an eloquent speaker, had a way of whipping up his flock into a frenzy. Not long into his sermons, one or two of the women would begin to shake violently. This would be followed by shouts of 'Praise de Lord! Praise im! Praise his holy name!' while the rest of the congregation would get louder, singing and clapping their hands, and the women would start speaking in tongues as the spirits entered them.

'De Holy Spirit has entered sister Ivy and sister Julia!' the pastor would scream, as he jumped up and down in front of his little podium like he was also possessed. 'Praise God, praise be to de one an only mighty God! He is speaking truth through our dear sisters today! Praise him!'

During these visitations, the affected women would throw themselves on the floor and writhe around, oblivious to any danger. Women who were entered by bad spirits foamed at the mouth and clutched at their crotches – the belief being that was the way the bad spirits got in, and that was the way they had to be made to leave. In contrast, the good spirits had the women behaving in a way that was – I reflected much later when I understood such things – almost orgasmic. The minister in the meantime would join the women writhing on the ground. It was a spectacle worth going to church for, particularly as no one could be sure which women would get what kind of spirit. In many ways, it was the best entertainment available for us villagers – we had never seen a television, and cinemas were something only the most well-travelled people had ever encountered. It was certainly far more entertaining than the Anglican church, but I'd joined the school choir, and choir practice took place there twice a week. Unlike the homely wooden school and the Pentecostal church, the Anglican church was built with granite and limestone. It had long, stained-glass windows that caught the sun and reflected vivid colours all around the inside of the building, solid shiny wooden benches with carved-out wooden pockets for holding Bibles lined the aisle, leaving a clear walkway to the altar. High above the altar a huge wooden cross took centre stage with a painting of the twelve white apostles beneath it. It was here that I felt most in awe of God and removed from the ordinariness of village life, but I was still unable to find answers to the questions that concerned me most, like the death of baby Leslie, or how Delphine had got him in the first place.

Four months before my eleventh birthday, I was sitting with Patricia in a small pasture by our house. We were plaiting the supple green leaves of two grass plants, pretending they were dolls, when I felt as though I'd wet myself. I stood up and a trickle of blood escaped down one of my legs. I ran, weeping, to my grandma, certain I was about to face my worst fear: death.

33

'Erna, yuh is fine, pretty gal,' she said, and she showed me the practicalities of how to take care of myself, before adding, 'Erna, yuh is woman now. Jus nuh come home with belly.'

I was finally starting to understand.

It was much later, though, that I learned of my own conception – long after leaving my island, and long after Grandma was no longer with us.

The full story of how I came into this world was told to me by my Auntie Madge, when she considered that I was grown-up enough to hear it. Auntie Madge was the second oldest of my grandparents' children and had been the first to leave for England, several years before my mother. Although my mother was a bright girl, her parents' finances didn't stretch beyond trying to educate their sons and their two oldest daughters. By the time she was twelve years old, school stopped for Miss Violet, and she spent most of her time after that at home, helping her parents to care for her four younger siblings.

She was only thirteen when my grandfather personally delivered her to her first employers. They were a married couple named Mr and Mrs Dee who had three young children and who both worked as teachers in one of the well-known technical colleges on the other side of the island. With no close family of their own, they were in need of reliable help. Mrs Dee was also offering the right girl a chance to learn a trade in dressmaking. My grandparents had heard about the Dees' search for a helper from a travelling tinker man.

'Wi not happy to see yuh go soh young,' my grandfather said to my mother, 'but de way tings is it will mean wi ave one less mout to feed.'

They told her that her work would be to look after Mr and Mrs Dee's children, as well as help out with jobs around the house.

'De same kind of tings yuh do here wit yuh brothers and sisters dem,' my grandmother added, by way of reassurance.

My mother had felt fearful and excited all at the same time. She liked the idea of earning her own money. She had four siblings younger than herself, for whom she had to take a lot of responsibility, and she felt that one less child to drag out of bed every morning, and force to have a wash and brush their teeth, followed by the nightmare of helping them to get dressed, seemed a much more manageable proposition. Yet she was worried – she had only ever left her village to walk the short distance to the school in the next village, where some girls were sent to learn the basics of reading and writing, or when she went to hunt for mangoes in Poros. As far as she was concerned, these other villages were just bolted on to her own, with the only difference being that one had a little school and the other a few more varieties of mango trees. She had really only known life in Little Hammon, with her parents, brothers and sisters, various aunts and uncles, and too many cousins to count. She had never seen a bus or a car, much less travelled in one, and now she was to be packed off across the island to work for strangers. My mother never found a way to ask her parents why it was that all of her brothers were either in school or had left the village to pursue further studies, while, apart from her second oldest sister, Madge, all her other sisters had left the village to go to work as domestic helpers. She knew that one of her big boy cousins had become a barrister (whatever a barrister was), because he went to school for a very long time and then attended all kinds of colleges in faraway places. He would sometimes return to the village for short visits, dressed in smart clothes and with lots of paper money in his pocket. Still, she had accepted that that was how things were and held on to her dream of one day having enough money to buy the material for a real fine church dress.

There was a storm brewing on the day my mother and my grandfather set out to meet her employers. She sat on the rickety bus watching the trees as they sped by, humming quietly every church song she could remember and even reciting the odd psalm. Throughout the journey, she held tightly to the little notebook in which was written the exact place where the driver had to set them down, and where Mr and Mrs Dee would be waiting. After what seemed like an age, the bus driver called out, 'Violet James! One stop!' Violet jumped up, her heart pounding, grabbed the battered brown grip my grandmother had put her few things in, and climbed off the bus. Grandpa stepped off behind her. She immediately warmed to the kindly looking couple standing by the overgrown mango tree, their three children making busy around them. It didn't feel to her like the family were strangers, and she felt that everything would be all right. Grandfather greeted the couple and spent a long time talking to them about her.

'Mi daughta is a pickney gal who know what hard work mean. She hanest and mannerable. An she kyan cook good, yuh jus ave to encourage har wit de seasoning. She kyan wash, iron and clean good. An she ave a good way wit de younger pickney dem.'

Formalities out of the way, Grandpa Sippa told the Dees, 'Mi an har grandmada grateful yuh could tek Violet in. She is a helpful chile and wi sure yuh wi look after har good.'

Mr Dee walked to the roadside where an old dusty black pickup was parked. He must be really rich to have a car, my mother thought.

'Violet, you can climb into the back,' he said. There didn't seem to be enough room for everyone inside. 'You will be comfortable there. The cushion and blanket will help with the bumps.'

Mrs Dee bundled the three children into the back seat. Mr Dee was already in the cab revving up the engine, which took a little time to splutter into life, when Mrs Dee climbed in next to her husband. The vehicle made a few more spluttering noises and pulled off. My mother waved bravely to her father, who quickly disappeared from view.

The drive to the family's house took nearly an hour. My mother loved the drive, especially when Mr Dee started driving alongside the first river she had ever seen. She was intrigued by the way it meandered away from the road and then a few minutes later appeared again. The river had lots of white and grey stones, some large and some small, and the rapid flow of the water over the rocks fascinated her.

'Is how de water so clean and pretty even doah it a run pon de ground?' she wondered. When the car got close to the river, she could hear the swishing noise it made, even over the noise of the pickup engine. She wanted more than anything for Mr Dee to stop, even for a moment – to let her put her bare feet into the glistening water.

Life with the Dees was a lot easier for my mother than life back in the village. It took her no time at all to settle into her new family. Mr and Mrs Dee treated her well, almost as if she was their eldest child. She certainly had the normal duties of an eldest child. She ate with the family and had her own tiny room next to the children's. She liked that Benjamin, Lucas and Juanita all had good manners; the boys were good at getting things done for themselves, so Juanita was the only one who needed her help, as she always managed to put on most of her clothing back to front, and even her shoes often got put on the wrong feet. The Dees drove the boys to their school, which was right next to the technical college where they both taught. One of Violet's jobs was to walk Juanita to the local village school. She loved skipping along each morning with this pretty, talkative girl. The Dees had their own water tank, so my mother didn't have to fetch water, and they had a lovely big iron stove. Once a week, the wood was brought to the house by the Dees' yard boy, who chopped it into the neat pieces needed for the iron stove. Violet did the cooking on weekdays, following all of Mrs Dee's instructions. On weekends, Mrs Dee would take over the majority of the household tasks, leaving my mother free to play and have fun with the children. Sometimes on Saturdays, the Dees would take her into town to help with the shopping, and at other times she remained at home with the children. Every Sunday, without fail, she attended church with the family. Mother loved going to church as it gave her the opportunity to wear the two new church dresses she had assisted Mrs Dee in making – delighted to have fulfilled her promise to herself of spending her first earnings on materials for new church clothes. All in all, Violet loved her life with the Dees, and everything seemed set to continue happily like this without interruption.

When she was suddenly returned to my grandparents, heavily pregnant and without a husband, they had wondered whether Mr Dee had taken advantage of their daughter. Violet had, however, protested her employer's innocence and confided in Auntie Madge that on her way to run errands, a gentleman who rode a horse and carried a shotgun had waylaid her. On a previous occasion when this happened, she'd managed to run to safety, but this time the man had appeared directly in her path and threatened her with his gun. He used his horse and the butt of his shotgun to direct her off the path, pushing her deeper and deeper into the dense cane field that lined both sides of the path. Then he dismounted his horse and pointed his gun at her, ordering her to remove her old brown work dress, followed by her under slip and, finally, her panties. Horrified at her nakedness in front of the stranger, my mother attempted to cover her prominent breasts with one hand and her private parts with the other. The man grinned at her, the veins on his forehead swollen and protruding, before hurriedly removing his trousers and undergarments. She let out a stifled scream at the sight of the stranger's fully erect manhood. Closing her eyes tightly, she waited for whatever was to be her fate.

The next thing she knew, she was being held firmly by the wrists on the ground, the sharp leaves of broken sugar cane plants cutting into her back and the force of the stranger's manhood inside her, seemingly ripping her apart. The last thing she remembered was the heavy stench of tobacco from his breath as he heaved himself up and down on top of her. When she opened her eyes, the man, his horse and gun were nowhere to be seen. Her legs were splayed apart and the tops of her thighs covered in a thick white mucus.

Looking around for her clothes, she saw they were close by and pulled herself up slowly, but immediately began vomiting as though she had been poisoned. She allowed her stomach to empty itself of its contents before gathering her clothing. Then she hauled on her dress, tucked her underslip and panties into her pocket and ran as fast as her legs could carry her to the nearby river. On reaching it, Violet leapt headlong into the cold, slow-moving water, even though she couldn't swim. Fortunately, the river was shallow and she emerged distraught and still feeling dirty, despite scrubbing her entire body until the more sensitive parts were red raw.

When her monthly failed to arrive, Violet knew she was with child. In her tiny room, she silently wept a whole years' worth of tears. She had little idea what she could or should do. Her only hope, she concluded, when she felt as though she had run out of tears, was to pay a visit to the 'Obeah man'. Every village had one, and it was said he could use magic to make anything happen. Fortunately, my mother knew exactly where the Obeah man lived. His was the little thatched cottage at the very end of the village that children ran past in terror, fearful that he would catch them and work his Obeah on them. Rotted fruit covered the area around his cottage as no one dared to steal from the Obeah man's trees.

The Obeah man was not at all what my mother expected. He was smartly dresed and looked no more than forty years old. With his fine, long fingers, he appeared more suited to being a teacher than some kind of strange healer. But since she had never met an Obeah man before, she had no idea how he should look. She was just grateful to have found him.

Violet didn't have to explain her predicament; the Obeah man was familiar with the plight of the many young girls who came to him – it would either be that another woman had stolen their man, or they had a belly that they did not want.

'Man, or belly?' was his only question. His job was to get the man back or get rid of the belly.

Violet was pleased with his directness – she hadn't wanted to talk about the circumstances of her belly with a stranger whose job was really the 'devil's work' – according to Grandma Melba – and something for which they would probably both be ultimately punished.

'Belly,' she responded.

The Obeah man gave Violet a medium-sized bag of assorted leaves, some of which she recognised: soursop, lemon grass, the dreaded cerasee vine, along with a few pieces of bark and some twigs from the sapodilla tree and some red sorrel – which she was sure had only been added for its colour, and perhaps to stop her from panicking over the concoction that would emerge once brewed. The Obeah man advised her to boil everything together in one large pot, then to leave it for three days, after which she should strain the liquid off and drink a full mug of the potion once daily for a week. He assured her that by the end of the week everything would be cleared from her body, while warning in the same breath: 'Still mi kyaan promise de medicines will work fa every woman. If its fiyuh destiny to give birth, even wit all my powers, I kyaan prevent destiny!'

Violet handed over an entire week's wages of two and a half shillings and hurriedly left the cottage, taking care not to be seen.

My mother's attempts to ingest the vile liquid each morning were accompanied by the most violent retching. It took all her will power to force the nasty-tasting drink to remain inside her, but she knew that her body needed to recognise the presence of the medicine if it was to do its job. In the evenings, after settling the children, she would sneak out the back door into the nearby woods, where she allowed her body to get rid of the bile that had built up inside her. Unfortunately, three months later, her childishly flat stomach now had a distinct roundness. My mother was not feeling her destiny.

It didn't take Mrs Dee long to see the obvious. She had got to know the church-loving young girl over the year she was with them, and instinctively knew that there would have been nothing consensual to explain the position she was in. She spoke briefly with Violet and assured her that when her pregnancy advanced they would send her home to have her baby, but they were willing to take her back into their employment, since she had proved herself a trusted and hard-working young woman. Mrs Dee was a kind, empathetic and God-fearing woman. She ensured that Violet never had to explain her predicament to anyone. She assisted her in whatever way she could, with clothing, a good diet, sufficient rest and, as my mother's time drew near, the Dees made sure that she got safely back to her parents.

Back at her family home, her mother told her simply, 'De baby wi come, Violet. Yuh nuh ave choice innah it now, chile. Yuh baby wi come safe, de Lord willing.'

My mother had experienced her baby kicking at her stomach many times, but on the particular Sunday morning of my birth, she woke to the most violent pains she had ever experienced. The stranger ripping her apart with his enormous pengie was bad enough, but this pain was on another level. She just wanted to close her eyes and never wake up again, but she couldn't and the pain just kept coming. She felt a need to scream as loudly as she could. Somehow, it felt that opening her mouth and just bawling 'Murder woe! Murder woe!' would help. But it was early and it was a Sunday and my mother couldn't bring herself to let all the villagers hear her carry on. She crawled on her hands and knees to her parents' room and frantically called out her mother's name, 'Miss Melba, Miss Melba, mi tink mi time come!'

Grandma Melba never went to her bed before preparing the fireplace in her lean-to kitchen that was situated alongside the main house, where she would balance her large cast iron pot full of water on three large stones. Realising that her daughter's time had come, Grandma sprang into action. She lit the fire under the pot and left it to boil while she got together the various items she needed to help her daughter birth her baby. Grandpa Sippa took his day clothes and left the room.

Grandma Melba spread a couple of old sheets on the floor close to her iron four-poster bed, then woke my Auntie Madge, telling her to fetch her Aunt Eula from her nearby house. The two women helped my mother out of her clothing and washed her body down with carbolic soap. When it seemed for a moment that she was about to succumb to the pain and pass clear out, Aunt Eula popped a little bit of smelling salt under Violet's nose. They placed her in a squatting position on the old sheet with Aunt Eula kneeling behind her, clasping her shoulders firmly. As the surges of pain became more rapid and ever more violent, Grandma Melba positioned herself in front of her daughter, gently massaging her stomach with castor oil and reassuring her that her baby was on the way.

My mother felt no sense of elation at my birth, only relief that I was no longer in her belly and that the pain had stopped. She didn't feel in any way maternal towards me, her new baby. She was fine with children, other people's children, the ones who could walk and talk and go to school, like her younger brothers and the Dees' children, but not with me. And so, within a few days of my birth, she left me in the care of my grandparents and returned to her employers.

It was strange to reflect, many years later when Auntie Madge told me this story, that maybe her lack of maternal feelings had been passed on to me.

# Chapter 6

One night, after Grandpa Sippa had finished telling us a long-winded duppy and Anancy story and the other village children had left, he told us that he had something important to say to us. 'Mi an yuh grandmada get news from yuh mada,' he said, looking at each of us in turn. 'She seh har papers come trough fi har fi travel to Hinglan. She want Petra to measure yuh up fi new clothes because she want fi tek picture wit all a yuh before she leave fa Hinglan.'

The news of my mother's plans didn't upset me: I always knew that I had a mother – who was separate to my grandmother – and although my Grandma Melba was the midwife for all my three younger siblings, I had no memory whatsoever of my mother being present in my grandparents' home. So I had no idea what she would even look like. Grandma Melba told me that when my mother finally left her job with the Dees, she took up an apprenticeship to develop her skills in dressmaking, something Mrs Dee had been teaching her. She said that, when my mother completed her apprenticeship, Mother and my uncle Lambert set up a small tailoring and dressmaking business in a two-storey Victorian house in Milverton, a town about fifteen miles from our village. My mother worked upstairs on an old Singer sewing machine, while Uncle Lambert worked downstairs in the front room. They were both good tailors and got plenty of orders from the district where they had their business.

It was our mother's cousin Petra who normally measured us up for new clothes, so Grandpa Sippa sent a message to her to let her know of Mother's request.

Grandma Melba made sure that we were all thoroughly scrubbed before parading us on the verandah to await Cousin Petra.

Sure enough, Cousin Petra wasted no time getting to our house – knowing she would be paid a whole two shillings for her work. She was a little breathless on arrival and Grandma suggested she took a rest on the verandah. She immediately threw off her rubber slippers and cleaned her feet on the floor cloth, before walking purposefully across to a wooden bench in the corner. Grandma offered her a tall glass of freshly made lime drink. The silvery segments that gave the drink its sharp taste floated gently at the top.

As Cousin Petra slowly sipped at her drink, appreciative noises seeped from her lips. She emptied the glass and let out a huge belch. 'Tank you, Miss Melba, tank you kindly,' she said. 'Now, come, children, so mi can set fi work. Which a yuh mi fi measure first?' She pulled absentmindedly at some small curled up hairs that were growing out of her pointy chin, then pulled down one of the tape measures that was hanging loosely around her shoulders. 'Sonny, come, child, yuh look like yuh a dead fi pee-pee, so come let me measure yuh up first and put yuh outa yuh misery.'

Sonny looked at Cousin Petra somewhat perplexed, not able to make the connection between wanting a pee and being measured for new clothes. Clifton and Patsy followed. I was last, as I was for most things, presumably because I was the oldest.

Cousin Petra had some special paper, which she pinned on to the clothes we were wearing. Each time she took a measurement she drew lines on to smaller bits of paper and wrote numbers at different points along the lines. We'd had this done before, when Cousin Petra had measured us for new school uniforms and special church dresses, so we knew the routine. Standing very still was a must, and any attempt to touch the paper that was pinned to you would result in a sharp slap on the offending hand. Once she completed her measuring, Cousin Petra deftly unpinned and removed the paper from our clothing. Then she gathered up all her bits, stuck her pencil behind her right ear, folded her tape measures and pushed them into her apron pocket.

'Bye, Miss Melba,' she called out, as she turned on her heel and began walking away across the dirt yard. 'Oh! An mine yuh pickney dem look after yuh grandmada now,' she said, without a backward glance.

Six weeks after our measurements were taken, Grandma Melba visited our mother for the day and returned with our new clothes. 'Yuh kyan do de trial tomorrow,' she said, removing from my head any idea that she was about to show us our new clothes.

The following morning, Grandma sent Patricia and I to fetch two buckets of water from the old concrete water tank hidden from view behind a row of orange and pomegranate trees at the bottom of our back yard.

'Cleanliness is next to godliness,' Grandma said, 'soh yuh children dem mus know seh new clothes dem have to go pon clean body.'

The old water tank was deep and covered in a slimy green moss. On the water's surface a myriad of weird small creatures leapt about as if giving some peculiar balletic performance. The buckets, when filled, weighed twice as much as Patricia and I did, and it took all our strength to haul the water up to the tank's edge while the slippery threadbare sisal rope threatened to snap with every tug. We were always relieved not to be dragged down into the murky darkness under the weight of the full buckets. Our cousin Everton had not been so lucky. He had fallen into the parish tank two years earlier. When the village men finally pulled him out, his mother didn't recognise him – his body bloated up to several times its normal size. The village men had to build a coffin big enough for a fully grown man to contain his eight-year-old body. Only a day earlier I had been in school with him and we'd ended the day playing cricket with the other village children. Everton's mother didn't speak for several weeks after his death, while her three other bewildered children gathered around her with defeated, tear-stained faces.

Patricia and I returned with the water to find the boys pressed behind the back door of the house as if held there by glue. They both hated carbolic soap and water, and as the time approached for their scrub down they started wailing. Clifton first, then Sonny joined in the chorus, 'Murder woe! Murder woe! Please, Grandma Melba, de soap wi go innah mi eyes. Murder woe!'

They were making such a commotion I was sure they could be heard in the village across the gully.

'Bwoy pickney, mi nuh waan fi call oonoo name twice!' Grandma Melba warned sternly.

Clifton and Sonny finally crept out from behind the door where they were trying to make themselves invisible.

'Stop de bawling now an step innah de tub. Nuh tempt mi fi tek de switch to yuh scrawny back end dem.' Grandma over-soaped the loofah and, brows furrowed, began scrubbing the boys with some force.

'Murder woe! Murder woe! De soap deh innah mi eyes. Murder woe! Grandma Melba, mi eye dem a hot me!'

Clifton had given up screaming and left it to Sonny to do his best. Grandma poured a bucket of cold water unceremoniously over them, tugged at their ears, which she wiped roughly, before ordering them to go and wait in the Hall.

Patricia and I fetched fresh water and scrubbed ourselves, careful not to miss any part of our bodies, as we had to pass Grandma's inspection. We dried off with what was left of an old sheet and pulled on our hand-made cotton panties, which Grandma had made from the same old sheet and were sized to last for at least another year. As we waited in the Hall for Grandma, I found myself thinking – as I had several times before – that there were no pictures of our mother in there, even though there was at least one framed photograph of all of Grandma and Grandpa's other children, along with their husbands or wives. I once asked Grandma why there were no pictures of our mother and her reply was, 'Cho, pickney gal, nuh bada yuhself wid big people business.'

Now, following my gaze as she entered the Hall behind us, Grandma Melba said, 'Dem seh a picture tell a tousand story.' Then she directed us all to sit in a row on the bed in readiness for the fitting of our new clothes.

Sonny was first to be helped into his beige-coloured khaki shirt and pants, while Grandma Melba palmed his newly shaved head and marvelled at Grandpa Sippa's deftness with a cut-throat razor. Sonny's entire outfit, including his socks and shoes, was too big for him, and he looked rather self-conscious in his new clothes. But Grandma simply declared, 'Handsome!' and grinned, flashing her ill-fitting false teeth. Conversely, Clifton's matching suit was too small, and begged the question of how accurate Cousin Petra's measurements had been. His long knock-kneed legs jutted from his too-short shorts and his shoes were at least one size too small. I watched quietly as he attempted to hide his discomfort to fit with Grandma Melba's nodding approval. She could just swap their clothes around, I thought.

'Tek de shoes dem off, pickney. Mi a go get fi yuh grandfada to fix dem up fi yuh.'

The shoes were off before Grandma could finish her sentence. Clifton flexed his released toes and his face visibly relaxed.

Next, Grandma brought out Patricia's dress, which was made with a combination of soft-pink and pale-blue cottons. The body of the dress was pink and the blue was used for a delicate round collar. There were front pockets and a separate waistband, which gave the appearance of a belt, only with holes and buttons rather than a buckle. Sewn into the underside was a double set of petticoats, made of a fine but stiff pink crinoline mesh, which gave the dress a wonderful puffed out look.

Our eyes were out on stalks. Neither of us had ever seen such a beautiful dress, and certainly no one else for miles around would have a dress like that.

Patricia spun round and round, like a dog in search of its tail, in an effort to admire herself. The shoes, when Grandma produced them, made my mouth drop open. Patricia looked at them and went into a hysterical frenzy of laughter – earning her a chiding from Grandma of 'Chile, stop yuh stupidness!' The black shoes shone like the seeds in ackee pods. A bow in the shape of a small rose sat atop each one and a thin strap at the ankle held them on with gleaming silver buckles. Patricia was mesmerised by her outfit.

'Please, please, God,' I begged, 'please let mi ave de same.'

'A wa yuh seh, pickney? Wah mek yuh call de Lard's name out in vain? A sinting wrong wit yuh? Duppy gwaan juk yuh or sinting?'

Grandma allowed Patricia to strut around for a while and then, when she heard some voices approaching the house, she instructed her to walk out on to the verandah. Grandma plonked her tiny frame down on a cushioned chair as she listened to the eccentric middle-aged twins Miss Merle and Miss Blossom cooing their approval. Miss Blossom helped out Grandma Melba and Grandpa Sippa from time to with the washing and ironing, but sometimes Grandma Melba complained that 'De dyam foolish ooman nuh know ow to mind fi har business. She always a poke poke bout.'

'Patricia, a soh yuh look beautiful, like a princess fram foreign,' said Miss Merle.

'A true dat,' echoed Miss Blossom.

The women sounded like one person having a conversation with herself in a cave.

'She pretty eeh, Miss Blossom.'

'A true! She pretty so till, Miss Merle.'

'She musa get dat frock fram foreign,' they said in harmony.

They tittered some more before shuffling off.

Grandma Melba stood up and displayed the kind of triumph that might be expected had she created the dress herself. But the moment Miss Merle and Miss Blossom disappeared from view she told Patricia to return to the Hall. 'Tek dem dere tings dem off, chile – quick quick! Before yuh spoil yuh mada handiwork.'

Grandma Melba was clearly proud of our mother and, for a moment, I too felt a sense of pride for this mother that I didn't know, but who had made us these beautiful new clothes, even if they were only for us to wear to say our goodbyes.

I could hear the boom-boom of my heart as it came to my turn for trying on my new clothes. I soon discovered that my dress was just as beautiful as Patricia's. It was made in the same style, but where the main body of her dress was pink with blue trim, mine was the opposite. I loved it! However, I could immediately see that the gorgeous patent leather shoes were at least one size too small for my fat feet. But come hell or high water I was going to make them fit. As I pushed my feet into the shoes, I felt my toes curl beneath me in protest. The tops of my feet puffed themselves up high above the pretty shoes. I winced again and again, without making a sound – my problem was the same as Clifton's. After what seemed like an age, Grandma bent forward and squeezed at each foot in turn.

'Mmm! Petra nuh measure any of dem right at all,' she said, a hint of resigned frustration in her voice. 'Mi a fi go see wah yuh grandfada can do. Mi nuh tink dis one a go easy fi fix though. Mi nuh tink dis shiny sinting gwaan budge dat easy at all.'

Even as she spoke, I'd already made up my mind that whether or not Grandpa could fix my shoes, I was wearing them for my photographs. I even thought of wearing them to bed every night, in the hope that they might stretch as I slept. There was still another month to go before our mother's arrival, time enough, I figured, for Grandpa to work his magic on both Clifton's and my shoes.

# Chapter 7

The month leading up to our mother's visit passed slowly, but we children could talk of little else. We boasted of the visit to the other village children. We wondered what she'd look like, or which one of us would look the most like her. We spoke incessantly of the beautiful things she'd bring us. I dreamt of a white-skinned doll with glassy blue eyes and wavy brown hair, like the one my cousin Precious's mother had sent her from England. The doll had proper clothes, including a tiny pair of plastic shoes. Patricia said that she wanted lots and lots of mint balls, and the boys agreed on a football like the one Uncle Lambert had brought back from America when he'd worked there picking oranges, before setting up his tailoring business. It was a red and white football, which we'd all spent many happy hours kicking and throwing, until a village boy named Denis sat on it and squashed out all the air. My brothers had shown the deflated ball to Uncle Lambert and asked him to fix it, but he told them he'd need a pump for that and no one in the village owned a pump – apart from the football there was nothing that needed pumping.

The day of our mother's arrival eventually came. She was due to arrive sometime in the afternoon at Preston, the small town nearest to our village through which the bus passed; once she got to Preston the rest of her journey would be completed on foot and donkey. It was a day full of excitement and strangeness at the same time. In my nearly eleven years, I couldn't come up with a single memory of our mother, and neither could Patricia, and definitely not the boys.

I woke early and watched as Grandpa saddled up Treasure Girl and Bugle Boy, who were, despite the latter's name, both female donkeys. Two donkeys meant that our mother would definitely be coming loaded up with wonderful things for us! When he'd finished, Grandpa heaved himself into Treasure Girl's saddle and grasped Bugle Boy's extended rein. As the donkeys trotted off down the dew-covered path, I did a little dance of anticipation. My mother was coming. My mother!

It wasn't just me who was giddy with anticipation. It seemed as if the entire village had heard of our mother's intended visit and, as the afternoon drew on, adults and children began to congregate on the edge of our yard like John Crows that had smelt carrion. The odd person would pass by, surprised at the gathering masses, and ask, 'A wah a gwaan?'

'Yuh nuh hear seh Miss Violet a come today?' someone would respond from the crowd. I hoped that they'd all melt away in the same way they'd arrived. Whatever our mother was bringing was not going to be enough to share among almost the entire village.

It was Treasure Girl who announced Mother's imminent arrival with her braying, something she always did when she was near home.

'Anybody wouda tink seh dat donkey is human,' Grandma Melba muttered.

The next thing I knew, Treasure Girl was standing in our yard with the person I presumed to be our mother sitting astride her. I searched her face for a memory, anything that would tell me I actually knew who she was, but nothing came.

She climbed gingerly off the back of the donkey, helped by Grandpa. Although we recognised nothing about her face, she looked every inch the lady that we'd imagined. She was small in stature like my grandmother, but light brown in complexion. Again, like my grandmother, she had a mass of hair, an elongated neck, and a face sharply defined by the highest of cheekbones. Her dress was beautiful! A simple purple paisley-patterned dress that had sleeves to the elbow and which showed off her slim figure. Her bottom kicked out in exactly the same way as Grandma's too. Pretty earrings dangled from her ears, set off by a matching necklace. Patricia and I just stood and stared at her.

Then Patricia pointed at her and blurted out, 'Look! Look at her shoes! I nevah in mi life see someting soh pretty!'

I could see what she meant. Her shoes were made of white leather, soft-looking and toeless, with little cone heels also covered in white leather. Her feet, unlike mine, appeared slim and dainty. I repeated out loud what I was thinking inside my head, 'Our mother is a natural born princess!'

'She's not a princess,' Patricia retorted. 'Mi did see a princess in a book at school. She was white like Teacher Cavallo and she had yellow hair.'

'Mi nuh care about your Teacher Cavallo,' I shot back, 'fi wi mada is a princess. She a black princess, because all princess who live here have to be black.'

'Anyway,' Patricia continued, ignoring my statement, 'mi did tell Teacher Cavallo dat when mi grow big, mi waan fi be a princess like de one in de book. She did tell me seh princess only live in faraway places, like Canada, de place where she come from.'

Clifton and Sonny were standing to attention like miniature soldiers, even though Clifton's peculiar knock-knees made him appear as if he was unable to stand straight. As our mother came towards us, our collective hearts could almost be heard hammering in our chests, along with the sound of rapid intakes of breath.

She paused for a moment, then bent slightly forward and said, 'Hello, my children.' She talked in what Grandma always described – whenever folks spoke anything but our local dialect – as a 'speaky-spokey' voice, even though Grandma herself was not averse to a bit of speaky-spokey when she felt she had a strong point to make.

Following her brief speaky-spokey greeting, Mother disappeared into the Hall, quickly followed by Grandma. The double wooden doors closed firmly behind them, leaving us with the feeling that our position was little different from that of the waiting neighbours. A month of excited waiting, rewarded with three words. A quarter of a sentence.

We didn't see our mother again until the following day, when, having scrubbed ourselves raw and dressed in our new clothes, we were invited to join her in the Hall. As we hoped, she'd brought lots of presents, which were separated into small piles, placed on the bed a few inches apart. She gave us all water and food canteens with straps around them, so that we could carry them like bags. The boys got underwear, socks, schoolbooks and a geometry set each. Patricia and I were given packets of panties with the days of the week emblazoned on the fronts. My sister was also given an elaborate crinoline underslip with layers of yellow and pink taffeta. I got a more traditional half-slip of white calico with narrow red and blue satin ribbons stitched around it. It was the kind of slip that every girl in the village had. I tried not to show my disappointment, while promising myself that I'd do whatever it took to get a few wears out of my sister's slip. Mother also gave us long pink and blue satin ribbons along with matching socks, which she told us were to be worn with our new dresses for our photographs. Finally, she gave us girls a packet of white handkerchiefs with little flowers embroidered on each corner.

We all thanked her politely for our gifts, although none of us had received any of the things we'd wished for. What was important was that we now knew that we had a real mother. That was all that mattered.

Grandma's gift was a long brown crêpe dress with perfect pleats. The dress hovered just above her ankles and made her look very stylish. She was well known in the village for finding a reason not to go to church – most Sundays remembering that she had either an animal that was about to give birth, or one that had wandered off that she had to go in search of. But on the Sunday after my mother had given her the new brown dress, Grandma topped off her new outfit with an elaborate beige hat and set off for church. Grandpa, on the other hand, had little interest in clothing. My mother brought him a bottle of good white rum and a bottle of blood-red syrup, which he sometimes used as a chaser. She might have lived away for a long time, but she hadn't forgotten her father's favourite drink.

It was Monday morning, and Mother had been with us for a whole week. The house stirred into life at around four in the morning, when Grandma Melba hurried out us out of bed with uncharacteristic haste.

'Come, pickney! All of yuh fi get up now. Yuh figet a today yuh mada a tek yuh to get yuh picture dem.'

In truth, we'd all stayed awake most of the night overcome with excitement.

'Erna, gallang with Patricia fi get de water, an mek sure all a yuh wash yuhself good.'

It was to be our first outing with our mother, and the longest bus ride we'd ever been on, as the photographer lived a long way from our village. Grandma made herself busy in the kitchen, where she prepared saltfish fritters and bammies for our lunch.

'Mi a beg yuh fi get mi two pound a parrotfish and two pound a goatfish,' Grandma said to our mother, who was checking how the breakfast was coming on. 'Dem should be nice an fresh caus de market nuh soh far fram de sea.'

Grandma reached down the front of her dress and removed a knotted handkerchief. She untied the handkerchief and handed two shillings to Mother who studied them for a moment before handing the coins back.

'Don't worry yourself, Miss Melba, I can take care of that,' she said.

Grandma put her two shillings back in her handkerchief, tied the knot and stuffed it back somewhere in her clothing. 'Mek mi go finish wit de food soh yuh kyan mek yuh way.' Grandma disappeared for a moment, but in no time she returned with a wicker basket wrapped in a blue-checked tablecloth. 'Plenty food dede to feed all a oonoo fi de whole day,' she said.

'Thank you, Miss Melba, for doing all that,' my mother replied.

Cousin Petra was waiting to comb our hair. She parted mine into fat bunches and made three plaits, one at the front and two at the back. Then she cut a pale blue satin ribbon into three pieces and tied a bow at the root of each plait. Patricia's short hair meant lots of small plaits with a pink ribbon wrapped around her head and tied in a large bow at the front. The boys had had their usual haircuts from Grandpa on the Sunday. We were all dressed in our finery, except for our shoes and socks, which our mother told us we should carry with us – so we set off for Preston wearing our rubber sandals that were made from discarded car tyres and would keep the worst of the red dirt at bay. Mother packed a rag, for cleaning our feet when we reached the photographer's house; only then would we be allowed to wear our fine shoes. Mother herself was wearing a navy skirt with a matching jacket and a white blouse. In a bag she carried her lovely white shoes that also matched her blouse. She looked every inch a beautiful black princess.

We walked to the bus stop in silence, all concentrating on making sure we didn't catch any part of our clothing on the roadside brambles. The bus was due to make one of its stops directly opposite a provision shop owned by Mass Julius and his wife Miss Ethel. We were relieved after our long walk to find half a dozen upturned Coca-Cola boxes intended for seats lined up along the shop's verandah.

We made a beeline for the boxes, but a sharp rebuke from our mother stopped us in our tracks. 'Wait!' she shouted, before producing two whole tablecloths from her bag, which she spread across the boxes before we were allowed to sit down.

Moments after we sat down, the loud continuous tooting of the approaching bus shattered the quiet of the morning – the cacophony was the only way villagers had of knowing that the bus was actually on its way and not broken down somewhere.

We clambered aboard the bus ahead of our mother and it continued its journey along the rough tarmac road, which went from one end of the island to the other. The island's many mountains meant that the road curved and wound its way like a meandering river. Every so often the battered old bus chugged up a seemingly impossible hill, its passengers loudly willing it on with shouts of 'Yuh kyan do it, driver! Wi kyan mek it!' And as it hurtled down the other side, the more nervous passengers jammed their dusty sandalled feet to the floor as if their actions would somehow assist the braking. The journey was long and uncomfortable. The dirty scraps of cloth still visible on some of the old sprung seats made it impossible to imagine a time when the bus was spanking new, with seats covered in gleaming upholstery. Children were not expected to occupy any of the seats while there were adults who could fill them, so while Sonny got to sit on our mother's lap for the very first time, the rest of us were jammed between the legs of any willing adults. Sonny sat there looking like a little king, with his belly sticking out and a satisfied smile on his face.

Since there were no official bus stops, the driver was constantly braking to a shuddering halt for embarking and alighting passengers, wherever they chose to be picked up or dropped off – on the very edge of a deep gully, or even in the middle of someone's front yard. The rule was that if the bus could be seen it could be waved down, and if a passenger needed to get off at a particular spot then someone just needed to shout, 'One stop, driver!' and this would be followed by a screech of brakes and loud engine noises, with the very same passengers who had requested the stop now shouting, 'Easy nuh, driver! Tek it easy, man! An nuh dead wi waan fi dead. Wi jus waan yuh fi stop de bus!'

I'd travelled on a bus less than a handful of times and I mostly enjoyed the experience, but I'd also caught sight of a couple of those so-called 'jolly buses' that had left the road with their passengers before ending up in one of the island's many gullies. Now, I distracted myself from my worry by eavesdropping on people's conversations and counting how many men, women and children I saw along the sides of the road as the bus sped through the countryside. Often, people boarded the bus who knew each other, and loud friendly chatter soon developed among the adults; children, as usual, spoke only if spoken to – unless they needed a toilet stop.

'Marning, marning. A nice marning it is!' Talk was often interspersed with a story about some recently dead relative. 'Is how long now Mass Isaac dead?' asked one woman, who seemed to have addressed her question to everyone on the bus. She continued speaking without waiting for an answer, 'Im was a good man, doah, and im did reach a respectable hage. De Lard giveth and de Lard taketh. Mi sure seh im will get plenty a Jehovah blessing. Im had such a lovely send-off. Everybody in di village did dede. People did love de man, yuh se! Dat is owcome dem did nickname him Beauty, because im did ave a beautiful spirit fi true.'

'Praise de Lord, sista! A truth yuh a talk. Praise him,' all the adults chorused.

A little while later, a woman who'd been quietly turning the pages of a well-thumbed King James Bible piped up, 'Yes, fi true! Mass Isaac lived a whole tree score year an ten, an im live a good life. Nuh like Mass Sylvester. Im nuh even sixty and de stroke tek im weh. Mi nuh seh im was a bad man! But a plenty people pon di island a dead sudden from dis stroke an pressure sickness.'

'Yuh mighta put yuh finger right pon de problem, Miss Lily,' another woman said. 'Mi wonder if dem a transport dese disease tings from Hamerica!'

Miss Lily, who clearly hadn't finished continued, 'Cause we nuh did ave dese kinda sickness pon de island. Tek fi mi mada and fada. Dem dead long time, but dem dead of ole age. Dem nuh dead of nuh kind a sickness. An di Bible seh a soh people fi live and dead. Yes, sah, tree score years and ten. De Lard word tell us Harmageddon a come, and mi sure seh it nearly deh pon us. Yes, sarh, we living in dark days.' Miss Lily drew in a deep breath and shifted uneasily on her seat. She was a large woman, fatter than anyone I'd seen in the village, and it had taken a lot of energy for her to make her speech. Sweat crept out from under her plaid head-tie and trickled down her pleasant, round face. She waited until her entire face was glistening before pulling a rag from her basket and dabbing it roughly about her face.

'Praise de Lard, sister!' chorused a number of the passengers in response to Miss Lily's statement. 'Never truer words said. Praise de Lard. Praise him. God bless yuh, sister. God bless yuh!'

The door at the back of the bus was badly damaged and couldn't be opened. This left the entrance beside the driver as the only one for exiting and entering the bus, and that entrance was missing its door. This meant that the conductor had to forcibly prevent waiting passengers from pushing their way on to the bus before those wishing to alight could get off.

He had his work cut out. He was tall with very long arms, which he stretched across the doorway. This mostly worked as a deterrent, but occasionally a fight broke out and the driver reacted by revving up his engine and setting down passengers a little further up the road. The waiting passengers then ran towards the bus and entered in a much calmer state, knowing full well that if any further fights ensued, they'd be left by the roadside and their only hope for another bus would be the next day at roughly the same time. I couldn't guess the conductor's age, but thought he had the face of an overgrown schoolboy. His eyes set deep in his face had very black irises, giving them the appearance of two glowing black balls surrounded by only a little white matter. He wore a matching khaki shirt and trousers, which shone from being ironed too many times. I watched as the muscles in his arms swelled when he lifted oversized bags, which he skillfully placed on his head before climbing up the little ladder on the back of the bus so he could deposit them on the roof. He was a calming character who greeted every passenger with a cheerful 'Good morning' and a flash of perfect teeth. It was the first time I ever fell in love.

As we neared the end of our journey, Mother began her preparations to get us to the front of the bus. She used her bottom to push her way down the crowded aisle while holding on to Clifton and Sonny. Patricia and I followed closely behind them in case the path got closed off. I was the last off the bus and my feet had barely touched the ground before it lurched forward, rounded a corner and disappeared from view, its horn warning the next set of passengers of its imminent arrival. I watched the bus disappear mostly with relief, but mixed with anticipation that I might see the conductor again on the return journey. We remained standing in the spot where we alighted while our mother took a good look around.

Suddenly, we heard a loud scream. Further along the dirt track, two boys were having a ferocious fight. In a split second the shorter, chunkier boy, brought his taller, skinnier opponent crashing to the ground with a well-placed kick to his back. Without saying a word, our mother ripped a slender low hanging branch from a nearby tree, scraped back the leaves in a single movement and marched towards the boys. Neither boy saw her coming, until the short boy felt the sting of the whip around his lower legs. The boy on the ground sprang to his feet and within seconds both vanished into the bush. Mother returned with a slight smirk of pleasure on her face. It was normal practice on the island to deliver a good beating to anyone's child caught in any kind of wrongdoing. The child would then likely be dragged home to parents, who often drove home the point already made by the stranger with a further beating. Nevertheless, we four children stared at our mother with renewed respect. Clearly, she was not someone to be messed with.

The photographer's house was tucked back from the road on the opposite side to where the bus dropped us off. It was only a few minutes' walk from the fish market, which we smelt long before it could be seen. Mother knew the area as it was in fact not too far from where she and Uncle Lambert had their tailoring business. Once the photographer's house came into view, Mother instructed us to sit on a nearby wall. She produced the piece of cloth and soaked it with water from her canteen. Then she told us to remove our rubber shoes and clean up our feet.

'Come, children, let's go,' she said, as soon as we had our new socks and shoes on.

We found ourselves walking down a path lined with fruit trees. Ripe mangoes hung heavily on their branches and the ground was hardly visible under a sea of rotten and recently fallen fruits. Coconut trees bowed regally above the other trees and here and there the odd fallen coconut sat intact on the festering carpet. We reached a spacious front yard that was littered with discarded plastic bottles, old tyres and a small mountain of rusty tins. A man and a boy of about ten years were making their way down the path away from the house, talking in an animated fashion, the boy stumbling as he looked up at his father. The man was clutching a brown envelope tightly to his chest. As we drew level, my mother and the man stopped, exchanged greetings, and quickly got into a conversation.

'Looks like we're on the same mission,' my mother said.

'Yes, yes,' the man replied. 'Young Albert and I are moving to Florida, in America.' The man spoke with a clear, precise town accent. It seemed, like our mother, he'd lived away from the country for some time.

Young Albert shifted uncomfortably from one foot to the other, his face wearing a grimace. He obviously wasn't happy with the plan.

'My wife's been there for the past seven years,' the man continued. 'She filed for the two of us and it's a good thing, too, because being mother and father to young Albert is not easy at all. Not easy at all,' he added, looking at his son with affectionate concern. 'That's not to say he's a bad boy in any way. In fact, he's a most obedient child. It's just that not a day go by when he doesn't ask about the mother. I know he miss her. But I also know he is not one hundred per cent sure about leaving the island, either. But you will soon get use to it, son,' he said, looking at the boy again. Albert nodded his head very slightly. 'My wife says Florida is gigantic, but apparently it's just one small section of America. And she tells me it's hot too, just like here, and that she even has mango and pear trees growing in the back yard, and that they bear good fruit. Her only complaint is that the place is flat like a bammy!'

I thought the man was never going to stop talking. It was as if this was his first opportunity to talk to anyone about their upcoming trip.

My mother said nothing until the man finally closed his mouth.

'It's my husband who filed for me,' she told him. 'We hope to make enough money to come back to the island and set up a little business for ourselves in five or ten years.'

None of us quite understood this thing about 'filing', but we knew that the word was somehow connected to people from the island travelling to foreign places. It was obviously a different kind of filing from what Grandpa Sippa did when he was sharpening his machete or the hoes we used on the farm.

This was also the first time I realised my mother had a husband. Somehow this fact had never been relayed to us children. My mother had a husband! I couldn't stop thinking about it.

Mother and the man exchanged a few more pleasantries and then bid each other farewell and God's speed for their travels. We continued along the path until a large, dilapidated house came into view. The white paint had flaked off its exterior and red roof tiles lay scattered on the ground around it. We walked up five concrete steps to a wide verandah that jutted from the front of the house. The verandah was lined with large terracotta pots filled with flowers we called 'Joseph's coat of many colours'. A few larger pots were planted with lush ferns. There were two round metal tables with two low-backed chairs tucked underneath them, and the thick layer of dust that covered them suggested that neither had been used for some time. Mother moved towards the door and we followed. She took hold of the bulbous doorknocker and banged twice.

We waited in silence for a little while, until an old man, with crumpled white skin and a shabby suit, opened the door. He stretched forward a scrawny hand with dirty, long fingernails. I watched for Mother's reaction as their hands met. A cursory smile moved across her lips.

'I am Mr John, the photographer,' the old man said. 'I hope your journey wasn't too hard? The road here is rough and is particularly bad close to town.' He dragged his words out as he spoke. Everything about Mr John was crumpled and aged, except his eyes, which sparkled like dancing stars. They were eyes that somehow you knew could see beyond the ordinary.

Mother mumbled something about the journey being 'not so bad,' then complained that the driver allowed too many people on the bus. Mr John nodded; he clearly understood all about bus journeys on the island. He turned and led us through the hallway down a narrow passage towards the back of the house. The inside of the house seemed vast and mostly shrouded in darkness, the only light coming from the windows at the front. I counted the doors as we walked past and there were ten in all, five on either side of the hallway. Mr John showed our mother into the very last room and waved at us to follow, all the while clenching a half-smoked cigar in his left hand, which clearly hadn't long gone out, as the heaviness of tobacco smoke still hung in the air. Then he left us alone in the crowded room for a few minutes.

I looked around the room and wondered whether the old man had taken us to the right place – there was a small oil stove, a single wooden bed, and a table and chairs, each with a different part missing; I was worried that the first person to sit on one might end up in a heap on the floor. Leaning against a wall, a lopsided wooden bookshelf housed several piles of assorted papers, and one battered book called *Modern Photography*. Frameless photographs of various people were stuck randomly on the stained walls.

On his return, he looked over us children with a curious expression, as though he'd forgotten that he'd met us only moments earlier. Then he ushered us into a much smaller room, which was very dark but mostly free of clutter. He struck a match and lit two Tilley lamps that hung on opposite walls, flooding the room with warm light. On the right side of the room, two large, shallow plastic tanks sat side by side on a thick wooden shelf, alongside a number of plastic bottles filled with different coloured liquids. In the corner, there was something covered with a large black cloth. The old man carefully removed the cloth, revealing a camera sat on top of a wooden tripod. He lifted the camera and the tripod and carefully placed them in the centre of the room, then climbed on to a wooden crate and stood behind the camera. He spent the next few minutes covering and uncovering the top of his body and the camera with the black cloth.

'Come over here, Miss Violet,' he said eventually, pointing to a spot about five feet away from the camera. 'Come, children, join your mother.'

We walked across and stood on either side of our mother – girls one side, boys the other. The photographer came over to us and physically moved our positions. He placed me to the left of our mother, Patricia to her right, and Sonny and Clifton in front of her. Then he extinguished one of the lamps, returned to the camera, climbed on to the crate and repeated his actions.

After a long pause he announced, 'That's not going to work. I think it will be best to do it outside, in the garden.'

He gathered up his contraptions and we followed him outside where he asked us to stand in the same formation in front of a sea of tall flowering plants. Then he climbed back on to his crate. 'When I wave my hand,' he said, 'shout Hinglan!'

He waved and we shouted.

A bright flash like lightning came from a glass thing with wires, making me blink in shock.

'All done!' he said, stepping off the crate. 'You can go off now and look round town, if you like. Come back in a few hours, the picture should be ready.'

We left Mr John's house and headed for a field close by, where Mother took our lunch from the hamper and placed it on a rug, which she'd carefully arranged on the grass. For plates she used the sliced banana leaves that Grandma had placed in the bottom of the hamper. Mother had hardly spoken to us on the entire journey and when she had, it was always in the form of an instruction. Now was no different.

'Wash your hands and sit down for lunch.'

We did as she asked.

'Thank you, Lord, for your bountiful provision. Amen.'

'Amen,' we echoed. Then we ate in silence.

After lunch, we headed to the nearby fish market where my mother purchased the fish Grandma Melba had asked for. When we returned to the photographer's house, we stared in amazement at the black and white image. I wasn't sure whether the girl staring back at me actually looked like me, but I could see that Patricia, Clifton and Sonny looked just like themselves, only all their clothes looked white. Our mother stood tall in the photograph, her cheekbones sharp beneath sad-looking eyes. I turned away from the portrait for a moment and glanced up at her and saw a tear the size of a raindrop leaking from the corner of her left eye. She caught my gaze and quickly reached for one of the pretty handkerchiefs she carried everywhere and dabbed it away. Then she thanked Mr John, took the brown envelope containing a single copy of the photograph from his wrinkled hands, and carefully tucked it into her bag.

'Well, then, that's that,' she said, and we headed back to the bus stop.

# Chapter 8

Only a few days had passed since our adventure, but when I returned to school I found it impossible to describe to my classmates the experience of having our photographs taken. Only Opal claimed to have had photographs of her taken before. Everyone else was fascinated to hear about the process. Marva, my other best friend, wanted to know what the camera looked like.

'It was big an black,' I told her and the other gathered pupils. 'It had a thick roun glass ting at de front wit a shiny silver ting round it, like a big ring. Then dere was dis little pole ting sticking up wit a silver plate ting stick pon it. In de front of dat was a strange see-through glass ting wit small wire tings inside.' They all sat and stared at me, confusion etched across their faces. 'Mi nuh know ow else fi explain it,' I said, hoping to pre-empt Opal, who seemed increasingly sceptical of my description.

'A lie she a tell!' she suddenly blurted out. 'Yuh know how she always love making up stories. I have plenty picture take of mi an de photographer man nuh use anyting dat sound like dat.'

Anger surged inside me. I was not making up stories. I simply couldn't find a better way to explain what I had seen.

My mother spent her final week in the village, before leaving for England, lounging about the house doing very little. She rarely ventured outside and, when she did, within a few minutes she would be heard complaining about what she described as 'This darn mosquito and fly-infested hell hole!' However, she was careful not to make any such reference in Grandma Melba's presence. That would be cussing language, as far as Grandma was concerned, and no child of whatever age would have the temerity to cuss in the presence of a parent. Our mother also probably understood that Grandma loved the village almost as much as she loved her four grandchildren and that it wouldn't do to hurt her feelings. When I asked Grandma what was wrong with our mother, she told me, 'Nutting nuh do har. Fi har head jus full wit har travel plans. Dis is a big someting leaving everyting behind.'

A few days later, Grandpa's friend Mass Charlie saw our mother off from the island's main airport. He lived in Kingston, close to the airport, and had agreed to accompany her as a favour to Grandpa. The next day, Grandpa told us that Mass Charlie had said that our mother insisted on carrying the framed photograph of her and her children in her hand for the entire journey. He said that she was barely able to take her eyes off the picture and that he watched her as she made her way across the tarmac towards the plane still clutching it against her chest. And so, with little fuss and no ceremony, our mother was gone. She'd spent less than two weeks with us. She'd brought us some nice things, but shown us little warmth. There were no kisses or cuddles. The only real difference for us was that we'd at last met the person who gave birth to us. Now at least we knew what she looked like, even though we had no idea what she felt like. After she left, all talk about her stopped as suddenly as it had begun. The only thing that changed was an air of sadness that developed around Grandma Melba. I guessed it was because our mother had gone so far away. I knew England was a faraway place, because Grandpa Sippa told me that it was a country on the other side of the ocean – he said it was much bigger than our country and that maybe our island could fit into England at least one hundred times.

'Yuh see dat big jet plane flying high up in a de air?' he said one day, just before mother departed. 'A one a dem a go carry yuh mada to Hinglan. De time change, chile. De island young people dem nuh want fi work pon de land. Innah Hinglan, dem nuh hafi work pon de land like we here. Dem ave plenty money dere. De street dem pave wit gold, so dem seh.'

'De plane a go stop an pick har up hereso?' Clifton asked.

'No,' Grandpa explained patiently, 'it not like de car or de bus. Dem have place call hairport on de island, which is jus a big road for de plane to put down an tek off again.'

Satisfied with Grandpa's answer, Clifton and Sonny drifted off to play marbles. But I was left with the image of golden streets in my head. The only gold I'd ever seen was the ring on Grandma's finger. I knew it cost a lot of money, because she told me that was why Grandpa left the island several times to go and work in Cuba, so he could earn enough money to marry her properly and put a gold ring on her finger. We children often watched the planes gliding through the perfectly blue sky. We didn't know how they got up there or how they could eventually come down, and Grandpa Sippa's explanation hadn't really helped. The noise made by the planes as they passed overhead was so loud that we would have to shout over each other to make ourselves heard. The thunderous sound was the cue for all of us children to rush to the highest point in the village, cup our hands over our mouths and shout together as loud as we could, 'Wi beg yuh, please! Drop some money fiwi! Drop some money fiwi!' And we'd continue yelling until the plane disappeared from sight.

# Chapter 9

Life in our village quickly returned to normal as we settled back into our routines of chores before school and chores after school. During school holidays we helped our grandparents as much as we were able to on the smallholding. We hated some of the chores, like walking miles in order to find firewood, which once found had to be chopped into small pieces and tied into large bundles that seemed to weigh more than we did. The elaborately wrapped headbands that separated our heads from the wood often felt useless as the weight bore down on our small bodies and caused our necks to disappear into our shoulders. Heavy buckets of water carried long distances had the same effect. Once relieved of the painful load, it would take some time for our bodies to feel normal again. But, despite the hard work, we were very happy children. That is, until one day, about two years after Mother left for England, when everything changed.

The first signs of wrongness started early in the morning when Percy, our proud rooster – who was a match for any alarm clock – failed to make even the tiniest of squawks. Grandma Melba had woken up anyway, and her first job was to find out what was going on with Percy. She was quick to return from the coop where Percy lived with his harem of twenty-one hens. In her hand she clutched several of his purple and red tail feathers. I gathered from her distressed explanation that poor old Percy had, at some point in the night, been persuaded with a handful of shelled corn to leave his perch and go up to the side of the coop. The holes in the wire mesh were just large enough for him to poke his head through to retrieve the corn. His killer had been waiting. He or she had promptly rung Percy's neck and ripped it clean off. The wire mesh was then opened up so the thief could retrieve Percy's headless body. Grandma had stepped on the bloodied head as she made her way up the path. His still-glassy eyes suggested that Percy's demise had probably taken place less than two hours earlier. We should have heard something, but, sadly for Percy, the hens who would normally squawk like crazy at the slightest disturbance had kept quiet. Grandma Melba knew that this was no ritual killing, but she decided to keep her counsel until she'd satisfied herself as to who exactly the culprit was; she didn't want any stupid talk of Obeahs and nonsense about people trying to do bad things to the James family. And anyway, she had a pretty good idea about what had happened to her rooster.

Grandma followed her nose and the odd feather and the trail led straight to Duppy Boy Briscoe's yard. There she discovered that Briscoe had hacked the bird in two and the old rooster was already bubbling away in his dirty Dutch pot with nothing but a red Scotch bonnet for flavour. Briscoe's only reaction when he saw Grandma Melba was to start brushing furiously at his clothing. Grandma just sucked her teeth and walked away. Briscoe was a middle-aged man whose odd behaviour had earned him the nickname Duppy Boy because, although in reality he was completely harmless, he sometimes resorted to doing bad things. He had this habit of wandering around the village talking to himself and brushing imaginary creatures from his body, which led many villagers to conclude that he was possessed by a duppy that prevented him from growing into a proper man. No one wanted the duppy to jump from his body into theirs, so it was best that he was left alone. Only the eccentric twins, Miss Merle and Miss Blossom, would stop by his little shack to deliver one of their strange exotic concoctions.

'Him nuh bada fi nyam anyting people give him anyhow,' Grandma Melba commented, 'so why anybody fi bada fi give him food?'

On the occasions that Briscoe stole food from his neighbours, it was usually a fowl or a small goat, depending on how quickly he could execute his plan and make his getaway. But all of this ceased troubling Grandma at around ten o'clock that same morning, when her mind swiftly moved on from the vengeance she'd been planning to something far more concerning.

Patricia, Clifton and Sonny came running towards her, breathless, their bare feet kicking up red dirt behind them. 'Grandma! Grandma!' screamed Patricia. 'De man a come wit telegram fiyuh.'

'What yuh talking bout, chile? What man, what telegram?'

'De Yellow Man wit de telegram,' Patricia repeated.

'Pickney! Move from me,' Grandma said, giving Patricia a little push. Then she slumped down on a nearby rock, shoulders hunched. Her soft dark face took on a look of defeat. Grandma was expecting the worst news, although as yet she had no idea what this news would be, or the nightmare that a few bland words on paper might unfold. Then the Yellow Man rounded the corner and walked over to Grandma.

'Morning, Miss Melba,' he said.

Grandma Melba acknowledged him with a nod.

He took a thin, sealed blue envelope from his pocket and rested it on her lap. Then he looked over at me. 'Good morning to you, Miss Nurse,' he smiled.

I glared at the yellow-skinned man with his one wonky eye. Then I rolled my eyes and moved close to my grandmother. It was the only one of my nicknames that I hated, and it was because the yellow one-eyed man had given it to me. I wasn't his nurse and, moreover, he'd probably brought my Grandma bad news in his horrible telegram. A long time passed and Grandma was still staring at the telegram. I wished Grandpa would return from over the hill where he was digging yams for dinner. He would have known what to do. Grandma mostly had her own ideas about things, but there were some situations when she couldn't think of a solution. It was at times such as these that she'd always ask Grandpa's advice. But he wasn't expected back for a few hours, so we just had to sit and wait for Grandma to come out of her shock. Finally, Grandma Melba picked up the telegram and handed it to me.

I opened it and read out the single line of words: '*Philbert. Arrive. Little Hammon. 3pm. Thursday 8th March.*'

I handed the telegram back to Grandma Melba. Without saying a word, she slipped the crumpled paper into her apron pocket and walked slowly over to the kitchen where she set to work cleaning away the ashes from the previous night's fire. I didn't hear her speak again until much later, long after Grandpa returned with the yams.

That night I crept up to the door that separated my grandparents' bedroom from the Hall and listened as she vented her rage to Grandpa.

'Why dis man a come a wi yard? Him wife jus join him innah a foreign. A wah him want wit us, Sippa?'

'A how mi kyan tell yuh, Melba? Mi jus as much innah de dark as yuh.'

'Well, mi nuh want him in mi ouse, soh help me God! Mi might do someting mi regret. Sippa! Mi a tell yuh! Mi nuh want dat ugly Satan devil man anywhere near mi pickney dem. Mi kyaan forgive him for de wickedness im do to Violet. Dat chile was nevah de same person after she meet dat devil man.'

I suddenly realised that the 'ugly Satan devil man' was my mother's husband. My mother had given birth to Patricia two years after I was born. Clifton and Sonny followed in quick succession, but the man who was to become her husband had left for England without knowing that she was pregnant with Sonny. Sonny was already four years old by the time he returned.

'A wah mi did seh from time, Sippa? Him a wolf innah sheep clothing,' I heard Grandma say.

Percy's death suddenly took on the appearance of an omen and it was certainly strange when, one week later, my mother's husband arrived at almost the exact time that was written on the telegram. It wasn't as if the island had a transport system that said the number nine bus would be leaving Spur Hill at such and such a time and would arrive at Preston station at another time.

He appeared suddenly, as if materialising out of thin air, boldly standing in front of our verandah. Grandma's mood immediately turned as dark as the swirling clouds that presaged yet another hurricane.

'Afternoon, Miss Melba,' he said. His mouth barely moved when he spoke her name.

I stood behind Grandma and watched him as his bloodshot eyes looked beyond her at the house. He was a bulky man in his forties, already greying and balding. He looked, Grandma told me later, exactly as she remembered him. His eyes had always disturbed her. They were too close together and the whites were always red. She thought of him as a man who was permanently angry. She didn't like him the first time my mother had introduced him in town. She didn't like him when she reluctantly attended their hurried marriage. And she didn't like him now. We continued watching him as he shifted uncomfortably from one heavy-booted foot to the other.

'I did say afternoon, Miss Melba,' he repeated in a louder, but still half-hearted greeting.

Grandma hissed, 'And I did hear you.' Then she turned on her heel and left him standing there.

We children had no idea why he was standing in our yard, or why he'd come, and clearly neither did Grandma. The only thing that was obvious was that he was definitely not welcome or wanted. When he finally uprooted his bulk, he took the path towards the next village. I suspected then that Grandma was a bit of an Obeah woman. Her face visibly relaxed as he ambled from view, but I could also tell that she knew he'd be back. That night I dreamt that a large hand pushed through the jalousie window in our bedroom and grabbed at one of my feet. I instinctively retracted my legs. When I woke in the morning the dream remained in my memory.

One week later he was back in our yard. Grandma sensed that he was coming hours before he arrived and commented loudly that the weird-looking patoo – which had flown overhead sometime earlier, its massive owl eyes visible in the brilliant morning sunshine – was bad luck. 'Everybody know seh de patoo nuh fi fly a day time. It eider a go bring death or someting final.'

This time, he made no attempt to greet Grandma. 'I come for my children,' he shouted. The words spluttered from his mouth and seemed to linger for a second in the air before hitting Grandma somewhere deep in her stomach. Nevertheless, she held herself straight as she addressed him sternly.

'Which children would that be?' she said in her best speaky-spokey English.

'The three over there,' he barked, any attempt at politeness gone from his voice. His eyes shot past me without registering my presence and a lumpy finger pointed towards my siblings who had all been busy making mud cakes out of loose earth at the edge of our yard, until they heard the angry voices. They were now standing to the side of me and Grandma. Each of them instinctively swung their heads to the left, following the finger towards some invisible place beyond them. When they realised that beyond them was just an empty space, they began looking at each other. Patricia looked at Clifton, who looked at Sonny, who looked back at Clifton and Patricia in turn.

'You are my children,' my mother's husband declared gruffly.

Confusion spread across their faces and they began shaking, as though a blast of cold air was passing over them.

Meanwhile, angry veins rose to the surface of Grandma's usually smooth dark skin. 'Pickney! All a yuh! Gallang. Go find sinting fi do. Mi ave tings to deal wit yasso.'

'Patricia, Clifton, Sonny. Come!' I called. They followed me to the side of the house where we squatted low and peeked around the edge of the verandah. 'Stop yuh noise.' I said, placing my index finger over my mouth for extra emphasis as we waited for the inevitable explosion.

'Mek mi tell yuh sinting,' Grandma shouted at the devil man. 'De only instruction Violet give wi wen she lef all dese pickney dem wit us is fi sen dem to school and bring dem up in de Lord's way. Soh mek mi tell you again! Leave wi yard an nuh come back.'

'Those children are all mine,' the man shouted, 'except for the bullfrog-eye gal. It's because of you she didn't even want to give my children my name. She told me how much yuh hate me! What did I do wrong apart from take her off your hands? Who you think was going to marry her when she did go and produce dat ugly bullfrog-eye pickney already?'

He was talking about me. I knew about my big eyes and I was used to being called 'bullfrog eyes', but only by other children, not by a grown man who happened to be the ugliest person I'd ever seen. I wanted to run out and kick him hard in the shins, but I knew that my grandma was more than capable of dealing with him. Her breathing could be heard from ten yards away and I imagined dragon-like smoke curling from her wide nostrils. I guessed that she'd removed her false teeth, which she always did when she was having a big argument or debating some issue, to stop them from flying out when she got into her arguing stride.

'Yuh wutlis ugly Satan devil man!' Grandma bellowed. 'A what mek yuh tink seh yuh got any right fi mi grandpickney dem? Yuh tek me daughta an yuh batter her till she half lose her mind. One time yuh did leave har nearly fi dead. Yuh breed har up every minute like she a dyam rabbit, and every time yuh dun wit har, yuh gwaan to one next woman an lef har fi fend fi harself!'

'Ole woman, mi not leaving here without—' the ugly Satan devil man started to reply, but Grandma Melba continued, speaking over him:

'An who ave to bring up de pickney dem dat yuh breed har up wit? Nuh, me an Sippa! Every last one a dem! She nuh keep one a dem wit har wen dem born. An dis a de first time yuh a lay yuh red eye dem pon de pickney dem yuh call fiyuh. Ah nuh forget seh me did meet yuh mada and even she, yuh own mada, tell mi seh yuh rotten from de core and dat yuh is de devil son! An bout yuh have de tarmarity fi call yuhself church minister!' Grandma was in full flow. With every utterance she made I felt more triumphant. There was no way she was going to let this man take my sister and brothers away from us. 'Yuh better come outa mi yard,' she roared, 'before yuh live fi regret yuh ever set foot yasso. Go weh fram mi!'

'Let's see which one of us is going to win this one, you miserable old witch!' the ugly Satan devil man spat, when Grandma Melba took a moment to breathe.

'Yes! Mek wi see!' Grandma fired back. 'Mi seh come outa mi yard – yuh brute, yuh Ugly Satan Devil Man, yuh!'

The last of the remaining white of his eyes sank into the redness, and his whole body shook with anger. With one furious backward glance, he strode away from the house. Grandma Melba shut her eyes and sucked her teeth hard. For the second time, Grandma sent the ugly Satan devil man on his way.

# Chapter 10

I woke early the morning after the ugly Satan devil man was ousted from our yard and hurriedly made up the bed in the Hall, which I'd sneaked into not long after the household had fallen asleep. By now this was an almost-nightly routine, so desperate was I to avoid the smelly, urine-soaked bed that I shared with my brothers and sister. I pulled on my yard dress and walked out into the cool morning air. I rubbed my bare feet hard against the thick dew-covered grass and admired the white of my soles against my dark brown skin. I decided that my toenails needed cutting and promised myself to look for a neat piece of broken glass, with which I could pare them down. Then I fetched the big grass broom and did the morning's sweep of the dirt yard. After that I set off with a bowl of corn to feed the chickens. My chores completed, I decided to wake my brothers and sister, anticipating the usual groans and moans of 'Lef mi, why yuh nuh lef me?' from Patricia, and Clifton, and Sonny, dragging the smelly sheet back over their heads each time I pulled at it.

At some point a lime tree had been planted too close to the house and now some of its branches grew across the entrance. As I climbed the last step to the verandah a jutting branch caught me across the face. I clamped a hand over my cheek to ease the stinging and hoped that blood hadn't been drawn.

When I entered our bedroom, the smells were as strong as ever, but even through my one open eye I quickly realised that the children were not in the bed. I stared at the crumpled mess and the empty bed seemed to stare back as if taunting me. Somehow Patricia, Clifton and Sonny had managed to get themselves out of bed very early without me knowing about it. They'd stolen my thunder. I always got up first, not them! It was my job to drag their lazy butts from the urine-soaked bed. But where had they gone? I rushed back the way I'd come, this time avoiding the branch, and ran towards the latrine. For some strange reason it was a place where they could often be found. One of them would be inside and the other two would be stationed directly outside, chattering and laughing, or even involved in a game of marbles or blind man's cradle. This wasn't necessarily about waiting their turn to use the latrine, they just seemed to enjoy being in that spot. But, on this particular morning, they weren't there.

'Patricia!' I called out, with no expectation that she would reply.

Grandma often said, 'That pickney gal have wax innah har earshole,' and I knew that if she did choose to come, she'd turn up in her own time, wearing her belligerent 'don't-ask-me-to-do-anything' face; Patricia seemed like a child with a secret life that only she knew how to access.

'Patricia! Clift-tonnn!' I called out, over and over again, but there was no response. In a final effort to try and locate them, I bellowed out all three of their names, 'Patricia, Clifton, Sonny! Answer me now, man!'

Grandma came towards me, brows furrowed.

'Chile, a wah do yuh, meking up dis whole heap a noise so early innah de morning?' she asked.

'De children dem nuh innah dem bed, Grandma,' I replied.

'Wah yuh mean bout de pickney dem nuh innah dem bed? Soh weh dem deh?'

'Mi nuh know, Grandma. Das why me a call out fi dem.'

Grandma walked back to the house. She flung open the doors to the Hall and walked through the narrow passageway that led to our room. She tarried briefly by the bed before reaching out and dragging the yellow-stained mattress and the excuse for a sheet from the broken jutting springs.

'Chile, drag dis disgusting stinkin ting and put it some place out of mi sight.'

I did as I was told and quickly returned to Grandma's side.

'Chile, you did see yuh Grandfada dis morning?'

'No, Grandma, mi nuh did see him dis morning.'

Her voice sounded weak with the worry. She knew Grandpa's movements well, so asking whether I'd seen him was odd. It was like she was trying to fill in time inside her head.

'Come, chile,' she beckoned to me, 'dem have to be somewhere pon de place.'

While we searched the village for the children, neighbours going about their early morning chores greeted us constantly.

'Marning, Miss Melba, marning, Erna.'

'Marning, marning,' we replied.

By early afternoon, we'd walked several miles and covered a number of our fields. There was no sign of the children. No one had seen them. All three seemed to have vanished from the face of the earth.

When we reached Little Lees, a particularly lush piece of land where everything grew in wild profusion, Grandma stopped and sat down heavily on the stump of a fallen tree. I sat quietly beside her. She opened her mouth as if to speak, but nothing came out. Grandma suffered from high blood pressure, which sometimes caused her to have heavy nose bleeds. As she sat contemplating what could have happened to three of her precious grandchildren, a trickle of blood made a slow-motion exit from her nose. I reached into my pinafore pocket and pulled out one of my still-dazzlingly white handkerchiefs. I moved closer to Grandma and wiped away at the rapidly solidifying blood.

'Dem gone,' Grandma whispered after what seemed an age. 'Im tek dem.'

It suddenly dawned on me what Grandma was saying. The children hadn't gone on an early morning hunt for mangoes. They weren't playing a prank on us. They were gone. Taken by the ugly Satan devil man. He'd returned to our house in the night. He'd sneaked up the back steps, woken the children, and persuaded them to leave with him. It was like the rooster attack, but without the killing. I was riveted to the spot. I recalled that fateful day when the telegram had arrived and when, a week later, at the precise hour that the telegram said he would arrive, the man with bloodshot eyes had turned up and greeted my grandmother who ignored him. I remembered his second visit, when he hadn't bothered with a greeting, but had spoken through tightly clenched teeth: 'I come for my children!' Then the dream came back to me of the hand reaching through the jalousie window. It wasn't a dream at all, it was real! The devil man must have been checking out the sleeping arrangements. Maybe he'd been coming back to our house regularly at night and had become familiar with our movements. Maybe he knew of my midnight excursions to the Hall and knew that I wouldn't be in the room when he returned to steal the children. Grandma had never entertained the notion that the children actually belonged to the ugly Satan devil man. She and Grandpa Sippa were the ones who'd raised them. His utterances were just left to hang in the air, until the moment that Grandma realised that her precious grandchildren had been taken from her care. Now there was nothing else to do but wait for Grandpa. There was no one to whom we could report the missing children. There was no police station, and no police. The most official thing in our village was the little sub-post office. This was a crisis and there was no one who stood in charge of a crisis. The worst thing that had ever happened prior to the children's disappearance was the stealing of the odd goat or chicken. And, like Briscoe, the culprit was usually quickly found and the matter left to the owner to deal with.

While we waited for Grandpa Sippa to come home, Grandma suffered a more serious nose bleed. I fetched the tin bucket from the back yard and held it under her head and watched as thick dollops of red blood poured from her nose. It only stopped when what looked like a pint of her blood had been deposited into the bucket. I led Grandma to her room and tucked her up in her bed; the events of the day had just proved too much for her.

Grandpa returned home in the early evening, loaded up with provisions and ready for his cooking marathon. I went part of the way along the dirt track to meet him and, in the time that it took us to walk back to the house, I filled him in on everything that had happened. Grandpa bent down, removed the stuffed jute bag from his head, and stretched himself back to a standing position, groaning slightly as he did so. His six-foot-four-inch frame refused to pull itself up straight any more, and he seemed like an over-tall tree, slanted slightly to one side, just like his nickname 'Leanside'. Grandpa didn't speak, but instead asked for a drink of lime water before removing himself to the breadfruit tree where he sat in quiet contemplation.

Later that evening, Grandpa dispatched me on an errand to purchase some lined writing paper. These days when he wrote, his hands would shake a little, so lined paper helped him to place his words in a more or less straight line. I returned with the paper and watched as he lit a Tilley lantern and then wrote at speed what turned out to be a very long letter to our mother. What we didn't know then was that it would be several months before we found out what had happened to little Sonny, Clifton and Patricia, and it wouldn't be from our mother.

# Chapter 11

In late May, Grandpa Sippa finally received a letter from his daughter Madge, in England. We were all – Grandpa, Grandma and I – surprised and worried to death that we had heard nothing from my mother for months, but 'no news better than evil news' Grandma constantly reminded me, until it became like a mantra.

Aunt Madge's letter began in the way that all letters between family in England and their folks on the island began:

*May 1968*

*Dear Mass Sippa and Miss Melba,*

*I hope when these few words of mine reaches you they will find you in the best of health. I am writing for two reasons: one, because Violet is sick with her nerves. And two, because when me and Herbie visited her, she told us that she got a letter from you and Miss Melba to tell her that Philbert come out and took the children away from you. According to Violet, his trip was suppose to be to look at some land he wanted to buy near his family up in Merchant Bay. There was never any talk about him taking the children away from your care. Violet has always been happy with the way the two of you look after them.*

Mass Sippa and Miss Melba, it seems that Violet isn't happy about this decision at all, and this situation has contributed to making her sick. Not one of us can make any sense of why her husband took the children from you and bring them to live with people they don't know.

I am sorry to tell you, but Violet's nerves haven't been so good since she arrived, and now this goings on with the children is not helping her situation at all. It seems one of his relatives, we believe it was his mother, wrote to Violet and told her that the children's aunt was beating them all the time and making them work without being given enough to eat. She also told her that the children no longer went to school. It seems that when Violet heard all of this her nerves took her so bad that she didn't know who she was by the time she got to hospital. The doctor treating her say that they had to give her something call ECT. We are not quite sure what that is, apart from that it's some kind of electric shock to her brain. They say it help to calm people down, but it seems to us it mostly makes people forget things because my poor sister hardly knew who we were when we visited. Still, since our last visit and as I am writing this letter, I can say that we have seen some improvement and she is expected to leave the hospital soon.

We are sorry for all this happening and sorry to be worrying you. But as we know, at the end of the day, they are his and Violet children and only them can sort the mess out.

Not much more to say now. We are both keeping well. England is still hard, just bills and more bills for everything! Not even water you can drink without paying for it. Nothing you can eat without putting your hands in your pocket. It's not like the island where you can just reach up and pick a mango, everything has a price. Still, enclosed is a few shillings that me and Herbie scraped *together to send for you. I hope it reaches you safely. Herbie send his best.*

*Take care of yourselves now, and may God bless you.*

*Your loving daughter, Madge*

Merchant Bay! This was the first inkling we had of where the children had been taken. Until now, we didn't know whether they were even still on the island. Our village was on the north-east side and apparently the children had been taken clear across the island to the south. The ugly Satan devil man may just as well have taken them to England. Our two donkeys, as sure-footed as they were, would never be able to manage such a long journey. Even if we could travel by bus to find the children, we had no way of knowing where we would pick up a bus for a journey that would probably take much more than a day. And where would we stay when we got there? And how would we get the children back from their flesh and blood father?

The days, weeks and months dragged slowly after the children were stolen. For a time, they occupied all of my thoughts. After all, we used to do everything together. My nights were filled with bitter tears. I'd sob quietly into the harsh calico pillow, and many a morning I woke still sobbing.

It was nearly a year after the ugly Satan devil man took the children when a second letter arrived from Auntie Madge. As impossible as it seemed, the news within was even more of a blow: the children had been taken to England at the start of the year.

I listened keenly from the side of the house as Grandpa Sippa slowly read the letter to Grandma Melba. The more she heard, the more I heard her shift uncomfortably in her wicker chair. I snuck a glance, as Grandpa read out that the devil man had never intended to buy land at all; he only came for the children.

A defeated expression on Grandma's face had replaced any last-minute hope she may have been harbouring of her grandchildren being returned to her.

'Come play hopscotch with me,' a voice sung out from behind a thick clutter of flowering coffee trees. It was my cousin and friend Dorcas. 'Come from de verandah, come play hopscotch with me!' she said.

In the months that the children had been gone, Grandma hadn't failed to notice the pervasive look of sadness that had settled in my eyes. Each time she was near, she would pat my head gently and sigh loudly before murmuring, 'Oh, life, life, life!' And so it was that she'd borrowed Dorcas from her mother, Miss Mavis, to provide me with much-needed company.

Dorcas came nearer and tugged at my yard dress. 'Come, Erna, come play now, man.'

Dorcas's mother had plenty of children and not enough food or beds, so she was more than agreeable to Dorcas going between the two homes. I had a new horse hair mattress and every trace of pee smell was gone from my room. On the nights that Dorcas came to stay, we shared my bed. I was happy that she wasn't a bed-wetter like my sister and brothers. We played games well into the night and we had two imaginary boyfriends, named Devon and Darren. We had discovered our bodies, and our boyfriends – who were, in reality, two lumpy pillows filled with bits of old rags – helped us to 'sin' on an almost-nightly basis. Although that kind of sinning was never discussed in church, we knew for sure that what we were doing couldn't be right. We were both convinced that our punishment would be to roast in the deep hellfire that the church minster preached about every Sunday. We'd seen a picture of what a hellfire looked like in the big orange-coloured book my grandparents kept propped up on a shelf in the Hall. Each time we sinned, we got down on our knees, faced each other, and prayed as hard as we could that we would never let our lumpy boyfriends touch us ever again. But we always did, safe in the knowledge that we could make things right with a prayer, asking for the good Lord's forgiveness.

But while Dorcas was helping me to recover from the loss of my siblings, Grandma was not the same person after the children were stolen. Her health began to deteriorate and she laughed less and often sat alone and in silence. Her nosebleeds were occurring more regularly, too, and I was worried more about her health than anything else. And even though I had Dorcas, I still missed my siblings' warm bodies next to mine, and their voices, and all the other daily things that were once so routine.

The news of the children now being in England overwhelmed our little household with sadness. Grandma seemed to know from the day they were taken that she would never see them again, and, on the day that Auntie Madge's second letter arrived, I believe she began the process of slowly dying.

The April storms arrived during the night with the usual drama. Howling winds and eerily creaking trees made sleep almost impossible. The old jalousie windows rattled in their partly rotted frames, so much so that I worried what we would find when day broke. Three nights later the storm was still raging. I was in and out of fitful sleep when I woke with a jolt and a deep sense of foreboding: Grandma was sick again. I just knew it. Leaving Dorcas fast asleep in the bed, I ran to my grandparents' room with our old enamel pail and propped it on Grandma's lap as she struggled upright. I sat by her side and clutched her grey hand in mine, watching as half a pail of thick coagulated blood poured from her nose. I shook Grandpa Sippa, who was deep in sleep and snoring so hard it was enough to wake the neighbourhood. He woke with a start and then, when he looked into the bucket, he knew immediately that Grandma was going to need hospital treatment this time around. He left the house before dawn to work with the village men to prepare a wooden stretcher to carry her to the roadside, so that a car could take her to the nearest hospital in Black Hill.

I was terrified. If death was coming to my beloved Grandma, it would mean that she would no longer be able to stand over me, her warm breath bathing me in love as she tried without success to rake through my unruly hair. Who would hitch up my slip when it showed below my dress? Who would scold me and then make me laugh till I cried? Being dead would take that all away. It would all end up with a nine night with hundreds of people eating too much curry goat and drinking far too much white rum. And when the nine nights were finally over, there would be a burial not too far from the back of the house.

The storm had pretty much washed away the dirt track that led to the main road, so the young village men, who were given the job of carrying Grandma on the wooden stretcher, had to drag themselves through rushing swirls of water and mud to reach the main road. That was not a lot better, the thin layer of asphalt having almost disappeared with the force of the storm. The truck used to transport Grandma to Black Hill Hospital was an old wreck of a thing and very noisy, but the men tried to make her as comfortable as they could. They lined the truck with straw covered with old sheets, before laying Grandma carefully in the open back. Grandpa and I scrambled in beside her. The driver did his best to compensate for the state of the road, and the truck drove slowly along, kicking up pebbles as it did so, a few of which landed in the back of the truck where Grandma lay, drawn and grey. Several torrid hours later we pulled up outside the hospital, where two porters rushed her at speed through the large entrance, followed by Grandpa and me. We were greeted by the overpowering smell of Dettol, but it was a far more welcome scent than the smell of a bucket of Grandma's blood. Grandpa and I were told to remain in the waiting area while the porters were joined by a doctor and a stern-looking matron who wheeled Grandma out of sight.

The waiting area was crowded with adults and children. Two seats along from us was a man with a heavily bandaged right arm with fresh blood still seeping from it. Next to him, a skinny young man peered anxiously out of his massively swollen eyes. He looked as though he'd collided with a knuckleduster. Opposite us sat a small girl, who kept bawling, 'Mama, mi belly a hot mi bad bad!' and next to her was a little boy, no more than two years old, with a massive bump protruding from his tiny head. In the middle of all of us, pacing up and down and talking constantly to each other, were two heavily pregnant women, one of whom looked far too old to be having babies. The women rubbed gently at their enormous stomachs as they paced and talked.

We sat in the waiting room all day, and eventually my exhausted Grandpa was told that Grandma was in a serious, but stable, condition, and that she would need to remain in the hospital for now. They would only allow us to look into the ward, so we said our goodbyes to an unconscious Grandma Melba from the doorway and left.

Grandpa had arranged for us to stay at the house of one of my aunts who lived not too far from the hospital, but he could only afford to stay away from our smallholding for a couple of days, so the following day, reassured that Grandma was in safe hands, we left Black Hill and returned to our village.

It was always hard when Grandma had to go into the hospital, for both Grandpa and me. The worst was the distance. In her absence Grandpa busied himself on the land. It was naseberry season and they grew in abundance around us. I kept myself occupied fruit picking with Dorcas. We'd fill our baskets with as much as we could carry and walk around our village and the next selling the fruit for one cent each to whoever we could.

Grandpa and I were kept informed of Grandma's progress by relatives and friends who passed by the hospital. Then, three weeks after her admission, Grandpa received a telegram to let us know that Grandma was ready to be discharged. The doctors had worked a miracle – Grandma had been pumped full of plasma and other people's blood and was well enough to return home. We waited all day for the truck that would bring her back, and then, just before sunset, Grandma arrived, looking frail and tired, but insisting that she was in good health. Her first words were a comment on the untidy state of the house, and this made me feel better than any doctor's pronouncement: Grandma was back! And she had returned in her very favourite fruit season: mangoes.

# Chapter 12

The storm had damaged the house as well as the roads and, while Grandma was in the hospital, Grandpa decided it was time to fix up the place to provide her with a bit more comfort. He took his inspiration from his younger brother Egbert, who had recently renovated his own house. Great-Uncle Egbert had had extra rooms built, new glass windows to replace the wooden jalousies, and a shiny new zinc roof in place of the old rusted one. His place looked so good that Grandpa employed the man responsible to renovate our old house as well. He was big man named Mass Booker, and he had a weird looping moustache that he twiddled while speaking. He was at least fifty years old – not as old as my grandparents, but still really old in my eyes.

He arrived at our house early one morning at the end of Grandma's first week at home, carrying with him a large canvas bag, which I later saw was packed full of all manner of work tools. Grandma, who was up and about and seemed back to her old busy self, offered Mass Booker freshly made coffee in the white enamel mug that she reserved for strangers. When not in use it was kept a couple of feet away from the fireplace, filled to the brim with ashes. Grandma said the ashes sterilised things. I'd watched her a few days earlier filling the same mug with warm ashes after she'd offered fresh mint tea to the Coolie Man who had passed through the village and had soldered our pots and pans.

Grandpa and Mass Booker talked for a long time. They drank more coffee and then Grandpa walked him around the house pointing out what needed doing. When at last they stopped talking, Mass Booker gathered up his belongings and left. Grandpa called Grandma and me to the verandah and told us we were going to have a new roof and a brand new kitchen, with a proper oil stove to replace the old paraffin one.

'Dat is nice, Sippa, tank you,' Grandma said when he told her, flashing Grandpa an almost girly smile.

In Grandma's new kitchen we would be able to sit around a proper table on proper chairs, instead of wonky stools and upended buckets with plates of food balanced precariously on our knees. I wondered whether eating around a table all the time would make Grandpa keep his false teeth in when he ate, or whether he would continue to remove them and pop them into the same handkerchief with which he often vigorously blew his nose.

Mass Booker returned two weeks later with more tools and a couple of young men who turned out to be two of his seven sons. It was reaching the end of the rainy season and the land had quickly dried, already wearing a cracked and parched appearance, as though it hadn't rained at all. Only the profusion of overgrown plants, flowers and weeds told the real story.

Over the next few days, the three men took measurements, marked out lines on the ground and wrote numbers in chalk on the walls. Half a dozen young village men, who normally sat around bleary-eyed with nothing to do but watch the days pass, each as uneventful as the next, got themselves on to Grandpa's payroll, and soon our village was buzzing with noise and redolent with the smell of the men as they lugged their heavy loads of cement, wood, zinc and whatever else was required to carry out the work from the track to the house. Grandpa shopped for provisions each day and used our largest three-legged iron pot to cook food for everyone.

On the days that I wasn't in school, I scrutinised the youngest of Mass Booker's sons. One night when Dorcas asked me why I'd screamed so loud, I couldn't tell her that my boyfriend wasn't a pillow any more, he was almost real, and his name was Daniel.

Shortly after Mass Booker began working on our house, a parcel arrived from England. In what I presumed was one of my mother's better moments, she'd sent me new clothing, as well as some useful things for Grandma and Grandpa. She had also sent me the doll that I'd always wanted. I was months away from my fourteenth birthday, a little old to be playing with dolls, perhaps, but I'd prayed for one so hard that, when it came, I played with it unashamedly, dressing and undressing her, combing her long silken brown hair, taking her little shoes and socks on and off and admiring her three-quarter length pantaloons with their frilly edges. She came with her very own flowery plastic carrycot, which had a mattress, a sheet, and a woolly cover. I remember wondering how cold it must be in England if even dolls were covered in woolly blankets. She was a lovely doll and I named her Elizabeth, which I thought was a really nice name, the same name as the England Queen.

One day as I played with Elizabeth in the yard I heard a deep voice behind me. 'Yuh is too big to be playing with dolls!' it said, accompanied by an enormous hand, which snatched my precious Elizabeth from me. It was Mass Booker. He was an educated-sounding man who spoke in a mixture of speaky-spokey and village patois.

Before I could react, I watched with horror as Mass Booker dropped my doll into the huge hole that had been dug as part of the construction.

I was so upset and angry that tears immediately exploded from my eyes, followed by unsightly dollops of yellow and green mucous that streamed from my nose and down my face. How could he not understand that, besides Dorcas, Elizabeth was my only proper company during the dark island evenings? She was my next best friend! Wiping my face, I drew myself to my full height and fixed Mass Booker with the nastiest, coldest stare I could muster. I wanted to ask him why on Earth he did this, but every island child knew the unspoken rules: you do not question the actions of adults, and you never answer back.

Before I could speak, Mass Booker addressed me again. 'But wait,' he said, 'now I'm looking at you good... Yuh look like somebody I know. Tell me, what yuh mother name?'

None of your business, was the answer in my head. 'Mi mada name is Miss Violet, sarh,' I said, knowing full well he wanted her surname, but as I was still angry about what he did to Elizabeth I decided to play the fool in the hope that he wouldn't ask me any more questions.

'Violet what?' he persisted.

'Mi mada name is Violet Pearl James, sarh.'

'So, yuh have the same name as yuh mother?'

'Well, no, sarh. Mi ave mi own name. Mi name is Erna Annette Mullings. Mi mada did give me my fada name, sarh, even though me nuh know who im is, sarh.'

Mass Booker twiddled his moustache and repeated what I'd said, 'Mmm. James and Mullings. Yes, man, me know her. So, Violet James is your mother and Big Man Mullings is your father. Hmmm.'

He didn't seem to be addressing me directly, so I felt no need to reply.

'But yuh say you don't know yuh father?' he asked, after a pause.

The man was getting on my nerves. I was thinking he was supposed to be building a house, not asking me lots of stupid questions.

'Yes, sarh, mi nuh know who mi fada is, sarh, but people seh im name is Judah Mullings, and dem seh him mussa dead long-time, sarh! Dem seh him was tief and him fall off truck an bruk him neck, sarh.'

'I think people telling you a whole heap of foolishness, child,' Mass Booker replied. 'Your father is far from dead. He's more alive than me! I know who he is very well and he is a big man where him come from. And, now I look at yuh, I see you have the same big buckteeth an half-coolie face like him.'

'Mi fada nuh dead fi true, sarh?'

Mass Booker didn't answer my question, but instead continued, 'You're his child for certain. All Big Man Mullings' children look the image of him. Him can't hide them. Soh wait, that must mean that Big Man Mullings did breed up the two sisters at the same time. Violet *and* Pookie!' He smiled to himself, but not in a nice way. 'Nuh, man, your father! Him nuh easy.'

He turned and went over to talk to his youngest son, Daniel, who was also my boyfriend who had no idea he was my boyfriend. My heart was skipping all over the place. I'd grown up without questioning the fact that my grandparents were, in every respect, my parents. My brief meeting with my mother did little to make me feel like I was actually her child, and all I had known of my father up to the point of this awkward conversation with Mass Booker was that I had his surname and that he was probably a thief who fell from a truck and broke his neck. Now, I was being told by this man who asked far too many questions that not only did he know my mother, but that he knew my father too, and that my father was very much alive. Suddenly, I was desperate to keep Mass Booker talking and I was happy for him to ask me a thousand questions if he wanted to. I needed to know more about the buckteeth man with his half-coolie face and why he was so sure he was my father. I was equally fascinated that Mass Booker said that my father did breed up two sisters, my mother, Violet, and her sister Pookie. I knew what 'breed up' meant and now I knew that I had at least one other sister on my father's side. I also worked out, from what Mass Booker said, that this

95

likely sister was also my first cousin, because she was my Auntie Pookie's daughter. The girl he referred to had to be Angelia. She was the only one of Auntie Pookie's many daughters who was the same age as me. I'd seen her at the house when I visited a few times with Grandpa at the end of market days; one of her sisters had even said that we had the same large eyes. Since my entire family was already full of all kinds of mix-up, I wasn't surprised to hear that I had a sister who was also my cousin. But as I watched Mass Booker scratching his head from under a partially removed cap, I had more important questions running around my head: did I really look like my father? Was he nicer than the ugly Satan devil man? Did he also steal people's children? Since my mother wasn't his wife, did he have a different wife? And, if he did have a wife, did they have other children? The idea of lots of new sisters and brothers played out like persistent sweet music in my head. It was like the world had suddenly expanded and I had a new and important role in it.

Interrupting my thoughts, Grandma Melba shooed me off to do my chores. I managed to complete them at lightning speed, wanting to present myself somewhere in the line of Mass Booker's sight, in the hope that he might tell me more about my possible father. But he managed to avoid seeing me for the rest of the afternoon, even when I sat on the edge of the step watching as he reckoned up with Grandpa at the end of the day.

June was mostly a wet month, hampering Mass Booker's progress on our house. He and his workers even downed tools for a couple of weeks. But by the last Monday of the month, despite being less than four hours since sunrise, the temperature soared high into the eighties. I was on my way to clean out the chicken coop, when I spotted Grandpa and Mass Booker standing under the breadfruit tree deep in conversation. I surmised they must be talking about the work on the house.

'Chile,' Grandpa Sippa said, 'Mass Booker here tell me seh him been talking to yuh fada and dat him waan fi meet yuh.'

I did a motionless jig – my father wanted to see me! 'Yes, sarh,' I replied, 'I would waan fi see im, if im waan fi see mi.'

'Mi wi a leave it fi Mass Booker to arrange, den,' Grandpa said.

That seemed to be that, and both men turned from me and continued with their conversation.

At the end of the day, Mass Booker called me over and asked if I could write. What kind of stupid question was that? Of course I could write, and probably better than him! But he was going to take me to meet my father and, however stupid I thought some of his questions were, he couldn't be allowed to read my thoughts.

'Yes, sarh,' I replied, 'I can write real pretty and I can spell good too.'

'Then can you write a letter to you father to tell him you want to visit him?'

'Yes, sarh, Mass Booker. I kyan write good. I'll write him a nice letter jus like yuh seh.'

'Well, then, write down this address,' he said. 'Mr Judah Mullings, Boldero Corner, Boldero PA. Write the address in the letter and don't forget to write the same thing on the envelope.'

That evening I sat at the dining table in the Hall and began composing a letter to my father. I wrote slowly taking care not to make any mistakes:

*Dear Mr Judah Mullings,*

*Good Morning, sir. I hope when these few lines of mine reaches you, it will find you in the best of health. The man who is working on my grandparents' house tells me he knows you and that you are my father. His name is Mass Booker. He said I have teeth just like yours and fine coolie skin. He said that you want to see me, and he told me to*

*write you this letter. That is why I am writing it. Mass*
*Booker said when you write back with a date, he will bring*
*me to your house. I beg you to write back soon, because*
*I would really like to meet you.*

> *Yours truly,*
> *Your daughter,*
> *Erna Annette Mullings.*

The following day, both Grandpa and Mass Booker read the letter. Mass Booker handed it back to me and nodded his approval.

'Yuh seem like a clever child. You can write good and yuh spell well,' he said.

'Tank yuh, sarh,' I replied.

Grandpa handed me a three-pence coin to purchase a stamp. I placed the letter in my pinafore pocket and ran as fast as my legs would take me to the Baldwin's store. One of two provision stores in the village, it sold most of the basic things that village people used on an everyday basis, and was home to the sub-post office – it also housed a men-only rum bar out the back.

Miss Baldwin, who was always to be found behind the counter, took the envelope and my three-penny coin. She examined the letter for some moments before asking, 'Mullings? A your fada yuh writing to?'

I nodded.

'Soh, is down a Boldero Corner him live? Sugar cane and mango country!'

Did the whole district know who my father was? Was it only me, his actual daughter, who'd had no idea that he even existed, never mind was alive and well?

'Mi nuh know, mam. Mi nevah been dere.'

'A wha yuh still standing here for, chile?'

'I tink seh yuh did a talk to me, mam.'

'Cho, foolish chile, away wit yuh!'

. . .

I'd always known my surname was Mullings and was happy that I didn't share the same surname as my sister and brothers. In fact, I preferred not having a father to sharing a surname with the man that I'd come to despise as much as my Grandma did. I skipped back up the path to our house, greeting everyone I met. I wondered whether they all knew just how happy I was in that moment? Could they guess my secret? Did they know that I was only days away from meeting my father for the first time? I couldn't tell them anything, not just yet, not until I saw him with my own two eyes and was sure that I hadn't dreamt it all up.

But it felt like an eternity before there was a response from my father. During every visit to the Baldwins' provision store and post office, I asked the same question: 'Anyting in de post for me, Miss Baldwin?'

The answer was always the same, 'No, chile, but mi will tell yuh when someting come in fiyuh.'

In the end there was no return letter, just a message from Mass Booker to my grandfather to let him know that my father had received my letter and was expecting my visit. There was no indication of when the visit would happen, just that I was expected.

Grandpa Sippa decided that the best time for me to go would be the start of the summer school break – only a week away. He would arrange for his good friend Mass Charlie to take me there. It seemed that Mass Charlie was in charge of taking people places, and Grandpa was confident that his old friend would be happy to help out. Grandpa himself rarely took bus journeys. His preference was to use our donkeys wherever possible; he did not have a lot of trust in the safety of our jolly buses or their drivers.

A few days later, Mass Charlie arrived and settled himself in the village, and then, before I knew it, it was time for him to take me on my long-awaited visit.

# Chapter 13

Early the following morning Grandma prepared breakfast for Grandpa and Mass Charlie. They sat together on the verandah where they sipped their coffee and ate their spicy turned cornmeal. After my morning wash, I tucked into the lumpy porridge that Grandma insisted I ate as the journey was long and it would keep my belly full. Lumpy porridge ordeal over, I pulled on the bright-red second-hand dress one of Auntie Pookie's daughters had given me. Grandma attempted to rake through my hair with a thick-toothed plastic comb. Each time she tried to pick up a bunch of hair in the comb, it felt as though my scalp was being lifted from my head. I hollered so loudly that she soon gave up.

'Chile, run to miss Petra an beg her fi do sinting wit dat hog hair!'

Miss Petra had a great technique. She would grab a large chunk of hair close to the roots tightly in one hand, comb out the the looser hair from the end, then work the comb toward the roots. Once the knots were out, it was easy to comb through all of my hair. In no time at all she'd combed and braided my hair and I was ready to leave for my father's house. I felt like a proper lady, dressed up in my new long-line brassiere with its myriad hooks and eyes, my red second-hand dress and my shiny black shoes. I was all set to leave when Grandma Melba called me to her and checked me over carefully.

'Mm, Erna, yuh look pretty still. Siddung wit mi awhile,' she said.

I sat beside her on the verandah, took her left hand in mine and began playing with her wedding ring.

'Grandma, can I have your ring when you die?' The strange question just popped out of my mouth.

I needn't have worried, Grandma replied with her usual calm, 'Mi nuh tink so, chile. When me dead mi ring fi go pass to mi youngest bwoy. Yuh uncle Dan.'

'But *I* would like it,' I insisted.

'Now, tek yuh tings and gwaan. Mass Charlie wait long enough fiyuh,' she said sternly.

I was going away for two whole weeks, so Grandma had packed a couple of changes of clothes – one yard dress, one half-slip, two pairs of panties and my church dress – and placed them in the battered grip I was using as a suitcase. She handed me a canteen stuffed with ackee and saltfish and bammies and placed it inside a jute bag. For good measure, she put four ripe mangoes and an avocado inside the bag as well.

'Lunch fi yuh and Mass Charlie,' she said. 'Aff yuh go now an yuh mine to behave yuself good, like mi teach yuh.'

I was halfway across the yard, heading towards Mass Charlie who was still sitting on the verandah with Grandpa, when Grandma called out, 'Chile, come back yasso. Fiyuh slip waan fi draw up. A yuh slip!' she repeated as I walked back towards her. 'It too long. It a show long down under yuh frock.'

Grandma hitched up my slip, tying the slender straps into knots on each side and tucking them out of sight. When she was done only a glimmer of white lace could be seen below the red dress. Grandma considered that a hint of lace was acceptable, but a great length of white cloth hanging below one's hem was not.

...

Mass Charlie, who was known for his love of walking, set a quick pace on our three-mile journey to Preston, where we would catch the bus that was vaguely expected around 9.30 in the morning. I was soon lagging behind. Mass Charlie stopped and waited for me.

'Let mi help yuh wit dat, chile,' he said, and I handed him the grip.

Only then did I realise that it was quite heavy and that I was doing all the carrying, what with the lunch canteen hanging from my left shoulder and the grip in my right hand. Now I was able to keep up with Mass Charlie and we reached Preston with half an hour to spare.

At approximately 9.20am the raucous sound of the horn signalled the bus's approach. People who had been ambling around suddenly converged towards the sturdy wooden sign that marked the bus stop. A number of passengers were making hurried last-minute purchases of fried dumplings and patties from Mass Julius's provision store. Promptly, on the half-hour, the bus arrived and screeched to a stop in a cloud of dust. We piled on in the order that we'd each reached the stop. Some of the passengers were heading to market, which meant a long wait while the bus conductor supervised them in loading their bales of produce on to the roof – including sacks full of yams and crates containing pigs and chickens, their squealing and squawking loud enough to muffle the sound of the engine. Mass Charlie managed to grab a single seat on the already-packed bus and sat me down on his knees. The journey time was dictated by the state of the road, and was slowed considerably in the places where it was still badly damaged from the last year's storm. The only respite from the constant bumping up and down came when the bus neared one of the many small towns along the route. Here, the road surface changed from gravel to tarmac, and the bus glided smoothly along for a few minutes, until it changed back to the gravel road a mile or so outside the town. Although everyone knew that there was only one bus a day, not everyone made it to a pickup point in time. Now and again, someone would dash out of the bush, awash with sweat, and race after the bus, sometimes managing to leap on to the small ladder attached to the back, where, if he or she was strong enough, they would hang on precariously until the driver decided to stop. Despite these constant distractions, it wasn't long into the journey before my thoughts began to turn to lunch.

'Mass Charlie,' I said, 'mi hungry. Mi kyan eat mi lunch now?'

'If yuh seh yuh hungry, chile, den it a good time to eat.'

Grandma Melba had carefully wrapped our food separately, so it was easy to remove my portion from the canteen, leaving Mass Charlie's for when he was ready. I finished my lunch long before lunchtime, and for a time kept myself busy counting roadside fruit and vegetable stalls as the bus whisked past them, reminding myself how lucky I was to live on my island. Makeshift sound systems pumping out reggae music kept the roadside sellers and higglers entertained, and when the bus drove by one it would slow a little and the passengers would sway to the music.

It was a whole hour and a half into our journey before we reached the small market town where the majority of passengers got off. The back of our journey was broken. The blood-red dirt road morphed into grey-coloured clay and, as the bus neared Boldero, the earth changed again to a chalky white. The lay of the land and the vegetation also changed. The craggy outcrops I was used to disappeared, replaced by flatlands and sugarcane plantations as far as the eye could see. As the bus trundled along the dusty road, I also noted a large body of water that was sectioned off into square pools.

Before I was able to ask Mass Charlie what the pools were, he volunteered the answer, 'Fish farms!' he exclaimed. 'Dem breed up certain type of fish in de water to make sure folk get dem fish on demand. It's not every time de fisherman dem bring wah people want fram de sea.' It sounded like a very strange story, but I feigned understanding.

Just then the driver shouted, 'One stop!' to remind Mass Charlie that we were getting off the next time the bus stopped.

The bus chugged on for a few more minutes before pulling up outside a low concrete schoolhouse. The handwritten sign on the weather-beaten board above its weather-beaten wooden doors read: *Boldero School House.* That must be where my brothers and sisters go to school, I thought, as we clambered off the bus.

The bus drove off in a cloud of white dust, leaving Mass Charlie and I on the side of the road. I looked across at the provision store on the other side and felt my heart leap in my chest. My father – for it was unmistakably him – was leaning against the wall, next to a shiny red and black motorcycle, looking straight at me. He was taller than I'd imagined, and well-built, without an ounce of spare flesh on his muscular frame. His short-sleeved shirt exposed the strong arms of a man who worked the land. He was a good-looking man with a fine brown face, exactly as Mass Booker described him to me. He was wearing a red baseball cap, which I soon discovered rarely left his head. Seeing us, my father straightened himself up and called out a greeting to Mass Charlie. He smiled as he did so and I was relieved to see that his teeth were nice, even if they were buck teeth just like mine, with gaps between them. Mass Charlie and I crossed the road towards him.

'Good afternoon, Mister Mullings, sarh,' I said shyly.

'So, yuh is de daughter your mada did try fi hide from me,' he laughed in response. 'Come, let me look pon you good, chile. An a soh yuh fayva Violet! Lawd a mercy! Yuh fayva har fi true.'

My father was full of surprises. How could a mother hide a child? I couldn't recall being hidden anywhere. I was always there in my village with my grandparents and my sister and brothers, before they were taken away. No one had come to claim me, like the ugly Satan devil man came to claim his children. A dozen questions whirred around my head, but before I could say anything more my father directed us out of the sun to the verandah, where we settled down on a couple of rickety benches.

'Miss Lettie,' he called out to the middle-aged woman who was sitting behind the store counter sewing something, 'bring a soda fa mi daughta! Mass Charlie, wah yuh a drink? Miss Lettie have Red Stripe and rum if yuh wi tek someting strong?'

'I'll tek a gill a de rum,' Mass Charlie replied. 'Beer is young bwoy dem sinting.'

Miss Lettie brought out two sodas and a generous helping of rum for Mass Charlie. My father, as I soon learnt, neither drank or smoked these days. The two men exchanged some brief talk about the journey, after which my father turned to me again.

'Lawd, Erna, yuh really fayva Violet. Yuh have everyting fi har.'

Not my buck teeth, I thought. I sensed that my father didn't know what else he could say to his long-lost thirteen-year-old daughter, and I didn't know what I could say to him. But all I cared about in that moment was that there was this man sitting two feet away from me who was partly responsible for me existing. At last, I had a mother and a father, as well as my grandparents.

'Soh, Erna, yuh a go a school?' my father said, after a bit.

'Yes, sarh! Mi go a school. Rose Hill School, sarh.'

'Yuh a learn good?'

'Mi tink soh, sarh.'

We finished our drinks and my father explained that his house was roughly half an hour walk away. Then he went over to where his motorbike was lent up against the wall.

105

'Miss Lettie,' he called out, 'mi a beg yuh, keep a good eye pon fi mi motor for me. Mi a come back later fi tek it off yuh hands.'

'It will be alright with me, Missa Big Man,' Miss Lettie replied with a smile.

'Missa Big Man,' I whispered to myself. That was how Mass Booker had referred to him on at least one occasion, too. He'd said something about my father being a big man in the village and I'd interpreted this to mean he was a tall man like my grandfather, but now I realised it was a measure of respect as well.

Once my father had sorted out his motorcycle, we set off for his house. The two men strode side by side, chatting as they walked, and I followed a short distance behind them. We turned right on to a gravel path and after about ten minutes we passed a group of children, a number of whom appeared to be a similar age to me. They were standing in a line on a series of flat white stones by a standpipe, waiting their turn to draw water. Containers of different colours and sizes sat on the ground next to them.

'Good afternoon, Papa, good afternoon, sarh!' the children chorused as we approached, but my father and Mass Charlie continued with their conversation without replying, seemingly oblivious to the children's greetings. The children stared at me but made no comment.

I walked on behind my father and Mass Charlie and occasionally glanced back, only to catch a number of curious eyes looking after me. Why had they called my father Papa? Perhaps I'd just misheard them. Yet they all seemed so familiar!

The walk, which was steadily uphill, soon became tiring under the relentless afternoon sun, but as we topped a small rise in the road a provision store appeared out of the heat haze like an oasis.

'Dis is my shop,' my father said when we reached it. 'One a yuh big sista run it fimi. And dats my house over dere soh.' He pointed towards a house that stood on a low hill about a quarter of a mile away.

My father's provision shop was typical of all such village shops, a slightly off-square, two-roomed concrete building, with a red-painted zinc roof and faded beige-coloured walls. On the verandah, which ran the width of the shop, were two roughly carved wooden tables with benches either side of them. Seated at one of the tables were four old men playing a game of dominoes, while a fifth man looked on. One of the men slammed his final piece hard on the table with a cry of 'Domino!'

'Carry mi winner Red Stripe, come gimme, man!' the winner crowed.

The three losers placed a few coppers on the table and the fifth man collected the money, went into the shop, and returned with a bottle of Red Stripe. While the men started setting up for another game, my father called to his daughter to send out two sodas and a gill of rum. The young woman inside the shop in turn bawled out 'JM!' and moments later a boy of about fourteen appeared carrying the soda bottles and the rum on a small wooden tray.

'Him a one a yuh bredda. His name Junior, but wi call him JM for short,' my father said, taking his soda from the tray.

As I gulped down the sweet fizzy liquid, I became aware that a small crowd had gathered. They looked from me to my father and back again. My father went over to a tall woman with feet large enough to match her height.

'Yes, man, she's a next one,' he said to her. 'Dis one grow with her grandparents dem.' He turned to me. 'Erna,' he called, 'come and say hello to your Aunt Berta. Berta a one of fimi younger sista.'

'Good afternoon, Auntie Berta,' I said to the tall woman.

'Yuh kyaan hide yuh pickney dem!' was all that Aunt Berta said in response.

While my father continued his conversation with his sister, I walked a little way from the provision store until I reached a spot where I was able to get a clear view of his house perched on the hillside across from a shallow gully. There were no other houses in the immediate vicinity. It appeared very large in comparison with my grandparents' home. The original wooden structure seemed to be sandwiched between two newer concrete buildings, their zinc roofs glinting in the afternoon sun. All three visible sides of the house had glass panelled windows and the walls were painted a light blue that matched the colour of the island sky. Half a dozen brightly painted red steps led up to the verandah and a large brown double front door. It was surrounded by at least four acres of land, most of which was rocky and dotted with large trees interspersed with patches of tall grass and clumps of red, pink and orange hibiscus and green mountain sage.

Then I heard my father call out to me and I ran back to the store.

'Come say goodbye to Mass Charlie,' he said when I reached him. 'Is time for him fi leave us.'

'Thank you, Mass Charlie,' I said, and he stood up and gave me a pat on the head before heading back towards the bus stop.

My father and I walked on until we reached the small gully that ran alongside the edge of his land. From its depths I heard, rather than saw, squealing pigs, cooing pigeons and loud roosters. Four dogs lounged on the path between the house and the shop. One large dog, with an attractive face and silky hair that made him look as though he'd just left a hairdresser, came bounding out of the gully towards my father.

'Yuh come look fi mi, Freddie?' my father said. He patted the dog a couple of times before shooing it off. 'Go bout yuh business now, Freddie. Move, bwoy!'

The children we'd passed at the standpipe came up the path behind us, chattering excitedly as they moved swiftly with their buckets on their heads. Their energetic pace betrayed nothing of the weight they were carrying, or of the relentless heat. As they reached my father, they greeted him for the second time, and again my father looked at them, but did not return the greetings.

'Mama mus a fi tired fi tek in Papa outside pickney dem,' one of the boys said loudly as he passed.

'Tyrone!' my father called out. 'Yuh waan fi come back here an repeat dat?'

'Sarry, Papa! It nuh nuttin mi said, sarh!'

'Mek mi hear yuh talk lakka dat again, dirty bwoy, an yuh scrawny arse will be sarry fi true!'

The others, who weren't brave enough to echo Tyrone's sentiment, cut their eyes at me and carried on walking.

Soon, they turned on to the path that led directly up to the house. As they mounted the first step, the front doors swung open and a tall, slender young woman appeared. She walked down the steps towards two large black plastic barrels that were placed to the side of the house and began helping each child in turn to lower their buckets and pour the water in. The empty buckets were then upended and left nearby. Water pouring over, the youngsters disappeared from sight.

'Finish up yuh soda, Erna,' my father's voice cut into my quiet watching. 'Yuh better come and meet Miss Iris. A long time she a wait fi meet yuh.'

I swallowed the remains of my drink and thought about what Tyrone had said. I felt nervous about meeting Miss Iris – what if she chased me away from her house and from her own children, or demanded that my father had nothing further to do with me? In the few minutes it took to reach the house, my belly heaved and churned so much that I worried that the moment I was introduced to her I would throw up all over her and that would spell the end of everything. The next minute, I found myself standing on the verandah and there, seated outside the kitchen door on a wooden stool, was Miss Iris herself, a rather fat brown woman. She was dressed in typical yard clothes, with a plaid scarf wrapped round her head, and a multi-coloured apron round her waist. In front of her was a small mountain of gungo pea pods. She was shelling at speed, dropping the peas into a large white basin covered in black spots where the enamel had chipped off. Miss Iris stopped her shelling, looked up at me and beamed the biggest, friendliest, most toothless smile I'd ever seen. Immediately, the churning in my belly was gone.

'Dis is de daughta mi tell yuh bout, Iris,' said my father. 'De one mi breed wit de gal from Little Hammon. Yuh memba seh de mada did bring har here when she was a baby, nine or ten month? Something like dat. Den mi nevah hear from de mada again.'

Miss Iris smiled some more, to the point where I felt confident enough to address her directly.

'My name is Erna, mam, an my mada name is Miss Violet.'

'Yes, chile. Mi know all a dat. It good fi meet yuh now, yuh is big pickney.'

'Tank yuh, mam.'

'But, Judah,' she said, turning to her husband, 'a soh she fayva her mada! She nuh ave nuttin fi yuh. Not a striking ting!'

My father's sister had said a few minutes earlier how my father couldn't hide his pickney, and now Miss Iris was saying that I looked nothing like him. Nothing was making much sense.

'A mus soh it go,' said my father, 'mi a go back out a road. You two kyan get fi know each other.'

I looked on as he strode back in the direction from which we had just come.

'Siddung an res yuhself, chile,' Miss Iris smiled. 'Soh, yuh granparents dem well, chile?' she asked, once I'd sat down beside her.

'Yes, mam, dem very well,' I replied.

'Mi hope seh dem have sumady to help dem while yuh deya wit yuh fada. Dem ave odder grand pickney dere wit dem?'

'No, mam. Mi sista and bredda dem gone an Hinglan. But mi have plenty relative in de village. Dem all help, mam. An mi grandparent dem strong.'

While Miss Iris continued to make small talk with me, one by one her children edged closer. The recognition that their father had indeed brought home yet another outside child registered in all their eyes.

'It look like yuh bredda and sista dem want fi get fi know yuh, Erna,' Miss Iris said. 'Yuh kyan go talk to dem if yuh want now.' And with that she picked up her bowl of shelled peas and disappeared inside the kitchen, leaving me alone with this crowd of siblings.

There was a long silence after Miss Iris left. All the young people's eyes were on me. I wanted to say something, but nothing came to mind. There were maybe nine or ten of them. I scanned their faces in the hope that one of them might want to say something to me. A boy with dark skin like mine was staring hard at me, so I stared back. The more we looked at each other, the more I felt as if I was looking into a mirror and an angry male image of myself was staring back. I was disconcerted, so averted my eyes, searching around for a friendlier face.

'All dem is Papa pickney, in case yuh a wonder,' a young man of about eighteen years finally piped up. 'Kenroy is my name, but people call mi Ken,' he said, holding out his hand.

'My name is Erna,' I replied, shaking his hand.

'Cho, man,' Ken replied, 'mi know dat long time. Wi fada talk bout yuh all de time! Tell wi seh yuh mada did bring yuh here one time when yuh a baby.'

'Fi true?' I said.

'Wah yuh mean, if a true? Mi fada seh soh, soh it nuh mus be true! Bwoy,' he continued, 'yuh did look frighten when you did see all a wi. But yuh nuh se nuttin yet! Papa ave plenty more pickney.'

'How many im have?' I asked, amazed to discover there were even more of us.

'People talk seh! More dan forty wid a whole heap a woman. Dem seh him have pickney spread up an down de country.'

'Fimi grandparents dem have sixteen, but mi nevah hear seh any one sumady can have forty pickney!' I replied.

The other children looked on, but said nothing.

'Yuh see your mada? Papa have pickney wit fi har sista too! Mi believe she a de same age as you and dat renking bwoy over dere, soh! De long black one who a look pon you bad.'

I looked across at the boy with the angry eyes. His steely gaze was still directed at me.

'Mi nuh tink seh im like me,' I said. 'Im look like seh im would kill me if im get a chance!'

'Nah mind him. A soh him stay wit people.'

I was wondering why Mass Booker hadn't made so much as a mention of my father's many children. A little preparation would have helped. For some reason, he'd seen fit to mention my aunt Pookie's daughter, but not the hordes of young people who now surrounded me. Of course, I hoped that I'd have a few brothers and sisters, but this was on another scale altogether!

'Yeah, man,' Ken continued, 'mi did meet yuh auntie daughter once. She look like yuh too. Same gappy teet!'

The fixation with my teeth was strange, because as far as I could see pretty much all of my father's children who'd opened their mouth that day betrayed the same slightly unfortunate inheritance, and that included Ken.

'But yuh ave de gaps dem, too! Look like all a wi ave dem,' I said.

'And de brown skin girl, dat fat one dat look like Mama,' Ken continued, ignoring my comment, 'she is another one born de same year as yuh.'

'Mi name is not brown fat girl,' the girl retorted. 'Mi name is Alvita Rose Mullings, an mi look lakka myself!'

'Alvita! Nobody nuh chat wit yuh,' Ken shot back. 'Yuh always ave too much fi seh about nuttin.'

'A wi next sista yasso mi a talk to,' Alvita replied, 'soh nuh seh nuttin else if yuh nuh want mi fi fix yuh mout.'

'Soh weh mi was?' Ken continued, as if this was a completely normal exchange. 'Oh yeh, mi fada pickney dem. Mi a one of five pickney fi mi fada born de same year.'

'Five different mada,' Alvita added, 'soh nuh bada tink seh yuh special!'

To my relief, this uncomfortable conversation was ended abruptly by Miss Iris calling for her girl children from the kitchen.

'Hazel, Yvette, Alvita, Adana, Hilret! Mi ready fi start de food now.'

Immediately, the five girls disappeared into the kitchen, leaving me alone on the verandah, as my new brothers had scattered in all directions.

As soon as Miss Iris started serving out the food, my father made an appearance, said grace and headed into the dining room, which, even though it was far bigger than our Hall at home, still wasn't large enough to accommodate his enormous family. The children took their food and slunk off to sit on what I thought were random stones and tree stumps scattered about the yard. It turned out, though, that each seating place was as demarcated as any chair around a table. Unsure what to do, I sat on a stone next to Miss Iris who smiled at me and carried on eating her food. And so, with little fuss, I was absorbed into the bosom of my new family.

# Chapter 14

Night fell quickly, as it always did on our island, and I joined the girls in lighting the lanterns, which we placed in each room. The house had a shower room inside, but Alvita warned me that none of us children were allowed to use it.

'Dem mek wi use dat old makeshift sinting,' she said, pointing towards a corrugated zinc-roofed outhouse on the edge of the gully. 'Tek two a de lantern down dere. Hang one pon de big nail inside, and hang de odder one outside pon de nail near de water drum.'

Only the girls used the shower house and the strict queueing system meant I was the last one in. The boys took their showers in the open, carefully positioning themselves on a few large rocks and then pouring water over themselves from a variety of buckets and water containers.

The adults hadn't told me where I'd be sleeping and I hadn't found the courage to ask, so I assumed that I would be with the younger girls. I followed them into a room, which contained a double bed, a wooden wardrobe and a dressing table with a mirror attached. Odd items of clothing hung from nails that were hammered into the wall. A strip of green cloth separated the younger girls' room from the older girls', but it might as well have been a reinforced door, as I discovered when I attempted to peer behind it.

'Do dat again,' said a voice, 'an one of wi a go bruk yuh arm fi yuh!'

The cloth fell instantly from my hand, drawing loud laughter from the younger girls.

'She nuh know who dem she a mess wit,' Hilret chuckled.

'She musa waan har arm bruk fi true,' Alvita chipped in.

I waited until the five girls had climbed into the bed before squeezing myself in on the very edge. That night I wished that I was back in my village, sharing my old bed with my proper sister and brothers. I hated being in the room with these five strangers. They all had each other and I felt that not one of them cared about me, not even slightly.

When dawn came, I rolled quietly off the bed, pulled on my yard dress and went outside. The sun hadn't yet risen over the hill and the morning still had a dewy, dreamlike appearance and a shadowy mist clung to the hillside. I walked barefooted a little way from the house until I found a large stone, which I sat on and examined the purple bruises at the top of my right thigh. The same two girls had kicked me several times during the night. I'd been at my father's home for less than a day and already I was feeling utterly miserable. Part of me wanted to stay and get to know my father, but an even bigger part just wanted the warmth of being back home with my grandparents.

I could hear the rest of the household waking up, so I reluctantly got up and walked slowly back to the house.

'Morning,' I called out to the girls with whom I'd shared a bed, in an attempt to be cheery.

'Tonight,' responded Alvita, who seemed to be the main spokesperson, 'don't even tink bout coming pon fiwi bed! Nuff a wi on it aready. Yuh better talk to Mama and Papa. Dem kyan tell yuh wey yuh fi sleep tonight, but it nuh go be wid us! Yvette, Hilret, Hazel, Adana, wah yuh seh?'

'Wi agree wit yuh, Alvita,' they chorused.

I agreed too. I'd rather have slept on the doorstep, or even between two rocks, for the rest of my stay than spend another night in bed with that lot.

Around mid-morning I heard voices, all talking over each other, echoing up the gully. I wandered down the path a way until I saw that there was quite a crowd gathered outside my father's store, so I strolled towards it, curious to know what was happening. As I approached, I could hardly believe the scene in front of me: there were young people everywhere. I did a silent head count, and, including those I'd met already, there were twenty-seven people in all. Most of the new arrivals seemed to be in their twenties, with the exception of one tall, skinny man with a long face and a goatee, who looked almost as old as my father, whom he was standing next to.

As soon as he saw me, my father introduced some of his other children to me. 'Dis is yuh big bredda Longers, Erna, him forty-year-old,' he said, pointing out the man with the goatee. 'Him real name a Elsworth, ahn him born when mi was fifteen year old. Im mada nuh did much older dan yuh is now,' he added, with a grin. 'Erselyn over dere is de oldest girl. JM dere is one a de younger bwoy. And Vinette, dat one dere, she a de youngest of all a yuh. Yuh wi get fi know all a dem, in time.'

Nine years old up to forty years old! Those were the ages of the children that my father had gathered to introduce to me. All the children lived on his land, some with their mothers, others with their own families. It was going to take more than two weeks to get to know these names, I thought. It seemed as if all the children in the village belonged to my father. There were enough of us born in the same year alone to form half a cricket team! Alvita was right, there was going to be nothing special about me in this gigantic family.

I passed that night on a makeshift bed on the concrete floor of an anteroom at the back of the house, which connected the dining room to the outside. It wasn't comfortable, but better than the donkey kicks from my half-sisters. It was daybreak when I woke to the sound of a door closing. I sprang out of bed and through the open window caught sight of my father walking briskly away from the house. He hadn't spoken to me much the night before, but I felt safe with him around. Now, I was worried that some of his children – the ones who seemed angry with me for turning up out of the blue – might take their revenge on me. So, instead of waiting for them to wake up, I decided to go and explore the area. I followed the gravel path that led up the hill away from the house. After fifteen minutes or so, I reached the far side of the hill, which was scattered with a number of neat houses. It appeared to be a thriving place with its own Baptist church, a school and another couple of provision stores. As I walked along the dusty main street, I was aware that every eye was turned on me. A woman who was leaning on a fence spoke loudly to her neighbour as I passed, 'Anada one a big man pickney!'

'Bwoy,' said the neighbour, 'mi stap counting long time!'

'Im nuh ave dat name fi nuttin, man ave to do im ting,' replied the old man who was sitting on his verandah next door, puffing on a huge cigar.

I carried on through the village and followed the road until I found my way to the banks of the Boldero River where I sat with my feet dangling in the cool water, listening to its soothing flow and watching fishes dart about in a shady pool under a stooping bamboo.

'Erna! A wah yuh do hereso all by yuhself? Yuh nuh fraid alligator bite off yuh foot dem?'

In one swift movement my feet were out of the river and I was looking up at my father, who must have crept up silently behind me.

'A joke mi a mek wit yuh, Erna,' he laughed. 'No alligator nuh in dis river, but plenty a dem down a Black Point. Tree years ago, a big rass one nyam a market woman whole. She did siddung innah de same place by de bridge weh she sell chocho fi years. Im mussa watch har fi a long time, before im mek im move. Dem tings clever like sumady.'

'Yuh mean seh de alligator nyam de whole woman, like im swallow har?' I cried, casting my eyes nervously at the river.

'Mi swear pon yuh mada life,' my father replied, 'yuh kyan hask anyone round here. People still talk bout it.' He held out his hand and pulled me to my feet. 'Come,' he said, 'I was tinking yuh might waan fi see mi limestone pit. Is a big someting,' he added, when he saw the doubtful expression on my face. 'Mi ave a contract wit de government. De money mi get from selling it help mi fi manage dis place.'

'What de government use de limestone for, sarh?' I asked him as I trotted along at his side. He walked with great big strides and it wasn't easy to keep up.

'Dem have road building programme right now, dem a use it for dat,' he said. 'Yuh know de nice road yuh see near de town dem? A fimi limestone dem a used to build dem. Government a plan fi asphalt up all de main road dem. Soh mi might become a rich man,' he chuckled. 'Yuh kyan see mi wife cow dem too, wi pass dem on de way to de pit. Iris ave...' he scratched his head as he considered the size of her herd, then added, 'mus be eighty a dem in all maybe.'

'Dat a whole heap a cow, sarh,' I said, wide-eyed in amazement at this statement. 'Miss Iris she musa rich woman too!'

My father just laughed in response.

Soon we were strolling through a field that was indeed full of Miss Iris's big fat cows. I spotted a couple of bulls and instinctively moved closer to my father.

'Dem nuh go bada yuh,' he said, 'dem only ave time far each odder.'

We passed through the field and scrambled up another hill on the far side. As soon as we reached the top, the limestone quarry came into view. It looked like a giant had bitten a huge chunk out of the land and the rock it had revealed was such a brilliant white it almost hurt my eyes to look at it. I watched as a massive noisy red machine, controlled by a man with a yellow hard hat on his head, scraped the limestone from the bottom of the pit. Two big trucks sat at the edge of the pit and about a dozen men were heaving baskets of the limestone into the back of the trucks.

'All dem man dem work for me,' my father said. 'Some a mi older bwoy dem down dere too.'

My father seemed proud of his wealth, but not, I thought, in a boastful way. He'd worked hard and built up a big business and earned himself quite a reputation into the bargain – in more ways than one, as I'd discovered.

An hour later we were back at his provision store, where my father ordered me a soda and then announced that he had to return to the quarry.

'Yuh wi be alright here on yuh own, Erna,' he said, with a nod to Aunt Berta who was serving behind the counter.

I thanked him and took my soda outside where I sat on the grass verge and watched as clouds scudded high above, forming the most fantastical shapes before fizzling out to leave the deep azure blue of a perfect island sky. I'd almost dozed off when I heard the sound of footsteps crunching on the pebbles behind me. I turned to see a postman bearing down on me, holding something in his hand.

'Yuh is Miss Erna?' he asked.

'Yes,' I said, confused.

'Your father told me I would find you here,' the postman said. He handed me a thin blue envelope.

It was a telegram. My heart sank immediately, as he pressed it firmly into my hand. I thought about the telegram Grandma had received exactly one week before the ugly Satan devil man arrived in our village. She knew for certain that it was bringing

119

bad news, and it turned out to be the worse possible news. I had that same feeling of certainty now: this telegram was not bringing good news. I was sure of it.

The postman tarried a little. 'Why yuh don't open it, miss?' he asked. 'It don't have to be bad news!'

I studied his face, in the hope that he could reassure me that he really hadn't brought bad news.

'I am sorry, miss,' he continued, 'but if yuh could just sign to show that yuh receive de telegram, miss, den I can be on mi way.' He handed me a lined exercise book in which I scrawled a childish signature. 'Tank you, miss. Like I say, it don't have to be bad news. Bye, miss. Tings will be aright.' He turned and hurried back down the path.

I stayed sitting for a long time, until the pounding inside my chest calmed. The whole village seemed to fall into a silence. Nothing moved, not even the fluffy white clouds that only a few moments earlier had dilly dallied across the sky. Then I tore open the envelope.

*MELBA DIED YESTERDAY. COME BACK WHEN YOU CAN* was all it said.

# Chapter 15

My beloved Grandma was dead. Dead! When I was much younger, I couldn't understand what being dead meant. I thought that people only died because they slept too deeply. I practised waking myself up, believing that if I could do this at will, I wouldn't die. The reality of death only struck me when Delphine's baby Leslie died. Then Everton drowned in the parish tank, and soon after Glenmore was thrown off his mule and smashed his head against a sun-baked dirt wall. He had startled the mule with a sudden scream when the bumblebee that he'd trapped in the palm of his hand stung him. Glenmore was eleven years old and was his mother's only son. It was after these harrowing events that I truly understood that not only was death the end, but that it appeared in many guises and could happen at any time to anyone. But I'd never experienced the death of anyone who meant as much to me as Grandma Melba.

My father returned home that evening to find me clinging to Miss Iris and weeping uncontrollably.

'Busta,' Miss Iris cried as soon as she saw him, 'har grandmada dead mussi yesterday, or de day before. See de telegram yasso. See fa yuhself!'

'But how dat happen?' my father said, picking up the telegram. 'Nah yesterday, mi did hear yuh a talk to har about har grandparents dem. And she tell yuh dem both strong!'

'Is true dat,' Miss Iris replied. 'Soh someting musa happen fi change tings soh fas!'

What my father and Miss Iris didn't know about, of course, was my grandmother's history of high blood pressure, or the half-bucket of blood that sometimes poured from her nostrils leaving her weak and delirious. They didn't know about the time, not that long ago, when the village men had to rush her out of the village to get her to hospital. Nor did they know that the reason she never combed her hair was because she couldn't tolerate any pressure to her head. But I was in no state to explain any of this.

I could see from both my father's and Miss Iris's faces that they understood my plight and, even though my father couldn't find words to console me, Miss Iris told me, 'Erna, chile, mi sarry. Mi know seh she was a mada fi yuh. But a soh life go, chile. None of us ave authority over it.'

The following morning, before I had even had breakfast, my father found me.

'Yuh want fi go back a yard today?' he asked, and I nodded. 'Den go get yuh grip an sort out yuh tings dem. Mi will tek yuh pon de bike to Santa Fe and get yuh into a car.'

I lost no time in gathering my few belongings. My father took my grip and I followed him to the back of the provision store where he kept his shiny red and black motorcycle. He strapped my grip to the back and wheeled the bike out on to the road.

'Come, Erna, climb on an hold tight pon mi waist.'

I settled myself on the bike and he sped off. A large part of the road between Boldero and Santa Fe was asphalted and once we reached this section my father picked up speed. We flew past row upon row of swaying sugar cane plants and before I knew it we'd dismounted in the square of bustling Santa Fe.

It was market day and the town was full of colour and the pavements were lined with higglers selling every conceivable kind of goods.

My father parked up the bike outside a shuttered building. 'Wait right yasso, Erna,' he said, 'mek mi go sort a car fi yuh.' And he vanished into the crowd.

I leant against the bike and watched as two women haggled over the price of a basket of sweetsop.

'Come down, auntie,' said the propsective buyer, 'yuh kaa hexpect mi to pay dat whole heap a money fi one little basket a sweetsop. Mi a give yuh two dollar fi de lot! Dat's mi last price.'

'Dat kyaan run, sarh,' the seller argued. 'Jus put one fifty cents an top an wi done.'

'Yuh is a hard sumady,' the buyer replied, 'but mi a feel generous tiday.'

A few minutes later my father was back. He removed my grip from the bike and we walked over to the taxi stand. It seemed like every taxi driver was shouting at my father at once.

'Me wi tek har, papa!' said a young man, despite having several people jammed into his car already.

'Mi ready, man! A weh she a go? Mi will get her dere safe! Mi a di best pon de road!' another young fellow claimed.

'Come nuh, papa!' a third chimed in. 'Sen har up wit mi. Mi a tell yuh seh, dem woulda gimme prize if dere was a competition!'

My father passed on these young men and chose an older man in a colourful island shirt who mocked the younger men and boasted that he was the best driver.

'Yuh young bwoy tink seh yuh a driver before yuh kyan walk,' he said. 'A nough accident oonoo people dem cause. Plenty!'

'Mi respect yuh, papa, soh mi nuh bada fi rise to dat one,' the first young man replied, before trotting off to find himself another passenger.

My father turned to me and put his hands on my shoulders and looked into my eyes. 'Erna, all a de car dem pack up wit people, a soh it stay at de beginning, but some a dem nuh go far, soh if im nuh pick up more people yuh might get some comfort.

Try not to tink too hard bout tings, and mi a hope to see yuh soon,' he added, as he squeezed me into the crammed car where I became the seventh passenger.

I wriggled into the space and then turned and waved goodbye to my father through the open window and watched him melt into the crowd.

'A true seh yuh little bit, yuh wi fit dere nice, man,' said the driver as I settled into the front seat between the gearbox and an unhealthy-looking middle-aged woman whose head was almost completely swallowed by a huge pink church hat. Behind us sat a further five people, including a man whose belly was so big I wondered why he didn't have his own car – since men with big bellies were always supposed to be rich – and a woman seated on the lap of a man I assumed must be her husband. The nightmarish journey seemed to take far longer than my bus trip a few days before. I sat quietly, trying to make sense of what had happened to my grandmother. When I had left my village, she was full of life, just as I told Miss Iris. She hadn't had one of her awful nosebleeds for some time, and my youngest uncle had been due to visit in a few days. Grandma had told me the news before I left, and even managed to show a bit of excitement. 'Im will still be here when yuh get back from yuh fada,' she'd assured me. And now she was dead. It had to be my fault. I told her that I wanted her ring when she died. Perhaps I was some kind of Obeah girl. I thought of all the things that would never happen again: I would never be able to tickle the bottom of her feet over and over. No more trips to the Top Hill to help her feed her pigs and goats. No more market days. She was never going to be around for even one more Sunday dinner. Never again would Grandma flash her shiny false teeth in one of her fits of laughter. I would never hear her calling out to Grandpa when she needed something fixed or had a problem to be solved, 'Yuh grandfada will know wah fi do!' Everything had died with her.

124

'Oh, God!' I wailed 'Please help me! What mi fi do? Mi grandmada dead pon me!'

'Chile, mi sorry to hear dat,' said the woman in the hat squashed up next to me. She placed a skinny brown arm around my shoulder.

'Murder woe!' I screamed bitterly. 'God, why yuh tek mi grandmada from mi? Wah mi did do?'

'Calm yuhself, chile!' the woman said. 'Yuh know seh de Almighty work in mysterious ways. Yuh grandmada gone join him in Heaven. Righta now! She a sit by his feet with angels pon her side.'

'But mi nuh waan har fi go to no Heaven!' I cried. 'Mi want har right here wit mi! Mi nuh wan har fi sit wit no angels.'

'Yuh wi see har again, chile,' the woman replied, more softly this time. 'Yuh wi see har soon innah de new order.'

I pulled my handkerchief from my purse and cleaned my face. This woman with her strange talk was in no position to understand or help. My tears were replaced by a mountainous headache and each jolt of the car felt like a clash of thunder inside my head. The woman stopped speaking and thankfully the rest of the passengers remained silent. That was until we drove past an overturned jolly bus resting precariously on the side of a steep precipice.

A man in the back seat who'd spent most of the journey clearing his throat commented, 'Lard, ave mercy pon de people dem soul! Mi hope nobody nuh dead. The stupid driver musa go too fas!'

The skid marks, which ran for several yards, suggested that the man was right. Suddenly there were more opinions.

The woman who'd been trying to console me piped up, 'Dem nuh see dat de good Lard a watch every striking ting dem do!'

'Driver like dem should be put in charge a donkey an mule! Dem nuh fi trust wit people life,' the taxi driver added.

Everyone apart from me roared with laughter. I was the

proud owner of two donkeys and I didn't get the joke. And anyway, the pain in my head was a constant reminder of why I was crammed into a wreck of car with a bunch of strangers. It was a relief when three people left the car at a village named Mountainside, including the man with the belly. The woman in the hat climbed into the back at that point, so I was left on my own in the front seat. By early nightfall, the taxi finally arrived in Preston. There had been no time to send word to the village of when I would be expected back, so I didn't expect Grandpa Sippa to meet me, and anyway he would have been too busy with arrangements. As it was, I would have to make my way to the village, alone and in the dark, with only the stars and the flickers of light from people's cooking fires to guide me. Although I'd never been frightened of the dark, or even by Grandpa's duppy stories, I still felt nervous about negotiating the tortuous path on my own.

The lanterns hanging on the verandah of Mass Julius's shop lit up the road where the taxi had stopped, and it was buzzing with customers, mostly old men, drinking white rum and playing dominoes. Mass Julius was leant up behind the counter talking with a couple of men about a new parish tank, which had been promised by the local council. 'Dem seh it will improve de water supply in the district, but dem is politician,' he said.

'Dem kyan look yuh straight innah yuh eye, shake yuh hand and still nuh do what dem seh dem will do,' one of the domino players added.

'A so de world stay,' Mass Julius replied. 'We ave to exercise patience. Dem nuh ave no choice but to do it now, but mark mi word, dem a go tek time still!' At that point, Mass Julius noticed me. 'Wi sarry to hear bout Miss Melba, Erna,' he said, walking towards me and placing his hand on my shoulder. 'Every striking soul around here a go miss har. Dere is not one sumady in de entire district dat roll a cigar like Miss Melba. Whole heap a man dem come aready fi ask, weh dem a go get

126

dem cigar and pipe tobacco from? Mi nuh know wah fi tell dem! Nuh heverybody ave dem kind a skill dat Miss Melba had. But a soh it go. One day we deya, de next who kyan tell?'

In my misery I hadn't thought about that part of Grandma's life at all. She was indeed the only person who rolled cigars in all the surrounding villages, and probably the entire parish, as Mass Julius had said. And her sales provided us with a steady income. Grandma had a keen understanding of the whole process of getting green tobacco leaves to the point where they could be made into cigars. She knew exactly how the cigars should look and even how they should taste, even though she never smoked a single one herself. Her cigars really were legendary, and Mass Julius's words made me realise that it wasn't only me and Grandpa who were going to miss Grandma Melba.

'Sorry, Mass Julius,' I said, feeling a pressing need to get on, even though I wanted to listen to the conversation, 'but mi ave to get back home in de dark, sarh, and mi did want fi borrow one bottle torch, sarh.'

'No problem, Erna,' Mass Julius replied, 'yuh need de torch fi stop yuh from bouncing up yuh foot dem in de dark.' He reached behind the counter and brought out an already-made-up torch, which he lit and then handed to me. 'Tek care how you goh now, Erna,' he said, 'an remember fi keep de torch from yuh face.'

Even though there were five villages to pass through before I reached my home, I was back in my village in less than an hour. The place was barely recognisable. There were people everywhere, talking, laughing, singing, praying. Behind our house a dozen neighbours were stooped over cooking pots. The competing smells of curried goat, jerk pork and fried fish filled the air. It seemed like people had travelled from all over the district and even further afield to attend Grandma's nine night, and this was only the beginning of the celebration of Grandma Melba's life. Many more relatives and friends would continue to arrive over the next six days and it was the job of the village women to make sure that everyone was fed throughout all nine days and nine nights.

No one had noticed me in the dark and, after a few moments of searching, I found my grandfather sitting talking with relatives on the verandah. He stood up when he saw me, his long frame looking more bent than ever, and pulled me to him. I dropped my grip and surrendered to his embrace. Tears sprang from my eyes immediately.

'It good yuh reach soh fas, Erna,' Grandpa Sippa said, wiping the tears from my face with his handkerchief. 'Yuh musa tired an hungry. Blossom round de back a cook food. Go get someting fi eat an den come back. Yuh need plenty food innah yuh body fi stay up all night.'

I'd barely eaten since the news of Grandma Melba's death, but, encouraged by Miss Blossom, I drank a small cup of peas soup before returning to sit at my Grandpa's feet where I fell to into an exhausted sleep to the gentle sound of many voices.

In the early hours I went to my bed, but didn't try to sleep again. There seemed little point in trying to force something I knew my head was not going to allow to happen.

Daylight only brought further feelings of numbness. I slid from the bed and picked up the enamel jug, in which I'd put a small amount of water the night before. I opened the door, cupped my palm and filled it, splashing water vigorously over my face. I put on the plainer of my two church dresses and made my way outside, where I headed for the breadfruit tree.

As is tradition, the village men had built the ceremonial lean-to where Grandma's body would rest in her coffin for the nine nights of ceremonies until her burial. It was constructed directly under the expansive foliage of the breadfruit tree; the one spot in our yard that the sun spared from its relentless heat. The lean-to was made from bamboo and wood, and decked with coconut palms and a huge array of lilies – the pungent smell of which remained with me long after the nine night was over. In front of the lean-to shrine was a duppy table, which was piled with food and bottles of white rum. The duppy table was there to keep Grandma Melba's spirit fed on her journey to heaven. Her duppy would join the living every evening during the nine night to eat, drink and listen to music, only leaving the festivities at midnight, when the villagers would feast from the table themselves. On the last night, her duppy would finally pass from the world of the living into the world of spirits, and only then could Grandma's body be considered to be at rest.

Her coffin appeared small under the elaborate lean-to. It rested on thick planks of newly cut cedar wood, laid across four of our Hall chairs. A stark white cloth hung loosely over it, though the coffin was currently still sealed from the night before. It would be opened again before sundown for two hours, a ritual to be repeated every evening at the same time until all nine nights had passed.

As I stood beside Grandma's coffin, relatives and friends began to arrive for the day of mourning. Various people greeted me briefly, offering their condolences. Among the mourners were several of Grandma's sisters and brothers, a few of whom were much older than her. It seemed so unfair that she was taken so early. But there was almost no time for me to fret, as every waking moment seemed to be filled with singing or eating and, as soon as one song ended, someone was ready with another. Many of Grandma Melba's favourite church songs and old spirituals were sung: 'How Great Thou Art', 'Amazing Grace' and 'We Shall Overcome', and her favourite psalm twenty-three from the King James Bible was repeated over and over:

*The Lord is my shepherd; I shall not want. He maketh me to lie down in green pastures: he leadeth me beside the still waters. He restoreth my soul: he leadeth me in the paths of righteousness for his name's sake. Yea, though I walk through the valley of the shadow of death, I will fear no evil: for thou art with me; thy rod and thy staff they comfort me. Thou preparest a table before me in the presence of mine enemies: thou anointest my head with oil; my cup runneth over. Surely goodness and mercy shall follow me all the days of my life: and I will dwell in the house of the Lord for ever.*

All day long people continued to arrive in the village, bringing with them even more provisions – firewood, water, baskets of fruit, vegetables, pots – everything that could possibly be needed to continue to feed the ever-growing crowd. The village men, who had made an early start digging Grandma's grave, could be heard singing a popular island call-and-response song as they worked:

*Hill an gully rider – Hill an gully,*
*Hill an gully rider – Hill an gully*
*A mek me beng dung low dung,*
*Hill an gully*
*A mek me feel up! Feel up!*
*Hill an gully – Hill an gully rider*
*Hill an gully*
*Took mi horse an come dung*
*Hill an gully*
*But mi horse done tumble dung*
*Hill an gully*
*Mi seh hill an gully rider...*

As I stood listening and mouthing the words of the song, Great-Aunt Eula appeared by my side.

'Erna, chile, yuh aright?' she asked, pushing a large mug of Horlicks into my hands. 'Yuh know de song?' she added when I looked at her doubtfully. 'Horlicks give yuh henergy. Henergy all day long! An just like yuh grandfada tell yuh, dis is a good way to start de day.'

'Tank yuh, Auntie Eula,' I said, before downing the sweet milky liquid.

A group of children were playing hopscotch in the yard, and round the back of the house the women were still busy with their cooking. Miss Gertie's teenage son Maurice, who'd been put in charge of sweeping the yard, was getting a telling off from her for not dampening the ground first. 'A dirt yuh want people fi nyam,' she scolded, 'yuh kyaan see seh de red dirt a fly everywhere!'

'A figet mi figet, Mama,' he replied, before running off to fetch a bucket of water.

I walked round the side of the house to find two young sisters who were washing up a constant stream of dishes. I offered to help and Miss Blossom appeared and handed me a bowl of yams to peel.

'Dorcas ask after yuh yesterday, Erna,' she said, after a few minutes of silent work. 'Yuh see har yet?'

'No, Miss Blossom, mi nuh see har yet.'

'Weh yuh nuh go look fi har den?' she replied. 'Mi kyan manage yasso. It better fiyuh to be round pickney dem yuh own age.'

I took Miss Blossom's advice and walked over to Dorcas's house where I found her hanging out her family's washing on a sisal rope stretched between two pimento trees.

'Hi, Dorcas,' I called out when I saw her.

She stopped at the sound of my voice, leaving a pair of khaki trousers hanging from one peg.

'Mi did hear seh yuh back, Erna!' she cried, rushing over to me, 'Mi was jus a finish de washing and den come look fiyuh.'

She grabbed me and hugged me tightly. Her younger brother Nathan was sitting on the ground plucking the feathers from a line of colourful little birds – he'd caught them by tricking them into feeding from a piece of string covered in sticky gum on which he'd placed bird food. We broke our embrace and looked at him and laughed. It was the first time I'd laughed since my return. Then we strolled over to the mango tree and sat down. Dorcas was keen to hear about my trip to see my father.

'Yuh ave ow many bredda an sista?' she asked, looking visibly shocked when I told her about my new family. 'Lawd, yuh fada nuh easy man!' She poked a stick into the soft earth. 'Dem like yuh?'

'Mi nuh really know fi tell yuh de truth,' I said. 'A short time mi did stay a de house. Mi nuh really get fi know any a dem yet. But mi know seh some a dem nuh like dem fada outside pickney dem.'

'But him a fiyuh fada too, Erna! Soh dat a fi dem problem.'

'Dem mada alright, though. She name Miss Iris an she was nice.'

It was like opening a tap, so desperate was I to share the overwhelming experiences I'd had with someone. Dorcas and I sat under the mango tree and talked until sundown.

'Yuh have bout an hour lef before yuh hafi go pass over Miss Melba coffin,' Dorcas said.

'Mi know, but mi fraid fi see Grandma Melba dead. Mi frighten seh she ago live innah mi head as a dead sumady forever.'

'Mi understan what yuh mean, Erna. Mi did go down a yard to see har not long after she did dead. She was lying on har back all wrap up. She did have two clothes iron innah har hand dem and har foot dem tie up together. Mi nuh know why dem do dat. But already, she nevah look like harself and dat is how I keep remembering har, but mi nuh fraid.'

Dorcas was still talking, but I had long stopped listening to anything she was saying. My entire body vibrated as I cried out uncontrollably. But, even as I was crying, I knew it would change nothing. I was terrified of seeing my beloved grandmother dead, but I was also driven by the knowledge that this would be my very last opportunity to see her ever again, even if it was inside her coffin.

The last residue of the evening sun was doing a shadowy dance under the mango tree. Much earlier on in the day, it had rained. Now, Dorcas and I silently focused our attention on a slimy fat earthworm that was digging itself back into a small mud patch.

'Yuh betta go now,' Dorcas said, 'before it get dark, an yuh grandfada ave to come look fiyuh.'

My legs trembled as I made to get up from the ground. They felt as though they were ready to give way under me.

'Steady, Erna, man.' Dorcas said. She was already standing next to me. She drew herself even closer and lifted my right arm, placing it on her shoulder. 'Let me come wit yuh, Erna. We can do dis together.' She offered.

The walk back to my house took nearly twice as long with Dorcas struggling to hold me up for most of it. I had quarter-filled our tin bath with water and left it to heat up in the sun prior to visiting her. Back at the house, she helped me drag the old bath into the tiny wash house next to the latrine. She stood outside the door and waited while I had a quick wash down. When I rejoined her, I was feeling a little calmer. I put on my best Sunday frock and asked Dorcas to do up the buttons at the back and tie my two trailing waist bands into a big bow. She brushed the front of my hair back with her hands.

'Let's go an fine yuh grandfada,' she said.

Grandpa Sippa was sitting on the verandah in Grandma Melba's favourite battered wicker chair. It had gaping holes in places, where the wicker had rotted and fallen off. Smoke curled around the long silver hairs in Grandpa Sippa's nostrils as he puffed on one of Grandma's Cuban cigars. Grandma Melba had kept a good stock of her left-over cigars, and she'd generously sprinkled them with overproof Appleton rum before placing them in an old George Horner biscuit tin, tightly sealing it closed. Grandpa still looked as drawn and tired as he did earlier.

'Mi ready, Grandpa Sippa,' I said, in a whisper.

Grandpa immediately sat up straight and seemed more alert. He popped the partly smoked cigar down on the wall nearest to him, pulled himself wearily up from the old wicker chair and walked down the steps towards me. 'Mi did worry seh, yuh gwaan run way an hide yuhself. Mi glad seh yuh come back innah good time. Mi know seh it nuh easy fiyuh, but de dead nuh nuttin fi frighten. De passing-over a long tradition from Africa time. It will help yuh grandmada go an har way to meet har maker.'

Grandpa Sippa placed a big reassuring arm around me, and together he and Dorcas led me the short distance from the verandah to the breadfruit tree, under which was Grandma Melba's open coffin. As if sensing our approach, the crowd that had already gathered, and was in the middle of singing a dead night celebration song, went quiet for a moment. Still holding on to my hand, and with Dorcas still determinedly by my side, Grandpa Sippa moved us deftly through the crowd. Suddenly, there was a clear space and I could see my grandmother's coffin directly ahead of me. I pulled hard on my grandfather's hand and he hesitated briefly before moving me closer. I was tall enough to see inside, though I didn't feel ready to look. My whole body began to shake again. I bit hard on my lips to stop my mouth from opening. I didn't want to cry in front of all those people. I hardly noticed as my grandfather, assisted by my rarely sober Uncle Cleveland, lifted me in a single coordinated movement off the ground. The two men held me flat on their forearms and steadied themselves before passing me three times over Grandma Melba's body. The whole ritual probably lasted less than a minute, before I was on the ground again. But, somehow, it felt a lot longer, and for a moment my head felt as though I'd been playing a vigorous game of hula hoop.

I looked around, but Grandpa Sippa was nowhere to be seen. My heart felt as though it was about to beat itself right out of my body. Then there was a tiny squeeze of my hand. Thank God! I thought when I realised that Dorcas was still right there by my side. A feeling of relief washed over me.

It was now time for me to look at my grandmother for the last time.

Grandma Melba was dressed in her favourite brown crêpe church dress, the one my mother gave her before leaving for England. Her hair was covered in an African-style white head-wrap. Another white cloth had been positioned beneath her chin, drawn up around her jaw, and tucked into place under the edge of her head-wrap. She looked beautiful and serene, except that the usual ebony shine of her face was now replaced by a strange grey colour and she laid as rigid as a dried-out cedar board.

The smell of death filled up my nostrils. It wasn't the first time I'd seen a dead body, but it was the first time I'd found myself having to linger over one. She was my grandmother and I knew that I wasn't allowed just to have a quick peek and disappear. Grandma Melba died during the island's hottest season and her body was already four days old, and there were still five more days to mourn her. I squeezed hard on Dorcas's hand, as myriad thoughts rushed through my head. How I wished I'd been there to help my grandma when she must have needed me most. Had I been there, maybe she would still be alive. In the end, just standing there looking at Grandma's unmoving body, the pain inside my heart and the smell of death all proved too much to bear. I pulled away from Dorcas and ran screaming in search of my grandpa.

'Mi beg yuh, Winston,' Grandpa called to his nephew, 'go bring mi dat rum bottle over dere soh.'

Winston brought the bottle over and poured a generous amount of the strong white rum into my grandfather's cupped hands.

'Come, chile.'

I moved close to Grandpa Sippa. He patted my face gently with the liquid. I inhaled deeply and the pungent smell shot up my nostrils, delivering a stinging pain that caused me to slap myself hard on the side of my head in my effort to ease the sensation that was both unpleasant and somewhat pleasant at the same time.

'Chile, trow yuh head back an drink dat down!' Grandpa commanded, handing me a gill glass of the rum. 'It wi clear yuh head.'

I drank the shot in one. A fiery warmth tickled my throat and lit up my belly. I tucked myself tightly into Grandpa's chest and fell silent.

'It was a big stroke dat tek yuh grandmada,' Grandpa said after a while. 'Mi did send fi de doctor, but dere was nutting him could do. Him seh she did gone de minute har body hit de ground. Mi poor Melba! Mi sure seh she did dead from a broken heart.'

I sat up and tried to take in Grandpa Sippa's words. 'Is what yuh mean, Grandpa? How dat could happen? Who coulda get innah her chest an break her heart open and kill her like dat?'

'Chile, yuh is young still, and mi nuh tink seh yuh understan so good. Yuh grandmada nevah get over losing de other grandpickney dem. From dat day till the day she dead, she never stop fretting. Lawd! God know seh she did miss dem children. Not a day did pass when she nuh talk bout dem.'

In that moment I understood that it wasn't me who had somehow caused my grandma to die. It wasn't because I'd asked her for her wedding ring. It was the fault of the ugly Satan devil man, who took her beloved grandchildren away. It was the sadness she felt in her heart that made her die.

The huge turnout on the day of Grandma's burial was befitting of the big-hearted, deeply loved woman that she was. The crowd spread all the way from the family burial plot to the entrance of the graveyard, and for several hundred yards either side. Only immediate family members and those who'd gathered early were able to get anywhere near the grave. Anticipating a large crowd, Grandpa Sippa had borrowed two loudspeakers from the dance hall crew, and a couple of his nephews had rigged them up to relay the service, call out the hymns and play Grandma Melba's favourite spirituals, which resounded over the treetops. Women spoke in tongues and moved their bodies in ways that I later learned were traditional African funeral dances that had survived the slave trade. And in true African style it was not the mourning of a death, but the celebration of life, that took place. Grandpa read the ceremonial words himself as our beloved Melba was lowered into the ground. Only when the grave was covered in lilies did I notice his tears.

# Chapter 16

Normal disappeared from my life after Grandma Melba's burial. It took more than two weeks for all the family and friends to finally leave, and once they'd gone our house felt emptier than ever and our village felt like the saddest and loneliest place on Earth. If I hadn't realised it before, it soon became obvious what a huge character my tiny grandmother had been. Everything seemed to have lost its heart and energy without her around. Nothing felt or tasted the same. I ate because I had to, rather than like before, when sitting down to a meal with my grandparents had been the big event of the day.

My grandfather tried his best to keep my spirits up, but his job had mostly been as a storyteller for us children, and I was no longer interested in hearing Anancy or duppy stories. Most of all, I missed the sound of Grandma Melba's laughter.

I still had a month of my school holiday remaining, so Grandpa decided it would be best for me to pay another visit to my father's house for a couple of weeks, rather than hang around in what he'd taken to calling 'de ole empty place.'

'Mi a beg yuh, Grandpa,' I cried when he told me, 'dere is plenty tings here mi kyan help wit! Mi kyan go a mi fada house pon de next holiday.'

'I understand you, chile,' he replied sadly, 'yuh have a good heart. Melba woulda proud a yuh. But it betta fi yuh fi spend time wit yuh fada an him family. De company will help tek yuh mind off tings an yuh will come back innah good time fi school. An true seh yuh nuh ave much time left pon de island, tings a go ave to sort out soon.'

'Wah yuh mean, Grandpa Sippa, bout mi nuh ave much time left pon de island?' I asked him, perplexed by this statement. 'Den a weh mi a go?'

'A fortunate Missa Booker know yuh fada,' Grandpa continued, 'because yuh fada wi ave to sign papers, so yuh can go join yuh mada in Hinglan.'

Join my mother in England? I suddenly felt as if Grandpa Sippa had taken a large rock and dropped it on my head and smashed me into the red dirt yard. Go to England? I couldn't believe that my grandfather was making plans to send me away. And, worse, that I was being sent to live with the ugly Satan devil man. Grandma Melba would have died a second time, had she been able to know that this could happen! Nevertheless, I didn't want to argue with my grandfather, so I accepted my fate with a heavy heart.

The next day, I walked alone to the bus stop. This time the bus journey unfolded in a kind of slow motion. The countryside held little of the interest of my first journey to my father's house. In fact, I barely glanced out of the windows. Even the noisy chatter on the bus couldn't block out my grandfather's words. It was as if I was trapped in a bad dream that had somehow got stuck inside my brain and, once there, it kept repeating on a loop. Had the driver not shouted out, 'One stop, Miss Erna! Yuh figet seh a yasso yuh ave to drop off?' I most likely would have ended up at the final stop.

Dusk fell in that sudden way it does on the island, and before I could complete the short journey to my father's shop, the night sky became so littered with stars that it appeared that the moon was having to fight for space.

The shop was busy as always. A few of my father's sons and some older men were sitting around drinking island beer and sodas. A different half-sister, a girl I'd only seen briefly before named Priscilla, was serving behind the counter. She had one of those faces that seemed never to have broken into a smile.

'Cock a rass!' she declared, looking at me. 'Papa outside-pickney de back yasso aready.'

'A big man daughta!' someone else hollered out.

'How come yuh a walk street soh late! Yuh nuh fraid a duppy?' said another.

I sat on a stool to wait for my father to turn up.

'Mama seh yuh fi sen ova one chicken and a two-pound bag a flour,' said Alvita, who had wandered into the shop. Then she seemed to notice me. 'Yuh back soh quick, Erna, yuh grandmada duppy run yuh?' she said.

'No,' I replied, 'mi jus back. Mi grandmada is resting in peace.'

'If yuh seh soh,' she replied, with a suck of her teeth. Then, after a pause, she added, 'Papa nuh deya yet. But im wi come soon.'

'Yuh sure seh Mama want de frozen chicken?' Priscilla asked Alvita. 'She nuh did kill fowl dis morning?'

'Mi a jus de messenger! Mama want de frozen chicken. She seh she a go pour boiling water pan it. De fowl she kill scrawny to ratid! It kyaan mek dinner fi all wi. An now Erna come tun up, it definitely nuh enough.'

Alvita took the frozen chicken and the flour and left. The chest freezer in my father's store was the first I'd ever seen. The poles that carried the electricity cables all the way from the road stopped at the shop, so he was able to keep a freezer full of dead chickens and rabbits.

'A how yuh comeback so quick, Erna?' Priscilla asked in a disapproving tone. Without waiting for an answer she called out, 'One a yuh bwoy go look fi Papa, tell im seh Erna deyah, again!'

For a moment none of the boys moved and it soon became clear that it was the youngest boy who was expected to go and

140

fetch my father. This boy, who was about a year older than me, was another 'outside' child. He had slicked-back coolie hair, which suggested his mother was probably Indian. He got up and ran at full speed up the hill to the house. A short while later I heard my father's voice. I stood up and went outside to greet him.

'Evening, sarh,' I said, before he could say anything. 'Mi know seh yuh nuh expect mi, but mi grandfada said it good fi mi to come stay wit yuh to stop mi fretting over mi grandmada, sarh.'

'Yuh grandfada right,' he said, 'yuh need plenty sumady round at a time like dis.'

Then I asked him about the subject that had been driving me to distraction ever since Grandpa Sippa mentioned it. 'Mi grandfada seh mi a go Hinglan soon, sarh, but mi nuh want fi go! But mi grandfada seh im kyaan look after mi now mi grandmada dead.'

My father gave me a long, level look. 'Is true dat,' he said, 'an mi jus a get fi know yuh. Wen yuh a leave?'

'Mi nuh know, sarh. Mi grandfada seh a yuh have to sign paper, but mi nuh know what kind a paper him did a talk bout, sarh.'

'Mi nevah know yuh mada ave belly until she carry yuh here when yuh a baby,' my father said, without any apparent connection to what we were talking about. 'Iris seh she would tek yuh in and yuh mada tell wi she wi tink bout it. Dat was de last time mi see de two ah oonoo. Erna, mi nuh did know if yuh did dead or alive. Is true still dat a whole heap pickney mi ave, but mi try fi own every last one a dem, if dat's what de mada want.'

I didn't really understand why my father was telling me this. It sounded like he was blaming my mother. He knew my aunt, so it couldn't have been that difficult to find me if he really wanted to.

Still, there was no time to be angry. I just wanted to spend as much time as I could in his company. If the plan to send me to England really was true, then there would not be many more opportunities to visit. Though, despite his proclamation about what happened after I was born, I heard no offer from him now to take me in.

Still, I could see that my father also wanted to build our relationship, and as the days passed I felt more and more at ease in his company. He began asking me to join him on little outings and I jumped at every opportunity to hop on the back of his motorcycle to wherever he was going. Being on the bike was nothing like riding my donkeys or even being driven in a bus or car. I loved the sensation of moving so fast on the dusty, open roads, the cool breeze on my face when the sun was beating down at its hottest. The outings were usually to check on his workmen and animals. Sometimes we'd hang out at the Boldero provision store, where he'd play a few hands of dominoes with the other village men, while I sat and watched and drank soda.

Grandpa was right: being at my father's helped me. It was a busy place, which meant that Grandma's face wasn't always the first that I saw in the morning or the last at night. When I wasn't hanging out with my father, I went to the market with my half-sisters and helped them with chores. From time to time, the boys entertained me with their endless squabbling and the odd fist-fight, seemingly intent on trying to kill each other. And then there was the day they tried – and failed – to get me to ride a bike, which left me with bruises all over and a badly dented pride. My least favourite activity was going to church with Miss Iris. Miss Iris had endless sins to pray about – mostly linked to my father's womanising – so she attended church on the three days a week that the church was open. My father, on the other hand, often walked straight past the church without even looking at it. And he never went inside.

'Sarh,' I asked him one day, 'yuh nuh waan fi go a church with Miss Iris?'

'Mi? No, sah!' My father threw his head back and laughed out loud. 'Dem place a fi mad people fi go jump up, jump up! Yuh nuh catch mi in a dat place, sah. Yuh see man deh!'

Apart from going to church with Miss Iris, I'd enjoyed my time at my father's so much that I felt quite sad when it was time to go. Most of my half-siblings had been accepting of me this time, and several of them had become friends; it appeared that Grandma's death and the news that I was probably going to England soon had stirred up extra interest in me. The day before I left, they rather optimistically placed orders for the things they wanted me to send to them once I was in England. My sisters mostly asked for clothes; Alvita said she'd like a watch so she could know the time. The boys wanted baseball caps. Longers was more ambitious: he wanted me to send money so he could buy a motorcycle like our father's. I nodded appeasingly at them all. While I didn't feel quite ready to say goodbye, I was nevertheless happy to be going home to my grandfather.

As I made ready to leave, my father rested his hands on my shoulders and said with a soft smile, 'Miss Erna! Mi wi miss yuh, man. De time too short, but mi did glad to know yuh and mi hope seh yuh wi write mi and dat yuh wi come and visit when yuh can.'

'Thank yuh, Papa!' I replied. 'Mi glad fi know yuh too, an mi wi definitely write yuh.' The word 'Papa' slipped effortlessly and unexpectedly out of my mouth.

My father just smiled and repeated, 'Yes, man! Mi ago miss yuh.'

Miss Iris and my half-siblings stood three-deep as I said my goodbyes.

'De bus wi reach Boldero school innah de next twenty minute, Erna,' my father said, after watching us all hugging for a minute. 'It betta yuh dere fi wait far it, dan get dere las minute.'

143

'Yes, Papa,' I said, and with that I climbed on to the back of his motorbike to cries of 'Sen some money fi wi!' echoing from my siblings.

'Erna, nuh tek notice of dem pickney,' my father shouted over the noise of the engine, 'dem too craven an gravalicious!'

My father waited with me at the side of the road, and when the bus pulled up, he put an arm around my shoulders and gave me a big hug.

'Mi wish yuh a safe journey an God's speed, Erna,' he said.

'Tanks, Papa. Mi promise, mi wi write yuh soon.' I boarded the bus and sat in the one remaining window seat.

'Remember yuh promise now,' he shouted, when I stuck my head out of the glassless window.

The bus moved forward and I waved to my Papa until he was out of sight.

# Chapter 17

The heat had built up inside the bus until it was like an oven, and I soon felt tired and irritable. I certainly wasn't looking forward to the walk to the village all the way from Preston. But when I climbed off the bus, to my delight, I saw Grandpa Sippa sitting outside Mass Julius's shop with Bugle Boy and Treasure Girl hitched-up to a nearby pimento tree.

'Mi miss yuh round de place, Erna,' Grandpa Sippa said as soon as he saw me.

'Mi did miss yuh too, Grandpa,' I said, giving him a hug, which given his height meant just above his waist.

We climbed on to the donkeys and began making our way back to the village, chatting as we swayed along the rough dirt tracks.

'How is mi chicken dem, Grandpa?' I asked.

'Mongoose call!' he replied. 'Dem grab two a de hen dem before de yard bwoy could do anyting. Yuh know seh mongoose fas. De yard bwoy fix up de fence round de coop, soh de rest of yuh fowl dem safe, fi now.'

I had been the proud owner of twenty-one hens until Grandma decided that Sensay, the mother hen, was too old and was ready for the cooking pot. Sensay had laid hundreds of eggs and was mother to my other twenty hens. She'd turned into quite a peculiar looking fowl, with her few remaining feathers sticking out all over the place. One Sunday morning, Sensay had failed to appear in the yard as usual with her adult brood trailing behind her. It turned out that Grandma had risen early, collected Sensay, and stuffed the old fowl's body under a tin basin. She used the rim of the basin to hold the fowl's head from her body and, with a flick of her knife, she sliced off my Sensay's head and then plucked her remaining feathers in readiness for Sunday dinner. My poor Sensay! Her headless body, once released from under the basin, would have danced about for a couple of minutes before surrendering to death. Thinking about this story and my Grandma brought everything back, and as we rode alongside each other I found myself welling up with tears. I could feel Treasure Girl's body tremble under my frame as if sensing my distress.

'Yuh waan stop a while, Erna?' Grandpa said. 'Mi know seh yuh nuh bawl bout de fowl mangoose catch.'

I nodded, so we dismounted and sat on a nearby rock.

'Erna,' Grandpa said with a sigh, 'yuh know seh, wi kyaan bring Melba back. An yuh know seh yuh grandmada had a good life. It was har time to go an when dat time come, only God Jehovah kyan stop it, but him nuh choose to, chile, because a de one ting wi all hafi go trough. Wi jus kyaan pick de time. Dat is all!'

The sun had nearly disappeared, so Grandpa lit the two bottle torches he'd brought with him and handed one to me. Bugle Boy and Treasure Girl had travelled the route so many times they could be ridden without us having to hold on to their bridles, which made it easy for us to carry our torches.

Grandpa's words had helped, but as we approached our house I began hiccuping so violently that my body shook. He dismounted from Bugle Boy, hitched her up to a nearby tree, and came over to Treasure Girl, leading her to the front of our verandah. Grandpa gently helped me climb down from her saddle, before tethering her to the same tree as Bugle Boy.

'Go an siddung in yuh grandma chair,' he said. 'Let mi go move de donkey dem fi de night.'

When he returned, I followed him nervously into the house. I could feel Grandma Melba's presence as strongly as though she were standing right there in the Hall. I sat on a chair and started to cry again, but this time it felt like I would never be able to stop.

Grandpa placed a hand on my shoulder and whispered, 'It hard to believe Melba gone fi true.'

He went to the kitchen and brought me back a mug of sweet tea. I drank it down and stuck a finger inside the mug to scrape out the condensed milk that had settled at the bottom.

'Go fix up yuhself an try fi get some rest, chile,' he said when I finished. 'Mi know seh a big ting dat Melba gone caus yuh nevah ave mada or fada, and mi know how much yuh di love and depen pon yuh grandmada. De good Lard wi pull us trough. Off you go now,' he added gently, and I trotted off to bed.

Grandpa and I quickly found ourselves a routine, where I did a bit more of the yard work and tending to the smaller animals. But he also put me in charge of the cooking. Sadly, like Grandma Melba, I was not the best of cooks; my sister, Patricia, despite being two years younger than me, had been much better at preparing a reasonable meal.

One evening, as Grandpa struggled to eat the mountain of hard food and chicken that I'd served up, he exclaimed, 'Chile, mi is sure yuh a cook fi duppy! Whole heap a duppy! De food plenty even for a big sumady like me! Ahn mi nuh waan yuh fi feel bad, but mi kyaan fine de taste. It come like yuh nuh bada wit one drop a seasoning!'

'Sorry, Grandpa Sippa,' I replied, 'mi will memba fi add more seasoning de next time.'

'Chile, wi ave every ting, salt, pepper, scallion, thyme, every striking ting! Yuh jus ave fi use de tings. It wi mek de food taste like food!'

And so, in our clumsy way, we carried on without Grandma Melba to keep everything in order. I continued to work as hard I could, in the secret hope that there would be no more talk of me being sent to England. I thought Grandpa and I were managing just fine, but one Sunday afternoon after we returned from church Grandpa called me over and handed me a letter from my father, which had arrived the previous day. The letter had only one sentence, written in ungainly capital letters and signed with a barely legible slant. It was addressed: *To Whom It May Concern.* I scanned the three lines:

*I JUDAH AUGUSTUS MULLINGS HEREBY GIVE MY CONSENT FOR MY DAUGHTER ERNA ANNETTE MULLINGS TO BE SENT TO ENGLAND TO JOIN HER MOTHER, VIOLET PEARL WILLIAMSON.*

My grandfather had forwarded those exact words to my father, the very same words that my mother had sent to him in one of her letters from England. I handed the letter back to my grandfather.

'Pickney! Yuh ah young sumady,' Grandpa said, in a voice full of emotion. 'Mi deya fa almost as long as Methuselah. Mi know seh yuh nuh waan fi leave dis place, but mi nuh know how fi tek care ah yuh without yuh grandmada. Dat was Melba job.'

I listened to Grandpa Sippa in silence. It was the moment that I'd so desperately wanted to avoid. I must have been in a state of shock, because my voice disappeared for two full days. But, whether I liked it or not, preparations for my journey to England began in earnest.

Grandpa Sippa took me back to Mr John the photographer to get my passport pictures taken. He also asked his good friend Mass Charlie to travel to the registrar office in town to get a copy of my birth certificate – the one that Uncle

148

Cleveland had given to my Grandma had long disappeared from the massive King James Bible where Grandpa kept important papers.

Mass Charlie arrived in the village with my birth certificate on the same day that a carefully wrapped brown paper parcel covered with colourful stamps bearing the face of Queen Elizabeth II arrived.

My birth certificate, which I'd never seen before, was a foot-long strip of cream-coloured paper. Written on it were my full name, the date and place of my birth, and my mother's name and occupation. The box where my father's name should have been was empty, apart from a black line drawn through it. The irony was not lost on me: despite the absence of my father's name on my birth certificate, he was the only person who could give permission for me to leave the island. What if Mass Booker hadn't known of his existence? What if the story that he was a thief, who had broken his neck and subsequently died, had been true? Then there would have been no father to sign anything and no preparations for me to go to England. Grandpa thanked Mass Charlie, took the birth certificate into the Hall and placed it inside the same Bible from which the original had disappeared. When he came back to the verandah, he sat down and carefully unwrapped the parcel. First, he removed and admired two checked shirts and a flat cap that were clearly meant for him. He appeared very pleased with the flat cap, in particular, which he immediately placed on his head. Then he pushed the parcel towards me.

'Chile, I tink de balance of de tings is fiyuh,' he said.

I pulled out a thick green-and-white jacket and matching skirt. A label on the inside of the jacket read: *80% Wool, 20% Nylon. Dry clean only*. The label in the skirt said the same thing. I slipped the jacket on and the lining clung to me like an uncomfortable second skin.

149

'Dem mus be yuh Hinglan tings,' Grandpa said. 'Your mada write dat it will be cold when yuh reach Hinglan. Soh she sen warm tings fiyuh.'

I took the strange clothes to my room and hung them from one of the three wooden hangers in my wardrobe. Although the summer holidays were coming to an end, Grandpa Sippa had suggested that there was little point in me returning to school in September, as my ticket was booked for the twenty-fifth of October.

I went through to the kitchen where Grandpa was boiling a pot of coffee. 'Erna, chile,' he said, 'mi know seh, yuh nuh go happy wit mi suggestion. But yuh Hinglan time a come soon. Yuh nearly fourteen now, chile, and yuh is old enough, so stop up dem tears now.'

But I couldn't stop the tears. It was my birthday the following day, but with Grandma having been so vague about the dates, I'd never celebrated my birthday before. In fact, it wasn't until I read the copy of my birth certificate that I discovered the actual date of my birth. But knowing the date meant little to me now: I was leaving my beloved Grandpa and my village forever, right on the cusp of becoming a young woman, and my heart ached with the tragedy of it all. I was going to England.

I tried over and over again to imagine what England would look like, but I couldn't. Would there be mountains and rivers like we had on our island? Did they have sun there? This question was a real worry, since most of the stories I heard said that it was always cold and usually raining there. I'd also heard about the white flakes that came out of the England sky called 'snow' and how they could cover up the whole of the England earth and stop people from even being able to leave their houses. I wondered if they had mango trees. I couldn't see how I could ever live in a place that didn't grow mangoes.

The following day, the day of my actual birthday, Grandpa presented me with a large, brand-new brown suitcase.

'Dis wi fit yuh tings and de tings yuh mada tell me fi sen fi har,' he said.

I didn't have much that I could put in it – the few items of clothing that I owned were mostly too tatty, and anyway they probably wouldn't work in the England weather – but I was still very grateful to Grandpa for my first ever birthday present.

# Chapter 18

In the days that ticked by until I left my island, I made a list in an exercise book of the things I wanted to carry with me to England. Top of my list were the complete set of *Nelson's West Indian Readers* by J O Cutteridge and my hog-hair comb, as Grandma called it, because it was the only one that could be pulled through my thick hair without snapping in half. I also included a set of soft red woollen ribbons (which had become the must-have fashion item for girls on the island) and a red hobble dress that had been passed down to me by a cousin. The last two items on my list were a chipped white Pyrex mug emblazoned with the words: *Out of Many One People* – given to all of us school children on the day our island became independent – and a little cloth bag full of the new decimal coins that I had been saving. The suitcase would still be more than two-thirds empty, leaving plenty of room for the provisions that I would be carrying for my mother.

As the date of my departure approached, Grandpa asked his sister Beryl, who lived in a town near the airport, to prepare bammy, fried fish, roast breadfruits and coconut cakes, and anything that she could think of that could be carried safely to England. In my mother's letter, she'd complained that island food was expensive and hard to find in England. She'd told

Grandpa that any little thing he could send would be a big help, and made an extra plea for one or two bottles of overproof white rum to use as medicine.

I began to count down the days with mounting dread. But then, a few days before the actual date arrived, Grandpa Sippa revealed one really good surprise that he had kept back from me.

'Erna,' he said, as we worked together in the yard that morning, 'mi a tek yuh a town fi mi sister house miself. An mi a stay up dere wit yuh till yuh leave fi Hingland.'

It was the best possible news. I'd expected that Mass Charlie would be taking me to the airport, given that Grandpa had never liked bus travel, but he wanted to stay with me for as long as he could. It was much more than I could have hoped for.

The day soon came for me to leave my village. Grandfather locked up the house and we set out in near darkness for Preston. The local bus took us to a depot, where we changed to a second bus for the long-distance ride to Great-Aunt Beryl's house. We travelled through villages and towns that I was seeing for the first time, and saw some of the big rivers that I had learnt about in school. I even spotted my first waterfall. We finally arrived at my great-aunt's house, having travelled on the two buses and a taxi over the best part of a day.

I loved Great-Aunt Beryl's house the moment I saw it. It was made of white-painted wooden slats and stood high off the ground on stilts. All the windows had glass in them. Grandpa Sippa told me that the house was very close to the sea, and, even though the sea couldn't be seen from it, instead of a usual dirt yard, the ground was covered in fine white sand that must have come all the way from the beach. The town seemed to be filled with children, and underneath the stilt houses was where they all played. I soon discovered that they loved what they called my 'down a country talk'.

'Say something, Erna,' begged an impish albino girl, 'it nice when you talk country!'

I equally liked listening to the town children's speaky-spokey accents and my last few days on the island were filled with fun and laughter. And although Grandma was rarely far from my mind, I no longer cried when I thought of her. But, as my final night on the island arrived, sleep became impossible: excitement had at last kicked in – not because I was about to leave for a place I had never been before that was half way round the world, but because I was going to get to see the great big aeroplanes close up. My feelings about actually getting on to one and flying away forever were an altogether different matter.

Great-Aunt Beryl's son Delroy drove Grandpa Sippa and me to the airport in his taxi. We left his mother's house a whole two hours early, as I wanted to see a little of what Kingston looked like, especially as it was where my mother had lived for a while. It was the most dramatic sight I'd ever seen – first, hundreds of shack houses seemingly piled up in an unholy mess on top of each other, then Delroy drove a short distance and we were surrounded by elegant homes with beautifully tended gardens. There were row upon row of stylish shops, and more people and cars than I had ever seen. Everything jumbled together in one great mass.

Delroy parked up and said, 'Erna, you might want to come and tek a look. Yuh might not see someting like this again over foreign.'

Grandpa chose to wait in the car.

As we walked over to the sprawling Coronation Market, my eyes were met with a mountain of colours, foodstuffs, clothing, household items, livestock. Dozens of stalls with folks cooking up all manner of food; it was like Sante Fe market magnified hundreds of times.

'Stop a mi stall noh, young gal,' said plump woman from behind a glass case filled with delicious looking patties.

I stopped in the hope that Delroy might see his way to buy me one, and sure enough he did.

Back in the car with Grandpa, the energy in the voices of the market traders and their customers, and the smells of all the various produce stayed with me as we drove away from the city.

Then, almost before I knew it, we were at the airport. Delroy carried my suitcase and we made our way towards the airport's only terminal. Just before we entered, Grandpa pointed to a balcony near the top of the building where a crowd of people stood waving at a steady stream of people as they made their way across the tarmac towards a huge plane with the words *Pan American* written on its side. Only Grandpa Sippa and I were allowed inside the terminal. Delroy handed me my suitcase while Grandpa reached inside his jacket pocket for my passport and ticket. A young man walking alongside the queue that my grandfather and I had joined stopped beside us.

'Sir, how many of you are travelling today?'

'Jus mi grandaughta hereso,' Grandpa replied.

'May I see her passport and ticket?'

Grandpa Sippa handed them over.

'Ah, she is a minor,' he said. He turned to me. 'Is it your first time travelling on a plane, Erna?' he asked.

'Yes, sarh. I nevah go on any plane before, sarh.'

'You will be fine, Erna,' he beamed, turning back to my grandfather and handing him my documents. 'Sir, once your granddaughter has cleared security, she will be cared for by a staff member until she lands in London. She will be well looked after, sir.'

Grandpa thanked the man and remained with me until we got to the front of the immigration queue. I felt my body trembling as I stood, not sure whether I was feeling excitement or fear. Then Grandpa took my hand and looked me in the eyes.

'Erna, yuh a leave wit my blessing,' he said. 'Mi wish yuh a safe journey. De good Lord will keep a close eye pon yuh.'

'Mi going fi miss yuh bad, Grandpa. Mek sure yuh look after yuhself till mi come look fi yuh.'

The customs woman took my papers from Grandpa Sippa.

'Keep this very safe, young lady,' she said, as she gave me back my passport – the first page was now sporting two colourful inked stamps.

Suddenly I was being swept through the airport building in a winding queue of adults, children and babies in arms. We were ushered briskly down a long corridor to a large swing door, which opened on to the tarmac. The massive BOAC aeroplane stood elegant in the distance. Dozens of men were scurrying around, some walking, others driving. High off the ground in the belly of the craft two men off-loaded all manner of luggage from a forklift truck. A man dressed in fluorescent orange clothing stood near the plane just waving a flag. As the various activities continued, airport personnel walked us to the plane. The roar of the engine blocked any thoughts I had in my head in that moment. But as I mounted the last step, I turned and looked back at the airport building. Grandpa was gone, and my whole life up to that point seemed to melt away before my eyes.

Part two

Part Two

# Chapter 19

The plane landed with a jolt at London's Heathrow Airport and raced down the runway as though it had no intention of stopping. I took a deep breath and offered up a silent prayer, overwhelmed with relief that we had actually landed. It was the second time on that long journey that we'd made it back to earth alive, in a machine that seemed to be held up only by great puffs of white cloud and the desperate hope of us passengers to survive. I'd barely moved for hours. When we made our first stop, somewhere in America for refuelling, I risked a trip to the bathroom, but while the aircraft was in the sky I feared that any extra movement would be enough to bring it tumbling to the ground. I might have been able to relax a little if so many people hadn't been moving aimlessly up and down the aisle like yo-yos, possibly risking everyone's safety. The hostesses had fussed and constantly asked people if they were okay; of course, no one was okay, we were all trapped! I refused all offers of food and took only tiny sips of water to avoid any further toilet visits. When we finally landed, my hamstrings were so tight that I was unable to stand up straight for several hours. As the moment came for us to disembark, the pretty blonde hostess, who had been so patient and kind throughout the journey, tried in vain to reassure me, 'Think how lovely it will be to see your mum and dad again!' she said.

'I don't want to see her, and my father don't live in England,' I replied crossly. Each time she gently mopped the tears that poured from my eyes, another torrent cascaded down my face.

The room where I waited for the immigration lady to complete the seemingly endless pages of different-coloured forms for my entry into the UK was dank and cold, and the suit my mother had sent me to wear offered little protection against the autumn chill. My knees visibly shook and my teeth chattered as my skinny body struggled to cope with the cold that seemed to invade every inch of me. I tilted my head as far back as I could in a desperate effort to stem further tears, but come they did, accompanied by my uncontrollable wailing. I felt as though I'd been torn from my island with no way of ever getting back. When the immigration lady finally handed back my plane ticket, I focused on the word 'minor', wondering over and over again what I'd done to find myself in such a terrible place.

'Ready to go, Erna?' she said. 'Your father is waiting for you.'

Oh, dear God, no. Please don't let it be the ugly Satan devil man, I thought.

'Where's mi mada?' I asked the kindly hostess who had waited with me in immigration.

'It's your father who's come to collect you, dear,' she said. 'Maybe your mother stayed behind to prepare a nice welcome for you?'

I felt like I was stuck in a nightmare with no way out. I was thousands of miles from everything I knew, trapped in this cold foreboding place full of people who looked extremely odd and talked in the strangest manner. I didn't want to be here in this England place. Something in the faces of the strangers told me that they didn't want me here either. To complete my misery, my mother had sent the one person I disliked most in the entire world to collect me.

. . .

I didn't look at him as I climbed into the back seat of his clapped-out Ford Cortina, ignoring his suggestion that I sit in the front. We travelled in silence along streets paved with asphalt, just like the big ones on my island; there wasn't a hint of gold anywhere. Peering into the semi-darkness, I could just make out endless rows of grey houses, all squashed together, each one with its own little front garden. Dense black smoke billowed from the rooftops. It was as uninviting a vision as I could imagine. Finally, the car came to a halt outside a house that looked exactly like all the others we passed. The front sloped down into what I at first thought was some kind of gully, but turned out to be a lower living area. Why would anyone want to live underground? I thought. Surely that was a place for the dead! Above the battered black front door stood a further three floors of heartless red bricks.

The ugly Satan devil man turned a key in the lock and the door swung open on to a hallway that felt even colder than outside. The only apparent warmth came from the hideous clash of flowery patterns on the carpet and wallpaper. He ushered me into a large living room and then left. A gas fire with pretend flames hissed out the possibility of warmth from an alcove. I sat at the end of the sofa closest to the fire. My stomach churned with fear. I focused my attention on the room, in which every surface was taken over by ornaments and plants. A cage full of plastic birds had prime position on a low glass table; a gangling rubber plant and a straggling geranium struggled for space in the far corner. The clash of patterns continued in the curtains, rugs and sofa; the one note of consistency was that everything was some shade of orange, red or brown. I shifted a little on the sofa and stared vacantly at the blank television screen – the first TV I'd ever seen – when a photograph in a wooden frame on the shelf above it caught my eye. It was the photograph we'd had taken before our mother left for England over three years ago. I stood up and studied it carefully. All four of us children appeared to have eyes too big for our faces, staring with bewilderment into the camera. Our mother stood tall behind us, her beautifully elongated neck beneath her sharp-jawed face with eyes that seemed to veil some secret pain.

'Your mother gone to Brixton to get food shopping,' the ugly Satan devil man said, sticking his head around the door frame. 'She should be back in the next half hour or so. I suppose you can't wait to see her?' he offered.

I didn't respond. I just sat and waited.

Suddenly, the front door slammed and I sprang to my feet. My mother walked past the open living room door, pushing a huge Silver Cross pram. Inside it, facing each other, were two fat baby girls, dressed identically in thick knitted pink dresses and matching bonnets, and obviously twins. Following sluggishly in her wake were three more children, a girl and two boys. They looked thinner than I remembered. Patricia still had very short hair, but her face resembled that of a much older person to whom life had been unkind. The boys no longer had their little bellies, and their bones stuck out. And Sonny now had a thick head of hair, instead of that shiny, smooth little head our grandparents so loved to rub.

My mother parked the pram at the far end of the hallway leaving the twins strapped in. I could hear them babbling to each other in a kind of call-and-response, one prattling away for a short time, then the other taking over when she stopped. The next thing I knew my mother was standing in front of me.

'Hello, my dear,' she said. 'I'm glad you arrived safely.'

She too looked strangely altered. Her head was covered in a flowery scarf, but the wisps of hair that escaped from underneath it were not her own but some kind of wig. She was wearing a thick brown coat and black wellington boots. I didn't respond to her greeting – I was afraid of giving her the impression that I was actually happy to be there.

'Cat got your tongue, child?' she said. 'You know it's rude not to answer when an adult is talking to you.'

I smiled weakly, but no words would come out.

'You must be tired,' she added in a softer tone. 'The plane journey is a long something.' She smiled broadly, as if she was genuinely happy to see me. Then she patted me on the head and disappeared.

I had imagined that when my siblings and I saw each other again we would be overjoyed. The scene that had played out in my head was of the four of us rushing into each other's arms and laughing loudly, with lots of rapid-fire talk as we tried to catch up with our lives. In reality, they just stood in the hallway and stared at me. After what seemed like a long time, we all moved through the connecting doorway to the back room, which was roughly the same size as the front room, but more square in shape. Faded pale blue paper with odd little green and red flowers decked all four walls. A large table covered in a frilly plastic tablecloth and plastic mats sat in the centre. In one alcove, next to a sealed fireplace, stood a tall wooden cupboard with textured glass panels and a drop-down shelf. The cupboard was painted the same blue colour as the walls. The children plonked themselves on the chairs around the table and continued to stare at me out of their sad-looking eyes. I had to look away from their intense searching and concentrated instead on the three framed portraits of Jesus on the wall. The Jesuses were all white with flowing hair, but all had different facial features.

I soon found myself wondering how it was that Jesus was always white, even on my island where the population was mainly black. Surely, he should at least be a mulatto?

I was quite lost in my thoughts when my mother reappeared and offered up a prayer:

'I thank you my God Jehovah for delivering this child safe into our hands. Amen.'

'Amen,' my siblings muttered.

Her prayer did nothing to initiate conversation, and in the silence that followed my thoughts returned to my island: waking up to the crowing cockerels, the orange glow of the sun as it rose gently above the horizon, the early morning dew on grass, the lushness and vibrancy of colours, the early morning banter of adults and children. In the meantime, my mother left the room again and then returned carrying one of the fat babies, whom she placed on Patricia's lap.

'Keep a good eye on Doretta for me,' she said, before turning to me. 'Erna, can you look after Barbette? Someone has to cook the supper.'

Barbette was protesting loudly that her sister was no longer with her, and she carried on crying until mother returned and plonked her on my knees. She stared briefly at my face before letting out the most almighty scream. In a desperate attempt to soothe her, I started jerking my knees up and down, but this only made her scream even louder.

Without a word, Patricia placed Doretta on the floor and whisked Barbette off my lap. The crying stopped immediately. A sly glance from Patricia said it all: Barbette didn't like new people. She put Barbette on the floor next to her sister where they babbled contentedly, reaching out their chubby little hands to touch each other. Grandpa Sippa and I had learnt of their birth from one of the blue airmail letters. Grandpa had mused about how Grandma Melba would have loved to have known that another one of her daughters had given birth to twins; twins were practically a tradition in our family, but Doretta and Barbette were the only pair who had actually survived.

'Your food is ready,' Mother said, emerging from the kitchen some two hours later. Little bits of wet flour still stuck to the back of her hands from making dumplings.

My siblings were out of their seats at speed. I followed them into a freezing bathroom, where strips of glossy pink wallpaper hung limply from the pitted walls, and worn lino covered the floor. We took turns washing our hands in the cracked sink, the water so cold it made me wince. Then we trooped back into the dining room. I gingerly sipped some sweet tea that my mother placed in front of me. The food on the table looked familiar, but when I tasted it, it had an odd flavour.

I realised that I was screwing up my face with every mouthful, so I said in my most convincing voice, 'De people dem give mi plenty food on de plane.' It was the first time I'd spoken since leaving Heathrow.

Suddenly, there was hysterical laughter around the table.

'She sounds really funny!' Patricia said. The boys giggled their agreement. 'They must speak really funny in your country,' she added, turning to me.

*They must speak really funny in your country?* I repeated the comment in my head. How could she have forgotten that it was her country too? Didn't she realise that it was they who sounded funny with their weird way of speaking?

'Children, stop with your nonsense,' Mother warned. 'And, Erna, there'll be nothing else on offer for the day, so you can eat what you've been given or leave it.'

I left it.

'How was Mass Sippa when you left him?' Mother asked, when Patricia was clearing the dishes.

'He was alright, mam. He seh fi tell everybody hello.'

Mother didn't respond, just murmured to herself and got up from the table.

It was just after eight o'clock when I finally climbed the stairs to the room I was to share with Patricia. My body felt like a block of ice. I sat on the edge of the bed, my knees knocking and my teeth chattering loudly. I wrapped myself in the thin blue coat that the ugly Satan devil man had given me at the airport, and listened to the rattle of the window frame as the wind whistled fiercely outside. Tears silently streamed down my face. My first day in England had remained resolutely cold and grey. Finally, I curled up in the ice-cold bed in the freezing room and fell into a fitful sleep.

# Chapter 20

By 7.30am the next morning, the house was buzzing with activity. I hadn't realised that my first visit to the bathroom earlier in the morning was my only chance to wash with warm water. When I tried later, the hot water was all used up and I was left to squat over a purple plastic bucket half-full of icy water, attempting to clean myself. Everyone else was quickly dressed and ready for their day: Patricia, Clifton and Sonny in their school uniforms, and the twins in their identical pink knitted outfits. My mother looked smart in her sky-blue auxiliary nurse's uniform, finished off with a little white cap and a white belt. The ugly Satan devil man was still on his night shift at the factory and hadn't yet arrived home. It concerned me deeply that once Mother and the children left for the day, I would be the only one in the house when the ugly Satan devil man returned. Moments later they were gone – Mother to drop the twins with their childminder before making her way to the hospital, and Patricia and the boys headed for their schools.

Before leaving the house, Mother mentioned that there was some chicken-neck soup I could heat up if I got hungry. Then she took me into the bathroom and pointed to a mountain of clothing. 'I want you to wash and hang these in the garden,' she said, 'and mind you don't spoil the colours! Wash all the white things separate from the coloured things.'

I tried to hide the shock that must have appeared on my face. On my island, I'd only been responsible for washing my smalls; my grandparents had paid Miss Merle, Miss Blossom's even more eccentric twin sister, to do the big washes and the ironing.

As soon as everyone had gone, I went to the bathroom and separated the clothing into colours and whites, threw all the white things into the bath and added some soap powder from a box I found in a cupboard by the door. I plunged my arms into the frigid water and started massaging the whites, but within seconds my fingers were numb. I withdrew them fast, dried them on a rough towel and went to the kitchen, where I searched out the biggest cooking pot I could find and filled it with water. Four pots of boiling water later and the water in the bath was just about warm enough for me to complete the washing. Rinsing was easy – I simply swished the clothes about in the bath with the help of a wooden spoon. After that, I made my way to the garden where I hung out the two lines of dripping wet clothes as fast as I could.

My chores completed, I decided to explore the rest of the house, where I discovered that, apart from the kitchen, bathroom, dining room and the bedrooms where we children slept, all the other rooms were locked. With nothing else to do, I decided to take a walk. I pulled on every item of clothing I had and, bracing myself against the cold, I left the house, took the first left turn I came across, and was amazed to find that it led me to a small park with undulating grassy mounds and stark, leafless trees. The park was empty apart from an old woman walking a dog and two young mothers pushing giant prams. I walked briskly around the edge of the park before returning to the house. I was cold and hungry, but I still wasn't looking forward to the chicken-neck soup. Grandpa had stopped serving me chicken-neck soup years before, when he'd seen me picking out the grizzly bits of flesh and depositing them in a tin can.

'Chile, a trow yuh trow good food weh,' he'd said.

'Mi nuh like de chicken foot and chicken neck, Grandpa,' I'd replied, 'dem look lakka foot bottom and dem taste grizzle, grizzle!'

I hesitated, but chicken-neck soup was all there was. I turned the knob on the cooker, but, unlike earlier, nothing happened. The hall light didn't come on either when I flicked the switch. It was the same story when I tried the switch in the bathroom and the bedroom. I was worried that I might have broken something with all that water boiling. I put the soup back in the fridge and found an over-ripe banana, which I ate slowly, relishing its sweetness.

Back in the bedroom, I sat in front of the paraffin heater, which Patricia had removed earlier from the boy's room. Compared to the rest of the house, the temperature was bearable, but the room reeked of the paraffin. I warmed my hands in front of its grille before climbing back into the bed, where I wrapped myself in the sheet, the blanket and the heavy blue candlewick bedspread.

My body was just beginning to warm up nicely when the slam of the front door made me jump. I listened as someone walked heavily downstairs into the lower living area. Moments later, the hall light came on and I heard whoever it was walk back up to the ground floor. I assumed it was the ugly Satan devil man and, sure enough, moments later he called out, 'Erna, you in the house?'

I ignored him by pretending to be asleep. I heard him climb up the stairs, then he stopped outside the bedroom door and turned the handle. I held my breath, but fortunately he made no attempt to enter; he simply reached inside and switched off the light.

. . .

It was Clifton who explained later that evening why the cooker and lights had stopped working.

'Everything in this house works on a meter,' he said.

'What's a meter?' I asked. 'How yuh mean everyting work from it?'

'Come,' he said.

I followed him downstairs to the room he called the 'basement'. The low-ceilinged space was lit by a single dull light bulb. Strange black patches covered the walls and the stench of damp stuck in my throat.

'Those are the meters,' Clifton said, pointing at two black metal boxes fixed to the wall. 'One's for gas, the other is for electric. When you put a shilling in, everything works.'

So the mystery of the lights not working was solved. I soon found out that every few days the house would be plunged into darkness until either my mother or the ugly Satan devil man came home and replenished the meters. That was, until I remembered the bag of coins that I had brought with me from my island. It dawned on me that the England shilling was exactly the same shape and size as the island dollar. I showed Clifton the coins when he came home from school. The electricity had been off all day.

'Maybe we can use dem in de meter,' I said.

'Yes, I think we could,' Clifton agreed, 'but my father will kill me if he finds out!'

'Im nuh go know it's you,' I replied, not really believing it, but thinking it was worth the risk.

I held the torch while Clifton took one of my coins and pushed it into the electric meter slot. After a moment, the lights came on.

'Yesss!' he cried triumphantly, clapping his hands.

Then he led me back upstairs and showed me that he'd worked out a way of jamming a sixpence halfway into the slot on the television, which made it run continuously.

For the next few days, Clifton and I kept everything in the house running non-stop. It was all going fine until the ugly Satan devil man sensed something was up and went to check the meter, where he found one of the island coins that we must have left there by mistake. He came back upstairs with a face like thunder and went over to the television and discovered the sixpence that Clifton had jammed in the slot. We watched in terror, but he didn't utter a single word. Instead, he sat heavily in the armchair, sweating profusely.

The ugly Satan devil man was a diabetic and had to inject himself daily with insulin. Mother told me that we had to look out for him, in case he forgot to inject, and that if we saw him sweating and shaking, then we had to shout 'sugar!' to remind him to take some. But now that it was happening we just sat there frozen with fear. Half an hour later, Mother came home and found him slumped in the armchair, with the four of us still sitting on the sofa, staring at him. She rushed to the bathroom and came back with an insulin-filled syringe, which she jabbed into his abdomen. After a minute or so, he began to recover, then, for a reason I was unable to understand, he grabbed hold of Patricia and began lashing her with his belt. The more she screamed, the more he hit her. It was only when she began screaming, 'I'm going to tell! I'm going to tell!' that Mother intervened, shouting, 'Philbert! That's enough!'

The ugly Satan devil man stared at her, wild-eyed and panting, and dropped the belt. Patricia ran crying to our bedroom. I gazed at my mother and her husband, trying to make sense of what had just happened. Then Clifton and Sonny started fighting and Mother screamed at us to go to our beds, and the moment was forgotten.

There were only four sources of heating in the house: the gas fires in the living and dining rooms and two paraffin heaters, one of which never left my mother's bedroom. The other one was shared between the other bedrooms and the bathroom, depending on who got to it first. The smell of damp that I had noticed in the basement gradually permeated the entire house and it seemed like every day a new black mould patch appeared on the walls. Despite the daily cold washes, the awful taste of everything, the freezing cold walks, the demanding chores, the lack of conversation and any fun, almost against my will, slowly but surely, I found myself becoming acclimatised to what felt like a nightmare place.

# Chapter 21

England was turning out to be stranger than I could ever
have imagined. I'd had no idea what I would find when I
got here, and now that I *was* here, I was discovering that
everything was at odds to the world that I'd grown up in. For
a start, the people were different – not just the white people,
but the black people as well. It was the dead of winter, and
the sight of everyone wearing thick overcoats, knitted hats,
scarves and boots just to go about their daily lives was weird
enough, but seeing black people dressed in the same fashion
was a whole other level of weirdness. What on earth could
have persuaded them to leave a place like my island, where
only grown men occasionally wore shirts with long sleeves, to
live in a country where everyone had to swaddle themselves
in layers of clothing? Another thing I hadn't expected was
that the black people came from all sorts of different places,
not just from Jamaica. I was often perplexed by the multitude
of accents and languages that I encountered. On my island,
everyone spoke patois – with a few regional differences – and
everyone talked to everyone else. Here in London, it seemed
that people didn't even know the names of their next-door
neighbours. I soon discovered that some of our neighbours
had come directly from Africa, but my mother warned me

not to talk to them, as she didn't like them, nor they her, it turned out. 'They think they are better than us,' she said, followed by her trademark suck of disgust on her teeth. But I was fascinated by them, especially the women, whom I often passed in the street. They were always dressed in elegant, wonderfully colourful clothing with dramatic headdresses. I would stop and stare at them while they walked regally by, barely registering my presence. It was the first time in my life that I heard the term 'coloured' used to describe people who looked like me. Back on my island, I had just been 'me'. I wasn't coloured, I wasn't black, I was just Erna Mullings. Sometimes people on my island would cuss each other for being too black, or too red, or too 'chinee', but there were no 'coloured people', and it took me a long time to get used to the term. No one walking down the road greeted anyone. On my island, it was the height of bad manners not to greet your neighbour, but here it was normal. It was an unfriendly, upside down world that made little sense to me, and somehow I had not fully understood that leaving my island was meant to be permanent. The worst thing about this England place was the slow realisation that I was going to remain here forever. I started to experience disturbed sleep and would wake often during the night, each time convinced I was simply having a bad dream and that at any moment I would wake up in my little house on my island. But then morning would come, and with it the terrible realisation that it was no dream, but a nightmarish reality that had already lasted far too long. More than anything, I wanted to get back on that plane and return to my home. For the first time in my life, I found myself feeling really angry with Grandpa Sippa. Why did he ever agree to put me on that plane? 'A de law of de land,' he had stressed, when I questioned him about it before I left. 'A de best ting mi kyan do fiyuh, chile. It wi get yuh a chance in life, an yuh wi be wit yuh mada, where yuh belong.' But I did not belong and I was never going to belong. The only place I belonged was back on my island with him, so I decided to write a letter to tell him so.

*November 1969*

*Dear Grandpa Sippa,*

    *I hope this letter of mine find you in the best of health. I hope you're not feeling too lonely. I am sorry that this is the first letter I am writing to you since I reach England. I wanted to write you before, but I thought I should settle myself and get to know the place a bit better, so I could tell you some good news. Well, Grandpa Sippa, although I have decided to write you now, I still don't have anything good to tell you yet. Maybe apart from that it's nice to see Patricia, Clifton and Sonny again and it's nice to meet the baby twins, Doretta and Barbette. I hardly recognise Patricia and the boys, though. They have all grown much taller and they are all a bit bony. Not like the twins who are really fat. Also, Patricia and the boys now speak with English accents. I can hardly understand what they're talking about sometimes, and they don't always understand me either.*

    *Grandpa Sippa, I can't find anything to like about this England place. The place is cold like inside a freezer and it never seem to stop raining. Sometimes the place is so foggy you can't even see the person walking next to you. The food is not nice either, Grandpa, but I like their tea. I drink lots of tea. It helps to keep me warm. I was right, too, they don't have even one single mango tree here. Not one. We can buy mango from the market, but one ripe mango cost nearly the same here as a hamper full of mango would cost us on the island. They have lots of trees, but most of them don't have fruit growing on them and most of them have no leaves, although Clifton tell me that will change in the spring time.*

*The worst thing, Grandpa, is that people don't even say hello to you in this place. The white people don't like the black people at all, and the black people don't like the white people much, and none of them talk to you. I used to try and say good morning to everyone I met in the street, but some people would look on me like I was mad, so I don't do that any more, and anyway the people always seems to be in one big hurry.*

*I can't say that I like living with Miss Violet and her husband either. Sometimes Miss Violet doesn't seem so well. She get very upset and don't talk to anyone for a long time, and she take lots of pills for her nerves. And I don't like her husband at all and I don't think Grandma Melba would ever want me to like him.*

*I am hoping to start attending school in January. I am looking forward to that because I miss learning. For now, I am mostly staying in the house, and I help Miss Violet with the twins sometimes.*

*Grandpa Sippa, I miss you and everybody. I miss our house and specially all the sunshine, and I still really really miss Grandma Melba. I don't think that will stop.*

*I am going to finish this letter now, Grandpa Sippa. I am sure that next time I write, I will have some good news to tell you.*

*God bless you and take care of yourself,*
*Your granddaughter, Erna.*

My days consisted of chores, going for brisk walks and, on Wednesday evenings and Sunday mornings, reluctantly accompanying my mother, her husband, and my siblings to their evangelical church meetings. The church was a large, ugly, single-storey building, sat back from the main road. It had a mixed congregation of both white and black people, but the whole place had a strange feeling about it. We were not the only children to be dragged along to the church, but, in my eyes, we seemed like the most normal. Given how dysfunctional my family was, this was quite a feat. All the other teenage girls were dressed like five-year-olds and behaved accordingly. There was one girl called Babsie, a tall girl of around fifteen, with a lopsided face. She was always dressed in flowery knee-length frocks with voluminous puff sleeves. Every week, she seemed to be on the verge of starting a conversation with Patricia and me, but the words never quite came.

'Hi, Babsie,' I said one Sunday morning, just before the dreaded sermon began, 'you alright?'

Babsie just stared at me from her lopsided face. Her mouth twitched ever so slightly, but no words came out.

'Maybe she's dumb,' Patricia said, as we walked away.

At precisely a quarter to ten on Sunday mornings, the pastor would sound a handbell and everyone would stream into the building. Once inside they would sit chattering away as if they actually liked each other, but as soon as they left the building the white people would revert to talking to their white brethren and the black people to theirs. Our mother's main reason for taking Patricia and me along was so we could look after the twins, which gave her time to chat to her Bible sisters. Inside, like the village church back on the island, there were no effigies of any kind. It was just a large plain room with benches, a platform and a reading stand. Men would stand up and read out pages and pages from the Bible and then a few tuneless songs would be sung. Then everyone would sit down again for yet more Bible readings. The women didn't receive the spirit or talk in tongues. There was no dancing or shouting of 'Praise the Lord!' The whole scene was as dry as two sticks being rubbed together. Only there was no fire or brimstone here. It was a passionless, joyless experience for Patricia and me, but these church visits were the highlight of my mother's week, and it was the only time she appeared chatty and happy.

It began to seem like my life would continue in this miserable vein forever, when one chilly Saturday afternoon the mood in our house lightened unexpectedly. My mother had spent the previous two weeks preparing for a party. It was our turn to host our extended family, which turned out to be a tradition started by my mother's eldest sister, Auntie Madge, as a way of keeping everyone connected. This was the very same Auntie Madge who had written to us about Mother's predicament two years earlier. She was a formidable character who, along with her husband, Herbie, had provided many of our island relatives with a room in her large house in Clapham, until they were able to rent or purchase a home of their own.

At around four o'clock on the Saturday, relatives began to arrive. Within a couple of hours, over forty adults and children had piled into our house, filling all the common spaces. No one looked casual: all the men wore suits and the women sported an array of fabulous frocks, bought specially for the occasion.

'Bwoy mi loving dis!' I said to Patricia as the house echoed with noise, laughter and the reggae music that our relatives had brought with them.

'Come, Violet!' a skinny man with straightened hair shouted, pulling my mother towards him. 'A long time you have a dance with your old school friend.'

He swung my mother around the middle of the room a couple of times until she managed to escape his grasp. 'I have to look after everyone, Linford,' she squealed, 'I've got no time for you and your crazy dances!'

Then someone put Millie Small's 'My Boy Lollipop' on, and all at once everyone got up to dance to the ska beat.

'The place too hot, though!' cried a male relative who had found a seat in a corner and was sipping from a bottle of brandy. 'The dancing will provide all the heat we need right now,' he added, wiping his brow with a handkerchief. Of all the days for my mother to have actually switched on the fire!

'You can start making your way through to the dining room,' Mother said, during a lull in the dancing.

She was like a woman transformed. She bantered with her relatives as they moved around the table collecting their food. 'I can't believe so many months have passed since we last saw each other, Vernie,' she twittered to a woman in a striking red dress, 'in fact, I think it was at the last get-together at your place.'

'Time is our enemy, cousin,' Vernie replied, 'but at least we are guaranteed to meet up at these gatherings. Well, as far as we can guarantee anything.'

Somehow, Mother had managed to make the whole affair appear as if fun and laughter were just how things moved in the house. But all too soon it was over and life returned to its normal dreariness, and it was hard to believe the party had even happened.

# Chapter 22

Soon enough it was December and coming up to my first Christmas in England. All the shops were lit up and filled with bright sparkling things. Every conversation, whether at the bus stop, on the train, or in the park, seemed to be about Christmas. People were constantly asking each other what they were doing for Christmas, what they wanted for Christmas, what gifts they were giving to whom, whether they were going away for Christmas or staying at home. The local high street was packed with shoppers who appeared to be in an even bigger rush than usual. I sat by the living room window and watched as our next-door neighbour, Mr Kelly, dragged a Christmas tree into his house. Everywhere I looked, people seemed to be dragging Christmas trees along with them.

It was a good time for the rag-and-bone man to tout for business. I heard his horse and cart clanking along the street at least once a week in the weeks leading up to the holidays, accompanied by his sing-song refrain: 'Make space for the new! If it's broken, we'll take it away! Make space for the new!'

One afternoon, as I made my way home from another of my brisk park walks, I found myself arriving back at the same time as Mrs Kelly. As we climbed the steps to our respective front doors, she turned and asked me, 'Is your ma around, dear?'

'No, mam, she gone to de hospital for work,' I replied.

'Oh, so she has! I don't suppose you and your brothers and sister want to see the tree, do you now, dear? Me and the boys put it up yesterday.' Mrs Kelly knew full well that our mother did not celebrate Christmas, and would not have approved of the invitation. 'It could be our little secret,' she continued, 'we wouldn't want to upset your ma now, would we? But you're children, after all, and every child loves Christmas. Santa coming and all that!'

Patricia and the boys let out yelps of joy when I told them of Mrs Kelly's invitation.

'I wish we could have a Christmas tree,' Clifton sighed.

'Me too,' echoed Sonny. 'All my friends at school have one.'

The Kelly's house was the opposite of ours in every way. Everything about it seemed perfect. The first thing I noticed when Mrs Kelly opened her front door was how warm it was. There was a long radiator in the hallway that was almost too hot to touch.

'In you go, dears,' Mrs Kelly sang, as she ushered us into her living room.

Inside the room, a granite fireplace glowed with orange flames that danced above a mound of white-hot coals. On the mantelpiece were framed photographs of John F Kennedy and the Pope, surrounded by pictures of family members and children taking their first Holy Communion. Next to the fire, inside an alcove, there was a miniature shrine that housed a tiny water font, alongside a statue of Mother Mary with a bleeding heart. The tree that I'd seen Mr Kelly dragging past a few days before was standing tall in the bay window. A doll in a full-length white dress, a pair of wings protruding from her back, and a white veil partly covering her blonde hair, sat at the very top of the tree.

'Why yuh put a dolly on top of de tree, Miss Kelly?' I asked her.

'Because it represents Jesus Christ, dear,' she explained.

'But Jesus was a man, Miss Kelly, and dat is a girl dolly.'

'You have a point, Erna!' she smiled thinly. 'I should have said she represents the Bride of Christ.'

I decided not to ask the next question that popped into my head, about why Jesus's bride was white.

Beneath the tree lay a pile of beautifully wrapped presents, each with an individual name tag. Patricia, Clifton and Sonny had moved over to the tree and stood staring open-mouthed in admiration at them.

'Those are mostly for our boys, Frankie and Aaron,' Mrs Kelly said. 'We've lots of family back in Ireland. They all send the boys little gifts for birthdays and Christmases.'

A tall bookshelf weighed down with books lined the wall opposite the fireplace. I was entranced by the sight of so many books in one house, but as I edged closer, trying to read the names on their spines, Mrs Kelly's voice stopped me in my tracks.

'I see that you like books, dear,' she said, 'you can come and look another time.'

I had a vague idea that Mr Kelly's job was something to do with the government and that Mrs Kelly worked as a schoolteacher. I guessed that was why they had so many books.

'Excuse me for one minute, children,' Mrs Kelly announced suddenly, 'and mind you don't touch anything.'

We stood as still as statues, almost too scared to breathe, until she returned with a china plate covered with thick, round, cream-coloured biscuits.

'These are proper Irish biscuits,' she said, as she handed me the plate. 'I baked them myself yesterday.'

'Thank you, mam,' I said.

'Mind you share them fairly,' she said.

No sooner had we taken one each and bitten into them, she started shooing us out of the house. 'Off with you now, then,' she said, 'and don't forget to give my regards to your mother.'

And with that she herded us out of the front room and through the front door.

My mother made it clear that she disliked everything about Christmas. She even refused to say the word unless she had to, replacing it with 'Christendom' whenever she had to refer to it – a word that she was not shy about using in public. A few days before the day itself, she took us to Woolworth's on the Old Kent Road. The boys were convinced that they were going to be bought presents, so they skipped happily alongside her. But Mother's shopping expedition had nothing to do with buying us children anything. She had taken up sewing again and wanted to purchase herself a much-needed sewing box for all her needlework paraphernalia. The wooden box turned out to be quite a large item and, along with various other purchases, we knew that it was going to be our job to carry them all home.

'This Christmas thing,' she announced loudly, as we followed her around the store, 'is a pagan celebration for heathens and the ungodly. And you can take your eyes off all that rubbish,' she snapped when she caught Sonny and Clifton looking wistfully at the pretend parcels under a huge Christmas tree. 'None of that devil worshipping stuff will be coming into my house!'

As I watched other people's children racing around the store, begging their parents to buy them one of the multitude of toys on display, thoughts of Christmas celebrations on my island came flooding back to me. Christmas wasn't something that was spoken about, it was just something that islanders did. Preparations would start with house painting, followed by an insane amount of house cleaning and yard sweeping. Everything inside and outside the house had to shine. A few days before the big day, village children would gather together and sing every Christmas song they knew, or just any old folk song with a good rhythm.

'Christmas a come an mi waan mi lama.'

'Christmas a come an mi waan mi deggeday.'

'While shepherds wash their socks by night and hang them out to dry' and so on, with all the versions children liked to sing.

The village men would build a makeshift dance hall in the middle of Mass Byron's yard, and would organise two big dances over the weekend leading up to Christmas. Villagers would flock from all around, dressed in their finest clothes. It was a time when copious amounts of white rum and Red Stripe beer were drunk by the adults and a ton of curried goat and chicken and rice and peas consumed. Once everyone was fed and watered, the dancing would start – to ska and bluebeat, all night through. The atmosphere was electric. We children would be given small amounts of money, which we spent on firecrackers that detonated with delightful noisy explosions, frightening old women and chickens alike. Christmas was a time for villagers to come together, for fun and merriment. But our mother's church did not observe Christmas and she in turn must have shut out her memories of island Christmases.

On our return from Woolworths, Mother unlocked the living room door, walked over to the gas fire and ignited it. This was something she did only when she couldn't avoid the fact that it was actually colder inside the house than it was outside.

'This is another level of cold,' she gasped, 'pneumonia weather!'

We all rushed forward and, with a bit of pushing and shoving, I managed to get closest to the fire. With my feet outstretched and my hands resting behind my head, I lay back on the carpet and felt my body slowly begin to warm up.

It wasn't long before Patricia had something to say. 'Some people's fingers and toes fall off in the cold,' she stated.

'And your eyes and your mouth can freeze shut,' Clifton added.

'That's not true,' Patricia countered. 'When did you see anyone with their eyes and mouth frozen shut? Only blind people's eyes are shut and that's cause they're blind, and nobody's mouth can close over unless it gets sewn up, stupid!'

'An yuh see people wit dere fingers and toes fall off, Patricia?' I asked.

'Course not, but I know it's true,' she replied.

Clifton began to laugh, just the way he did when he was a very small boy and had suddenly remembered something that he thought was funny.

'I did a pee in the garden when it was really cold and it turned into ice,' he said.

'How is that even funny? It just means you're nasty,' mocked Patricia.

Nevertheless, we all started laughing and, despite her retort, Patricia laughed the hardest. For a brief time, it was as if we were back on our island, laughing together and having fun.

Then a small voice came out of Sonny, 'Erna, your boot a burn up!'

Suddenly, I could smell burning rubber and could feel the heat on the toes of my right foot. I snatched my leg away and removed the boot. As I did so the burnt area detached itself from the sole. My brand-new boots were ruined!

'What in the name of Jehovah is going on?' barked my mother, entering the room with a face like curdled milk. The smell of burning rubber was unavoidable. She marched over to the fire and turned it off.

We were already on our feet, ready to skedaddle as fast as we could, when she yelled, 'Not you, Erna, wait!' I stopped dead in my tracks. 'I want you to know,' my mother said in an icy voice, 'that you're going to wear those boots until they're ready to fall apart.'

'And a happy Christmas to you too,' I muttered.

'What did you say?' Mother glowered.

185

'Nothing, Mother,' I said.

'Good,' Mother replied, ushering me into the corridor where Patricia, Clifton and Sonny were hovering. 'And that's the last time I want to hear you blaspheme. The word Christmas is a pagan term. There is only Christendom. Now, upstairs with you, and give me some peace!'

# Chapter 23

I wasn't sure whether Patricia and Clifton's stories about fingers and toes falling off and mouths freezing shut were true or not, but I decided that, just to be on the safe side, I would start wearing the pair of mittens and the knitted red-and-black-striped scarf and matching tea cosy hat that Mrs Kelly had given me. I wanted to wear them straight away, but I knew that mother hated the fact that Mrs Kelly was always knocking on our door with various offerings, so I thought if I left it for a bit she might forget. Mrs Kelly's sons, Frankie and Aaron, were a similar age to Clifton and Sonny, so she would sometimes give my mother clothes parcels for them. On one occasion she even gave us a huge cut of Irish beef.

'Excess to need,' she'd said, explaining that she had brought the meat over from County Cork in Ireland where she came from.

Mother never refused these things, but as soon she heard Mrs Kelly's front door slam, she started cursing her. 'That woman is just renk,' she exclaimed, 'she must think we are some kind of paupers that she keeps giving us her second-hand tat!'

But, no matter what she had been given, she always carefully packed away the things and, in the case of the clothes, the boys were soon dressed in Frankie or Aaron's unwanted garments. And so, despite her huffing and puffing, Mother quickly made space in the chest freezer and slipped the beef inside. Imagine my surprise when, on the twenty-fifth of December, she served up the very same piece of beef without alluding to its origins, or to the day we weren't celebrating.

When Christmas was over, I breathed a sigh of relief that I wouldn't get into any trouble for accidentally blaspheming again, but the holiday had brought one welcome change: Patricia, the boys and I had finally begun to talk about our time growing up on our island. They all had questions for me, even though they were mostly about mangoes, which was the fruit that they, like me, loved and missed the most. Sonny wanted to know why mangoes didn't grow in London, to which Clifton replied, 'Because it's too cold here, stupid! There's not enough sun to make them ripe.'

I laughed out loud, recalling that these were the kind of details Clifton had always noticed. I tried to ask them questions about the place their father had taken them to when he'd spirited them away from our grandparents' home, but the boys immediately clammed up and Patricia shifted uneasily before saying, 'It was alright, but we missed you and...' then her sentence trailed off. She quickly got up and moved away as if to emphasise that the conversation had ended.

That same night in bed Patricia interrupted my reading. 'When we came to London, our father told us that we shouldn't use your name or our grandparents' names in his house,' she said.

I put my book down, fascinated to hear what my sister had to tell me.

'One time, he caught me and Clifton talking about Grandma Melba and Grandpa Sippa, and he beat us really bad.'

I was really sad to hear this. I had been so happy to learn that she and the boys had missed our grandparents and our island as much as I did, and that they also missed me just as much as I missed them. At least we were back together now, the four of us. I didn't count my mother and the ugly Satan devil man as family.

At the start of January, Patricia, Clifton and Sonny went back to school and I carried on as before with my days of washing and walking. But one Saturday morning, towards the end of the month, I woke up to my first sight of snow. It had been the one thing I had longed to see in England. The ugly grey streets were transformed into something magical and dreamlike. I watched for hours with my nose pressed to the cold windowpane as the countless white flakes rushed silently to the ground. Rooftops groaned under their new soft white mantles and the roads, the pavements, even the cars, disappeared under a sea of white.

'We have to go to the park,' Patricia cried, 'so we can see how pretty it is!'

We pulled on our boots and rushed to the front door.

Outside, we padded through the deep snow counting the different footprint patterns as we went, all the way to the park.

'I wish I had one of those!' Sonny said, as soon as we entered the park. He was pointing towards two children whizzing down a steep slope on a wooden sledge.

'It looks like fun,' I agreed, and we stood and watched for a few minutes. I could have stayed all day, looking at the snowy trees and the happy children, but my toes, exposed by my burned right boot, were already freezing, and I decided it was time to go. 'Come on,' I said, 'before the cole a kill me! Mi have to get back to the house.'

Reluctantly, the others trudged back home with me.

We returned to discover Mother and the ugly Satan devil man in a terrible mood. At first, I thought that they must have had some kind of a fight, but it turned out that it was *us* they were angry with.

'Did you give them permission to leave the house?' Mother asked her husband.

'No! Did you?' he replied.

She sucked her teeth loudly and turned her attention to Patricia.

'Patricia, what did I tell you to do this morning?'

Before Patricia could give any kind of answer, her father jumped in, 'It must be woman she thinks she is now! She must believe is she make decisions in this house.'

The boys darted off to their room, while I sat half-way up the stairs furiously glaring at the ugly Satan devil man and my mother who hovered behind him like his evil assistant.

'I'm sorry,' Patricia mumbled under her breath.

'You said something?' the ugly Satan devil man said in a menacing voice.

'I'm sorry,' Patricia repeated.

Without warning the ugly Satan devil man grabbed Patricia and began to beat her with his belt.

'No!' Patricia screamed. 'What did I do? I didn't do anything!'

Her screaming seemed to fire up her father even more. His eyes were bright red and there was a rage inside them that terrified me. In a flash, he brought his belt down on Patricia's back, her backside, her legs, whatever part of her body presented itself to him as she squirmed in his grasp. With each lash of the belt, I grimaced in sympathy for Patricia. Despite her guttural screams, not a single tear rained on her face. It was as though the anger she was feeling prevented them.

'Enough, Philbert, stop now,' Mother said eventually, reaching out and restraining her husband's arm. 'We don't want this devil child's blood on our hands.'

Just as quickly as it had begun, the beating stopped.

'Get out of my sight!' Mother shouted. 'Next time you won't get away so easy.'

I was shocked and confused. I couldn't understand why Patricia was being singled out. It wasn't the first time that we'd gone to the park. I had no idea what was different about this occasion.

# Chapter 24

When my siblings' February half-term arrived, I took a deep breath one morning and walked up to my mother while she was doing her ironing. 'Mi did wonder when mi kyan go buy mi uniform, soh mi kyan go school with Patricia,' I said.

'You're plenty old enough to look for a job and take some of the burden off your father and me,' she replied, without looking up.

'But mi ave to reach sixteen to stop school an work!' I protested.

'I could get you a job as an orderly in my hospital,' she said, ignoring my statement.

The mention of hospital brought back memories of Grandma Melba, propped up in a hospital bed bleeding heavily from her nose.

'But mi nuh like de sight of blood! An mi nuh waan fi work in no hospital. Mi waan fi go a school!'

My mother looked at me as if I had lost my mind.

'Blood?' she mocked. 'Did I mention the words nurse or doctor, Erna? I said hospital orderly. It means you have to clean up after people.'

'Well, mi nuh want fi do dat eider.'

'You have to make yourself useful,' she said. 'You can't sit round the house like some kind of Queen Bee doing nothing.'

'But I want to go to school!' I protested.

Mother eyed me carefully.

'You can start looking after the twins by taking them to and from Mrs McPherson's,' she said.

I gazed at her in dismay. 'Mi wi look after dem, till mi start school,' I replied. There was no arguing with her, but in my head I was determined I would be starting school not too far in the future.

Each morning, I pushed the twins in their Silver Cross pram to Mrs McPherson's house, which was four streets away. Mrs McPherson was a frumpy white woman who only minded black children. As well as the twins, there were four other kids she looked after. Whenever I sneaked a look in the front room, they were always sat on the floor with blank expressions on their faces, a few fluffy toys around them, in which they showed little interest. The house was small and dingy and smelt of the scruffy white Yorkshire terrier that always preceded Mrs McPherson.

'Out of the way, Trixie, make some room for Erna!' Mrs McPherson said, as I rolled the pram into the hallway on the first day of my new career. As usual, one twin began to cry, followed by the other.

'Hand over the little dears,' she said, 'they'll stop that racket the minute you're gone.'

Mrs McPherson repeated that exact phrase the following morning too, with a tight smile that didn't match the jovial tone of her voice, and each day I left her house with a mixture of relief and sadness. Once I'd got that chore out of the way, I would head to the library to sit and read in the warmth. I had secretly joined the library before Christmas, and I was able to borrow six books on my card, and twice as many when I used my mother's card, which sat untouched on the hall table.

'It's good that you love reading so much dear,' the librarian commented on one of my visits, 'but I'm not sure your parents would approve of your choices.' She peered at me over her glasses, waiting for my response.

'Oh, no, these are for my mother, you see,' I replied. 'I don't even look at them.'

Mills and Boon, Georgette Heyer and Ian Fleming's *James Bond* novels became my most trusted companions. Once I'd completed my chores, I would climb back into bed with a hot water bottle and a book. The words transported me to worlds far more interesting than my own. For hours at a time, I could escape my dreary existence into romance and adventure. If the day was sunny, I would walk to the local park and sit on the bandstand and watch people going about their business. Elderly couples, people walking dogs, parents of small children not yet in school – everyone seemed to have a purpose apart from me. Then I would take a slow stroll back to Mrs McPherson's and wait while she changed the twins out of their filthy nappies and food-spattered clothing.

'Yuh aright with how Miss McPherson tek care a de twins?' I asked my mother one evening, as I helped her prepare dinner in the kitchen.

'You think you can look after them better?'

'Dem always wet and dirty wen mi go pick dem up,' I said.

'And I asked you if you think you can look after them better?' she replied.

'No, mam.' I stared at her, trying to gauge her mood.

'What is it?' she said eventually.

'Mi want to go school on Monday,' I said.

Mother said nothing in response she just carried on stirring the big aluminium pot on the gas stove. I looked at her and realised that she was never going to relent. If I was going to do something about this, I was going to have to do it on my own.

The following morning, after I dropped off the twins, I set out on a mission to find myself a school. A thick fog had enveloped everything, which made it difficult to see more than a few yards ahead of me, but nevertheless, after half an hour of wandering, I found myself standing at the entrance to a formidable red-brick school building. A group of children were playing chase in the playground. One of them noticed me and ran over to the gate. She was a tiny girl with a head of white-blonde hair and glinting eyes the colour of the sky on a clear blue day.

'Do you want me to get you a teacher?' she asked.

'Mi jus want to ask someone how to fine a big school,' I said.

The little girl screwed up her face. 'I'll get a teacher,' she said emphatically, before walking off.

She returned accompanied by a pretty young woman in an orange mini-dress and green overcoat.

'How can I help?' she asked in a kindly voice.

'Mi looking for a school for me to go to, miss,' I said.

'Oh, you mean a secondary school?' she replied.

I nodded.

'Well, there's Catford Girls' School, just off the Bromley Road,' she said, pointing in a vague southerly direction. Seeing that I needed more help than that, she gave me precise directions.

I thanked her and set off down the road trying to remember the left and right turns. I lost my bearings almost immediately, but then, through the fog, I saw a burly man coming towards me.

As he drew level, I began to ask him for directions, 'Excuse mi, please, sarh, I'm looking for—'

'Why don't you go back to where you came from?' he spat, before I could finish my question. I felt a hard jab to my side and stumbled off the pavement. 'Bloody nig-nog,' he added, without looking back.

The next person I asked was more helpful, and eventually I reached the gates of a school building almost identical to the first one. A man dressed in blue overalls was sweeping the playground.

'The reception's through there,' he said, pointing towards a pair of large blue-painted doors with the word *Entrance* above them. 'Turn left when you get inside.'

He held the gate open for me and I walked across the asphalt playground with my heart racing in my chest. Once through the doors, I entered a long corridor, and was immediately startled by dozens of teenage girls rushing towards me. I drew my body up against the wall and waited for them to pass. I continued onwards until I reached the open door of a small office and peered inside.

'Step forward, child,' commanded a tiny, neatly dressed woman, looking up from her typewriter.

I entered the room nervously.

'You look like you've walked for miles,' she said, eyeing me up and down. 'Would you like a cup of tea?'

'Yes, tank you, mam.'

'Sit down there then, and don't touch anything,' she said.

I sat on the hard plastic chair and waited. Several minutes later she returned with a steaming mug of tea, which I grasped with both hands, allowing them to absorb the heat.

'Do you have an appointment?' she asked, sitting back behind her desk.

'No, mam. I want to come to dis school, mam.'

She picked up the black telephone and spoke briefly. Replacing the phone on the receiver, she said, 'Miss Wells will see you as soon as she is free.'

A book on her desk titled *Jane Eyre* caught my eye.

'Can I look at de book, mam?'

'Help yourself,' she said, her fingers still tapping away.

I flicked through the pages and stopped when the word 'Jamaica' sprang out at me. I was completely absorbed in the book when, a few minutes later, a small, stoutly built white woman entered the room.

'I am Miss Wells,' she said, in a strident voice that gave the impression of a much larger person. Her short grey hair framed

196

a face full of wrinkles. Silver spectacles with round lenses sat on the tip of her pointy nose. She seemed rather old to be a teacher. 'Come with me,' she instructed.

She led me to another office, although this one was larger and had framed awards on the walls. 'Please, sit down,' she said, motioning me to a wooden chair. 'Miss Robinson told me you are enquiring about continuing your education here. When was the last time you attended school?'

'Last year, mam. Jus before I come to England, mam.'

'And you say you're fourteen years old.'

'Yes, mam.'

'Please don't call me that "mam", or whatever it is you're saying,' she said.

'Mi sorry, mam. Mi mean, mi sorry, Miss Wells.'

She peered at me over the top of her spectacles.

'Okay, consider yourself registered. We'll expect you Monday morning, then. Oh, and tell your parents you'll need these.' She handed me a piece of paper with a list of the items I needed for school.

'Tank you, Miss Wells.' I said. 'Tank you very much!'

Later that day, after I'd collected the twins from Mrs McPherson's, I presented the piece of paper to my mother. 'Dis is de list de teacher give mi fi mi school clothes,' I said.

She eyed me carefully and I thought I detected a hint of admiration in her voice. 'So, you're going to school against my advice?' she said. 'Well, I hope the books will feed you,' she added, sucking her teeth with contempt. She read through the list, then dug into her purse and handed me a five-pound note. 'I don't know where this teacher is coming from with her multiply by two,' she said, 'what's wrong with water and soap when clothes get dirty?'

'Nothing, Mother,' I said, quickly pocketing the five pounds.

Patricia was standing by, quietly listening.

'I'll take you to the shop, Erna,' she offered. 'We can go on Saturday.'

I looked at my mother, who was gazing at me with an amused expression on her usually stern face. I had won my first victory. But victory, as they say, is fleeting.

# Chapter 25

'Patricia,' I said, as we walked to the uniform shop the following Saturday, 'is why mek yuh father beat yuh soh much?'

She looked down at her feet. 'Can't you just call me Patsy,' she said, 'like everyone else?'

'Patricia was yuh island name,' I replied. 'But me can practise saying Patsy. An yuh nevah answer mi question.'

'It's nothing. He likes beating us. That's all.'

'It's okay, yuh don't have to tell me nutting if yuh nuh want to. Yuh school nice?'

'I like it. I have loads of friends. That's the best part. And the teachers are okay too, I suppose. Better than being in junior school, anyway.'

A bell rang over the door as we entered the uniform shop. A man seated behind the counter stood up, exposing a huge belly, which forced him to shuffle sideways on to the shop floor.

'You're a bit late getting your uniform,' he said, 'changing school, are you, luv?'

'Yes, sarh. I did go to a school in another country, sarh.' Patsy stamped hard on my foot. 'Is why yuh do that?' I asked.

'It's *sir*, Erna,' she hissed. 'You sound mad when you keeping saying that "sarh" word!'

'But yuh could just tell me. Yuh nuh have to mash up mi foot!'

I handed the man the list.

'Okay, that's your lot.' he said, placing the items on the counter a minute later.

'Buy the plain one,' Patsy whispered in my ear, 'it's easy to turn into a mini-skirt. Roll it up when you leave the house and down before you get back home.'

My first day began with filling out enrolment forms with Miss Robinson, and so I was late for my first class and, as I walked in, twenty sets of eyes stared at me. I reached up and touched my head, concerned that I might have forgotten to remove the pair of cut-off tights I used to cover my hair at night.

Then the teacher's voice roared over the silence of the staring girls, 'Erna Mullings, unroll that skirt at once and don't ever enter my class in that state again!'

Within seconds, my skirt was back to its normal length. I made a beeline for the back of the class where the only other three black girls were seated.

During the first break, a bunch of white girls gathered around me and chanted, 'Erna Mullings, the mini is for the road, not for school! Mini for the road, not for school!'

It was a tough first week. Everything was unfamiliar, the way lessons were taught, the moving from class to class, the speed at which everyone spoke, the different accents. There was a black girl with a Liverpudlian accent, and Irish girls who sounded like they were from the Caribbean. And then there was Mr Anand, who was Indian. He taught Maths – the subject I feared the most – and wore a rather obvious toupee. Mrs Gregory, the sour-faced geography teacher, ripped my first attempts at homework from my exercise book and bawled me out in front of the class. 'Don't you know anything, Mullings?' she said. 'You write on both sides of the paper, not just the right! Are you simple, or something? You are wasting good paper.' It was all so different from the schooling on my island. For a start, all my teachers had been black, apart from the Canadian Teacher Cavallo and my fellow pupils were all village children. I had had no problems understanding anything or anyone. But in this school, I felt like a dunce.

At least I made a couple of friends: a wan-looking white girl with short mousy hair, named Katherine Smith, and a smart Guyanese girl with a bouncy Afro, named Jennifer Richards. Jennifer and I took an instant liking to each other.

'Tell the truth now,' Jennifer challenged Georgina Blake, one of two Jamaican sisters we sometimes hung out with in the playground. 'Out of Erna and me, who has the best Angela Davis Afro?'

'You both do,' Georgina replied.

'I agree,' her sister, Rhea, echoed.

'Who's Angela Davis?' I whispered, once we were out of earshot of the Blake sisters.

Jennifer eyed me in amazement. 'Girl, you've got a lot to learn!' she said.

Jennifer was the most single-minded person I had ever met and she had no problem making herself understood. Her hand constantly shot up in class in readiness to ask, or answer, questions. 'Miss! Why is Africa so small on that map? It's a big continent, Miss, but on this map Africa looks like it's smaller than England, Miss, and that can't be right, Miss. Even Guyana is bigger than England, Miss, and Africa is a continent, Miss.'

'It's a matter of scale, child,' Miss Sour-Face had replied to that one.

Jennifer was a good friend to have, and for the first time since I'd arrived in England I felt that I had made a real connection with someone.

'I've lived here since I was seven,' she said one afternoon, as we travelled in the school coach on our way to the playing fields for a game of hockey. 'We came here after Dad died in a

201

gold-mining accident. I don't remember him really, but we have pictures at home. My mum is my best friend, apart from you, now. I can talk to her about anything, even boys.'

'Yuh real lucky, Jennifer,' I replied. 'I can't imagine my mada being mi friend. We barely speak. In fact, I can't wait to go back to mi island. I don't find anyting soh far to like bout dis place.'

'I'm used to it,' Jennifer said, 'but I'll definitely go and visit Guyana when I'm older. It's a beautiful country.'

I hated hockey. I was always left with badly bruised ankles from being deliberately whacked with the opposing players' hockey sticks. After limping off the playing field one afternoon, I suggested to Mr Copeland, who was in charge of sports, that perhaps we should play cricket instead.

'Cricket is for boys, Erna,' Mr Copeland said. 'Hockey is for girls'

'But, sir, everyone play cricket on my island!'

'Well, we're not on your island, are we?' he said, rolling his eyes.

Jennifer, who'd been listening in, started laughing as soon as Mr Copeland had walked away.

'Well, well, so we have a proper feminist in our midst, after all,' she said.

'A what?' I asked.

Jennifer took me by the arm and led me towards the changing rooms.

'Erna,' she said, 'I think it's time I taught you the facts of life.'

'I already learnt those from mi grandma,' I replied, stung by her criticism.

Jennifer stared at me with her eyes crinkling in delight. 'Oh, Erna,' she said, 'you do make me laugh!'

# Chapter 26

I had started school in the depths of the winter and it was hard to imagine a time when it would not be cold. But when I woke early one late-March morning to see the leafless cherry trees suddenly ablaze with beautiful pink and white blossoms, I felt that perhaps there was some hope in this England place, after all. The days began to warm up and the first time I walked out of the front door wearing a dress and a pair of espadrilles, it felt like a miracle. No coat, no knitted hat and scarf, and definitely no clunky ugly wellington boots. Oh, the feeling of the warmth of the sun on my body again! With my eyes closed tightly, I imagined myself sitting on a low wall in my village, a basket of mangoes by my side, slowly eating my way through them as their delicious yellow juice escaped down my right arm and ran all the way to my elbow.

The months passed quickly now, and everything that had seemed dead sprang into life. Even the people seemed different. On our street, laughter replaced surly conversation and people greeted each other with pleasantries and observations about the lovely weather. I was amazed. People did greet each other! At school, in the weeks leading up to the summer holidays, my classmates chatted eagerly about going away with their parents to romantic-sounding places, like Cornwall, Devon and Dorset. Some even boasted of going abroad to France or Spain.

'Are you going to the seaside?' I asked Katherine, on our last day at school.

'Only to visit Nan and Granddad,' she replied. 'They moved to Hove when Granddad retired. Nan said she wanted to feel the sea breeze on her face every day right up until her time comes. They like it when we visit, but it'll only be for a week.'

'Well, I'm staying right here,' Jennifer said, 'in Catford-on-sea. My mum says she has to work to keep food on the table. No time for holidays.'

'What about you, Erna?' Katherine asked.

'Me? My mother says she doesn't understand why anyone would pay good money to go and sit in the houses of people they don't know,' I replied. 'And, to be honest, I don't get it either. All I've seen on the telly are white folks lying around half-naked on the sand with the sun burning them up. How is that fun?'

Katherine laughed at my description of a typical English holiday. 'I suppose it must seem funny,' she said, 'all these white people who want to get a tan, when they're always saying they don't like coloured people!'

Jennifer rolled her eyes without comment.

Just before the end of the summer term, I finally received a response from Grandpa Sippa. His letter was brief, and not quite what I had expected, but I still read it with tears in my eyes.

*June 1969*

*Dear Erna,*

*I hope when these few line of mine reaches you, they will find you in the best of health. Your letter reach me safely, but, as you know, I always have to wait for my hands*

204

to steady, so I can do the writing. I read your letter and the most advice I can give you, Erna, is keep your head in your studies and don't mind big people and dem business.

I can't understand what happen in England, but everybody I know who go there settle down after time. I am sure you will settle down soon. If you mother feeling better, maybe you could remind her to put a little something in an envelope for me. Me sure that you can still remember, Erna, that life not easy over here at all, especially now. That is all I have to say for now. Look after yourself, child, and may the Lord God bless you as always,

Your grandfather, Sippa.

Grandpa's letter left me feeling sad. I wished that I could've been there on my island, looking after him. But I knew full well that he would not want that. His firm belief was that being in England was what was best for me. So, I wiped my eyes, took a deep breath, and resolved that I would try and make the best of this England place. Summer, however, brought its own challenges. Despite my shaky start, school had brought routine and structure to my life. Without school, there was either playing with Patsy and the boys in the local park or the garden, or the rare treat of watching telly to alleviate our boredom. And that was only when the ugly Satan devil man wasn't hogging the box. The only drama series he liked were the ones with cops and robbers in them. It was sport that he truly loved, and he watched everything that was on. He particularly liked boxing, which involved what Mother called 'getting up to his antics' while he watched – during a match, he would leap to his feet and shadow-box Clifton and Sonny, simultaneously shouting at the telly as if he was ringside.

'Go on, throw him an uppercut! No, man, I said uppercut, you idiot! Swing man, go in with a right hook!'

The only thing he watched apart from sport and cop dramas was anything with Shirley Bassey in it. He would fixate on the long split in her dress, drooling with pleasure, while I squirmed with disgust. Mother, on the other hand, never watched a single television programme. Her preference was to entertain herself with just one particular song, which she played repeatedly on the old record player until it drove me mad. It was titled 'Honour Your Mother and Your Father' – a verse from the Bible that had been turned into a hit record by Desmond Dekker. It was her mission to make sure that the church should remain ever-present in our house, even if it came in ska form.

Most days we would head for the park with a football and a rounders bat and ball that we bought with the pocket money that Auntie Madge gave us. We never got anything from our mother or the devil man. Playing these games took me back to a carefree place where life felt simple and joyful. This routine of park, garden and telly seemed like it would be the pattern for the entire summer, until an announcement from our mother one Saturday night caught us by surprise.

'I want you all up by six o'clock tomorrow morning, latest,' she said. 'We are going to the seaside.'

The seaside? None of us had even seen the sea since our arrival in England and it was hard to contain our excitement.

The following morning, we woke to discover a mountain of food that Mother had prepared the night before, and she presided over the transfer of this bounty to a robust-looking green Ford Transit van, with bench seats and windows along the side, which had miraculously replaced the devil man's old Cortina – possibly with this trip in mind. Bubbling with excitement, we clambered in and set off on the tortuous journey from South London to the coast.

This was my first trip outside of London and, once the excitement had worn off, I was disappointed that there was so little of interest along the route. The images in my head of forests and rivers and white sandy beaches were replaced by a seemingly endless crawl through grey London suburbia. When we finally arrived, three hours later, Southend was nothing like my tropical fantasy either. It had a dismal gravel beach that was dotted with dog's mess. But my dashed expectations were forgotten when we discovered the Kursaal amusement park and the accompanying funfair rides that sprawled along the seafront, past the old pier that stuck out into the choppy grey sea, which had its own miniature railway. To my utter amazement the funfair included a roller coaster and a rotor ride, where you climbed inside a large barrel that spun around so fast you stuck to the sides. Mother gave us five shillings each to spend as we wished – a small fortune and the first time she'd ever given us money for any leisure activity – so we were able to enjoy as many fairground rides as we liked, and stuff our faces with ice-cream, candy floss and sugary pink sticks of rock. It was the best day I'd had with my family since my arrival in England. It was also the first time I saw my mother looking genuinely happy with us – playing with the twins, running up and down the beach with them, laughing, digging a hole in the sand and helping them to build a wobbly sandcastle.

When we got home that evening and the younger children had gone to bed, I thought it might be a good time to tap into this softer side of my mother by asking her about my father. The ugly Satan devil man was on his night shift, so I went to my mother's room at the top of the house and knocked gently on the door.

'Its Erna', I forewarned her.

'Come in,' she said. She was sitting on her bed, propped up with pillows, trawling through an Avon catalogue.

I sat down tentatively on the far corner of the bed and was surprised not to be bawled out. Instead, she smiled broadly, and in that moment she looked exactly like Grandma.

The conversation began well enough. 'Did you love my father?' I asked her simply.

She glanced up from the catalogue, but gave no answer.

I tried again. 'It's just that Papa did ask after you when I went to visit him.'

Mother began rapidly turning the catalogue pages. 'Well, do you hear me asking after him?' Her tone was sharp and angry.

I quickly changed the subject. 'You must miss Grandma Melba,' I said. 'I don't think I will ever stop missing her.'

My mother slammed the catalogue shut and tossed it to the floor. 'It's you who killed your grandmother!' she suddenly bellowed. She leapt off her bed and flounced out of the room. 'And get out of my room,' she shouted, as she slammed the door hard behind her.

I was speechless. I tried to absorb her words, before pulling open the door and racing after her, anger rising in my belly. I caught up with her just as she was about to descend the last few stairs.

I grabbed at her dress. 'What do you mean?' I asked her crossly.

'You know what I mean!' she shouted. She pushed me away from her, turned swiftly and started walking back up the stairs.

I watched her with mounting dread. Our relationship had sunk to a new low. The end of the holidays could not come quickly enough.

# Chapter 27

I spent the rest of the holidays revising with Jennifer and Katherine, trying to figure out the things I'd been struggling with in the classroom. My final year in school began and I buried my head in my books. I finally got round to reading *Jane Eyre*, having first spied it on the school secretary's desk the day I arrived to register. I read it over two nights. By the end, I was head over heels in love with gruff Mr Rochester and I desperately wanted to be his Jane. Mills & Boon and *James Bond* novels weren't cutting it for me any more; I had graduated to the tragic heroines of Thomas Hardy and I was particularly taken with the fate of Tess in *Tess of the d'Urbervilles*. Hardy's writing had a depth I could relate to and I was feeling a need to expand my reading and knowledge in general. I decided it was time to ask Jennifer, who was an avid reader herself, for recommendations. We'd started spending our weekends together, often on long walks, exploring places I had never been to, and had no idea existed: Hilly Fields, Brockwell Park, Greenwich Park, Horniman Gardens, and further afield to Battersea Park, and Crystal Palace with its hundred-and-fifty-year-old model dinosaurs. We even ventured as far away as Richmond Park in the west, and Hampstead Heath north of the river. I was amazed by the size of this city I was living in, and by the incredible variety and beauty of its green spaces. Now our talk was all about books and I was bowled over not just by how widely Jennifer read, but by her interest in black writers and poets. As we strolled through Camberwell Old Cemetery, among the tumbled gravestones one crisp February afternoon, Jennifer casually tossed some names at me.

'Ever heard of Maya Angelou?'

'No! Who's she?'

'Really, you've never heard of her?'

'I said no, didn't I?'

'Wow. Who are *you* reading then, Emily Brontë?' she mocked.

I felt humiliated. I loved Emily Brontë! But I couldn't admit that to her now that I realised that I was doing something deeply unfashionable in her eyes. But then I had no idea what writers were fashionable in Jennifer's eyes.

'No, of course not!' I replied.

'Well, who then?'

'Tell me about this Maya Angelou,' I said, not just to change the subject, but because I loved the sound of her name.

Jennifer glanced at me, pleased she had my attention. 'She wrote this book,' she said, 'it came out a couple of years ago. It's absolutely fantastic, Erna. It's about things you will relate to.'

'What's it called?'

'*I Know Why the Caged Bird Sings*.'

I liked the sound of it as much as I liked the sound of her name.

'Tell me more,' I demanded.

In the course of the next few hours, Jennifer opened my eyes to a whole new world. I heard about Paule Marshall's novel *Brown Girl, Brownstones* and its tale of Selina Boyce, a young girl growing up in a small black immigrant community, and about brand-new writers Toni Morrison and Alice Walker.

We strolled up to St Augustine Church, perched high on One Tree Hill, sat on a bench and gazed over South London towards the Thames, its meandering line marked by the buildings that followed its course.

'How comes you're so into black books?' I asked.

'I get it from Mum, I suppose. She is proper radical. She's into all the 'Black is Beautiful' stuff and I'm beginning to really understand where she's coming from, Erna. Mum says that black people have to learn their history or things will never change for us.'

'What does that mean, what needs to change for us?'

'Think about it, Erna! You've been filling your head with all that romantic crap, but how many times have you found a black character in anything you've read? And, if you have, what role does that character have? Do you recognise anything about yourself or our people in anything you read? Do you even know why you read, Erna?'

'What kind of question is that?' I said. 'I read for enjoyment, of course.' I thought about it for a moment longer and added, 'Reading takes me to another world, away from the madness of my home life.'

'But whose world, Erna?' she replied, ignoring my last statement. 'I bet it's not a world you know or understand. Same as on the telly, everything is seen through white people's eyes. And when black people show up in anything, they're either slaves or servants or something.'

'But where do you get the books from? I don't think I've ever seen a single book by a black writer in the library.'

'You haven't seen any because they're not there. Mum passes her books on to me when she's finished reading them. Her cousins send her books from America, but she also goes to this bookshop in Stroud Green called New Beacon Books. It's amazing, Erna. Honestly, you've never seen anything like it, row upon row of books all written by black people!'

I gazed at the South London landscape, leafy and innocent in the sunshine, and suddenly I saw a world entirely different from the one I thought I inhabited. Somewhere down below us, the suburban streets led to Brixton and I had the strongest yearning to be among my own people, the kind of people I grew up with.

'Come on,' I said, standing up, 'let's get out of here. I'm starving!'

Brixton was the one place in London where I felt at home. Once a month Patsy and I happily accompanied our mother when she went food shopping there. Mother loved the market, because it reminded her of our island. And I loved it for the same reason. We got off the bus outside the Town Hall and crossed the busy junction to reach Coldharbour Lane. Immediately, I could feel the buzz and energy of the place. We turned left down a passageway that led into the maze of streets that housed Brixton market. Reggae music blasted from makeshift sound systems and the sweet smell of Caribbean cooking tantalised my nostrils.

'I could kill for a piece of jerk pork,' I said, pointing to one of the barbecue joints where a queue was formed.

'Must be good, man,' Jennifer said, 'look at all those people!'

The dread-man running the stall was inundated by customers, but eventually we reached the front of the queue.

'Can I have a portion of jerk pork and sweetcorn?' I asked.

'Little sista, I man sorry,' he said, 'but is bare chicken and corn I man a serve. You can't insult Rasta like that, little sistreen, yuh mus know seh Rastaman don't handle pork! But you is young still, so no hard feelings. Try de bal'head stall over there if it's pork you want.'

The bal'head man's jerk pork was delicious. Licking our fingers, we took a stroll through the market.

Women with accents from every island wandered up and down the narrow lanes, seemingly unable to make up their minds at which stall to shop.

A large woman in a bright orange shift dress squeezed an avocado pear at the stall beside us. 'This pear was picked too young,' she announced, before replacing it and heading for a different stall.

'Yuh can chop off a small piece of that yam,' said a woman in a red and yellow turban, 'to make me see how it look.'

The stallholder picked up the huge yellow yam and hacked a piece off the end. 'Nothing but the best here!' he grinned, exposing a mouthful of nicotine-stained teeth.

'I've just remembered,' Jennifer said, 'there's a lady who sometimes sets up a black book stall in the market. I think she comes over from the bookshop where Mum goes. Let's see if we can find her.'

We scoured the market, but the lady was nowhere to be seen, so we wandered back on to Coldharbour Lane. A few black men passed us with white girlfriends, and sometimes with a mixed-race child in tow, without drawing so much as a glance from other passers by. As we walked past the Prince of Wales pub, a man fell out of the door and stumbled headlong into us.

'Oi, watch where you're going!' Jennifer shouted, pushing him away from her.

'Sorry, sister,' said the man, 'me jus looking for de toilet.'

'Ugh, he's probably going to use a doorway,' said Jennifer, grabbing my arm. 'Come on, let's get out of here.'

We ran back to the high street and caught a bus up the hill. When I got to my seat on the top deck, I gazed out of the window with a feeling not dissimilar to that of leaving my island. The thought of returning home to Catford filled me with dread.

# Chapter 28

The rest of my final year in school passed like a whirlwind. With Jennifer and Katherine's help, I studied hard and managed to bag myself a handful of CSEs. I soon learnt that there was a two-tier system of examinations, with the kids in grammar schools taking O-levels and those of us in comprehensive schools taking the less well-regarded CSEs. Nevertheless, I was now a 'proper reader' and, with a Saturday job in Woolworth's, I was able to buy books whenever I wanted. I was discovering new writers from across the colour divide, and every possible space in mine and Patsy's bedroom became a place to store my books.

This was a great annoyance to Patsy, who complained loudly to me one day, 'Erna, you and your stupid books! You've even started putting them in the wardrobe. It's not like we're flushed with space in here, is it?'

'I'm sorry, Patsy,' I replied, 'but maybe you should read some of them, instead of just complaining about them?'

She sucked her teeth at that suggestion and walked out of the room.

During my final week of school, Miss Wells gave my class a lecture on the importance of the world of work. Later that day, I discovered that she'd spoken separately to the white girls about the importance of sitting their A-levels and going to university. I was shocked and determined to have it out with her.

The following morning, I stood nervously in the corridor, waiting to talk to her. As soon as she emerged from the classroom, I broached the subject.

'Erna Mullings, I can assure you, you're not university material,' she said, walking briskly towards the staff room.

I had to skip to keep up with her.

'You must understand, your peers have been educated in the British system since primary age. It's a matter of familiarity,' she continued.

'Yes, Miss Wells. I understand,' I said in a voice that only thinly disguised the sense of unfairness and underlying anger that I felt. 'But—'

She cut me off before I could finish my sentence, 'The school careers officer is working very hard to ensure that all of you girls who have chosen to join the job market will have something lined up before you leave us.' She gave a tight smile. Then she entered the staff room and slammed the door in my face.

I stood in the empty corridor, trying to think what to do. Nothing Miss Wells said sounded like I had any kind of choice in the matter, so it seemed that I had no other option than to surrender to the inevitable, no matter how unfair it was. When she summoned me to her office on my last day of school, I felt more nervous than on my very first day, when I'd walked into the school and asked to be enrolled.

'Sit down, Erna, this will only take a minute,' she said. She looked at a letter on her desk. 'We have found a company willing to offer you an interview as an invoice typist.'

I hadn't given much thought to the actual type of job I might be offered. Apart from a vague idea that it would be nice to be a writer, I had little idea of what jobs were out there in the big bad world. 'What's an invoice typist, mam?' I asked. I hadn't used the term for a long time, but my nervousness had got the better of me.

It still irritated Miss Wells. 'How many times, Erna? Do not refer to me in that manner, and for God's sake don't call anyone at your new job that either!'

'Sorry, Miss Wells,' I muttered. Then I lifted my head and stared straight at her. 'It's just that I had set my heart on becoming a writer, Miss.'

A look of contempt spread across her face. 'You're setting your sights way above your station, young woman. Do try and remember where you came from!' She picked up the letter from her desk and handed it to me. 'I'm sure you'll do very well here.'

It was pointless arguing with her, and so it was that two weeks later I went to work as an invoice typist for Jenkins & Jones, a commodities importer based in a dilapidated four-storey building off Tottenham Court Road. At the same time, Jennifer was sent to an international engineering firm in Paddington where she'd been found a role as a booking clerk.

'I'm giving this a year,' Jennifer told me, the day before we embarked upon our new careers. 'Mum says it makes sense to get a bit of money behind me, but then I'm off. I'm going to study law at university.'

As always, I was impressed by Jennifer's determination, and wished that I had the same faith in myself. But soon the mind-numbing routine of my job made me think that perhaps Jennifer was right, and that maybe I should follow my dreams, after all. Day after day I punched out numbers on an old Imperial typewriter, surrounded by the clatter of typewriter keys and the chatter of the other typists in the office. The high point in my working day was the rattle of the tea trolley being pushed along the corridor by a sad-looking woman named Norma. My short lunch break was usually spent in a little park in Soho Square, catching up on my reading. The one solace I had was day-dreaming about life on my beloved island, and soon the idea of returning there became an obsession. I decided that the only reason I was doing this job was to make enough money to go back.

# Chapter 29

My life had become one of routine and predictability. In the end, I barely noticed that time was passing – I'd been working at Jenkins & Jones for over two years and the situation at home had hit rock bottom. The relationship between my mother and the ugly Satan devil man had never been affectionate, but at least I'd never seen him being physical with her; it was everyone else he took his frustrations out on. But now her mental state seemed to be deteriorating almost daily, and the arguments between them spiralled; physical violence quickly became a feature of their relationship. On one particularly bleak winter morning as I got myself ready for work, I heard an argument erupt between them downstairs. I opened the bedroom door just in time to witness his heavy hand slap my mother's face so violently that her head rocked backwards with the blow. I raced down the stairs, missing every other step, and leapt between them.

'Touch her one more time,' I screamed, 'and so help me I will find a way to fuck up your life once and for all!'

He was clearly shaken by my intervention and he raised his hand as if to hit me, but my eyes held his and the offending hand froze for a second in mid air before dropping back by his side.

'Yes, you wouldn't want to do that,' I challenged him, 'you really wouldn't want to do that.'

He stood gazing at me with hate in his bloodshot eyes, but, before I could say anything more, my mother rushed out of the house without her coat or even her shoes. The ugly Satan devil man made no attempt to stop her, and my anger with her for marrying him meant that I did nothing to prevent her from leaving either. Instead, I went back upstairs and finished readying myself for work, relieved to be escaping the nightmare for the rest of the day.

But escape was only temporary. The moment I walked back into the house that evening, Patsy confronted me in the hallway. 'They've taken her to the hospital,' she said. 'The Maudsley, the same place where she works.'

'Oh my God, what happened?' I said, removing my coat.

'She was found by some woman who lives in our street, wandering way down the hill near the high street, barefoot and cold, talking about "God coming for his world." The woman waved down a passing police car and they called an ambulance.'

'How did you find out?'

'The police came round just after I got back from school.'

I looked at my sister's stony face and realised that she was either in shock, or felt no sympathy at all for our mother. Or maybe both.

'What about…him?' I had to ask.

'I haven't seen him,' Patsy replied, before trudging upstairs to our bedroom.

The prospect of having the ugly Satan devil man in the house without my mother around was not appealing, but fortunately Auntie Madge stepped into the breach and dealt with everything in her usual efficient manner. When I spoke to her on the phone the next day, she told me she'd been to visit her sister, and that she was okay, although a bit confused about what was going on. She said the ugly Satan devil man had been there too, but she didn't know where he was now. She assured me she'd go in every day to check up on Violet, which was a huge relief.

As it turned out, the devil man took no responsibility whatsoever for the younger children while Mother was in the hospital, leaving Patsy and me to handle everything: cooking, washing, organising the boys and the twins, while at the same time juggling work and school. Thankfully, Auntie Madge and Uncle Herbie were never far away and would arrive at the house with cooked meals every other day, as well as providing Patsy and me with some extra cash to tide us over.

At work I put on a brave face and greeted my colleagues with a warm smile, but inside I was burning with a fiery rage. Unfortunately, there were days when my distress was evident, at least to Mrs Partridge, the office manager.

'Erna, what is it that's preoccupying your mind so much that you can't concentrate on your work?' she asked one day, waving an invoice that I'd mistyped in my face.

'My mum is a bit poorly at the minute,' I replied. 'She's in hospital and a lot of stuff at home has fallen on me.'

'Oh, I'm sorry to hear that, Erna. I hope she feels better soon,' Mrs Partridge said, peering at me over her half-moon specs. 'But you do still need to concentrate on your work.'

'Yes, mam… Mrs Partridge,' I said.

She handed me the offending invoice and I returned to my desk, relieved that she hadn't asked me any more questions. Work, dreary as it was, had become a sanctuary from the crazy world at home. It was a few months since I had turned eighteen and I yearned for escape. My thoughts began to turn dark.

One night, when the twins wouldn't go to sleep and Patsy had retreated moodily to the bedroom, I had a wild vision of myself tiptoeing on to the landing on hearing the ugly Satan devil man's heavy footsteps climbing the stairs. In my mind, I waited for him to reach the top step and then jumped out and shoved him forcefully in the chest, sending him tumbling back down, his body landing on the hallway floor with a mighty thud. Whatever the horrible orange-and-brown carpet was hiding underneath, it was hard enough to crack his skull wide open. Blood gushed from the wound, creating a massive red patch on the carpet. I imagined myself walking casually down the stairs to where he was lying, kneeling beside him, and whispering in his ear, 'It's only what you deserve, you ugly Satan devil man.' As I looked down on his twisted body, the swirling clouds of darkness, which seemed to hang perpetually over the house, lifted. It was only a fantasy, but it proved to be eerily prescient.

# Chapter 30

Apart from reading, Jennifer was my only solace. We met up one lunchtime a few weeks before Christmas at a café near Oxford Circus. Once we'd sat down with our sandwiches and coffee, Jennifer gazed at me with concern etched on to her face.

'What's going on, Erna? You look really tired.'

'Thanks!' I laughed.

Jennifer just sat there, looking at me, waiting for me to continue. And everything came gushing out, accompanied by floods of tears.

'Oh my God, Erna,' Jennifer said, when I'd finished my sorry tale and was drying my eyes with a paper napkin, 'it all sounds horrendous! We've got to think of a way of getting you out of there.'

'That's easier said than done,' I sniffed.

'I know that,' she replied, 'but at least you can start making steps towards it.'

'Like what?'

Jennifer took a sip of coffee and looked at me over the top of the cup.

'Well, how about giving up that awful job and taking the university plunge? You're always on about wanting to be a writer. Why don't you look into something along those lines?'

'I don't know really. I can still hear Miss Wells' words ringing in my ears. Do you remember when she told me that I was not "university material"?'

'I didn't think you'd take any notice of what some old racist white woman told you, Erna! If we listened to people like that, most of us wouldn't even bother to get out of bed. Come on, girl, you've got brains, and you can't waste them being a glorified typist for the rest of your days.'

'Don't forget, I've got my mother to contend with, Jen. And all she's ever wanted, from the moment I got off the plane, was for me to get a job and support myself.'

'And you will be able to continue to support yourself, Erna!' Jennifer replied. 'You can get a grant. In fact, you'll probably be better off. It's not like you're earning a fortune, is it?'

I gazed at my friend sitting there brimming with a fiery confidence, and I felt a flutter of hope in my chest.

The very next day, during a lunchtime visit to the library in Charing Cross Road, I came across a leaflet advertising introductory evenings for the newly established Open University. As I read through, it struck me that this could be the way for me to study for a degree without having to give up my job. Unlike Jennifer, I had no one that I could fall back on if money became a problem. I took the leaflet home with me and hid it in my clothes drawer, as if it was something too dangerous to leave out in the open.

All week at work the leaflet played on my mind until I couldn't avoid it any longer. On Thursday night I pulled it out of the drawer and read it again. I decided to take the plunge. The next day, after work, I travelled to the Finchley Road in north-west London where the Open University had a faculty in a large red-brick Victorian building. The open evening was in full swing when I arrived: Open University representatives milling around, handing out the university prospectus and chatting with the would-be students. There was a reassuring number of black and Asian people there, and maybe a few more women than men, but the biggest surprise was the age range of potential students, which spanned fresh-faced eighteen-year-olds to folks who looked to be in their seventies. By the time I left the building, I'd signed up for an English degree, which was not only affordable, but also offered the flexibility I needed, with no requirement for me to attend a physical university every day. Two weeks after I'd signed up for the course, I received a large package containing all sorts of English Literature study books, a dozen cassette tapes, and information on how to access weekly tutorials on BBC radio and television.

In no time at all, I found myself immersed in academic reading and essay writing. I attended every evening and weekend seminar that home chores allowed. I woke at the crack of dawn to listen to tutorials, either on the radio or on the television, and often late at night I would catch the repeats. Every spare moment was spent in the library, which offered a desk and a quiet space away from the distractions of home. For the first time in my life, I felt like I had a future.

# Chapter 31

Six-weeks after she was admitted to hospital, Mother came home. She looked thin and fragile, but mentally she seemed more settled. It was Auntie Madge who suggested that she might benefit from a trip to see their younger sister Lurline in New York. Auntie Madge looked at us older children – Patsy, Sonny, Clifton and me – to see if we appreciated what she was saying.

'Your mother needs a break,' she said, 'and I can think of no better place than with our sister. Those two were as thick as thieves as girls. They'll have plenty to talk about.'

Lurline had settled in Queens and found herself a job as a private carer for elderly white folks who were still living at home. She'd left the island a year after my mother, and the sisters hadn't seen each other since.

To begin with, Mother resisted the idea, saying, 'Madge, you know that I'm not well enough to make that kind of trip!'

I was amazed that, for the first time, she'd actually admitted she was ill, but Auntie Madge wasn't fazed at all, and she soon convinced her that a trip to see Lurline was exactly what she needed. And she wasted little time in planning Mother's departure.

Auntie Madge was the one person that my step-father appeared wary of, and he said nothing as she went about her plans to deprive him of his wife for another fortnight.

Two weeks later, Auntie Madge and Uncle Herbie drove mother to Gatwick Airport and waved her off to New York.

Within days of Mother leaving, it became obvious that something wasn't right with Patsy. It was as if, on an emotional level, she'd stepped into the space previously occupied by our mother. A few weeks earlier, we'd both been pulling together to manage a difficult situation, but now Patsy was irritable and ill tempered, especially with the boys, blaming them for things they hadn't done and cussing them terribly. Several times I had to intervene to stop a full-blown fight from erupting. In fact, she reminded me, scarily, of her father. I even caught her pinching the twins a couple of times.

One day, I was standing next to her in the bathroom while she was getting ready for school, as she pulled her hair back to put it in a band, I noticed a tiny bald patch just behind her left ear. It occurred to me then that I'd been aware of her habit of picking at this area of her head in a rather absentminded manner, but somehow I'd never given it much thought. Seeing the result of this close up shocked me. What else hadn't I noticed while I was out at work all day, preoccupied with my own concerns?

Patsy became aware of my gaze and turned to me with a scowl. 'What you looking at?' she asked.

'I was just thinking what a beautiful young woman you've become,' I replied.

'Huh,' was all she said to that.

She checked herself one more time in the mirror and pushed past me out of the bathroom. I was late for work so I simply filed away what I'd witnessed in the part of my brain where I stored all the things that upset me, and got on with sorting out my own unruly hair.

When I spoke to Jennifer about it in a whispered phone conversation a few days later, she had a practical take on it, as always.

'Well, what do you suppose is going on?' she asked me.

'I wish I knew. It's just a whole heap of madness. My family seems totally weird compared to everyone else's. My mother is mad, her husband is evil, and Lord knows what's happening with Patsy. She always seems angry, Jen, and not just angry, sad as well. She's got the same look in her face that she had when I saw her for the first time after I got to London. It was as though she had the world on her shoulders. And now she's literally pulling her hair out. What I am going to do?' I wailed.

'This might sound harsh,' Jennifer said, 'but I am one hundred per cent certain that what you need to do now is concentrate on your studies. Education is the key to whatever we want to be different about our lives, Erna. This means that you can't let your mum, Patsy, or anyone else distract you from your goals. I'm not saying you shouldn't care. Of course, you must. But you can't make them your responsibility forever.'

Deep down, I wasn't convinced by Jen's argument, but, in the state I was in, I clung to her advice like a liferaft.

'You know what Grandma Melba would have said about you? "Dat pickney gal ave old head pon young shoulders."'

Jennifer burst out laughing. 'Your grandmother sounds like such a character!' she said.

The following morning, just as I was about to dash out the door, a familiar thin blue envelope addressed to me in Grandpa Sippa's distinctive scrawl landed on the doormat. I picked the letter up and stuffed it into my bag. I didn't want to take the chance of leaving it on the hall table in case the ugly Satan devil man threw it away. As soon as I got home that night, I sat down on the bed and gently prised open the envelope, taking care not to tear through any of Grandpa's words. As I poured over the letter, I could hear the soft, reassuring tones of his voice:

*Dear Erna,*

*Greetings in the name of the highest god Jehovah. I hope that when these few lines of mine reaches you, they will find you in the best of health. Sorry it take time to write you back, but my health wasn't so good for a time. The hands having been shaking so bad, I couldn't steady them at all to do the writing. You have plenty cousin who would do it for me, but I still like to try and help myself. Anyway, God is good. And for now I am feeling as good as I can be, my advance age considering.*

*I know you like to hear how things going on down here. The drought finally come to an end. It was a tough time. We had a lot a water problem in the district. Fight bruck out all over the place sometime, when people take more than their allocation of water. But, God willing, we see the end and now everything just spring back to life. Erna, me find it hard to mention it, because me know how you like your mango. Right now, them so plenty, them a splatter splatter all over the yard. Every day the yard boy have one big job to do clearing them up. But the hog them happy now more than people with plenty mango to fill dem belly. And it not just the mango! Whole heap a fruit plentiful all over the district right now. I would be glad if I could find a way to send some mango for you. I am keeping a look out for somebody who a travel to England and see if them will carry two over for you.*

*I hope things settle down better than how you describe them last time. It seems life in England not easy at all. Plenty people get themself stress up. You must try to support your mother the best you can. I am sorry to hear nerves still a trouble her. I pray with God's help she will recover soon.*

*Erna, now I have to tell you something important. Me still a miss your Grandma Melba something terrible, but*

*I need a woman more permanent round the place, because there is plenty things me just can't manage any more now age overtake me. I know that you won't be happy about it, Erna, but I am considering marrying Miss Blossom. It is maybe too much to ask you to understand, because you are still a young woman, but me still hope and pray that you will.*

*Everybody here miss you, Erna, but England is where your life is now and you have to try and make the best of things.*

*I will leave you for now with God's blessings,*

*Your grandfather, Sippa.*

I must have read the words *I am considering marrying Miss Blossom* a dozen times and still they made no sense. How could Grandpa Sippa even think for a moment that he could replace Grandma Melba with any other woman? And Miss Blossom of all people! I remembered her as one of the eccentric twin sisters who sometimes helped out with the washing and ironing when Grandma Melba was unwell. She was a nice enough woman, but marrying Grandpa Sippa was a whole different thing. A terrible doubt began to seep into my head: had Grandpa Sippa loved Miss Blossom all along? Maybe he didn't really love my grandma. Otherwise, how could he think of marrying anyone else? I blinked away my tears and threw the letter on the bed. There was only one person who could help me to understand this. I began a silent conversation with my grandmother: I don't know if you have heard the latest news, Grandma Melba. I don't even know for sure if you can see or hear anything where you are, but I like to believe that you can. There have been so many times that I have felt that you're right here with me. Watching over me, keeping me safe, making sure I do the right thing. So I hope that you can hear me now and that you will help me to understand how you feel about Grandpa Sippa's news and what I should do. Maybe you're happy about Grandpa

Sippa marrying Miss Blossom, but I don't feel happy, Grandma Melba. Grandpa Sippa is your husband and he should stay your husband forever. But if you're okay with it, please, give me a sign.

I stared out of the window at the night-time sky, but there was no sign from Grandma. After a minute of silent contemplation, I took a deep breath and considered that since Miss Blossom had been around forever, then maybe it was okay for Grandpa Sippa to marry her, just as long as he didn't believe she could ever replace Grandma Melba. I felt much better now I'd come to this conclusion, so talking to Grandma had helped, after all. In time, I will write and give him my approval, I thought.

# Chapter 32

I'd been desperately looking forward to the weekend, but on Saturday it rained heavily for the entire day. I tried to read, but a persistent migraine made that impossible. The pain was so bad that I couldn't even listen to my pocket radio. The night brought some relief, in that I could legitimately try to sleep, with a hot water bottle wedged in the crook of my neck and my body wrapped tightly in the bedclothes, half of which I had to wrestle back from Patsy. I laid as still as I could with Patsy tossing and turning beside me, in the hope that a night's rest would ease my headache. Eventually, I succumbed to a fitful sleep. I was in the middle of a dream where Patsy and I had climbed out of the bedroom window in our old house in the village to escape some nameless menace, when my dream was broken by the sound of muffled voices and the quiet clunk of a door closing. I listened in silence for a minute, then reached out to pull the sheets back over me. Then I sat upright in bed. Patsy wasn't there.

At that exact moment I heard my mother – for it was unmistakably her voice – screaming, 'Get out! Get out!' to some unseen person, followed by the nauseating voice of the ugly Satan devil man begging her, 'Violet, quiet yourself down, woman, you want to wake the whole street?'

Unable to comprehend what was happening, I slipped out of bed, pulled my dressing gown on, and crept on to the landing. I peered downstairs to see my mother, her suitcase upended on the floor, standing with her legs apart and her arms folded. In front of her was the ugly Satan devil man dressed in a nightshirt. Behind him was Patsy.

The devil man looked up and saw me watching them.

'What are you looking at, you witch?' he shouted.

Ignoring him I started walking down the stairs.

'Erna, go back to bed,' my mother said.

I stopped halfway down and stared at her.

'What's going on?' I said.

All three of them stared up at me. Then Patsy, who had been frozen to the spot, turned and ran past me up the stairs. I looked up at her, then down at my mother.

'What the hell is going on?' I demanded.

I could see my step-father's face, strained and grey in the dull light of the bare bulb that hung from the hallway ceiling.

'You bug-eyed bitch,' he screamed, 'this is all your fault!'

My fault? I couldn't believe what I was hearing. I started to walk down the stairs towards them.

'Stop!' my mother shouted. 'You've got to stop.' Then she slumped to her knees. 'All this has to stop,' she said.

Sweat poured from the devil man's bald head and his eyes turned blood red. Mother watched in silence as he walked off in the direction of the bathroom. A moment later, he re-appeared carrying the purple bucket – I had left my smalls soaking in it. He pushed past Mother, knocking her off balance, opened the front door and hurled the bucket into the street.

Then he turned and stared up at me. 'When I come back, I don't want to see you in this house,' he shouted. Then he stalked through the door and slammed it shut behind him.

I remained staring at my mother.

'Has anyone collected the twins?' she asked suddenly, as if it was the most normal question in the world.

'The twins are in their beds,' I growled. 'But you've got to tell me what the hell is going on. And what on earth are you doing here, anyway? You're meant to be in New York!'

'I came back early,' she said, 'me and Lurline didn't get on.' Her voice was toneless, devoid of any emotion, and her face looked shrivelled and worn out in the dull yellow light. She climbed slowly to her feet and started dragging her suitcase along the hallway.

I turned and fled back up the stairs. When I reached the landing, I could hear the sound of sobbing coming from inside our bedroom. I took a deep breath and opened the door. Patsy was curled up on the bed, her face buried in a pillow. When she heard me enter the room, she turned her head towards me and gazed at me with wet eyes.

'What's going on, Pats?' I asked gently.

Patsy studied my face carefully before speaking. Then she wiped her eyes and sat up. 'There's something I need to tell you,' she said. 'But you've got to listen, Erna.'

I could feel my heart beating very fast. Suddenly I wasn't sure I wanted to hear what she was going to say next.

'I've never told anyone before,' she continued, 'because I knew no one would believe me. But I trust you, Erna. You're always asking me why my father takes all his anger out on me...'

'Yes,' I replied, 'it's never made sense to me.'

'Well, it's because,' she blurted out, 'before you got here, he had been having sex with me. And tonight he was trying to again.'

'Who? Doing what to you?'

'My father,' she said, in between gulps of breath, 'he's been having sex with me.'

'Patsy, I don't understand,' I said. 'Are you seriously telling me that your own father...' I could hardly say the words '...has done…*this* to you, his own child? Pats! This is serious stuff. Are you quite sure of what you're telling me?'

'I am one hundred per cent sure, Erna!' Patsy fired back. 'And I'm not talking about once, either. It's happened loads of times. And don't tell me I'm crazy! That's exactly what he used to say, when he did it: "No one will believe you, they'll just think you're mad and a liar."'

I stared at my sister open-mouthed.

'I am begging you, Erna, someone has to listen. Please!'

The pain etched on Patsy's face left me in no doubt that she was telling the truth. 'Oh my God, I'm so sorry, Pats,' I said, stroking her arm, 'I didn't mean to doubt you. It's just…well, I'm finding it hard to take in, that's all.'

She looked at me and nodded slowly.

'But…but when did all this start?' I said.

With tears flowing down her cheeks, Patsy told me how her father had started abusing her shortly after he kidnapped her and the boys from our grandparents' home, when he'd taken them to his mother's house on the other side of the island. She was ten years old at the time. She told me how at first she had no idea that what her father was doing was wrong. Then, one day, when she protested that he was hurting her, he took her to the graveyard and warned her that if she ever told anyone, he would put her into one of the graves with all the dead people – a threat that scared her so much she stopped speaking for several months.

'Didn't anyone try to find out why you stopped speaking?' I interrupted.

'Of course they did,' she replied, 'especially his mother. But she gave up trying when she couldn't get a word out of me. Then his horrible sister, Auntie Ruby, tried to beat the answer out of me.'

'Oh my God, Pats, this is so awful,' I said. 'I just hope that wherever Grandma Melba is, she can't hear any of this. It would kill her all over again.'

'When I got to England,' Patsy said, 'it started again. He would give me sweets afterwards, and then it was money when I got older. I didn't spend any of it, I just hid it under the carpet. "It's our little secret," he'd say. "You wouldn't want to get your daddy into trouble now, would you? Especially when you're my favourite!"'

It was almost too painful to hear. Patsy went on to tell me that when she was little, it hurt a lot. He would hold his hand over her mouth to stop her from crying, which made it hard for her to breathe, so she stopped crying.

By now Patsy was shaking so violently that I took the blanket and wrapped her in it and held her tight. Her bony shoulders felt sharp, even under the thick material.

'Jesus Christ, Pats, I just want to grab the biggest, sharpest knife I can find and plunge it into the evil bastard's heart the moment he walks back through that door! Now I understand why Grandma Melba named him the "ugly Satan devil man," because he surely is the devil himself.'

'The ugly Satan devil man?' Patsy asked through her tears.

'Don't you remember, that's what Grandma called him when he first turned up at our house and said he wanted to take you away? She never referred to him as anything else after that.'

'The ugly Satan devil man?' Patsy repeated. Then she started giggling, and soon we were both crying with laughter.

'Thank goodness we can still laugh,' I said. I looked at my sister, at her pretty, tear-stained face, and the obvious question dawned on me. 'So, doesn't Mum know what's been happening?' I said, wiping my eyes.

Patsy stopped laughing and stared at me. 'Well, she pretends that she doesn't, but she knows everything,' she said. 'Once she caught him trying to fix his clothes up while I was crying on the floor. She just scraped me up by my arm and gave me a slap across the face and told me to stop bringing my nastiness into her house.'

'You've got to be kidding me, how the hell does that work?' I cried. 'I mean who is this woman? How on earth can she call herself a mother when that's the way she reacts to her child?'

Patsy swore that our mother never said another word about the incident. It was as though she just put it out of her mind and continued to behave as if ours was a perfectly normal family. 'It got better when you arrived,' Patsy continued, 'because I was never alone in the house with him any more. But then he started to beat me instead.'

'No wonder he hates me,' I said, 'he couldn't get away with it when I was here, and Mother couldn't pretend that nothing was happening.'

'Exactly,' Patsy replied.

'And that's why you shouted out that you were going to tell, when he beat you. God, I wish I'd figured it out before,' I said.

'For a long time, I hated everyone. Even you,' Patsy said quietly.

I felt a burning anger for my sister. If it was possible to hate my step-father any more, I did now. 'I'm so glad you've told me,' I said. 'We should find a way of making the dirty bastard suffer for the rest of his life.'

'Well, at least you believe me,' Patsy replied, 'but I'm still terrified he'll kill me if he finds out I told you.'

'He can't just kill people, Pats. Anyway, he's just a big coward. You know what Grandma Melba would say, "Im will get im comeuppance."'

Patsy looked at me with a glimmer of hope in her eyes.

'You need justice, Pats,' I continued. 'We've got to think of a way of dealing with this. Maybe we should go to the police.'

'No!' Patsy cried. 'We can't! Imagine the shame. I couldn't face it.' She reached up to the side of her head and picked at the already thinned patch. Then she fixed me with a determined look. 'I think we should kill him, Erna,' she said.

I started to laugh, until I realised that not only was she

deadly serious, but that I agreed with her. 'Maybe we could poison him, or do something to him when he's asleep,' I said.

'You mean, like, suffocate him with a pillow?' Patsy asked.

'Yes, but we have to bide our time,' I said, 'let the dust settle. They mustn't know that you've told me.'

Patsy nodded.

'And in the meantime, you're going to have to buck up your ideas at school. You can't just let everything fall apart now. We have to act as if everything is normal, until we can work out what we're going to do.'

Patsy laughed out loud at the mention of acting as if everything was normal. But even though part of me knew that the whole conversation was utterly mad, we carried on discussing the different ways we could kill the ugly Satan devil man until we got tired of talking and slipped into the sleep that we both so badly needed.

# Chapter 33

Patsy and I became experts at avoiding all contact with our mother and the ugly Satan devil man. We slipped in and out of the house and even in and out of rooms like ghosts. We recognised every footstep and knew exactly when to remain in our room, or when to make a silent exit from the house. It was as though they both sensed that the secret was out, because the crazy rows that erupted between them got worse. If they were in the house together, they would be guaranteed to be having an argument, and the verbal insults got nastier, with little regard to what the younger children had to endure. Despite living in almost total chaos, Sonny and Clifton somehow remained immune to it, and were excelling in secondary school. Perhaps it was because school offered them the safety and routine that was absent from their home, in the same way that my work and my studies offered me a sense of stability.

Patsy had taken to watching murder mysteries on the telly, and after each episode, she would suggest a new idea. 'I think poisoning him is the best option,' she said one evening, when I returned from work. 'Then we could melt his body in acid. That's what this man who killed his wife did with her body in today's episode. He put her body in a barrel of acid and in minutes all that was left of her was her fillings!'

I wanted to humour her, and my anger certainly hadn't abated, but my natural island common sense had reasserted itself. 'Pats, I totally understand what you're thinking, but let's be serious, we are not going to kill anyone. The most sensible thing would be for us to try and persuade our mother to chuck him out of the house.'

'But you know that ain't ever going to happen!' Patsy protested, and I knew that she was right.

It was a relief to get a chirpy phone call from Jennifer one evening, a few weeks after Patsy's revelations. She'd left her job and, true to her word, had started a law degree through an access course at South Bank Polytechnic in Elephant and Castle.

'I'm really enjoying the course,' she gushed, 'all I'm reading now are these huge law books, there's no room left in my brain for anything else!'

'I'm not sure if that's a good thing or a bad thing,' I laughed.

'Oh, it's a good thing! Anyway, how are you doing, how's your course going?'

I hesitated for a moment, trying to decide if I should tell my best friend what had happened since I last spoke to her.

'Is everything okay?' she asked, noting the pause.

I decided it wouldn't be fair on Patsy to tell Jennifer what had happened and so I put on a brave face and lied. 'Oh, no, you know, just the usual craziness at home,' I said, 'nothing is easy in the circumstances. But the course is going really well. I've got a study week coming up at Sussex University in Brighton, which I'm really looking forward to. A whole week away from this house will be like a holiday.'

'That's great!' she said. 'It's important to have something to look forward to, and summer school will be a totally different environment. Anyway, I'm just touching base, trying to distract myself from the essay I have to write, but I promise, we will catch up properly soon.'

My week on the university campus took me out of the bubble in which I'd been living and placed me in an entirely different world. Nearly all of the university's full-time students had left for the summer, freeing up their rooms to be rented by the summer school attendees. The buzz inside the main auditorium was ten times that which I had experienced that first day I arrived at the Open University building on the Finchley Road. Once we'd registered, we were encouraged to mill around and introduce ourselves to each other. It felt overwhelming, but I was fascinated to meet all these new people and discover their reasons for studying with the Open University and what they were studying.

I met Sean, a scrawny thirty-two-year-old white guy from Kilkenny in Ireland, at the start of the first lecture. He'd taken a good look around the lecture room before making his way over to the empty seat beside me. It was a warm day and he was dressed in a short-sleeved crumpled white shirt and khaki shorts that looked as if they were as old as he was. He had a small, neat face and a head of frizzy brown hair that made me wonder whether he had some African ancestry.

'I'm Sean,' he said as he sat down next to me, 'nice to meet you.'

'I'm Erna, nice to meet you back,' I said, with a quick smile.

I was sweating profusely, despite being dressed in a simple Indian cotton dress. The lecture was soon underway and although I was concentrating very hard on what was being said, I was also aware that Sean kept stealing glances at me. I silently vowed that for my next lecture, I would be more strategic about choosing my seat. This week at the university campus was a big deal for me and I didn't need the distraction. Once the lecture was over, I slipped outside and walked across the manicured lawns towards a giant oak tree. In the distance, beds of poppies and cornflowers lit up the green space. A barefoot young woman in a red t-shirt and denim shorts was doing a handstand on the grass. I sat down between the tree's exposed roots and began flicking through my notes, not all of which were easy to decipher. I was so absorbed in my study that I didn't notice him until he was right next to me.

'There you are,' he said. 'I've never seen anyone move so quickly. It's almost as if you were trying to get away from me!'

'Not at all,' I lied. 'I just needed to look over my notes to try and make sure things stay in my head.'

'Good, I'm glad I didn't scare you away, then,' he said. 'Can I join you? I mean I could go and sit on my own, but this is an opportunity to get to know new people, don't you think?'

'I guess so,' I replied, putting my notes down.

'So, where are you from?' he said, sitting down next to me.

'London.'

'Whereabouts in London? I use to live in Gospel Oak a few years back myself.'

'South-east. Catford. A strange place, full of people who don't like people who look like me. But, hey, everyone's got to live somewhere.'

He laughed at my description. 'That sounds a bit like where I'm from,' he said.

'Well, judging from your accent that must be Ireland,' I replied.

'How on earth did you guess?' He winked. 'Is it because I look like a leprechaun?'

I couldn't help laughing, despite my irritation at being interrupted. 'How come you're doing an English degree at the Open University then?' I asked him.

'What do you mean?' he said.

'I thought most white people just went straight from school to university.'

He frowned at me. 'Now that's a bit of a generalisation, Erna. Most ordinary white folks don't get that chance. But, since you asked, this is my second outing at university. I studied medicine at Glasgow, but only because the choice was either to go into the priesthood, or become a doctor like my father.'

I sat up at this.

'Oh, so you're a doctor. Wow.'

'Not exactly. There was no fucking way I was going to become a priest. I might have been brought up a Catholic, but religion is not for me. And I didn't figure out that doctoring wasn't for me either until I was in my last year. Same difference, as far as I was concerned. You know, playing God? So, I left the course, grabbed a backpack and went travelling around India. Came back without a fucking clue what to do with my life, which is why I'm here,' he laughed. 'I've always liked reading, so studying English made sense, but I need a job as well. So here I am.'

'Well, before you ask, this is the only way I could afford to go to university myself. No free ride in my family. But I love the Open University set up and everything I'm learning.'

'Well, I like you already,' he said with a broad smile. 'You seem like a girl who knows her own mind.'

'And one who knows that the next lecture is about to start,' I said, clambering to my feet and brushing myself down.

'I hope you don't think I'm being too forward, Erna, but I think you're stunning. There wasn't another woman in that lecture theatre who came even close to you in good looks,' he added, standing up next to me.

I was shocked. No one had ever spoken to me in this way before, and suddenly I felt like the small girl from the village again. I blushed heavily and reached up to wipe away the perspiration that had suddenly appeared on my brow.

'Oh, thanks, that's a really nice thing to say. But this is a summer school, not a dating agency,' I said, gathering my things and putting them into my shoulder bag.

'Well, take it from me, you're really very beautiful, Erna. I love how your skin just glows,' he said.

Even though I felt no rush of feelings towards this skinny white bloke who was standing far too close to me, I still felt special and rather flattered. I didn't have any experience of being chatted up, and the only person who had ever told me that I was beautiful was my long-dead grandmother. Then I thought of Patsy, who constantly attracted the attention of men, even ones who were years older than her. She had grown into a stunning young woman, with her long legs and honey-coloured skin. But, not surprisingly, she hated the attention. '*He* used to tell me how pretty I was,' she'd confided in me, 'when he wasn't beating me.' All I'd ever experienced was having my black skin and large eyes commented on, usually in ways that suggested that I'd been born with some great misfortune. So I was intrigued that this white guy was interested in me, and that it was partly because of my ebony skin that he liked me so much.

Sean followed me back to the lecture room and I began to realise that I wasn't going to get rid of him. And that maybe I didn't want to. We sat together for the remaining lectures that day and later shared a meal in the café in the main hall. Afterwards, Sean invited me back to his room.

'Are you okay?' he asked, as he clicked the bedroom light on.

The light was disturbingly bright and I hung back in the doorway. If I stepped forward, there would be no turning back, but if I hesitated I was afraid I'd lose my courage and run.

Sean walked over to the bedside table and switched the lamp on. Then he came back and leaned behind me to pull the door shut, so that I had no choice but to enter the room. He turned the main light off and reached down into a backpack on the floor, pulling out a bottle of Lambrusco.

'It was all they had at the offy,' he shrugged, noting my expression, 'apart from lager. And I don't like lager.'

He tore the foil off and popped the cork, which flew across the room and hit the window as red wine foamed out of the bottle and spilled on to the bedspread. I burst out laughing, the whole scene seemed so absurd. Sean laughed too, shaking his head. Then he grabbed a tall glass from the bedside table, filled it and handed it to me.

'It's the only one there is,' he said. 'I wasn't expecting to be entertaining anyone.'

I sat on the edge of the bed and sipped the sweet fizzy wine. Sean sat down next to me and put an arm round my shoulder.

'I'm guessing this is your first time,' he said, 'although I thought you Caribbean girls…' he didn't finish his sentence.

'What, you think we're all easy, is that what you're saying?' I made to stand up, but he held me firmly in place.

'No, no, that's not what I meant at all,' he replied in his soft Irish lilt. 'I'm sorry, I'm an idiot. You're nervous, I get it.' He took the glass from my hand and placed it on the bedside table. Then he leant closer and stroked the side of my face with two fingers. 'You really are beautiful, you know,' he whispered.

The next day I woke to find Sean sitting on the edge of the bed, pulling his khaki shorts on. The sun was already glaring through the flimsy orange curtains.

'What time is it?' I said, blinking in the bright light.

'Seven-thirty.'

'What?' I replied, pulling the sheets over my head. 'I'm not ready to get up!'

'I like to have an early breakfast,' Sean said, standing up, 'sets me up for the day.' He leaned over and kissed me on the top of my head. 'You don't have to get up, though.'

I peeked over the edge of the sheet. I felt barely able to look Sean in the eye.

'Thank you for last night,' he said. He extracted a white t-shirt from the backpack and pulled it over his head. 'I like you very much, Erna. We should definitely make the most of this week, don't you think?'

243

I didn't have the courage to tell him that I felt sore and confused and had all these questions whirling around my head, like what exactly was the point of sex, apart from to make babies?

'Are you alright,' he asked, when I made no response.

'Yes, I'm fine!' I lied, pulling the sheet down for a moment. 'It's just all rather new for me.'

For the rest of the week, when we were not attending a lecture, or having sex, Sean and I hung out with a group of white socialist types that had coalesced around a scruffy Trotskyite lecturer named Paul, who reeked of the strong French cigarettes he smoked and had the revolting habit of picking his long toenails, which peeped out from his equally scruffy sandals. He seemed oblivious to the wincing disgust of anyone who happened to be in his company. His saving grace was that he was an eloquent and informed debater, and there were many debates over the week on all kinds of subjects. It was the first time that I had come across a bunch of white people who didn't just skirt around race and the general treatment of women. Trotsky Paul, as Sean and I named him, would usually engineer and facilitate these debates.

He took me aside one afternoon, when we were all sitting under the oak tree, and told me in confidence not to join in with any of the debates on race. 'We white people need to come to our senses,' he said in a low voice, so that only I could hear. 'We need to face up to what colonising other people and destroying their way of life has done to all of us, and stop expecting them to solve the problems which we have created. But I don't want you rescuing us, Erna,' he added, with some passion.

During one particularly stirring debate, Trotsky Paul reeled off the names of black activists who spent their lives fighting the cause. 'Martin Luther King, Michael X, Malcom X, Angela Davis, Rosa Parks, look what happened to them,' he said, 'white people have managed to kill or imprison most of them. And

244

for what? Fighting for their human rights. And let's not forget our very own C L R James,' he added. 'Alright, granted he isn't strictly an activist, but he is a great social commentator and the best cricketing historian who ever lived. That alone makes his name always worth mentioning.'

I was enthralled. Jennifer had first opened my eyes to the reality of racism and the existence of a previously hidden wealth of black culture, but Trotsky Paul took my understanding to a whole new level. There were even occasions when he mentioned the names of black writers that I was hearing for the first time. The few white people that I was friendly with didn't talk politics, and I had a couple of work colleagues who routinely made disparaging comments about black people. 'I don't mean you, Erna, you're a really nice person,' was a typical comment. People like Trotsky Paul were an entirely new breed of white people to me. People who were passionate about human rights, whatever their colour and wherever they hailed from. They were talking the same language as black activists and the debates were intense and covered everything from politics to the Arts.

Unfortunately, Sean, as it turned out, was not one of the intellects. His interest was focused on what he called 'the exotic'. 'I am fucking a beautiful African princess!' he cried out one night, in a moment of passion.

After my initial doubts about sex, the floodgates had opened and I couldn't get enough of it, even though I began to feel weary of Sean beyond the confines of the bedroom. Sean's other main interest was talking about the boat he claimed to own with his doctor father back in his native Ireland. He went on and on about all things pertaining to boats and sailing, most of which went completely over my head. On our last day on campus, I joked with him about whether he would take me home to meet his parents.

'Er, sorry, Erna, I don't think they would understand,' he said. 'I don't believe either of my parents have ever even seen a coloured person in the flesh. My mother would likely have a heart attack, and probably my father too. They've seen Kenny Lynch and Shirley Bassey on the telly, but that's as far as their interest goes, I'm afraid. They just wouldn't understand and I wouldn't want them to hurt your feelings, Erna.'

'Thanks,' I replied, 'I hope you enjoyed the conquest.'

'Ah, come on now, that's not fair!' he protested.

'Oh, please,' I replied, 'just listen to yourself.' I already knew it was over with him, but I still wanted to give him a piece of my mind.

I left the campus with all kinds of emotions. I was secretly pleased that I had slept with a white man, but angry that I wasn't good enough to meet his parents. I was worried that I had let the entire black race down by allowing a white man to take my virginity, but, at the same time, I was pleased that I was no longer a virgin. And I was left with an interesting question: would sex be different with a black man? I made up my mind that no one would know of my escapade; certainly not my sister – about whom I felt a huge pang of guilt for even enjoying sex – and definitely not Jennifer, whom I knew would not approve in the slightest that I had allowed a white imperialist to steal away my most precious commodity.

# Chapter 34

I got off the train at Catford station and walked home feeling about as carefree as I had felt since arriving in England. It was a beautiful sunny afternoon and I was mulling over the week's successes: not only had I navigated my first romance, but I felt like I'd learnt so much about myself, and maybe even my place in the world. I was looking forward, with confidence, to the day that I could say that I had a degree in English Literature, with honours. Nevertheless, the moment I turned into our street my heart sank and the reality of life at home came flooding back. But even that couldn't prepare me for what I would encounter when I entered the house.

The first thing I noticed was the silence.

I put my suitcase down and called out, 'Is anybody home?' but there was no answer. I flicked through the mail on the hall table, picked out a letter that was addressed to me, and walked towards the stairs. As I passed the front room, I thought I heard a stifled sob. I looked through the open door and then stopped and stared in disbelief. Patsy was kneeling over her father's prostrate body. He was lying in front of the sofa, as if he had fallen off and been unable to climb back up. He was deathly grey and some kind of foam was leaking from his mouth.

'I'm pretty sure he's dead,' Patsy said, before I could say anything. Her voice was icy.

'Oh my God, Pats, what happened?' I cried out as I hurried to her side.

'I don't know,' she said. 'I found him like this.'

'But when?' I asked, reaching out and taking her arm.

She allowed me to help her upright. I could feel her shaking. 'I didn't know what to do,' she said.

That's when I noticed the syringe sticking out of his stomach, where his shirt had ridden up.

'Have you called for an ambulance?' I asked her firmly.

She shook her head numbly.

I ran back into the hall and dialled 999 and explained to the operator that I'd found my step-father unconscious on the floor, and that I thought he might be dead. Then I hung up and ran next door and held my finger on the doorbell until Mrs Kelly opened the door.

'Goodness gracious, what on earth is it?' she cried.

'It's my step-father, Mrs Kelly,' I said, 'I think he's dead.'

'Wait there!' she commanded.

She disappeared inside and returned moments later with a cardigan over her dress. She motioned for me to follow her and we ran back inside our house. Patsy was still standing looking at her father's body when we entered the room.

'Goodness me!' Mrs Kelly exclaimed when she saw him lying there. She knelt down beside him and felt for a pulse in his neck.

I could hardly breathe. I had the strangest sensation of two conflicting emotions – shock and elation – fighting inside me for precedence.

Mrs Kelly looked up at Patsy and me and shook her head. 'He's gone, dears,' she said. 'Have you called for an ambulance?'

I nodded.

'I better call Doctor Jarvis as well,' she said, and she darted into the hall.

I could hear her panicked voice informing the receptionist of what had happened, as the sudden wail of a siren filled the street. Seconds later the ambulance came to a halt outside. Mrs Kelly let them in, telling the two black-uniformed men the little that she knew.

While they attended to my step-father, Mrs Kelly ushered Patsy and me into the kitchen and put the kettle on.

'A cup of hot, sweet tea is what you need,' she said.

We stood in awkward silence in the kitchen. I didn't know where to look. Then I heard one of the ambulance men talking to someone in the hall. Mrs Kelly poked her head out of the kitchen door.

'It's Doctor Jarvis,' she said, turning back to us. 'Do you know him yourself, girls?'

Patsy stayed silent and I shrugged. 'I've never seen a doctor.'

'Well, he's a good one. Your father certainly knew him. I bumped into him at the surgery several times.'

'Step-father,' I replied.

Mrs Kelly stared at me for a moment, then the kettle sang. While she busied herself making a pot of tea, Patsy slumped into one of the chairs by the table. I sat down next to her.

'Everything's going to be alright,' I whispered.

She looked at me with wide round eyes. 'Is it?' she said.

'Here you are, dears,' said Mrs Kelly, placing two mugs of steaming tea on the table in front of us. 'Drink that down. It'll help you with the shock.'

As we sipped the hot, sweet liquid, Doctor Jarvis entered the kitchen.

'Oh, hello, Mrs Kelly,' he said. Then he turned to me and Patsy. 'Hello, girls, are either of you related to Mr Williamson?'

'I'm his step-daughter,' I said, 'and Patsy is his daughter.'

'Well, now I know this is a very difficult for you,' he said, 'but I need to ask you some questions.' He looked at us carefully before continuing. He had a kindly face and I guessed he must've done this kind of thing many times before. 'From a brief examination of his body, it looks like Mr Williamson died within the last hour, or so. Were either of you with Mr Williamson at any time during the last hour?' he asked.

I looked at Patsy who was looking at the floor. Reluctantly she lifted her head and stared at the doctor.

'I was,' she said.

'Okay, Patsy. Now, this isn't about blame, or anything, and no one is in trouble here, but I just need to establish a few facts.'

Suddenly I was reminded of all the crime dramas that Patsy watched and a strange feeling came over me when I looked at her.

'I was on my way to the bathroom, when I heard these weird noises coming from the front room,' she said. 'So I looked in and saw him sliding off the sofa. He was sweating tons and shaking all over and this white foamy stuff was coming out of his mouth. He tried to say something, but I couldn't hear what it was. He was looking straight at me. His eyes were strange. Like he was begging me to do something. Then I noticed the syringe on the floor and I realised he must've been trying to inject himself. So, I picked it up and stuck it in his stomach.' Patsy looked at the doctor pleadingly. 'That's where he injects himself, and Mum always says we have to be ready in case something like this happens. I was just trying to help!'

'It's okay, Patsy,' Doctor Jarvis said. 'You didn't do anything wrong. That would normally be exactly the right thing to do if someone had missed their insulin injection. Approximately what time was this?'

Patsy looked at me. 'About five minutes before Erna came home,' she said.

'And when was that?' Doctor Jarvis asked me.

'About fifteen minutes ago, I guess,' I said. I felt like I needed to defend Patsy's actions. 'I could see Patsy was in shock. I called the ambulance right away,' I added, looking at Mrs Kelly for confirmation.

'That's right,' Mrs Kelly confirmed. 'Erna ran round to mine right after.'

Doctor Jarvis looked at his watch.

'Okay, that puts the time of death at around 2.45pm,' he said. 'Thank you for being so helpful, both of you. I know how hard this must be for you.'

At that moment we heard the sound of our mother's voice. I ran out of the kitchen, followed by Mrs Kelly and the doctor, just in time to see Mother disappear into the front room. In the hallway, the twins, Sonny and Clifton were standing frozen to the spot, looking lost.

'Patsy,' I shouted, 'come and look after the boys!' Then I ran into the front room to find Mother sitting on the sofa, looking down at her dead husband.

She was rocking back and forth and howling like an injured animal.

'Do try and calm down, madam,' one of the ambulance men was saying.

'Calm down!' she bellowed. 'Does this look to you like a calm situation?' Mother turned and looked at me. Her eyes were wild.

Patsy had crept into the room and was standing beside me. Clifton and Sonny hung back in the doorway.

'My husband is dead, and I bet on my mother's life that those two devils are responsible!' Mother screamed, pointing at Patsy and me.

'Now, now, Mrs Williamson,' Mrs Kelly said. 'You're in shock, dear. Why don't you come into the kitchen with me and the girls can make you a cup of tea?'

'Oh, so you want them to kill me too, do you?' mother replied. 'I don't want those witches to make me anything, certainly not something they can easily poison me with!'

Doctor Jarvis moved past Mrs Kelly and sat down on the sofa next to my mother.

'You're upset, Mrs Williamson,' he said. His manner was gentle. 'I fully understand how difficult this must be for you, but no one killed your husband. It looks, to all intents and purposes, that Mr Williamson died of natural causes. But it will be up to the coroner to decide the exact cause of death.'

Mother practically knocked the doctor off the sofa as she leapt to her feet and pushed the ambulance man away from the ugly Satan devil man's body.

'Jehovah God, what have I done to deserve this life? What is to become of me now, Philbert?' she ranted, shaking her husband's body as if she could get an answer from him.

Doctor Jarvis looked helplessly at Mrs Kelly, who took the cue and reached out and placed a hand on Mother's shoulder. 'Now, now, dear,' she said, 'we've got to let the ambulance men and the doctor do their job.'

Mother went limp and allowed Mrs Kelly to help her to her feet.

Doctor Jarvis adjusted his jacket and stood up. 'I'm very sorry, but we do need your assistance to complete a few bits of paperwork, Mrs Williamson, and then we will need to take your husband to the hospital mortuary.' He added, 'You're welcome to accompany him, if you like.'

'Why,' mother replied, 'are you planning to bring him back from the dead?'

Despite her deranged state, with Mrs Kelly's help, the doctor and the ambulance men managed to persuade Mother to do what was needed, and, with her tacit permission, Mrs Kelly took the twins and the boys next door, leaving Patsy and me alone in the house for the first time since I'd arrived back from Brighton. We instinctively avoided the living room and retreated to our bedroom. Patsy went and stood by the window and stared out at the garden. I wanted to hug her – she seemed so frail – but something in her posture told me that she wasn't ready for touch. After a moment, I sat down on the bed.

'What were you doing at home alone with him, Pats?' I said.

She turned and looked at me. 'Bunking off school. I didn't expect him to be here.'

'Are you going to tell me what happened, then?'

'What do you mean?' She scowled.

'I mean, not that story you told the doctor.'

Patsy eyed me carefully. 'Are you saying I killed him, Erna?'

I shook my head. 'No! But how did he get into that state in the first place?'

'I don't know,' Patsy shouted. 'He was like that when I got home!'

'It's okay, I believe you,' I said. 'Come on, sit down here next to me.'

I patted the bed and Patsy sat down beside me.

'I'm glad he's dead though,' she whispered, 'aren't you?'

'Yes, I am,' I replied. 'It looks like our prayers have been answered and you won't have to suffer any more, Pats.'

Patsy nodded slowly. I took her hands in mine, and then, for the first time in ages, we hugged. Moments later, Patsy began to sob and my tears began to flow too. I held her thin body tight and sent a silent prayer of thanks to Grandma Melba.

# Chapter 35

Things began to change quickly after my step-father's death. Mother seemed lost without him to anchor her in reality – no matter how awful that reality had been. When she finally returned from the hospital that night, she single-handedly dragged the vile orange and brown carpet from the living room and dumped it in the street. Then she set about scrubbing the entire room with bleach. It was well after midnight before the banging and shifting finally stopped.

The following morning, she collected the boys and the twins from Mrs Kelly, but she left it to Patsy and me to organise them all going to school. When I returned home from work that evening, I found her sitting in the kitchen staring vacantly into space. I hoped that this was only a temporary condition, and that she would eventually snap out of it, and maybe even begin to enjoy her life again, after years of suffering. Sadly, I soon discovered that my hopes were utterly unrealistic.

Mother never returned to work after that fateful day, and, what was even more shocking, she gave up going to church. In fact, she mostly stopped living. She became this shadowy figure who spent her days wandering aimlessly around the house, wearing a worn-out housecoat over an old, stained nightdress. The only variation to this routine was bizarre: every Saturday, without fail, she would somehow manage to get herself washed and dressed and go shopping. She would then cook for the younger children, although she herself barely ate. She filled her days by humming her church songs, mumbling under her breath and occasionally reading psalms out loud. On the rare occasion that she was forced to speak to Patsy or me, she would preface every comment with something disparaging.

'I wish to God that I never brought either of you devil children here,' she said one evening, as she stood at the kitchen door scrutinising us as we prepared a meal for ourselves and the younger children. She'd long refused to eat anything either of us cooked, convinced that we had murdered her husband and were trying to do the same to her. 'I know I am being punished for my sins,' she continued. 'Look at what they have done to me, oh Lord!' she cried, as we pushed past her carrying plates of food for our hungry siblings.

Mother's grip on reality wasn't helped by the coroner's report, when it finally came. Death by misadventure was the verdict. The devil man had needed his daily insulin injections to survive, but on the day in question he had collapsed due to severe hypoglycemia, and it was the injection of insulin that Patsy had delivered that killed him, from diabetic shock. The coroner was in no doubt that this was nothing more than a tragic accident. But for our mother it was the final confirmation of what she had long believed: that Patsy and I were the devil's children who had killed her husband and wanted to kill her too. The verdict brought no peace to Patsy or me, either. The doubt I'd felt when Patsy had told me what happened that day lingered, and, whether it was justified or not, I couldn't escape the idea that Patsy had murdered her own father, and that I had encouraged her to do it. Neither did the death of the ugly Satan devil man bring Patsy the relief that I'd hoped for. Rather than blossoming without the shadow of her father looming over her, she seemed to be struggling with her feelings more than ever, and this often came out as aggression towards the younger children, and even towards herself. There were times when she would fly into sudden fits of rage, or tear at her skin as though she had no feelings left. And for me, living in a house with my mother and Patsy in the state they were in began to feel like I too was being tortured. The one positive was that Auntie Madge and Uncle Herbie never relented in their support for us. As soon as it got to the point where I felt unable to cope, I decided to talk things over with them. The outcome of that conversation was as swift as it was dramatic.

'Herbie and I have talked to your mother about taking on the care of the younger children,' Auntie Madge informed Patsy and me during her next visit. 'To be frank, your mother knows she is no longer in a position to look after the children properly. It's not that she doesn't love them – she does – but she is just too sick to cope. Most of their care is already falling on you girls, which isn't fair on either of you. And they'll end up with the Social Services if no one in the family can take them. Herbie and I would rather take them on than see them go to strangers.'

'That's fine by me,' Patsy said, the moment Auntie Madge suggested the plan.

'Me too,' I agreed. 'You're absolutely right, Auntie, it's all getting too much for me, what with work, studies and everything. And I'm sure Clifton and Sonny and the twins will love living with you and Uncle Herbie. It's certainly far better than them living here.'

'Okay, then that's decided,' said Auntie Madge. 'But what about you two girls? Do you think you'll be able to cope living here with your mother?'

Patsy and I looked at each other. Could we cope? I wasn't sure.

'What's the alternative?' I asked.

'The alternative is putting your mother in a mental hospital,' Auntie Madge said.

Despite everything, the idea of that happening seemed so awful that I felt it was worth trying to keep her with us.

I was soon to learn how misguided my ambition was, and once she became aware of how unwell our mother had become Mrs Kelly started bringing us a mid-week meal.

'Anything else you need, dears, please just knock,' she'd say, whenever she popped up at the door. She never came in, but would always ask, 'How is your ma doing today?'

The truth is we'd become so used to our mother's deteriorating mental state that we already considered it to be normal, so we'd usually just tell Mrs Kelly that Mum was doing okay.

One Saturday morning in late November, as the leaves were starting to fall more copiously from the huge plane tree outside the house, I sat down to write to Grandpa Sippa.

It had been ages since I last wrote to him, and I needed to tell him what was happening with my mother. It wasn't an easy letter to write, and I signed off by saying that I hoped he was well and that Miss Blossom was looking after him. As soon as I had sealed the envelope, I burst into tears. Memories of my simple island childhood with Sippa and Melba came flooding back and I felt a deep longing to return to that time. I was sitting with my old, worn-out coat wrapped tightly around me as I wrote my letter, but it offered little warmth. Now that I'd finished, I popped it into my coat pocket, and pulled on a pair of leg warmers and my boots. The knitted scarf that Mrs Kelly gave me all that time ago had turned out to be my most favoured, warm and luxurious item of clothing. I swaddled my neck and upper body in the thick wool and stepped out into the windy autumn afternoon.

Every so often, a gust of wind lifted a few dozen leaves from a pile and sent them swirling a few feet further down the path. At the end of our street, I stopped and posted my letter, before heading towards the local high street. I needed a new coat, but couldn't afford a new one, so I decided to try my luck at the Oxfam charity shop that I'd passed many times, but never considered going inside before. It wasn't really the done thing in my family to buy secondhand clothing, but I'd noticed in passing that there was often good quality stuff in the shop's windows.

The musty smell that permeated the shop became less noticeable as I browsed through the racks. I tried to make myself as inconspicuous as possible in order to hopefully avoid being spotted by anyone I knew. However, this also necessitated the odd glance towards the shop front, in case a complete disappearing trick to the back of the store was required. It was during one of these furtive glances out the window that he caught my eye – a good-looking black man, tall with loose dreadlocks hanging way down his back. When he saw that I'd noticed him he winked at me, and then, to my surprise, he walked into the shop. I spun around and picked up the first thing that came came to hand.

The next thing I knew he was standing behind me. 'I wouldn't buy that,' he said, pointing to the small wooden African carving of a woman with a fat round belly that I was clutching, 'if I were you.'

'Why not?' I replied.

'Well, you know what they say,' he laughed, 'and you definitely don't look ready to be a mother!'

I had no idea what he was talking about. 'I like it,' I lied, 'and I'm going to buy it anyway.' I moved past him towards the counter.

He followed.

'I like your spirit, sister,' he said. Then added, 'My name is Fitzroy.'

I ignored him. I had only recently opened a bank account and proudly took out my cheque book to pay for the little carving.

'How much?' I asked the young woman at the counter.

'Oh, that's fifty pence, I think,' she said.

I felt a bit silly paying by cheque, but I'd taken it out now.

'We don't take cheques for such a small amount,' said the young woman.

'But I don't have any cash on me,' I pleaded.

'I'll cover that.' Fitzroy produced a little leather coin purse and handed a pound coin to the young woman.

'Thank you, but you didn't have to do that,' I said. 'How will I get to pay you back?'

'Easy!' he replied. 'Your name and address are printed in your cheque book.' Then he repeated what he'd clearly seen over my shoulder in my cheque book. 'So, you live in South London? Maybe I'll come and visit you one day, Erna Mullings.'

I turned around angrily. 'How dare you look at my address? That's private! Now I don't really care if I can pay you back.'

I took my carving and flounced out of the shop to the echo of his lightly mocking laughter. As soon as I was outside, my legs wobbled and my heart pounded hard in my chest. He really was a handsome man. I particularly liked his luscious full lips and sparkling smile. I walked back home with a spring in my step. It was only when I got to the front door that I realised I'd completely forgotten why I'd gone into the charity shop in the first place.

The house was in total silence when I entered. With no one around, I lit two of the rings on the old gas cooker – one to warm me up and the other to boil water for my favourite drink, a super hot mug of tea, which I loved for its ability to deliver instant warmth to my body.

I moved towards the window and was about to take my first sip, but, as I lifted the mug towards my mouth, I almost dropped it. My mother was standing, stark naked, in the vegetable patch at the bottom of the garden, apparently having a conversation with herself.

I cracked open the window to call to her, but realised that, if they hadn't already seen her, me shouting at her would likely attract the attention of the neighbours. I dashed to the back door and threw it open.

'Mum,' I hissed, 'come inside now. Please!'

Mother stopped her conversation and turned towards me. 'Do you mind, I'm talking to Philbert!' she said angrily.

'You can do that inside?' I offered. 'Come on, you'll catch your death of cold out there.'

My mother looked down at herself in amazement. 'What am I doing here?' she asked.

I ran across the scruffy lawn and took her hand. 'Come on,' I said.

She allowed me to lead her back inside the house as passively as a small child. I took her back to her bedroom and sat her down on the bed. Then I grabbed a dress from her wardrobe and handed it to her.

'Put that on,' I said.

She obeyed me without question.

'I've got to go and call Auntie Madge,' I said, 'so you just wait there till I get back. Okay?'

She nodded her assent. I ran back downstairs. My previously freezing body was now steamingly hot. I dialled Auntie Madge's number. As soon as she answered, I told her that I couldn't cope any longer.

'It's okay, Erna,' she said soothingly. 'Herbie and I will sort things out.'

I felt an incredible sense of relief when Uncle Herbie's brown Austin Cambridge estate pulled up outside the house half an hour later.

'I'll call the ambulance,' Auntie Madge said, the moment she walked through the door. 'You need to go and get your mother's things in order.'

She instructed me to collect various items of clothing and toiletries from Mother's room, which she then packed neatly into a suitcase. Uncle Herbie helped me get Mother downstairs and led her to the waiting ambulance. It was the last time Mother saw the house she'd lived in since she'd arrived in England eight years earlier. I stood at the top of the steps and watched the ambulance disappear down the road, followed by Auntie Madge and Uncle Herbie in their car. Patsy was nowhere to be seen.

It wasn't until much later on that evening, as I sat alone in the front room, that I finally allowed myself to think of my meeting with the enigmatic Fitzroy.

# Part three

Part Three

# Chapter 36

It was an unseasonably warm, muggy March day when I went with Auntie Madge to visit Mum in hospital.

The consultant who met with us didn't mince his words, 'I'm afraid to say that Mrs Williamson is not responding to her medication in any kind of beneficial manner. In fact, she appears to be deteriorating and we're trying electric shock therapy as a last resort.'

'Goodness me, you tried that years ago,' Auntie Madge said, in an exasperated tone.

The consultant looked at his notes. 'Yes, I can see that,' he replied, 'but her diagnosis at the time was depression. What we're looking at now is paranoid schizophrenia.'

I found everything about the Ladywell psychiatric wing of the Maudsley hospital depressing. The walls of the consultant's office were bare, apart from his various certificates of achievement; the ward where my mother lay catatonic from her latest round of ECT was stark. Despite everything I'd endured since arriving in England, I felt nothing but sadness for my mother, and I'd secretly begun to hope that she wouldn't recover from her treatment, that she would slip away from this life and finally find some relief. But what the consultant said next terrified me.

'The reason I said last resort is because your mother has tried to commit suicide,' he said, staring fixedly at me.

'What?' I turned and looked at Auntie Madge, who seemed equally shocked. 'Did you know about this?' I asked her.

She shook her head.

'And it's not the first time,' the doctor continued.

Auntie Madge sat bolt upright in her chair.

'Then why is this the first time you're telling us?' she said.

'We see no point in upsetting relatives unnecessarily,' he said.

'Unnecessarily?' Auntie Madge cried. 'Well, why are you telling us now then?'

'Because we may have to move your sister to a secure ward,' the consultant replied.

My poor mother! I was trying to think how I was going to tell Grandpa Sippa what was happening with his daughter. Auntie Madge had heard from Miss Blossom that Grandpa had been seriously unwell, and so we'd agreed to keep the deterioration of his daughter from him, but, surely, he deserved to know?

This conundrum was still weighing on my mind when I walked into our house two hours later to find Patsy lying on the sofa reading a magazine. Patsy had left school of her own volition, pretty much straight after Mother was hospitalised. She'd barely been attending anyway, and rather than try and get her to go back, the school seemed glad to be rid of her. Her behaviour had become increasingly erratic and she'd been suspended on numerous occasions. While this situation seemed perfectly acceptable to Patsy, it certainly wasn't to me. I was fed up with returning home from work to find her lounging around, and what made it worse was her attitude towards me. I'd tried to encourage her to do something positive with her time, but she always had a reason not to. My suggestion that she could do a college course had been met with derision – 'You're the one with the brains,' she'd said. 'As for me, I don't want to see the inside of a classroom ever again. What's the point of having my head filled up with a load of useless information that I'll never use! None of it has helped so far, has it?'

'Well, jobs don't come looking for you, Pats,' I'd replied, 'and if you're not going to go to college then you're going to have to find something else to do. And anyway, I don't see why I should be the only person bringing in the money. You're seventeen now Patsy and you can bloody well start pulling your weight!'

But that was months ago. Today I wasn't in the mood for her excuses. I swept her feet off the sofa and addressed her directly. 'I'm sick of finding you like this, Patsy!' I said.

Patsy threw the magazine on the floor and tried to walk past me, but I stopped her.

'Mother's in a bad way,' I said.

'What's new?' she replied.

I was about to tell her what was going on when the doorbell rang. It was late on Friday afternoon and we weren't expecting visitors. When the bell rang for the third time, Patsy glared at me before going to answer it. I picked up her magazine and glanced at its cover. It was a copy of *Vogue*, and I was amazed to see that it featured an incredibly striking looking black woman: Grace Jones.

'It's for you!' Patsy shouted from the hallway.

'Who is it?' I shouted back.

'The person says you should come to the door,' Patsy shouted in an exasperated tone.

I put the magazine down and walked towards the hall, crossing paths with Patsy in the doorway.

'Aren't you the lucky one,' she said with a smirk, as she pushed past.

At first, the low evening sunlight obscured the figure. Once my eyes adjusted, the person I saw standing on the top step was the man who'd flirted with me in the charity shop in

November. He was wearing a large black beret that covered his dreadlocks. For a moment I couldn't recall his name.

'I was in the area and thought I would check on you,' he said. 'I hope it's not a bad time?'

I burst out laughing, it seemed so absurd, although something in the tone of my laughter alerted him.

'Ah, so maybe it is a bad time,' he said.

'Well, it's certainly a long time,' I replied, leaning against the door frame.

'I know that, sistreen,' he grinned in response, 'and, now that I see you again, I feel sorry for that.'

'Well, I certainly never expected to see you again... Fitzroy,' I said, self-consciously pulling my hair into shape.

'Ah, so you remember my name, Erna. I must've made an impression then.' He smiled.

I turned at the sound of Patsy coughing as she walked back into the hall. She stopped at the bottom of the stairs, staring past me at Fitzroy. I turned back to face him.

'Now isn't a good time. I've just come back from hospital. My mother is seriously ill.'

His expression changed immediately to one of sadness. 'Oh, I am very sorry to hear that, Erna,' he said gently. 'Maybe another time?'

'Yes, that would be nice,' I said.

He turned his back on me for a second, then turned round and handed me a card on which he'd scrawled something. I stared at the card. It read: *Fitzroy Gibbons BA (Hons), Lecturer in Sociology, Thames Polytechnic.*

'Call me,' he said, turning to leave.

'Bye, Fitzroy!' Patsy called out.

Fitzroy stopped for a second, stared at Patsy through the open door, then smiled at me again and walked down the steps into the street. I closed the door softly and turned to face my sister who was staring at me with an amused look on her face.

'Where did he turn up from?' she said. 'I have never heard you mention a man before, ever! He is cute, though,' she added, 'and that's one huge Rasta hat. He must have some real long locks under that!'

'It's none of your business, Patsy,' I said. 'And by the way, he came to see me. Not you.'

# Chapter 37

On the Sunday after my visit to my mother, Patsy and I travelled to Clapham Common to have lunch with Auntie Madge, Uncle Herbie, Clifton, Sonny and the twins. The journey took nearly an hour – we had to change at Denmark Hill and then walk to their house from Clapham Junction – but we barely spoke the whole way. We'd argued fiercely after Fitzroy's visit, and I was still too angry with her to trust myself to broach the subject of her getting a job. Patsy seemed content to ignore me. In fact, she seemed far more interested in the attention she was getting from men. It was a marked difference in her that concerned me, even though I felt it might mean that she was starting to get over the abuse she'd suffered at the hands of her father. Nevertheless, the lack of conversation gave me a chance to think. It occurred to me that living in that dilapidated old house wasn't doing either of us any good, and that maybe we should move somewhere smaller, but, more importantly, somewhere without the constant reminders of the ugly Satan devil man and our deranged mother.

Auntie Madge and Uncle Herbie lived in an impressively large Victorian house that overlooked the wide, open space of Clapham Common. It was the perfect place for Clifton, Sonny and the twins – they got all the love and attention they needed from their Aunt and Uncle, and they had a huge area to go and explore. But the boys still greeted Patsy and me as if they hadn't seen us for months, and insisted on dragging me out to the garden to play football with them. However, they soon tired of my pathetic efforts, so I left them to it and went back inside to help Auntie Madge prepare the lunch. On the way to the kitchen, I found Patsy watching television with the twins and Uncle Herbie in the living room, which I was happy about, since it gave me the chance to talk to Auntie Madge on my own.

Auntie Madge was chopping vegetables. She pushed a bag full of muddy potatoes towards me to wash and peel.

'It was a terrible thing to see your mother so bad on Friday,' she said. 'How are you coping with it all, Erna?'

'I don't know,' I shrugged, 'I think I've become numb to it, Auntie.'

'You've had a lot of craziness to deal with, that's for sure,' she said.

She opened the oven to release a cloud of steam, then shut the door again.

'Can you peel those potatoes quick now, Erna, I need to get them roasting!' She placed her cut vegetables in a large pan and then joined me peeling the potatoes. 'It's just a crying shame what has happened to my sister,' she said, 'she was such a lovely young woman. Never would have harmed a fly. I am sorry to say this about your dead step-father, but something about that marriage started destroying her from the day it took place.'

I looked at her and wondered how much she knew about what had happened. She was an astute woman, so maybe she knew more than she let on.

'You know what Grandma Melba called him?' I said.

'No, chile, what did she call him?' she said, scooping the peeled potatoes into a colander and rinsing them under the tap.

'The ugly Satan devil man,' I replied.

Auntie Madge burst out laughing. 'Oh my, Miss Melba had a way of seeing right through to the heart of things,' she said. Then she came and placed a hand on my shoulder. 'I know he was a bad man, Erna,' she said, 'and me and Herbie was always sorry to leave you children there in that house with him and Violet in the state she was, but the one time I tried to talk to her about it she damn near bit my head off.'

'You don't have to apologise, Auntie,' I said. 'You and Uncle Herbie have done more than enough for us, really.'

'Well, that's kind of you to say, chile,' Auntie Madge replied.

She poured the potatoes into a roasting tin, covered them in oil and stuck them in the oven above a huge roasting chicken.

'I wanted to ask you something,' I said.

'Go ahead.' Auntie Madge seated herself at the kitchen table and indicated that I should sit too, so I pulled out a chair and sat opposite her.

'Well, I've been thinking about moving out of the house. It doesn't feel right, just me and Patsy living there.'

Auntie Madge nodded. 'That house is not a happy place, Erna. Your mother was never happy there, and sometimes I doubt anyone ever will be.'

'So, you agree then?'

'Of course. Too many ghosts. Anyway, on a more practical note, your uncle Herbie and I have been discussing renting out the house, so your timing is perfect. That way the mortgage payments can be kept up and we can bank something for your mother, when, God willing, she returns to us. Whatever is left can go towards helping with the children's care.'

So that was settled then. I breathed a huge sigh of relief. The rest of our conversation was social, talking about friends and family and memories of our island. The good mood continued over lunch and even Patsy came out of her shell and joined in. On the journey home Patsy continued to be charming and chatty, so I decided to broach the subject of moving home with her. I needn't have worried, she agreed with alacrity, and also agreed that I should do the looking and said she would be happy with whatever I found.

I blocked out the following four weekends, so I could visit all manner of properties in the local area: Bromley, Penge, Forest Hill, even venturing as far as Dulwich, which was considered very hoity toity by the denizens of Catford. A number of white landlords, upon opening their doors, closed them again as soon as they saw that I was black. A few did so without uttering a single word, while others stated that the room was no longer available. This was often minutes after I had made a call from a local phone box, using my poshest accent and had been assured that the room was free. One bloated middle-aged man took the time to tell me exactly why he would not be letting a room to me: 'We don't let rooms to your sort,' he snarled. 'I suggest you go and look in Brixton. Plenty of your kind hanging around down there. Or, better still, you could go back where you came from.' The man's words resounded in my head as I travelled back home that night. I wanted to cry. I must have visited more than twenty addresses without being offered a single suitable room.

When a second cousin suggested that we could stay with her and her husband in exchange for baby-sitting at the weekends, it seemed that my prayers had been answered. However, when I visited the house, while my cousin was making tea in the kitchen, her husband suggested that we girls could keep him company with a bit of loving when his wife wasn't around.

As soon as I got home, I called Jennifer. It was her mother who answered the phone. She told me that Jennifer was out, but she had a way of sensing problems and, with little encouragement, I poured my heart out to her instead. She listened without interruption.

'It's okay, Erna,' she said, when I managed to draw breath, 'there is a reason for everything and an answer to most things.

And, as it happens, you may have called at just the right time. I might be able to help you girls out.'

'Oh, thank you so much, Mrs Richards,' I replied. 'I'm very grateful for anything you can do to help!'

'Don't thank me yet,' she advised, 'I'm not offering any guarantees.'

Mrs Richards explained that some friends of hers were planning to move to Saint Lucia for at least three years and were looking for someone responsible to take care of their house in Streatham on a long-term basis, so the rent would be negligible and the house would remain furnished. 'Is this something you think you and your sister could manage?' she said.

'Definitely, Mrs Richards. I'm very… I mean, my sister Patsy and I are both very responsible.'

Mrs Richards assured me that she would speak to her friends and that she would put in a good word for us, but no guarantees, she reiterated.

Three days later, I got a call from Jennifer to say that her mum had arranged for us to go to Streatham to meet the couple the following weekend. I thought that Patsy would be overjoyed at the idea of moving out of our gloomy house of ghosts, but she seemed indifferent, and when the weekend came she disappeared into the boys' room, which she had made her own after they had moved out. I decided that on balance it was probably better that I went on my own anyway.

Number forty-two Payton Street, Streatham, was a neat, modern house with a white painted exterior and a flat asphalt roof, one of seven that were wedged in the middle of a terrace of three-storey Victorian houses. Mrs Richards' black Morris Minor was parked directly outside the front of the house and Jennifer hopped from the passenger seat as soon as she saw me. I was dressed in a sober outfit of grey skirt, white shirt and grey jacket that I felt made me look very adult and responsible. It must have done the trick, for the couple, Mr and Mrs

Campbell, who were as neat and tidy as their house, offered me the tenancy almost immediately. I explained that my sister had to work on Saturdays – a lie that caused me some anguish, but one that I felt was necessary in the circumstances. I walked out with a set of keys in my hand and the bubbling excitement of knowing that, at last, my life seemed to be taking a turn for the better.

Three weeks later, having tidied up our mother's house the best we could, we handed the keys to Auntie Madge. It was a glorious May afternoon and I took it as a sign that our move was blessed by the gods. Sweating in the heat, Uncle Herbie managed to pack everything we owned into his Austin Cambridge estate, and with Patsy sitting on my lap in the front seat, he drove us to our new house.

When I walked through the door for the second time, I felt instantly at home.

Patsy dropped her suitcase on the wooden floor with a squeal of pleasure. 'But this is fantastic, sis!' she cried.

I followed her, laughing, into the kitchen.

She turned and looked at me with shining eyes. 'Everything's so clean and new!'

'I told you!' I shouted after her as she ran upstairs.

'Well, she seems happy, at least,' Uncle Herbie grunted, as he heaved a large box full of my books through the door.

I ran over and gave him a hug.

'Thank you for doing this, Uncle Herbie,' I said, 'we're so grateful.

He stretched upright and wiped his hands on his trousers. 'Think nothing of it,' he said, smiling.

I ran upstairs to find Patsy in the back bedroom, looking out of the window at the tiny garden.

'This is my room,' she stated.

'Okay then,' I laughed, 'just as long as you're happy, Pats!'

She walked towards me with a serious expression on her face. 'Erna, I've been so horrible to you,' she said. 'I hope you can forgive me?'

'Of course I can,' I said, reaching out and pulling her towards me, 'after all you've been through.'

Half an hour later all our possessions were piled in the front room. I waved Uncle Herbie off from the front door and called out to Patsy who was somewhere upstairs: 'I'm going to take a quick walk down our new high street, Pats. Fancy joining me? We can unpack later.'

'I'd rather stay here,' she called back. 'You go ahead.'

It was so hot outside that the tarmac was melting. I took a right turn at the end of the street on to Streatham High Road. It was heaving with people and traffic, but I luxuriated in the feeling that there was no one here who knew me, or my family. I walked past an African food store and a beauty parlour selling cosmetics just for black women. I peered inside to see two women in colourful turbans fanning themselves against the heat. On the opposite side of the road, there was a small florist's next to the railway station. I'd developed a love of flowers from Grandma Melba, who had always placed freshly cut heliconia or oleander or hibiscus on the Hall table every Sunday. As I crossed the busy road, I recalled the time that I'd spent almost a pound of my salary on a bunch of pale pink roses with a stem of gypsophila and some ferns, which I'd placed in the middle of the dining table. When Mother had arrived home, she'd taken one look at the flowers and declared haughtily, 'I don't want anything dead in my house!' And with that she had picked up the vase and thrown it, along with the flowers, into the bin. Now I had a home of my own and I could do whatever I wanted. I bought a beautiful bunch of red roses and skipped back towards the house, so joyful was the feeling of liberation. On the corner of Payton Street there was a phone box. I hesitated for a moment, concerned that Patsy might be wondering where I'd got to, and then decided that there was no time like the present. I stepped inside the red, glass-panelled cubicle, and pulled out my purse. Inside its back zipped pocket was Fitzroy's card. I looked at the number, took a deep breath, and called him.

'Nice flowers,' Patsy said on my return, 'and no Mum to chuck them in the bin. Mind you, more fool me for hoping you had really gone to get us some fried chicken!'

I walked into the kitchen and searched for a suitable vase.

'We're going to have to start doing our own cooking, Pats,' I shouted, 'take-aways will have to be for special treats. We can do this if we work together.'

I cut the stems of the roses and placed them in the glass vase that I found in the cupboard next to the sink. I half-filled the vase with water and then walked back into the front room and placed the flowers on the dining table.

'By the way, did the Job Centre people ever come back to you, Pats?'

She was lounging on the sofa, and half sat up, resting the open glossy magazine across her chest. 'Nope,' Patsy said. 'But I will be sure to tell you when they do.'

'Patsy,' I said, heatedly, 'surely any work is better than the dole, unless you're aspiring to be the next Grace Jones?' Despite myself, her attitude had triggered me, which I immediately regretted.

Anger flashed across her pretty brown face, causing it to contort and redden. 'What do you want me do? It's like everyone wants me to have some kind of shit job! Is that how much you think of me, Erna? I know I don't have an education, like you, but that doesn't mean I want to shovel shit.'

'I don't mean anything like that, Pats. I'm just trying to say there are jobs out there that you could do until such time as you're ready to do something else. It's not fair that I'm out working every day, while you stay at home and read magazines.

It's not fair that I've been carrying us both, Pats. Can you not see that?'

'Where exactly are the jobs out there?' she replied. 'Go on! Give me some examples. Actually, don't bother. I know the kind of job that I'm probably qualified for. Prostitution! Is that what you want me to do?'

I was deeply shocked, but I tried to remain calm. 'I was thinking more that the Job Centre people could point you in the right direction. They can properly go through things with you and help you to see what kind of work would best suit you.'

'Erna!' she yelled. 'I've been to the Job Centre, not once, not twice, I've been there countless times, and each time they say the same thing, that they can easily find me a job cleaning offices or something. I am not doing that. Never!'

'Well, that's plain out of order, Patsy, and whoever said that should be reported. But at the same time, you need to have some idea of what work you want to do, or better still, you could go to college and learn a skill,' I said.

'Not your "go to college and learn a skill" mantra again,' Patsy replied with a roll of her eyes. 'You know what, I'm tired of waiting for you to come home and behave like Miss La-de-dah. It's not like you've had to put up with the shit that I have. All you do is boss me about and go on and on about the poxy degree you're doing.'

'That's not fair. I got my job without having any previous experience, and the same with getting on my degree course. Anyway, you can't use the past as an excuse for the rest of your life. And, like I said, I just can't afford to keep paying for everything on my own.'

'I don't remember asking to live with you,' Patsy said spitefully. 'It was you who invited me to share this house. You knew I had no job and no money.'

'Look, I'm not trying to pick a fight with you, Pats.'

'Well, you could have fooled me,' she shouted. 'Please! I don't want you spending any more of your precious money on me. I should have known that living with you would be a bad idea.' And with that she flounced upstairs to her new bedroom.

I picked up the copy of *Vogue* that she'd discarded. It was the same one she'd been reading when I'd come home from the hospital after visiting mother almost two months ago. Grace Jones' chiselled face stared back at me from the front cover. Maybe Patsy could do this modelling thing, after all, I thought. She was certainly tall and good looking enough. I placed the magazine on the dining table and stared at the gorgeous red roses. But how quickly everything good seems to slip away, I thought.

# Chapter 38

I was mindful of Patsy's flirtatious attitude towards Fitzroy when he'd shown up unexpectedly at our old house, so I was determined to be ready to leave the moment he arrived to take me out. It was the first Friday evening after we'd moved into Payton Street. Patsy was flicking through the latest copy of *Woman's Own* magazine downstairs and I was working on my hair upstairs in my bedroom when the doorbell rang. I looked at my alarm clock. Fitzroy was half an hour early.

'Suppose no one else is going to get that,' Patsy complained from downstairs. 'It's for you!' she shouted moments later.

'I know it is!' I shouted back.

I couldn't believe my best-laid plans had fallen apart already. I wasn't even dressed and I still had big yellow sponge curlers in my hair to make sure it was nice and bouncy for my first date. I pulled my kimono together and ran downstairs, giving Patsy a push as I moved towards the door.

'Serves you right,' she laughed, as she caught sight of my face.

Fitzroy was standing in the doorway.

'I hope I'm not too early?' he said.

'Only half an hour,' I said.

He looked immediately apologetic. 'Man, I'm sorry bout that.' When I didn't move, he added, 'Is it okay if I come in?'

'Oh, yes, of course,' I said, moving aside to let him enter the front room, simultaneously gripping my Afro pick a little too tightly and feeling very conscious of the curlers covering half my head.

Patsy sniggered from the sofa, where she was watching us over the top of her magazine.

'Patsy, don't you have something to do upstairs?' I said.

'I was just going to make some tea,' she said, 'do you want one, Fitzroy?' She gave me a smug sideways look and started walking across to the room towards the kitchen.

Fitzroy's eyes seemed glued to the movement of her backside.

'Patsy,' I shouted, 'go upstairs now!'

She stopped in her tracks and turned towards me. 'I just wanted to be polite to our guest, but excuse me,' she said, before walking slowly back across the room and then sashaying up the stairs.

Fitzroy's eyes followed her until she reached the landing, then he focused back on me.

'So that's your sister?' he said.

'Yes, that's my little sister, Patsy. Would you like a cup of tea anyway?' I said.

'No, thank you, water's fine for me,' he said, sitting down on a dining chair. 'I try to avoid the colonialists' favourite beverage.'

I ran to the kitchen, poured him a glass of water and walked back into the front room. 'I won't be a minute,' I smiled, handing the glass to him. 'I've just got to finish getting ready.'

He took a sip from the glass and I could feel his eyes on me as I walked up the stairs.

'You look lovely, Erna,' he said to my retreating back.

Fifteen minutes later, I climbed into the passenger seat of Fitzroy's blue Volvo estate wearing my favourite red dress. He leant across me with a smile, pulled my seatbelt over me and clicked it in place. Then he started the engine and pulled away from the kerb, reggae music thumping from the large speakers in the back.

'So, where are we going then?' I said, as we sped northwards down Streatham High Road towards Brixton.

'The Keskidee Centre in Kings Cross,' he said, 'have you heard of it?'

I shook my head.

'It's a really cool place, Erna,' he said, 'the first black Arts centre in Britain. You're gonna love it!'

'And what are we going to see there?'

He looked sideways at me. 'A new band call Misty in Roots,' he replied. 'I take it you like reggae music?'

'I love it,' I said.

We parked up in a street somewhere behind King's Cross Station and walked the rest of the way. The Keskidee Centre was housed in a big old building that looked like it had once been a school or a church, stuck on its own at the corner of the road, at the end of a row of terraced houses. Inside, it was buzzing with people, many wearing traditional African dress and men sporting Rastafarian colours with huge hats covering their dreadlocks. Fitzroy seemed perfectly at home and he introduced me to several of his friends as we made our way towards the back room to see the band. Photographs of black artists, musicians, writers and activists lined the wall.

'Well, what do you think?' Fitzroy said.

'It's fantastic, Fitzroy,' I replied. 'It feels pretty cool to be among so many black people for a change.'

'What I love about this place, Erna, is that it's got something for everyone,' Fitzroy said with a smile.

I looked at him standing there, tall, hawk-nosed and handsome, and I felt something melt inside me. The rest of the evening passed in a joyous whirl of music and conversation and laughter, and before I knew it we were back inside Fitzroy's car heading home to South London. When we reached my house,

Fitzroy climbed out and came round to open the passenger door for me. As we walked to the front door, I experienced the same thumping of heart that I had felt the first time we met.

'Well, that was a perfect evening,' I said, pulling out my key from my purse. 'Thank you, Fitzroy.'

'The pleasure was all mine, Erna.'

'Do you—' I started to say, but he interrupted me.

'I have to prepare for a tutorial tomorrow, so I better get going,' he said.

'But tomorrow's Saturday!' I protested.

'I know that,' Fitzroy smiled, 'but my students have their finals coming up and they've asked me to help them prepare, so that's what I'm doing.'

'Oh, I see,' I said.

'You look so downhearted, Erna. It's nice to see,' Fitzroy said. 'Anyway, I'd like to invite you over to mine for dinner next Friday, if that's okay for you?'

'Umm, I'll have to check my diary,' I replied.

Fitzroy burst out laughing. 'Just let me know,' he said, and then he leant over and kissed me full on the lips.

I stood on the doorstep and watched him climb back into his car, which gave me a few moments to recover myself enough to enter the house and face Patsy. As it turned out, I needn't have worried: she had already gone to bed.

# Chapter 39

In the week following my first date with Fitzroy, I found it difficult to concentrate on my studies or anything at work. Several times, Mrs Partridge reprimanded me for shoddy typing, but I just didn't care. I was floating in a haze of romantic expectation that I realised was exactly like the feelings described in the Mills and Boon stories I had devoured so avidly when I first arrived in London. Somewhere inside, I knew that it wasn't exactly a practical feeling, but since it was the first time I'd felt like this, I didn't want to disrupt it with anything trivial like work. So, I suffered Mrs Partridge in silence and looked forward to Friday night with mounting anticipation. Now and again, I thought about Sean – the skinny white Irish lad who had courted and won me so easily the previous year at summer school – but these thoughts were only fleeting intrusions on my romantic reverie.

The journey from Streatham to Peckham Rye station only took twenty minutes. Nevertheless, Peckham was an area I knew nothing about, having avoided it like the plague due to the fearsome reputation of its local school when I was a pupil at Catford Girls. I had diligently marked the address on my A-to-Z street map, but as I made my way through the unfamiliar streets, I realised that I had no idea what to expect. My imagination had conjured up all sorts of outlandish dwellings for Fitzroy, so I was surprised to discover that his house turned out to be a tiny white-painted cottage with a dark-blue front door, situated almost exactly in the middle of a row of identical buildings that faced a small park. Not knowing what I should bring with me – this being my first ever dinner date – I had bought a bunch of carnations from the flower stall next to Streatham station. When Fitzroy opened the door, he seemed amused that I had brought him flowers. He stepped away from the entrance and waved me into a functional room painted a brilliant white. One wall was covered with built-in shelves, filled with books and journals, with a space in the middle that housed a wooden desk. A neat stack of hand-written papers held down by a paperweight sat on the desk, alongside a blue china jug filled with pens and pencils, and a portable typewriter. Beneath the window was a proper hi-fi, not the old-fashioned kind of record player like the one we'd had at home, but one with a turntable and an amplifier, and either side of them, sitting on the off-white carpet, were two large speakers and hundreds of neatly stacked records. On the far side of the room, in front of a closed-off fireplace, there was a two-seater maroon-coloured leather sofa. A brown corduroy beanbag and a chunky black coffee table completed the furniture.

'Let me take those,' Fitzroy said, holding his hand out for the flowers.

I handed them to him and smoothed my dress, wondering whether to sit or follow him into the kitchen, which I could see through the doorway opposite.

'What would you like to drink, Erna?' he said, disappearing through the doorway.

I didn't know what to say. The first thing that came into my mind was rum, but that didn't seem ladylike.

'How about some wine?' he called from inside the kitchen. 'I've got a bottle of red one of my students gave me.'

I had a sudden memory of the foaming Lambrusco that Sean had uncorked that night in his room at Sussex Uni.

'Yes, that would be lovely, thank you,' I said.

I gazed at the bookshelves and was proud to recognise several books that I'd read as part of my degree course. At least I wouldn't be completely out of my depth. But I couldn't see a single work of fiction.

'Here you go,' Fitzroy said, returning from the kitchen and handing me a brimming wine glass. He raised the one he was holding. 'Here's to…' he looked at me quizzically, 'well, what shall we drink to?'

'Us,' I said, clinking my glass against his. I could smell something spicy wafting through the doorway. 'What are you cooking?' I said, taking a sip of the wine.

His white teeth gleamed in a broad smile. 'I'm making run down, sister!' he said, his Jamaican accent suddenly much more obvious.

'Oh, my Lord,' I said, 'food of the gods!'

An hour later, while Fitzroy cleared the plates from the tiny kitchen table, I went upstairs to find the bathroom. This really was a two-up, two-down cottage, but I liked it very much. It had a homely feel. I gazed at my face in the bathroom mirror. The wine had gone to my head and I felt a bit giddy.

'Well, Erna,' I said to myself, 'you better slow yourself down, girl, or you're going to make a mess of this evening.'

Fitzroy had been a charming host so far, but I still felt jittery, as if this was my first time all over again. I splashed cold water on my face and dried it with the rough blue towel that hung behind the door. It had a heavy perfumed smell that I couldn't place, and for a moment I wondered what on earth I was doing. Then I adjusted my dress and walked back downstairs to the sound of Bob Marley singing 'Stir It Up'. Fitzroy was sitting on the sofa with his feet resting on the bean bag, nodding his head in time with the music. He stood up when I entered the room, took hold of my hand and started dancing with me. Then he pulled me closer and I closed my eyes. I felt his lips against mine.

Fitzroy's bedroom overlooked the road and was lit only by the street lamp opposite. We tumbled on to the bed in a tangle of limbs and clothes. I let my hands run over his warm, hard-muscled body while he kissed me from my neck down to my navel. He ran a finger down my cheek and then kissed me on the lips, gently at first and then he thrust his tongue deep into my mouth. I tasted the flavours of run down and wine. Our movements, synchronised to the beat of the music vibrating through the floor, sped up, and then Fitzroy entered me. I let out a gasp of half-pleasure, half-shock. He was much larger than Sean had been, and far more self-assured. As Fitzroy drove into me, I felt like I was sinking into a whirlpool of deliciously satiated lust. Maybe it wasn't fair on Sean, but this was what I had been dreaming of throughout my teenage years. When I came back to myself, Fitzroy was panting beside me and both of our bodies were covered in sweat. He turned to look at me, his eyes and teeth glinting in the faint light.

'You're mine now, Erna,' he smiled. Then he closed his eyes and seemed to fall immediately asleep.

I gazed at his handsome profile, wondering what exactly that comment meant, and whether I liked the implication of it, or not. But before I could make up my mind, I too closed my eyes and succumbed to the warm embrace of the bed.

I woke to the morning light streaming through the window. I could feel Fitzroy's long body beside me. I closed my eyes and listened to the deep rhythm of his breathing. All sorts of thoughts flitted through my head, but foremost was the desire to call Jennifer and tell her everything that had happened since I last saw her.

I felt Fitzroy stir and looked sideways at him. He smiled, then yawned and stretched his arms wide, before rolling over and kissing me full on the lips. Then he sat up and climbed out of the bed.

'I'm going to make some coffee,' he said, 'want some?'

'Yes, please.' I smiled, leaning up on one elbow.

As he left, I lay back in the bed and gazed at the white ceiling. There was a small tan-coloured damp patch that reminded me of the outline of my island. I could hear Fitzroy rattling about downstairs and then the thump of reggae, followed by the enticing smell of coffee. A few minutes later, he appeared in the doorway holding two white mugs. He placed one of the mugs on the bedside table next to me and then walked round the bed and climbed back in holding the other one.

'What would you like to do this morning?' he said, taking a sip of his coffee. 'I was thinking maybe we could go to Brixton market.'

'Oh, so no students to teach then?' I said archly.

'No, no students today,' he laughed.

'Well, yes, then. I'd like that very much.'

He put his mug down and reached over and kissed me long and hard. When he'd finished he looked into my eyes. 'I man am grateful to be your first, Erna,' he said. 'It is a blessing.'

I sat upright in the bed and stared at him. 'What makes you think that?' I said.

His brow furrowed. 'What?' he asked, sitting upright and staring back at me.

'I mean, you're not my first.'

'Who took you, then?' he said, almost angrily.

'That's none of your business,' I replied, feeling angry and confused at the same time.

'You led me on, Erna!' he exclaimed.

'I beg your pardon?' I replied. 'I did nothing of the sort!'

He looked at me, almost with sadness and shook his head. 'Jamaican girls,' he said, sucking his teeth. 'I should have known!'

'God, you sound just like Sean!' I said.

'Sean? Who's Sean?' he said. 'The man who took you first?'

'Yes,' I replied. 'A self-centred bloody Irishman!'

Fiztroy's eyes were wide in shock. 'A white man?' he said, climbing out of the bed and facing me. 'You mean to say I'm following a white man?'

'Yes, a white man,' I replied. 'For God's sake, Fitzroy, does it really matter?'

'I think you better leave, Erna,' he said.

I couldn't quite believe what I was hearing, but when I looked at him standing there, his body stiff and his eyes hard in his face, I realised he was deadly serious. I jumped out of the bed and pulled my clothes on while he stood and watched me. Part of me wanted to sob, but another part of me, the proud granddaughter of Miss Melba, refused to give him the satisfaction. I looked at him one more time, searching his eyes for a hint of compassion, but there was nothing; it was as if he had turned to stone. I opened the door and ran downstairs, picked up my purse from the coffee table and fled.

# Chapter 40

It was already a hot day when I walked through the front door of our house in Payton Street an hour later. My body was sticky with sweat and I longed for a bath and some kind of oblivion, but the phone was ringing and there was no sign of Patsy, so I guessed she must still be in bed. With a sigh, I sat down on one of the dining chairs and lifted the handset to my ear.

'Hello?' I said wearily.

'Erna, it's me,' I heard the voice say.

There was a noise from the stairs and I looked up to see Patsy in a white t-shirt, rubbing her eyes. 'Who is it?' she said.

'Auntie Madge,' I replied, turning back to the receiver. 'What is it, Auntie?'

I thought I could hear a catch in her voice. 'Erna,' she said, 'I don't know how to break it to you darlin', but it's your mother.'

'What? What about my mother?' I asked. I stared at Patsy who was looking at me expectantly.

'Lord, it's a terrible, terrible thing,' Auntie Madge said.

I could hear that she was crying now and tears sprang from my eyes involuntarily too.

'What happened?' I asked her.

'I'm so sorry to tell you this, Erna,' Auntie Madge replied, 'but last night Miss Violet took her own life.'

I put the phone down on the table. Patsy was standing next to me now. I gazed up at her pretty face and she burst into tears. I stood up and we hugged each other tight. Then Patsy buried her head in my chest.

'It's Mum, isn't it?' she said.

I nodded and felt her body convulse. Through my tears, I gazed at the red roses that had withered in the vase and wondered why I hadn't thrown them away yet. I must do that now, I thought. I'd often wondered about this situation and how I would feel. Would I be upset? Would I miss her? The answer that always came back was a vehement 'no'. But at no point had I ever wished death on my mother. The realisation that we would never have an opportunity to resolve our differences hit me hard, and I found myself weeping like the child who wept for the loss of her beloved grandmother only a few years before. Now, I had no grandmother and no one to call mother either.

That afternoon, Patsy and I made our way to our Auntie Madge's house. A number of other family members had already arrived to console us, as well as to start making plans with Auntie Madge and Uncle Herbie about Mother's funeral.

When we arrived, there was little reaction from the children – none of them seemed able to comprehend the enormity of what had taken place. The twins greeted us and went straight back to whatever game they were playing, and Clifton just said, 'We know, Erna,' before hugging me and Patsy in turn.

All thoughts of my night with Fitzroy were buried beneath the turmoil that had followed, and right now all I felt was numb. But I knew I couldn't break down; I had to be practical, for my siblings' sake, if not my own. I looked at Auntie Madge's kind face and drew my strength from her.

'Girls, come and help me sort out some dishes for the food,' Auntie Madge said, 'there's plenty of mouths to feed.'

We followed her into the kitchen, where she handed us each a tray of hard dough bread to butter.

'Best to keep yourselves busy,' she said, picking up a knife and starting to butter a slice herself. 'I know this is probably a hard time to think about anything,' she continued, 'but what kind of send-off you think your mother would want? I mean, did she want to be buried, or cremated?'

'I don't know, Auntie Madge,' I replied. 'I think Mother's original intention was not to die at all. She used to go on about being one of the chosen few.'

Auntie Madge looked at me with a slight smile.

'But, seriously, if you feel it matters, I would say she would want to be buried. Cremation isn't an island thing. What do you think, Pats?'

'I wouldn't fancy either option,' Patsy replied. 'But if I absolutely had to choose then it would be to be buried. At least we can go visit then.'

'I agree,' Auntie Madge nodded.

'But the manner of Violet's death is most disturbing,' said Uncle Herbie, who had joined us in the kitchen. He shook his head vigorously. 'I hope it doesn't preclude a proper Church burial.'

'Now, now, it will be fine. The Lord knows she was an innocent woman,' Auntie Madge scolded him.

The fact was, as Auntie Madge went on to explain, my mother died from internal haemorrhaging, two hours after jumping from the roof of the psychiatric wing she was housed in.

'How on earth did she even get up there?' Patsy asked me later, when we were alone in the front room.

'Apparently, she escaped from her ward while the staff were dealing with another patient. Then she climbed to the top of the fire escape and jumped before anyone could reach her,' I said.

It was a horrifying death to comprehend, and for the first time I felt I had a glimpse into the agony that my mother must have been going through to take her own life. At the same time, I felt angry that life had failed her so badly.

'Surely there'll be some kind of enquiry?' Patsy said. 'Something like that shouldn't happen in a hospital.'

'Oh, yes, they'll have to do an inquest,' I replied.

'Well, at least Mum is out of her misery now,' Patsy said, with a shrug of her thin shoulders.

I looked at her in surprise.

'I wish we could go back to a time long before all of this,' she said. 'Back to our island. Back to our grandparents. Long before we even knew that the ugly Satan devil man existed.'

'I have wished that almost every day since I arrived here,' I said.


I returned to our little house in Streatham later that night, leaving Patsy to help Auntie Madge. She had complained bitterly, but I desperately needed to be on my own for a while and, in the end, she seemed happy to remain with Clifton, Sonny and, particularly, the twins, who always showered her with affection.

As soon as I got home, I went straight to bed and fell into a troubled sleep.


Sunday morning, I was up bright and early. I had got into the habit of writing to Grandpa Sippa on a Sunday. I went downstairs and made a coffee, before settling on the edge of the bed, with notepaper and pen.

*June 1975*

*Dear Grandpa Sippa,*

*I hope when these few lines of mine reach you they will find you well. I know Auntie Madge sent you a telegram about Miss Violet passing. It makes me sad, Grandpa Sippa, that I hardly ever seem to have any good news to tell you.*

It's a terrible time for us here at the moment. With Miss Violet gone, it means my brothers and sisters are orphans now, but Auntie Madge and Uncle Herbie are doing a great job of looking after Clifton, Sonny and the twins. Patricia and I are living on our own now, in a lovely house that my friend Jennifer's mother found for us, and we can look after ourselves, although, if truth be told, Patsy can be difficult sometimes, Grandpa. But I don't complain because I am sure things will work out for the best, despite everything that's happened.

We haven't started planning Miss Violet's burial yet because we have to wait for the inquest to be completed. I feel bad, Grandpa, because even though I am sad that Miss Violet has gone, I know that I didn't love her like a daughter should love a mother. In fact, I never really thought of her as my mother. She was not like Grandma Melba, who felt like she was my real mother, and this has never changed, Grandpa. I still miss her every day.

On a more positive note, I am still studying hard and really enjoying my course, although this does mean that I haven't had time to find myself a husband yet. I hope some day that I do meet someone, because I would like to have a long, happy marriage like you and Grandma Melba. But it's not easy to find a husband in England, Grandpa. All the nice men seem to have girlfriends, or they're already married, and the single ones seem nothing but trouble. I don't know why I am even telling you this, it's not like you can do anything about it. But I do want you to know that my happy memories of you and Grandma Melba are what keep me going through all the dark times.

I have enclosed ten pounds for you. I hope it can help with something you need. I will write again soon, hopefully with some good news. Please say hello to Miss Blossom from me.

*May God bless you, Grandpa.*
*Your loving granddaughter,*
*Erna*


I put the pen down and stared out of the window at the street, tears blurring my eyes. My heart ached for Grandma Melba's comforting presence. She would have known how to deal with Fitzroy and Miss Violet's death, and everything else. No matter what the situation, Grandma Melba had a practical way of handling it. The only other person I knew like this was my best friend and I couldn't believe I'd waited this long to speak to her. I picked up the phone and called her straight away.

'Jen, I need to see you right now,' I said as soon as she answered. 'Can you come over?'

'I'm on my way,' she replied.

Half an hour later, the doorbell rang. I ran to the door and flung it wide open.

'What on earth's the matter, Erna?' Jennifer said as soon as she saw my face.

'Oh, Jen,' I cried, collapsing into her arms, 'it's all too much.'

'Come on,' Jennifer said, guiding me to the sofa. She sat down next to me, put an arm round my shoulder and handed me a scrunched up tissue that she found in her jacket pocket.

'Tell me what's happened,' she said.

Between violent sobs, everything poured out of me: Fitzroy, Sean, my mother's suicide, Patsy, the ugly Satan devil man – I held nothing back. When I'd finished, Jennifer stared at me, shaking her head.

'It's almost too much to take in, Erna,' she said. 'But what I don't understand is why you didn't tell me any of this before?'

'I couldn't, Jen,' I replied, wiping my eyes. 'While I was in the middle of it, I felt like I just had to keep going and, somehow, I'd get through it all, but if I stopped, then I'd break down. Do you understand?'

'Not really,' she said, with a small laugh.

I looked at her smiling face and then I laughed too. It was such an incredible tale of woe it all felt suddenly ludicrous, as if it had happened to someone else and not to me.

'Come on,' Jennifer said, standing up, 'I'm taking you out for a treat.'

'Oh, God, I must look a right state,' I said.

'You look as beautiful as ever, Erna.'

On Streatham High Road we found a Wimpy that was open. We sat down and without hesitation ordered knickerbocker glories and coffee. The huge ice-cream desserts arrived in glasses that were nearly as high as our heads. After a minute of silence, during which we demolished these fantastic creations of sweetness, I put my spoon down with a contented sigh and stared at my friend.

'Did you ever read *Tess of the D'Urbervilles*?' I asked her.

'No,' Jennifer said, 'should I have?'

'Well, it's just that I feel like I'm mirroring her life, in a weird kind of way.'

'Oh, is that bad, then?' Jennifer said.

'Well, yes,' I replied, 'she gets hung in the end!'

'Hmm, definitely bad then,' Jennifer agreed, licking her spoon.

We paid our bill and then strolled arm in arm through the quiet streets to Streatham Common. Its green spaces were busy with gaggles of young men playing football and people strolling along like us or walking their dogs. I looked up at the cloudless blue sky and sighed.

'Life always goes on, doesn't it, Jen,' I said.

'It always does, Erna.'

Then she grabbed my hand and pulled me towards one of the impromptu football matches.

'Come on,' she cried, 'let's show 'em how to do it!'

'No!' I cried, resisiting her pull, as tears started to run down my face. But they were tears of laughter, not sadness.

# Chapter 41

Mother's funeral, organised with heartfelt enthusiasm by Auntie Madge and Uncle Herbie, turned out to be a typical Caribbean affair, attended by well over one hundred and fifty relatives and friends – some of whom I'd met at family get-togethers over the years, but many others whom I had no idea even existed. People came from as far away as Birmingham, Coventry, even Bristol. And they came in every shade of black and brown. The only people conspicuous by their absence were Mother's church brethren, of whom not a single one showed up. There was no nine night like we had for Grandma Melba, because we'd waited nearly three weeks for the coroner to complete his report, and nine nights weren't exactly allowed in England, anyway. But despite Mother's antipathy towards the world she found herself living in, she was given a proper, food-filled, rum-soaked, reggae-rousing send-off. And, of course, her favourite tune – 'Honour Your Mother and Your Father' – topped the playlist.

I wondered what she would have made of it all, since she was not a woman who saw much to be celebrated in life. I guess it's a good thing the dead can't talk, I thought. And, in happy contrast to her gloomy world-view, all her relatives that she'd grown up with had nothing but nice things to say about her.

'I wish we could have known that side of her,' Patsy said to me, after the speeches had finished and the dancing had started.

'I agree, Pats,' I said, 'and I'm really glad to know that there was a time in her life when she was actually happy. I've spent so much time feeling angry with her and blaming her for choosing the life she did, but now all I feel is sorry for her.'

Patsy stared at me over the rim of her glass of rum punch.

'I feel sorry for her,' she said, 'but I can never forgive her for what she allowed to happen to me.'

'No, I understand, Pats,' I said.

Nevertheless, as the evening wore on and the drinks flowed, and the conversation became lyrical, I began to piece together an entirely different picture of my mother – as an interesting and intriguing woman. In all my time of knowing her, she had never spoken about herself to me. But, despite having given birth to six children, being married to a maniac and being mentally ill for years, she had still managed to retain her youthful body shape and perfect skin. Her only exercise, which I didn't think was undertaken in any conscious sense, was when she would go off walking for miles, although she mostly did this when she was suffering from some kind of breakdown. Patsy and I had often whispered to each other about the way men would look at her when we accompanied her to the market, or even to church, but she never gave any indication that she was aware of these admirers. It still came as a shock, however, when an older cousin, whose name I managed to recall was Pamela, took me aside and confided that my mother wasn't quite as innocent as she seemed.

She took a long drag from her cigarette and then fixed me with a serious look. 'You know, Auntie Violet had a bit of a wild streak about her,' she whispered.

'What was that?' I said, not sure I'd heard her right over the booming music. She also seemed to have partaken a little too freely of the punch.

'Everyone has a little mystery about them, ain't that so, cousin?' she persisted.

'Pamela, I wish I knew what you were talking about!' I replied.

'I'm not talking ill of Auntie,' Pamela said, taking my hand and pulling me towards the garden. 'Honestly, I wouldn't do that, but I tell you that the only time I ever saw her happy was when she started something with this young guy called Barry. They really cared for each other, you know, even though she was years older than him. He was happy and she was happy. That wasn't long before you came up.'

I gazed at the other mourners in the garden to make sure no one could overhear us before I replied. 'Are you saying that my mum was having an affair?' I hissed.

'Barry is the twins' father, Erna. Auntie Violet got pregnant when your step-dad wasn't even in the country.'

For a moment I thought I was going to faint. I took a step backwards and reached out towards a handy branch to steady myself. 'Jesus Christ, Pamela!' I said.

'Well, I thought you should know, now that you're old enough to handle it and they're both gone,' she said. 'No one can hurt her now, can they?'

'You're saying that my mother had an affair?' I repeated.

'Yes, she did, Erna. Auntie Violet had a really unhappy marriage, but then you know that. Everyone could see that, and when Mr Williamson realised that the twins weren't his, well, if things could have become worse between them, that was like the final straw. I'm not sorry to say it, Erna, but I didn't like him and could never make myself call him Uncle. Anyway, Auntie had to give up the man she loved. They hid the affair from their church people, but close family knew, and not everyone blamed her. It was after she finished the affair with Barry that the breakdowns started coming thick and fast and her hospital admissions got longer and longer, until, according to what Auntie Madge told my mum, her brain just scrambled.'

'Excuse me, but I have to sit down,' I said.

I fumbled for a garden chair and sat heavily on it, causing its back legs to sink into the grass, which nearly tipped me over.

'Do you mind if I have one of your cigarettes, Pamela?'

'Not at all, Erna,' Pamela said. 'It's a lot to take in, I know that.'

Suddenly my mother's behaviour began to make some kind of warped sense. It was as though she saw in both Patsy and me something of herself that she didn't like, or maybe even something of herself that she had lost. Weirdly, I began to feel a kind of respect for my mother. It was heartening to learn that she probably wasn't okay living in a mentally and physically abusive marriage, and that she had found some sort of courage for a short time to do something about it.

Pamela leant down and lit my cigarette with a silver lighter that she took from her handbag.

I drew deep on the cigarette. The foul taste and the smoke hit me simultaneously. I dropped it to the ground, coughing and spluttering. 'Well, that didn't make me feel any better,' I said to my cousin, when I recovered.

'Its not the best habit to develop,' she laughed.

I reached out and took hold of Pamela's hand. 'Please, I beg you, Pamela, they might be dead, but the twins and my brothers and sister are very much alive, and I don't think they ever need to know any of this,' I said.

'To be honest, Mum would never speak to me again if she knew that I'd even told you,' Pamela said.

'Thank you, Pamela. Thank you for telling me. You don't know how much this has helped me.'

'No problem, darling,' Pamela said, patting my arm.

I watched her totter back towards the house, still managing to look elegant in her black crêpe dress, and said a silent prayer of gratitude for being part of such a wonderful, rich, dysfunctional family.

# Chapter 42

Patsy and I stayed with our aunt and uncle and the younger children for a few days following our mother's funeral. We needed family around us. A feeling of profound emptiness had injected itself into my head and my entire body. Patsy appeared equally shaken up and unhappy.

Our mother's difficulties had weighed much heavier on us than either of us had realised. We had both battled in our own inept ways to try and look after her, even when she made it clear that she didn't welcome any of our attention.

'I know its hard,' our aunt said, over breakfast on the third day of our stay. 'She was my little sister.' Her eyes were glassy with the tears she was holding back. 'It shouldn't have been her time yet, but God knows why he makes the decisions that he does.'

'I think I'll take the boys and the twins for a little run on the common,' Patsy said, getting up from the table.

'You go ahead, Patricia,' Auntie Madge encouraged. 'They could all do with some extra TLC right now.'

As soon as Patsy disappeared from view, I turned to Auntie Madge. 'There's something I wanted to ask you,' I said.

Auntie Madge raised an eyebrow.

Taking a deep breath, I began, 'I wondered if you know how my mother became pregnant with me?'

She took a long sip of her coffee. 'That's quite a question,' she said, after a moment. And then she began to tell me about how Mother had worked for the Dees, and how she'd come to be pregnant and had gone to see the Obeah man. 'When it was clear there was no stopping you coming into this world, she told me all that happened on that day. Her exact words to me were, "Him just throw me down."'

It took Auntie Madge a long time to tell me all the details that my mother had told her, and as I listened tears fell freely down my face. By the end of her story, I was sobbing, and all Auntie Madge could say to me was, 'Hush yourself, child. God has a purpose for us all. He knows why he sends us these trials.'

Christmas came and went. Although our mother was no longer around to object to its celebration, Patsy and I had long accepted that Christmas just wasn't done in our family. Like our mother, we pretty much ignored all the jollities that seemed to spill out everywhere around us. Instead, we decided to claim New Year as our own, so, on the thirty-first of December, Patsy and I stayed up to celebrate the arrival of 1976 at home with a bottle of cheap cava a colleague at work had given me as a Christmas present.

I was feeling very happy at the prospect of having an extra day off work to put my feet up and pig out in front of the telly. Patsy had actually made an effort to clean up the house, and for once we managed to get through almost the entire evening without an argument. I was cutting her plenty of slack, because even though she seemed to have handled the loss of our mother with little outward sign of it affecting her, I knew that deep down she was still very damaged from everything that she'd been through. And in the weeks leading up to Christmas I'd become concerned that she seemed to have lost her zest for life.

Up till then, she'd spent all the money she got from the dole on women's magazines and told me that she was still pursuing her dream of becoming a model – though I saw no evidence that she was doing anything about it; she spent most of her time at home, absorbed in the words and pictures of other women's lives. At the beginning of the summer, she had started going out on the odd weekend, dressed to the nines in outfits that she'd cannibalised from the clothes she found at the charity shops on Streatham High Road. One skill she'd learnt from our mother was sewing, and I often marvelled at the creations she conjured from scraps of material, or dresses that were far too big for her. Some nights she didn't return home at all, but when I tried to confront her about it, she would scream at me to mind my own business, and then lock herself in her room.

Tonight, though, she seemed happy to be at home with me, and we were quickly drunk on the cava and giggling like schoolgirls watching some puerile comedy on the telly.

'Well, do you have any New Year's resolutions?' I asked her, as I drained the dregs from the bottle into our glasses.

Patsy looked at me with amazement, as if I'd asked her if she wanted to be an astronaut, or something. Then she swallowed what was left in her glass and stood up. 'I haven't got any resolutions,' she said.

'Really? There's nothing at all you want to achieve this year?' I persisted.

'No, absolutely nothing,' she said, stretching and yawning at the same time. 'I'm tired. I'm going to go to bed.'

'Don't you want to wait up to see Big Ben?'

'I don't care for no Babylon Big Ben,' she retorted.

'Huh, where did that come from?' I said.

'Where did what come from?'

'I've never heard you express a political opinion before,' I replied.

Patsy shrugged her shoulders. 'Maybe I'm just taking an interest in my roots and culture,' she said.

I eyed her in amazement. 'Well, I'm very pleased to hear that,' I said. 'It's good to know you're interested in something apart from fashion.'

'Trust you to take the piss,' Patsy snarled.

I put my glass down and stood up.

'I'm sorry, Pats,' I said. 'I didn't mean to be sarcastic. I'm pleased, I really am.'

'Well, I'm glad you're pleased, sister,' she said as she headed for the stairs.

'I am,' I replied. 'And, for what it's worth, I'm looking forward to this year. My degree is going really well and I've decided to talk to my tutor about how I can go on to train as a teacher.'

Patsy eyed me from the bottom step. 'You'd make a good teacher,' she said. 'You're good at bossing people around.'

I caught the hint of a smile on her face and burst out laughing as I watched her clump her way upstairs to her bedroom. It felt like a small victory. But as winter ended and spring began, and everything started blooming again, my relationship with Patsy seemed to worsen, not get better.

It was a blustery evening in March, well beyond midnight, and the third consecutive night that I had had to get out of bed to open the door to stop Patsy's incessant banging.

'What on God's earth is going on with you, Pats?' I said, noting her dishevelled state. 'You've got to tell me, right now.'

'Nothing,' she said, pushing past me into the house.

'Well, just so you know,' I shouted at her retreating back, 'I was accosted by the neighbours when I got home from work this evening, and they said that any more of that loud music you play all day long and they'll be calling the police. And what have you done with your key this time?' I added in exasperation.

Patsy stopped halfway up the stairs and turned to face me. 'It's none of your business,' she shouted, 'and you best keep out of things that don't concern you.'

'But you've made it my business, Pats,' I replied. 'I'm exhausted from getting up night after night to prevent you from breaking down the front door, not to mention waking up the whole street. And how many keys have I replaced now? This can't continue, Pats. We could end up losing this place, and then what?'

Patsy's glazed eyes registered little interest in anything I was saying.

'You look terrible, Pats,' I said. 'Do you need a doctor, or something?'

'No doctors. I'm okay,' she slurred.

'Well, get some rest then,' I said, 'and we'll try to sort out whatever it is in the morning.'

I followed her upstairs and climbed into my bed, but it was hard to go back to sleep, especially as I could hear Patsy pacing around in her room. At some point I must have drifted off, because I awoke with a start and saw from the illuminated dial on my alarm clock that it was five in the morning. All I could hear was the wind sighing in the plane trees that lined the street. I got up and crept across the landing to Patsy's room, but before I could even open her door I felt a cold breeze from downstairs. I ran to the top of the stairs and looked down to see the front door swinging open. Patsy was nowhere to be seen.

After a week had gone by and she still hadn't returned home, I called Auntie Madge. I was consumed with worry, but Auntie Madge seemed surprisingly indifferent.

'It's either drugs or men, or both,' she said. 'Your sister was here a couple of days ago demanding what she described as "her inheritance" from your parents' property. She was on edge the whole time. She said she needed money for food, but I don't believe it was hunger that was making her behave so badly.'

'But she gets money from the dole, Auntie Madge. It's not much, but I pay for all our food, and everything else. I hope you didn't give her anything?' I said.

'I am afraid I did, Erna,' Auntie Madge replied. 'I didn't feel that I had a choice. She was in an awful state and I didn't want the younger children to get wind of it. And there was a man leaning up against the car she arrived in. I was caught on the hop so I gave her twenty pounds, which was all I had in my purse. I tried to tell her that there were problems with the house, but I don't know how much of that she took in.'

I had no idea that she had changed her mind about wanting money from the house. Mother had left everything to her six children in her will, and her husband having died intestate meant the house and everything in it had belonged to her. But Patsy had been adamant that she wanted nothing that came from either her mother or her father. Uncle Herbie had been dealing with the sale of the house, but it was in such a bad condition that he'd had to arrange for it to be renovated first, so there was no inheritance for any of us yet. Anyway, I was pretty sure that drugs were at the bottom of Patsy's change of heart, because the way she'd been acting before she disappeared was as if she'd had a complete personality change. But the one thing she had never done before, at least not to my knowledge, was bring a man to the house.

'Who was this fellow who was with her then?' I asked.

'Oh, he was one of those rasta people,' Auntie Madge said. 'He told me he was taking care of Patsy, helping her through her difficulties, though I very much doubt it.'

'So, are you thinking this man doesn't mean Patsy any good, Auntie?'

'Erna, I can only tell you what I have seen with my own two eyes. I just don't trust these rasta people. For all I know, your sister may have got caught up in something she may not be able to get herself out of. Can you believe she didn't even ask after the children?'

I suddenly felt guilty, as if this was all somehow my fault. 'I am so sorry about Patsy's behaviour, Auntie Madge,' I said. 'I promise you, I'll give her a good talking to when she comes home.'

'Erna, your sister is a grown woman,' Auntie Madge replied, 'and you don't have to apologise for her actions. She's going to have to learn to take responsibility for herself at some point.'

It was the end of April before Patsy finally showed up back at our house. I had spent nearly every night waiting up for her, and then late one Friday evening, just after I'd gone to bed, I heard the tell-tale scraping around the front door lock as Patsy struggled to insert her key. I leapt from my bed, dashed downstairs and pulled the front door open. Patsy pushed passed me, her head hunched on to her chest, and staggered towards the kitchen, before tripping headlong over the pile of books that I'd left beside the dining table. She muttered something to herself before crawling to the sofa and promptly passing out. I found a blanket in the cupboard under the stairs, which I draped over her, before heading back to bed, feeling safe in the knowledge that there was no way she'd be getting up any time soon.

She showed no sign of waking the following morning and I thought it best to leave her to sleep off whatever it was she'd taken. It was early evening when she finally surfaced and wandered into the kitchen. Her face was creased in an ugly grimace and her hands trembled as she tried to reach for the mug of strong black coffee I poured for her.

'Let it cool down a bit,' I said, placing the mug on the counter.

'Erna,' Patsy said in a pained voice, ignoring what I'd said and picking up the mug, 'you have to understand, I've told you before, I'm not like you. I'm tarnished goods. Dirty goods. The only people who want me are others like me.'

I was so horrified I couldn't think what to say to her in reply. Patsy glared at me for a moment before continuing.

'Look, I have to go, Erna. I need my thing.'

She attempted to walk out of the kitchen, but she only made it as far as the doorway.

'You need your fix, is that what you mean?'

'No, Erna, I don't need no fix. You got me all wrong, girl.'

'Well, at least let me help, Pats,' I said. 'I could arrange for you to talk to someone. A psychiatrist perhaps.'

'So that's what you think is it?' Patsy railed, this time managing to keep her balance as she headed into the front room. 'My little problem, is it? My life gets totally screwed over and I get the blame, and my own sister tells me I'm mad. Thanks for nothing, Erna. You and your psycho-whatever can fuck right off!'

'Patsy,' I cried, chasing after her and gripping her hand to prevent her from leaving, 'I'm trying to help you, can't you understand that?'

But Patsy seemed oblivious to what I was saying. 'You must be mistaking me for Mum,' she continued, 'but let me tell you right now, no one is going to bang me up in some crazy hellhouse for the rest of my life. I'd rather be dead. I used to believe you really cared, Erna, but you know what? You just wanted to fucking gloat all along. The only person you really care about is Erna. You're Mum's daughter alright! Fucking only care about yourself.'

I grabbed Pasty's arm in frustration, but she shook it loose.

'Pats,' I shouted, 'how can you say such horrible things, when all I have ever done is try my best to help you? I don't know what more I could have done, and I certainly don't have a clue what to do now. That's why I think you need to talk to someone who can help you get that stuff out of your head, so you can put it behind you once and for all. I'm your sister, Patsy, not some bloody doctor, and I love you, don't you understand?'

When she didn't respond, I tried to grab her again, but once more she squirmed from my grasp.

'Pats!' I pleaded.

'No, Erna, I have to go. I've had enough. I have to go.'

She headed towards the front door before spinning around to face me. She pulled herself up to her full height and addressed me in a low, calm voice. 'We waited, Erna. We waited. Clifton, Sonny and me. We thought Grandpa Sippa and Grandma Melba were going to come and get us. Come and take us back to the village. Sometimes when I was in the house doing one of the endless chores that my horrible Aunt Ruby piled on me, I would swear I could hear Grandma Melba's voice out in the yard. I would rush to the window, but it was never her. They never came, Erna. No one came.'

I listened to my sister's words with tears streaming down my face, but I had no idea what else I could say to make her feel better, apart from to tell her what I remembered.

'Pats, for months we had no idea where you'd been taken. Grandpa Sippa and Grandma Melba never gave up searching for you, but what could they do? They were old and there was no way for them to cover the whole island looking for you. When they finally found out where you were, there was still nothing they could do. Your father had every right to take you. You were his children.'

'Whatever, Erna. The fact is, right now, I really don't care who knew what, when.' And with that she strode out of the door and slammed it behind her with all the force she could muster.

I stared numbly at the still vibrating door. Then I dragged myself back to the kitchen and sat down and wept. Her coffee was still on the counter where she'd left it, untouched.

Over the next month, Patsy apparently returned home several times while I was at work, her rapidly reducing wardrobe being the only clue I had to her elusive visits. She was never far from my thoughts, though, and I constantly wondered where she was and whether she was okay. Sometimes, I would imagine a policeman turning up at the door to tell me that her body had been found in a ditch somewhere. In the end, I felt I had no choice but to blot out my worries all together. My exams were rapidly approaching and I was spending every hour when I wasn't at work revising for them.

I was sitting at the dining table one evening immersed in my studies when the phone rang. As soon as I answered it, I recognised Auntie Madge's voice and my heart skipped a beat. I was convinced she was going to tell me something bad had happened to Patsy. I took a deep breath and steeled myself for the worst, but I was surprised to detect a note of joy in Auntie Madge's voice.

'We've sold the house!' she was saying.

I had to shake my head, so uncertain that I'd heard her right, but she continued in the same happy vein.

'Your uncle signed over the deeds with the solicitor this morning,' she continued, 'so there's going to be some money for all of you.'

'Oh my God, that's fantastic, Auntie,' I said, as the truth of what she was saying finally got through to me. 'Thank you so much, both of you!'

'You don't have to thank me,' Auntie Madge said, 'you children deserve it after all you've been though. It's not a fortune, Erna, but there should be about a thousand pounds for each of you, after all the costs have been covered and a little put aside for the younger children's care.'

One thousand pounds? It was a fortune to me. I finished the call and went into the kitchen to make myself a cup of coffee. Suddenly, a world of possibilities opened up before me and, as I waited for the kettle to boil, a parade of fantasies passed through my mind. I saw Jennifer and me traversing the globe,

310

looking sophisticated as we swanned around art galleries and ancient ruins. I went into the front room with my coffee, sat down at the table and picked up the copy of Chaucer's *Canterbury Tales* that I'd been reading. 'The Merchant's Tale' was surprisingly bawdy and, despite the difficulty I had with the language, I was enjoying it immensely. I took a deep breath and carried on where I'd left off. One step at a time, I thought.

The following Saturday morning I went downstairs to find an envelope stuck through the letterbox. It was covered in colourful Jamaican stamps, but instead of Grandpa Sippa's spidery handwriting, the address was written in a bold, simple style. I tore the envelope open to discover that the letter was from Grandpa Sippa, but it had been dictated by him to one of his grand-nephews. I instantly wondered if his eyes were starting to fail him.

*May 1976*

*Dear Erna,*

*I hope when these few lines of mine reach you, in the name of the Most High, they will find you well. I am telling this to your cousin Sherwin because my health has gone down and I cannot write no longer as you can see, and I am more or less housebound now. But still, I can't complain.*

*I have not heard from you for a long time now, but I know you England people keep a busy life. My brother Basil and his wife want me to come and live with them in St Catherine, but I am too old now to make that kind of journey. And that place is like going to foreign for me. I am happy here in the village, Erna. Miss Blossom is getting on herself, but she still strong and she treats me well and there are still plenty family around who all help me out best they can. We are both born and bred right here in the village and this is where I want to die and bury. I don't want for a thing and I don't plan to spend my last few days on this earth being a burden to other people. But I long to see you, Erna. I long to see Patricia, Clifton and little Sonny again. But I am beginning to worry in my heart that it's not to be.*

*God's blessing be upon you. Please write when you can.*
*Your grandfather, Sippa.*

My heart ached reading his words. I put the letter on the table and stared out of the window, thinking that the news about the sale of our old family house was providential. I was just about to read it again when I heard a key turn in the lock and looked up in surprise to see Patsy walk through the door. It was an even bigger surprise to see that not only was she completely sober, but she was glowing with health and looking more beautiful than ever. Her attitude hadn't changed, though. She ignored me and walked straight towards the kitchen, so I followed her and watched as she perched daintily on a stool.

'It's good to see you, Pats,' I said. 'How are you doing?'

She surveyed me coolly, as if I was a complete stranger. 'I have nothing to talk about, Erna,' she said, 'not a blessed thing. I guess you must have forgotten our last little catch-up? I don't want to hear anything else from you and I certainly don't want any of your advice.' She got up and opened a cupboard, pulling out a packet of Ritz crackers, which she dipped her hand into. 'In fact,' she continued, 'I just want you to leave me the fuck alone.'

Before she could put the crackers in her mouth, I narrowed the gap between us and slapped her hard across her face. Her eyes opened wide in shock as she clamped a hand to her jaw.

'What the—' she started to say, but I cut across her.

I could feel my body trembling with adrenaline. 'You know what, Patsy,' I said, 'be a victim. The role suits you very well. I am done with you taking out your crap on me. You can piss off and go and live your victim life somewhere else. I will learn to not give a shit, just like you want!'

I stalked out of the kitchen, grabbed my purse and jacket, and exited the house into the summer sunshine. Without thinking where I was going, I ended up at Streatham Common and walked briskly across it towards its southern boundary. When I reached Norwood Grove I turned round and headed back. The inside of my head hurt. I was as angry with Patsy as she was with me. I left the common and headed for a local café where I sat down and ordered a coffee.

Patsy's house keys were lying on the mat when I returned to the house. Every last item of her clothing was gone, as was the little sound system I'd spent nearly a week's wages on. At that moment, I realised that I hadn't had a chance to tell her about our inheritance, or even talk to her about the state of Grandpa Sippa's health. But I shrugged my shoulders. Auntie Madge could tell her about the money, if she ever got in contact with her again. I inhaled deeply, and when I released the breath it was one of pure relief.

# Chapter 43

Living without Patsy freed me in a way that I couldn't have imagined, and although not a week went by when I didn't think of her, I took solace in Auntie Madge's words about Patsy needing to take responsibility for herself. Now I was able to concentrate on my own life again, which included a growing interest in grassroot politics. When the time between my work and my studies allowed, Jennifer and I attended various women's groups that were springing up all over London. Often these were situated in squats, and I started to realise that there was a whole way of living that suited me far better than the one inside the cultural bubble I felt I'd been trapped in for so long. And the idea of championing women's rights was something I was inexorably drawn to. Jennifer and I were determined to make a difference and, while life in London was by no means perfect, I felt more settled than I had done at any time since my arrival. And amidst all these new-found interests, and the many lonely evenings and weekends spent in libraries, at times doing little more than biting my fingernails, I managed to pass my summer exams. I had gone from a village girl with a disrupted education to sustaining myself and being on my way to becoming a Bachelor of the Arts. I felt as though I could move mountains, and to celebrate my exam success Jennifer arranged to take me out. But when I asked her where we were going, she just told me it was a surprise.

When we got off the tube at King's Cross station, I guessed where she was taking me. 'We're going to the Keskidee Centre, aren't we?' I said, as we exited the Underground into the rubbish-strewn streets surrounding the station.

'Oh, you've been there before?' Jennifer asked.

'Yes, with Fitzroy,' I said.

Jennifer stopped walking and turned to face me. 'Shit. Do you want to go somewhere else?'

'No,' I said, 'I'm not going to let anything to do with him ruin our evening out!'

'Good for you,' Jennifer replied, taking my arm, 'we're going to have a wonderful night, I'm sure of it. We're going to see this Nigerian writer, Buchi Emecheta. I heard about her at New Beacon Books. She'll be reading from her new novel. It's called *The Bride Price.*'

'I like the sound of that!' I said.

As we walked arm-in-arm along the gloomy streets that threaded between King's Cross and Islington, I couldn't help noticing the prostitutes soliciting for business and the endless stream of punters' cars cruising up and down looking at them. I shuddered to think that Patsy could have ended up like this and squeezed Jennifer's arm tighter.

'Tell me something,' I said.

'Tell you what?'

'I don't know. Have you been to the Keskidee before?'

'Oh, yes, several times. Mum knows the bloke who founded it, Oscar Abrams. He's Guyanese, like us, so we feel especially proud of it. The keskidee is a beautiful bird native to Guyana, did you know that?'

'No, I didn't,' I said, 'but from now on I shall think of you whenever I hear it.'

'What, because I'm a beautiful Guyanese bird?' Jennifer laughed.

'Exactly!' I said, poking her in the ribs.

The Keskidee was buzzing when we arrived, much like the time before, and we made our way upstairs towards the room where Buchi Emecheta would be reading. As we edged through the crowd on the first-floor landing, I noticed a striking woman in a flowing green-and-blue tie-dyed dashiki, with numerous colourful bangles on her long slender arms and a canary-yellow scarf tied around her greying locks. I was just about to ask Jennifer if she knew who she was, when the woman approached us.

'Jennifer, isn't it?' she said, holding out her hand. 'Yvette is a friend of mine. I'm Monica,' she added, 'Monica Clacken.'

'Oh, yes, I remember you,' Jennifer said, shaking her hand. She turned to me and said, 'And this is my friend Erna. Erna, this is my mum's friend, Monica.'

'Very pleased to meet you, Erna,' Monica smiled, and we shook hands as well.

'Likewise,' I said. 'I love your dress!'

'Thank you, Erna,' she said. 'I think everyone's going in,' she added, 'shall we catch up afterwards?'

'Yes, I'd like that very much,' I gushed, feeling suddenly very young and naïve in the presence of this sophisticated woman.

'What's wrong with you?' Jennifer hissed as we made our way into the room. 'You're blushing like a schoolgirl!'

'Oh, I just feel a bit out of my depth,' I said.

Jennifer pulled me round by the arm to face her. 'Listen to me, Erna,' she said, 'you're just as cultured as anyone else here. You're Erna Mullings, on her way to having a BA Hons, for fuck's sake, and don't you forget it!'

'Yes, Miss Richards,' I replied.

The reading was incredible, and the subject matter – the price of virginity, as if it could ever be commodified – seemed extremely pertinent. We left it in high spirits and wandered out on to the landing, waiting for Monica to come out. While we were standing talking, Jennifer looked downstairs and suddenly grabbed my arm and started pulling me towards the far side of the landing.

'What are you doing?' I asked, shaking her hand off.

'It's your sister!' she hissed.

'What?' I couldn't believe what I was hearing. 'Where?'

'Downstairs, with a man,' she replied.

I felt my heart go cold inside my chest. 'I've got to see,' I said.

I walked back to the top of the stairs and looked down on the crowd in the foyer, and sure enough there was Patsy, looking incredibly chic in a black dress, large hoop earrings and red high heels. Standing next to her, with his arm around her shoulders, was Fitzroy.

For a moment, I thought I might fall down the stairs, so I grabbed hold of the stair rail to steady myself. Then, as I stared down at the glamorous couple, they moved off towards the theatre and disappeared from my view.

Jennifer materialised by my side. 'Are you okay?' she said, touching my arm.

I took several long, deep breaths.

'I'll be okay in a minute,' I said.

Just then Monica appeared in the doorway, scanning the crowd. As soon as she saw us, she walked over, her smile fading when she noticed that I was leaning up against the wall.

'Are you alright, Erna,' she said, 'you look like you've just seen a ghost?'

I took another deep breath and stood upright. 'I have,' I said. 'Two of them.'

'How about we get out of here and go for a drink,' Monica said, 'and then you can tell us what just happened.'

I gripped Jennifer's hand as we followed Monica downstairs. I didn't know if I could handle facing Patsy and Fitzroy together, but the crowd had already entered the theatre and the foyer was empty. When we got out on to the street Monica crossed the road and headed towards a silver-grey Mercedes convertible. Jennifer and I exchanged a glance as Monica unlocked the car. She pulled the driver's seat forward and turned to us and said, 'I'm sorry, one of you will have to squeeze into the back seat, is that okay?'

'Sure, I will,' Jennifer said, climbing in.

I walked around the car and got in the passenger side.

'I thought we could go to this little place around the corner from my house,' Monica said, starting the car with a roar.

'Where do you live then?' I asked, wondering where on earth she was taking us.

'Notting Hill,' she replied as she manoeuvered out of the parking space.

'Um,' I started, despite feeling Jennifer kick me through the seat, 'I'm just a bit worried how we'll get back, we live in South London, you see, and…'

'Oh, don't worry about that,' Monica said, 'you can stay at mine.'

It seemed Monica's word was final, so I sat back and enjoyed the luxury of driving through London with the top down in the most expensive car I'd ever been in, the warm summer breeze blowing through my hair. Twenty minutes later we parked up in a tree-lined square of Georgian houses that, though they looked rather dilapidated, still clung to their former grandeur. In the middle of the square was what appeared to be a small private park fenced off by black railings.

'Welcome to Powis Square,' Monica said, as she let Jennifer out. 'That's my house over there,' she added, pointing to a four-storey stucco-fronted house with a large white portico. 'But first, I promised you girls a drink.'

Just around the corner from the square was a terrace of similar – though even more dilapidated – buildings, the ground floors of which were turned into shops. The fourth one along had the words *Globe Café & Restaurant* written in red above its white-painted front. Although the place appeared to be shut, Monica strode to a battered black side-door and knocked loudly. The door opened and a stocky black man in a green tracksuit top and jeans peered around it. He took one look at Monica, nodded and stood aside to let us in.

We followed her down a narrow stairwell to the smokiest room I had ever been in. It was filled with people of all colours, drinking, talking, playing games and listening to calypso. Monica ordered three glasses of rum and coke with lime from the tiny bar and we found a table next to a group of men playing dominoes. Once we'd sat down, Monica raised her glass and we followed suit, clinking them together.

'So,' Monica said, taking a sip from her drink, 'tell me about those ghosts.'

I looked at Jennifer, trying to decide whether I wanted to talk about my sister and Fitzroy.

Monica watched me and, noting my confusion, raised her glass again. 'Mi seh crick,' she said, in a broad Jamaican accent.

'Mi seh crack!' I replied, and we both started laughing.

'What's the joke?' Jennifer said, looking bemused.

'You're from Jamaica?' I said to Monica.

'Born and bred,' Monica replied. 'I still have a house there, high up in the hills above Kingston.'

'Oh, I'd love to go back,' I said. 'Especially as my Grandpa is so old now, I want to see him before he dies.' It was out of my mouth before I'd thought about it, but it was true. I was desperate to see Grandpa Sippa.

'Well, you must come and stay with me,' Monica said. 'I'm going back there soon, why don't you come?'

'Go on, Erna,' Jennifer urged, 'it will do you the world of good to go home.'

The music changed to up-beat ska and the men on the table next to us slapped their dominoes down with ferocity. I felt as if a great weight had been lifted from me.

'This place is the heart of the carnival,' Monica was saying to Jennifer, 'you must come this year if you haven't been before.'

I looked at the two women sitting opposite me: my best friend and my newest friend. How lucky I am, I thought. And then it dawned on me.

'Babylon Big Ben!' I cried out, banging the table so hard the glasses shook.

Monica and Jennifer turned to me in surprise.

'She must have started seeing him way back then,' I said. 'No wonder she was acting the way she did. She was feeling guilty!'

Suddenly it all made sense. Patsy had been flirting with Fitzroy from the moment he'd turned up on our doorstep, and clearly the poor bastard couldn't resist. Who could? My darling sister was stunning. I was in such a good mood I felt minded to forgive her. I gulped the remains of my drink and stood up. 'Who's for another round?' I said.

My friends drained their glasses and nodded in unison.

I don't know what time we left the Globe, in fact I couldn't recall returning to Monica's house, but I woke in a seductively comfortable bed in an unfamiliar room. Morning light was seeping through thick curtains and my head was pounding. I sat up and noted a sleeping form under the covers of the single bed next to mine, which I assumed must be Jennifer's.

I climbed out of the bed and pulled my dress over my head, then went over to the window and opened the curtains a crack. The window was barred and beyond it was a low white-washed wall topped by trailing plants in earthenware pots. Past them I could just make out the street through black railings, so I guessed I was in the basement of Monica's house.

Outside the bedroom door, I found a small bathroom where I doused my face under the cold tap and then drank from it. Feeling somewhat refreshed I decided to explore further. A few yards along the corridor it turned sharp left where a staircase began and beyond that was a door that led to the back garden. The door was open and sunlight was streaming through it, so I followed my nose and emerged blinking into a large back garden. Monica was sitting at a round wrought-iron table reading *The Guardian*. There was a jug of orange juice on the table, surrounded by plates, glasses, a butter dish, pots of jam and slices of toast in a silver-coloured toast rack.

'Good morning,' Monica said, putting the paper down. 'How are you feeling today?'

'A bit groggy,' I said, 'but I'll live.'

'Sit down and have some breakfast with me,' Monica said, pouring some orange juice into a heavy glass tumbler.

I sat on the wooden chair next to hers and lifted the glass to my lips. The juice was cool and freshly squeezed and tasted heavenly. Birds were chirping busily in the shrubbery that lined the elegant lawn. It was a far cry from my family home in Catford.

'Do you remember our conversation last night?' Monica asked lightly, but I could see straight away that it was important to her.

'No, not really,' I replied, 'it's all a bit blurred.'

'You were talking about why some families hurt the children they've gone to all the trouble of bringing to this country,' she said.

'Oh, was I?' I reached over and buttered a slice of toast and took a bite.

Monica smiled. 'I'm sorry,' she said, 'this sounds a bit like an interrogation! We can talk about it another time.'

Another time? That must mean she wants to see me again, I thought. The thought pleased me. 'No, it's okay,' I said, 'it's a subject close to my heart.'

'Yes, mine too.' She smiled, and took a deep breath before continuing, 'There were thirteen of us, seven girls and six boys. The six youngest were born here, while the rest of us were left on the island, shared out between two sets of grandparents.

I was three when my parents left. My grandmother used to show me a picture of this delicate looking woman. "This is your mother," she would tell me. But I didn't remember her, or my father. Then, when I was eleven, they sent for me. Leaving the island and coming here was such a wrench, I didn't think I'd ever get over it.'

I nodded at the familiarity of her story. 'But you did,' I said.

'Yes,' she sighed, 'I did.'

'And you seem to have done very well for yourself,' I added, with a wry smile, looking round at the grand house behind me.

'I married badly, but I divorced well,' she laughed. She finished her glass of orange juice and then topped up hers and mine from the jug. 'Here's a question for you Erna,' she continued, 'if I were to ask you whether there was anything the people around you could have done at the time to prepare you for coming to England that might have made the whole process easier for you, what would you say?'

I picked up my glass and swished the juice around.

'I don't know,' I said, 'maybe just someone talking to me about it might have helped. I mean, it was a *fait accompli*. I had no say in it whatsoever and everyone around me just accepted it: I was going to England and that was that! Don't get me wrong, it wasn't all bad. I can remember feeling excited, as well as being completely freaked out about it, but that was just about the prospect of seeing my sister and brothers again. The truth is, I was terrified about leaving the island and…' I paused as I relived the moment in my head, the sheer horror of it all '…and coming here was like a nightmare that never seemed to end. I don't believe my mother or my step-father were ready to start living with three children that they hardly knew, and then, when I turned up, it just made everything even worse.' I swallowed my drink and looked at Monica. 'You know, it was so extreme, it felt like my whole world had been pulled out from underneath me.'

'I know what you mean.' Monica nodded. 'Like you fell off your island and there was no one there to catch you.'

'Exactly!' I said.

'I think the reasons why people hurt their own children are complex,' Monica said, returning to her original theme, 'but at the bottom of it, I'm convinced it's to do with their own unresolved traumas. It's like anything, I suppose, some people are very conscious about not repeating things that have happened to them, and others less so...'

Monica left the statement hanging. I guessed she was referring to herself, and I was considering whether to press her further when Jennifer appeared in the doorway, yawning widely.

'How long have you two been up?' she said.

'Hours,' I replied. 'Come and get some breakfast.'

As I watched Jennifer tuck into the remaining toast, I thought about what Monica had just said. I was pretty sure my mother had suffered enough trauma, starting with how she got pregnant with me at the age of thirteen. But maybe the ugly Satan devil man had too.

An hour or so later, as we were leaving and thanking Monica for her hospitality, she reminded me of her offer to stay with her in Jamaica.

'I'm going back in a couple of weeks,' she said, 'and my home in the mountains is less than an hour from the airport, so, if you'd like a pit-stop before going to visit your grandfather, please come and be my guest. Just give me a ring once you've decided on a date and I'll have someone meet you at the airport. The offer is there!' She handed me her card, which had her name, number and occupation – psychotherapist – etched on it.

I looked up at her and fanned the card before placing it inside my purse.

# Chapter 44

On our way back from Notting Hill, Jennifer broached the idea of moving in with me.

'Much as I love my mother,' she said, 'I'm fed up with living at home, and now Patsy's moved out of yours, it seems like the perfect solution, don't you think?'

I did think. I could not have been happier and agreed without a second's hesitation.

And so it was that the following weekend Jennifer and Yvette turned up in Yvette's Morris Minor. We had grown up enough, it seemed, that we had transitioned seamlessly to first name terms all round. Soon Jennifer's belongings were piled in the front room and Yvette left us to do the unpacking with a cheery wave that rather undermined my sense that she was sad to leave her only child behind.

As soon as the front door closed, I turned and gazed at Jennifer's mound of belongings with concern. I wasn't expecting her to have quite so much stuff, or to be quite so bossy about how to proceed with unpacking it all. She'd already said she liked my house because it had so many bookshelves, but before we could even stop for a much-needed cup of tea, she demanded that we start stacking her book collection, under her careful instructions.

'Alphabetical order, please,' she said, 'and all my black writers must stay together. No mixing.'

The irony of that statement seemed to escape her, or maybe it was intentioned, but her attitude made me laugh out loud.

'Okay, I understand,' I said, 'no mixing! But how about colour coding them? Like all the orange Penguins together, or these green Viragos?'

'Hmm,' she pondered, 'yes, I like that idea. But make sure you still order them alphabetically,' she insisted. 'And my Women's Press books should all be totally together, like give them an entire shelf to themselves. Most of them are life-changing books, Erna.

Each time I picked up a book I didn't recognise I scanned the author's page and back cover, making a mental note of anything that piqued my interest. I was just about to open one with a yellow cloth cover, intriguingly titled *Their Eyes Were Watching God*, when Jennifer grabbed it from my hand.

'Zora Neale Hurston,' she squealed, 'that book should have a *handle with care* label on it!'

'Oh, well, I'd love to read it,' I said.

'Not that one, Erna,' she said firmly, and she placed Zora Neale Hurston very gently on the shelf between Lorraine Hansberry and Nella Larsen, as though she were dealing with a delicate flower. 'It actually belongs to Mum. It was out of print like forever ago, and she's only lent it to me on the understanding that I would like to live a long, happy life. But seriously, Erna, we're going to be doing this for days if you keep stopping to check every book. Can you just put them up please!'

I eyed my best friend wryly. 'I'm going to put the kettle on,' I said, walking towards the kitchen.

For a moment Jennifer didn't register what I'd said, then she put the book down that she'd just picked up and came after me.

'Oh my God, I'm sorry, Erna,' she said. 'I'm behaving like an absolute tyrant. You must be wondering what on Earth you've let yourself in for!' Jennifer studied my serious expression with concern, until I burst out laughing.

'It's all right,' I said, shaking my head. 'Luckily I already know what a nutter you are.'

Jennifer breathed a sigh of relief and came over and hugged me from behind. 'I'm so glad we're doing this,' she said, 'really, I couldn't be happier.'

I looked out of the kitchen window at the little garden beyond. The colourful blooms that I'd planted in spring had gone over already. I filled the kettle and clicked it on. 'Me too,' I said.

A few days later, I gave my work notice that I would be taking ten days holiday at the end of the month, and in my lunch break I went and booked my return flights to Jamaica at a travel agent's around the corner on Tottenham Court Road. As I walked out of their office clutching my precious tickets, I thought about the city that I'd been so desperate to escape from for so long. London has a way of putting even the most resistant non-believers under its spell. In the end, it matters little where you come from, the city will envelop you and make you one of its own. In no time at all you will find yourself convinced that there is no other city like it anywhere in the world, even if you've never travelled to any other city. London had definitely worked its charm on me. It had become familiar, a home from home, and apart from lacking wall-to-wall sunshine, pretty much everything else that I had on my island could be found somewhere in the city. There were thousands of fellow islanders living and working here, and we had found ways of keeping our island culture alive and vibrant. Most of our island foods could be found in markets and convenience stores across the city – although they were not freshly picked or dug straight from the land – and there were dance clubs and shebeens tucked away in every neighbourhood that had a sizeable population of Caribbean people. And even though I still hadn't been to it myself – something I planned to correct when I got back from my trip – every August bank holiday the drama of the Notting Hill Carnival unfolded, bringing all the disparate communities together. Almost without noticing it, my attachment to my island had been slowly chipped away. But my decision to make the return journey had also brought back a yearning for my island culture. I was looking forward to the simple things, like not being in a minority, waking up in a country where no one stared at my black skin. Where strangers wouldn't reach out to touch my hair without invitation. Where I wouldn't be asked foolish questions, like 'Why did you come here?' or 'Why would you leave all that sunshine behind?' I was looking forward to not being an exotic, or a statistic, and not feeling the need to define myself through the eyes of another community. I had forgotten what it felt like to be in *my* world, where everything was familiar. I was looking forward to feeling normal again. And then, of course, there was Grandpa Sippa. Dear God, if you really exist, I prayed, please keep him safe and well until I get there. Then I realised that I needed to let him know as soon as possible about my plans. I had missed my Grandma Melba's death and I didn't want my grandfather to leave without saying goodbye too. As soon as I got home that evening, I called a cousin on the island whose number I'd got through the offices of Auntie Madge's family network. He was able to pass on the message that I was coming back to the island, and two days later he called to relay my grandfather's response. It was a joy just to hear a pure island accent again.

'Uncle Sippa seh fi tell yuh dat im know you wouldn't let im dead before yuh come see im,' he said down the crackly line, 'and him seh once im buckup pon yuh again, im can dead in peace. I am sure de ole man waiting for you, Erna.'

'Thank you, thank you,' I replied, tears misting my eyes.

. . .

I spent the last few days at home going through everything I needed to take with me, checking I had presents for Grandpa Sippa and Miss Blossom, and enough left over for everyone else who I might bump into, and marvelling at the size of the two suitcases that I'd mananged to fill to the brim.

The day before I was due to travel, Patsy turned up at the house. It was a Saturday morning and I was in the kitchen making breakfast. Jennifer answered the door.

'It's your sister,' she called out.

I was in the middle of stirring scrambled eggs. I pulled the pan off the heat and walked out of the kitchen into the hall, suddenly conscious that I was wearing only a large white t-shirt.

'Hello, Erna,' Patsy said, as she stepped inside.

Jennifer was still standing by the door, holding it open. She closed it once she'd checked my face and seen that I was okay with this unexpected visitor. Then she walked past Patsy and sat down at the dining table, where she picked up a book and pretended to read.

'Hello, Pats,' I said.

For a moment we stood facing each other from opposite sides of the room. Then I wiped my hands on the sides of my t-shirt and walked towards her, until we were a few feet apart. Patsy stood still the whole time, watching me. She was wearing a blue denim jacket over a red t-shirt and black jeans, and her hair was wrapped in a red, gold and green bandana. She looked over at Jennifer before speaking.

'Auntie Madge told me you're going back to the island,' she said.

'That's right,' I replied. 'I'm going tomorrow.'

'I wanted to say...' she paused and looked around at the front door before turning back to me. 'I wanted to say I'm sorry, Erna.'

328

I thought I could hear the faint sound of reggae from outside.

'Did Fitzroy bring you here?' I said.

Patsy looked about as uncomfortable as I had ever seen her. I had a flashback to when I'd found her standing over the ugly Satan devil man's body. My little sister. I fought back the urge to hug her, because another part of me wanted to punish her.

'Yes,' she replied.

I looked at her – slim and beautiful and radiating health – and then I gazed past her to the window.

'So, it's working out for you then?' I said.

She nodded. I could see tears in her eyes. I stepped forward until we were face to face, and then I reached out and pulled her towards me and hugged her. She burst out crying then.

'I've missed you, sister,' she said through the sobs.

'I've missed you too, Pats,' I said.

She stepped back and I released her from my embrace.

'Will you say hello to Grandpa Sippa from me, and tell him that I love him very much?' she said.

'Of course I will!'

'Thank you, Erna.'

I nodded. 'It does my heart good to see you looking so well, Pats.'

'Me too,' Patsy said, looking from me to Jennifer and back again. 'You look happy, Erna.'

'I am.' I smiled and Patsy smiled back.

She walked to the front door and opened it.

'I'll see you around, Erna,' she said, and then she slipped out, closing the door softly behind her.

I heard a car door open and the brief thump of music, then it slammed shut and the car drove off down the road. I turned to look at Jennifer who raised her eyebrows at me.

'All's well that ends well?' she said.

'Very funny.'

As I walked back into the kitchen to finish making breakfast, I realised my heart was on another of its pounding missions. Thank you, God, I whispered inside my head, picking up the saucepan again. I believe Pats is going to be fine.

# Chapter 45

Almost seven years after I had waved a nervous goodbye to my Grandpa, I boarded a huge British Airways jet and returned to my island. I was no longer a frightened, angry fourteen-year-old girl, but a fully grown twenty-year-old adult. Even so, the idea of flying home set the butterflies racing in my stomach.

Ten hours later, I stepped out of the plane into the heat of the Caribbean sun – it felt intense but familiar as I shuffled down the steps that were secured to the second exit door of the aircraft. For a moment, I was tempted to get down on my knees and kiss the tarmac, but instead I took in the distant mountain range that seemed to wrap me in its embrace and breathed a deep sigh of relief. Then I hoisted my small backpack over my shoulder and followed the line of passengers into the terminal building that, to my Londoner's eyes, appeared small and provincial.

Tightly clutching the blue passport that proved I was no longer a citizen of the country in which I was born, I took my place in the queue of returnees and tourists. A mosquito sang past my ears, avoiding my attempts to swish it away. The queue was painfully slow, but at last I was propelled out of customs into a noisy crowd of excited relatives and hopeful taxi drivers shouting out the names of the people they were there to meet. I stood there, dazed for a moment, until I became aware that someone was shouting my name.

'Miss Mullings, over here!' The male voice sounded deep and smooth, like melting molasses.

I looked in the direction of the voice to discover a friendly faced, slim young man dressed in black trousers and a gleaming white short-sleeved shirt. The young man and his voice didn't match at all. Somehow, I expected a more robust-looking chap. He was holding a card with my name on it. I waved my acknowledgement and, noting the oversized suitcases on either side of me, that I had managed to haul from the baggage reclaim, he rushed over.

'Good afternoon, Miss Mullings,' he said with a beaming smile. 'My name is Conrad. Miss Monica sent me to collect you. Welcome back to our beautiful island! I hope you had a good flight?'

'Yes, thank you, very good. A bit of turbulence here and there, but otherwise it was fine.'

'Oh, that's good to hear,' he smiled, grabbing a suitcase in each hand. 'The car is parked just across the road, Miss Mullings.'

I followed Conrad outside into the wall of heat and stood fanning myself with my passport while I watched him force one of my suitcases into the boot and the other one on to the back passenger seat of his car. When he'd finished, I slipped into the front and Conrad got into the driver's seat next to me. He leaned round and dipped into a cool bag, retrieving a plastic bottle of water, which he handed to me.

'The weather is very hot here at the moment,' he said, 'but it'll be cooler up in the mountains.'

He started the car and joined a small traffic jam of tooting cars jostling for the exit, and then we were on our way. I opened my window wide and closed my eyes, breathing in a cocktail of petrol fumes and salty ocean tang. For a few minutes, we were enveloped in the dazzling light that danced off the sapphire Caribbean sea, and then we left it behind and began the slow, dizzying ascent into the mountains. On every side, deep gullies slashed through the lush green forest and enticing smells came wafting through the open windows. It was still mango season and now and then we passed groups of women sitting at the roadside, their baskets brimming with Julie mangoes, East Indian mangoes, green skins, bastards and number eleven mangoes, and suddenly I was transported back to my grandparents' front steps with my tin pan full, devouring them like they were about to become extinct.

'So, how is England, Miss Mullings?' Conrad's question cut through my thoughts.

I sat up and blinked the drowsiness away. 'Oh, good and not so good,' I said. 'But I'm sure you could say the same about anywhere.'

It had been over fifteen hours since I'd left home and I was beginning to feel the effects. When I opened my eyes again, the last golden rays of sunshine were dipping behind the dark blue mountains. Conrad made a left turn on to a gravelled road – the wheels spun and the engine roared as the car made its final climb before coming to a stop beside a long, low wall draped with pink and orange hibiscus.

'We are here, Miss Mullings!' Conrad beamed.

I opened the passenger door to deliciously perfumed mountain air. The winding road had taken us high above the city and we seemed to be floating between the thousands of twinkling city lights far below and the star-studded night sky above. Fireflies dashed madly about and I shuddered to recall how I used to catch and dissect the little flying bugs in my attempts to discover the source of their glow. Beyond the open gate and across an immaculate lawn, wide stone steps led up to an elegant two-storey plantation house, with yellow lanterns hung above the porch and along the ornate iron-laced balcony that ran the length of the frontage of both floors. Suddenly a huge tawny dog came bounding down the steps, barking furiously, and behind him a figure appeared in the doorway, silhouetted by the porch lights.

'Lion, stop that incessant barking,' Monica's distinctive voice rang out in the warm night.

I watched her descend the steps as Conrad heaved my luggage from the car.

'Don't mind old Lion,' she said, as she approached the gate, 'he sounds fierce, but the only things he scares are the birds!'

She looked incredibly relaxed and elegant in a blue tie-dyed dashiki, her long locks exposed.

'Oh, Monica, it's lovely to see you,' I gushed.

We hugged warmly and then she held me at arms length as she inspected my face with a smile.

'I'm so glad you made it, Erna. Come in, come in!'

We followed Conrad as he struggled up the steps with my suitcases; Lion taking up the rear, his long shaggy tail wagging.

'I hope I'm not being too forward,' Monica said as we approached the front door, 'but I've taken the liberty of planning a little dinner party tonight. I wasn't sure exactly how long you'd be staying with us here in the mountains, so I thought it would be nice to introduce you to a few friends.'

A rotund, dark-skinned, middle-aged woman wearing a red flower-print scarf and matching apron appeared in the doorway.

'I'm sure you must be tired,' Monica continued, 'so maybe you'd like to have a bath and a nap before dinner and then we can catch up?'

'Oh, that would be perfect,' I replied.

'Jessie,' Monica said, 'please show Miss Mullings to her room.'

Jessie led me upstairs to a large room at the back of the house that overlooked the rolling gardens, which were only partially revealed in the pearly moonlight. Beautiful pieces of handmade furniture gave the room a lovely warm feeling. A four-poster bed rose high up from the floor, necessitating a cute wooden stool to help climb into it. My two suitcases stood side by side at the foot of the bed.

'Your bathroom is through there,' said an irritated sounding Jessie.

I had the distinct feeling that she thought me just another jumped-up islander who had lived abroad and was now back thinking I was better than everyone else. She wasn't alone in that feeling; I was almost giddy with the conflicting emotions of guilt and appreciation that I was feeling, but in the stark contrast between the world of my island-past and this unexpected island-present, I also considered that maybe it was okay for me to be here, in this house, at this time. Maybe I deserved it.

The bathroom was luxuriously appointed and with a small squeal of pleasure I lowered myself into the warm water for my very first roll-top bath. After a few minutes I found myself nodding off, so I had a quick splash before climbing out. I dried myself, rummaged in my case and located one of the new pairs of white cotton pyjamas that I had bought specially for the trip. I hoisted myself up on to the four-poster, and laid out flat on my back with my eyes tightly closed. I couldn't be sure whether I had actually fallen asleep, but it felt like no time had passed at all when I heard a gentle knocking at the bedroom door.

'Miss Clacken seh har friends a come soon,' Jessie said through the half-opened door.

'Thank you, Jessie. Please tell her I'll be down shortly.'

I rolled off the four-poster and came to my feet. I felt even more tired than I did earlier. I went into the bathroom and splashed my face with cold water and returned to my bedroom where I checked the time. I had slept for nearly an hour.

I opened a suitcase and pulled out my clothes, trying to decide what would be appropriate for such a stylish occasion. In the end, I chose a simple green dress and a pair of red leather sandals. I opened the door and peered across the landing at the grand staircase. Sounds were coming from below, so I followed them downstairs, where I discovered a huge kitchen at the back of the house that would not have been out of place in an English country mansion. Red earthenware tiles covered the floor and two of its walls were lined with sage-green wooden cupboards. A substantial dresser containing beautiful glassware and ceramics stood against another wall, alongside a massive metal frame fixed to the ceiling, from which hung dozens of highly polished copper pans. Next to the door, a substantial wine rack was filled with bottles. Pots simmered on the huge stove and at a solid wooden table Jessie and a young woman in a white apron were busy helping Monica put the finishing touches to the dinner. Hearing my hesitant cough, Monica turned to me with a smile.

'Are you feeling rested?' she said, walking towards me.

'Much better, thank you,' I said. Only too aware that I had picked up that uniquely English habit of saying I was fine, when I felt the opposite. 'Your house is absolutely divine, Monica!' I added, gazing round the vast kitchen.

'Come on,' she said, taking me by the arm, 'come and meet my guests.'

I followed her across the tiled hall, through a doorway next to the front door that opened on to a large dining room. Standing around the gleaming mahogany dining table, chatting and drinking wine, were three people who could not have looked more different if they tried. They stopped talking and turned to me as we entered the room.

'This is Erna, everyone,' Monica said, 'she just got here this afternoon.'

'Welcome to Jamaica, Erna!' said a middle-aged woman in a dramatic yellow linen dress, with closely cropped hair and perfectly rendered red lipstick. 'Or should I say, welcome back? I'm Irene,' she added, holding out her hand.

'It's welcome back,' I said, shaking her slim, silver-beringed hand.

'Irene is a professor of history at UWI,' Monica said. 'And this is Daisy,' she continued, introducing the young woman standing next to Irene, who looked like the twin sister of Angela Davis. She was dressed casually in a blue shirt and white jeans and sported a huge Afro. 'Daisy is my favourite artist, she painted that wonderful picture over there,' Monica added, pointing to a vast, colourful watercolour on the wall opposite the window. 'And last, but not least, this is Forrest.'

Over a long and delicious dinner I discovered that Forrest, bushy-haired and spectacled, was a writer and sculptor from New York with roots on the island. He seemed to take a fatherly interest in me and was fascinated by my tales of growing up in Little Hammon. He was convinced that we were distantly related, as his grandmother hailed from a neighbouring village. I, in turn, was fascinated by his tales of New York and the writing community of which he was a part. Most of the rest of the conversation, in which everyone took an active part, was about my island: the many changes that had taken place since I'd left, and those things which remained the same. There were plenty of gaps in my knowledge, of course, not least because I'd grown up in a part of the island where life was uncomplicated, but my growing understanding of the political landscape in England, along with my interest in the Arts, meant that I felt confident joining in. I was aided by Monica's assiduous attention to my comfort and the seemingly unending supply of wine. I felt not only warmly included in this august company, but joyous about the many exciting things that were happening on the island. I discovered that my island was arty, academic, politically active and sporty. My island was making waves on the world stage.

The wine worked its magic on us and we ended the evening singing and dancing along to the lilting rhythms of our beautiful island home. Even Forrest joined in. Then the jet lag caught up with me and, after profuse promises of future meetings, I reached the sanctuary of my room, where I collapsed gratefully on to the bed and did not emerge until late the following morning.

# Chapter 46

We'd just returned from an extensive tour of Monica's delightful gardens when Jessie appeared at the top of the steps saying a man had arrived and was asking for me. I ran up the steps towards her and then around the side of the house to the front drive where I found a tall, well-dressed young man, lounging against the ticking bonnet of a shiny blue American pick-up truck. He looked at me with amusement.

'Same Erna with har buck teeth,' he laughed, 'but bwoy, you sure put on some weight. Must be the good life in old England Town!'

'Tony?' I said. I could hardly believe my eyes.

'What, you mean you don't recognise me, cousin?' he smiled, standing up and walking towards me.

'Well, I do now,' I said. 'Oh my God, look how you've grown up!'

He held his hand out, but instead of shaking it, I gave him a big hug. Then I held him at arm's length and studied him.

'My, how you've filled out,' I said, 'but it suits you. And you're darker than I remember.'

'I was just thinking the same about you,' he said, 'but the other way round. Yuh use to be real shiny black like yuh grandmada, but now we look like we're de same colour. Too much England cold for you and too much island sun for me, I reckon!'

'Hello, who's this?' said Monica, appearing on the drive behind us.

'This,' I replied, 'is my cousin Tony, and I'm just about to remind him what happened last time he mentioned my buck teeth!'

Tony burst into loud laughter. 'Yuh want fi try to fight me again, Erna?' he grinned. 'Pleased to meet you, mam,' he said, turning to Monica.

'Likewise,' Monica replied.

'Bwoy it some place you got here,' he added, 'look like my cousin moving in high circles now!'

'Will you have some breakfast with us?' Monica asked. 'Jessie's just about to serve it on the terrace.'

'No, tank you kindly, man,' Tony said. 'I've already eaten today. I'm happy to wait for Erna though.'

'Well, come and sit with us anyway,' Monica said.

'I appreciate you coming all that way from the country to collect me, Tony,' I said, as we followed Monica back around the side of the house on to the terrace.

'Anything for the old man, mi glad to help out,' Tony replied.

However, after accepting a cold soda, Tony asked if he could be excused and he followed Jessie into the house.

'Well, it looks like you're leaving us already,' Monica sighed.

'I'm sorry to be going so soon, Monica,' I said, 'it's so beautiful here, but I'm desperate to see my grandfather.'

'Of course,' Monica said, 'he sounds like an amazing man. I hope he's okay.'

After breakfast I returned to my room and re-packed my suitcases with a bittersweet mixture of regret and relief and then went downstairs to find Monica to say goodbye. Even though we'd only just met, she felt like an old friend and I was looking forward to seeing her again in a few days' time. When we walked back to the drive, we found Tony sitting on the wall chatting to Angela, the young woman I'd seen in the kitchen the night before. Lion, who was lying on the gravel in front of them, clambered to his feet as we approached and Monica petted him fondly. Tony had already loaded his truck with my cases and he seemed anxious to get going, so I hugged Monica and thanked her again, and, with a final wave, I climbed into the front of the pick-up next to my handsome cousin.

'It's better to start out early, while we still got the light,' Tony said, as soon as I'd got in, 'and keep yuh backpack somewhere on the floor in front of you,' he added, 'safer that way.'

Then he started the car with a roar and in a spray of gravel we were off. I just had time to wave to Monica and catch one last glimpse of her lovely home and then we were bouncing down the track towards the main road.

'Strap yourself in, Erna,' Tony said, 'we do the seatbelt ting here now too.' He laughed, handing me a bottle of water. 'Yuh going to need plenty water, the journey to country is long and hot, maybe even longer than it was when you were here, caus some of the country roads well mash up now, what with us getting a hurricane somebody or another practically every year. The woman ones are particularly lethal,' he added with a wink, as we swung on to the tarmac road and headed north.

I lay back in my seat and gazed in delight as we drove through tiny villages, past rushing rivers and gaggles of children who waved as we passed. The whole time, Tony chatted away about the chicken business that he'd set up in the district after returning from America, where he said he'd managed to make a bit of money.

'You look like you're doing good though, Erna,' he said, peering sideways at me, 'but just a little precaution. People tek one look pon yuh and them know seh yuh is from foreign. So, I would avoid too much of de talking. Even more than de clothes and de walk, the English talking mek people want to bada yuh more.'

'I hear yuh, coz,' I replied, 'but mi sure seh, mi wi drap back innah de lingo in no time. Yuh nevah really lose it when yuh

341

born pon de island, man. Dis is jus fimi landing voice an yuh nuh se seh mi put on jeans an t-shirt like heverybody helse.'

Tony roared with laughter. 'Yuh nuh easy, Erna, dat's nat bad at all! But de people will still know seh yuh come from foreign. Someting happen to the England people dem, man. Give dem five years in that cold place and they all sound foreign.'

'So how was my Grandpa doing when you saw him last?' I said, reverting to my London voice.

'Saw him before I left out. He is good, man. His hand shake like the clappers, but his mind is as sharp as his old cut-throat. Yuh remember the cut-throat, Erna?' Tony laughed. 'How Uncle Sippa use to scrape every last hair from Sonny head? To be honest, part from the nerve ting with his hands and the legs not carrying him any more, he's doing real good for his age.'

Suddenly we emerged from the misty depths of a high mountain pass to a spectacular view of the north side of the island.

'Oh my God, that's breathtaking!' I said, grabbing my backpack. 'Can you pull over over a minute so I can get a picture?'

'If we keep stopping so often we're never going to reach country today!' Tony said.

'Sorry, Tony,' I said, 'I hadn't realised we'd stopped that often.'

'You seem to want to take in every bush and tree! I understand, this island is our very own paradise, but one week is not long for your visit. You'll see a lot to remind you of what you left behind, for sure. That is why I can't leave it again,' he added, pulling over on to the verge. 'True the money ting nuh run here properly, but bwoy I'd rather live in paradise with little money than in hell with plenty money.'

'Well, I'm taking in everything I can,' I said, climbing out and stretching my legs.

'You tink you could live here again?' Tony, said, joining me on the side of the road.

Shading my eyes with my hand, I gazed at the vast blue ocean stretching to the horizon where it merged seamlessly with the cloudless sky.

'It's too early to tell,' I said, 'but I'm loving it so far!'

In no time we were driving along the coast, with palm trees and fishing villages swishing past in the late afternoon sun. I was still pondering Tony's question. Even though I was loving every minute, moving back for good was not a question I had considered in a long time, and it was certainly not something I could answer after less than two days back on the island.

'We will do a proper stop soon to get you something to eat,' Tony said, handing me another bottle of water. 'There's some nice little fish places up ahead. I take it you still like your fish?'

'I still like my fish,' I said, smiling.

Ten minutes later we pulled off the main road and bumped towards a cute little beach restaurant with a large sign, which read simply: *Jed's Place*. But before we reached the restaurant, which was really no more than a wooden shack, we had to run the gauntlet of women trying to stuff plastic bags of cooked king prawns through the windows. The women continued to bombard me after we parked up and I stepped from the car. It was as though I was the first customer they'd seen in days.

'Come nuh, miss. Tek wan bag from mi noh, miss!' pleaded a large woman in a blue and white headscarf.

'Yuh waan cane? Pear? Mango? Wi ave hevery ting yuh need, Miss Hinglish,' her skinny companion added.

'She nuh Hinglish! She a Hamerican,' said the first woman.

'No, man! Yuh se she a wear shorts an bobby socks?' her companion cried. 'She a Hinglish woman, man!'

The two higglers got so involved in their debate about where I was from that they appeared to have forgotten that they were trying to sell me their wares.

'Ladies,' I interrupted, 'mi is from right here soh. Just been away awhile.'

343

'Wi know dat, man,' the skinny one said, 'but yuh ave foreign stamp all ova yuh now. And mi right still. A Hinglan foreign yuh is.'

'Yeah, man, yuh right still,' I laughed.

'Mi know seh yuh a try hard fi still drop de lingo,' the large woman said, 'but it nuh sound artentic again. Soh jus do yuh Hinglan ting, man. Is aright.'

'Sistren,' Tony smiled, taking my arm, 'if you don't mind?'

The two women sucked their teeth and returned to their debate as they wandered back towards the highway, lugging their plastic bags along with them. We made our way to a bamboo table that faced the gently rippling ocean and a young man in cut-off denim shorts and white t-shirt appeared from inside the shack and handed me a menu.

'Snapper good today, miss,' he beamed.

'Thank you,' I said, taking the menu.

'Mi wi come back wit de drinks,' he said, without asking what it was we wanted to drink. He returned a moment later with two glasses filled with ice-cold coconut water, which we received gratefully. I sipped at my drink while Tony ordered our food. It sounded delicious – I chose the snapper and roast breadfruit and Tony ordered char-grilled mahi-mahi with a full complement of island hard food. While we waited for our food to arrive, I gazed towards the sea where a small fishing boat bobbed at anchor. There was no denying it, I was in paradise. Then the food came and I tucked in with relish. I considered that if anything could bring me back to my island, it would probably be the food.

'I don't know if you came to this beach before yuh lef fi Englan,' Tony said between mouthfuls of fish, dumpling, banana and yam – I'd never seen a person cram so much food into their mouth at one time – 'but it used to be a beautiful piece of coastline until storm Gilda eat up most a de beach a couple o' years back. Dem dead corals use to be way out a sea, but when de storm done, dis was all dat was left of Jacob's beach.'

I followed Tony's pointing finger, but it still looked beautiful to me.

Soon, Tony and I were back on the road and I could feel my stomach churning with excitement. By five in the afternoon, we reached the outskirts of the village. We'd already met the deep red earth and scorching heat some time back, and the temperature inside the car had built to an almost unbearable level as we were forced to keep the windows shut during the final stage of our journey to keep out the swirling red dust.

'I can't afford to use the air condition, Erna,' Tony had explained, 'even for visitors. It eat up de petrol too quick.'

To be fair, we had managed most of the journey with the windows cracked wide enough to allow the Caribbean breeze to flow through. Driving conditions on some of the preceding roads had been fairly treacherous, but the village road still had a few nasty surprises, with potholes and craters which looked like they could swallow small trucks and which taxed even Tony's admirable driving skills.

'Is that Rose Hill School?' I shouted, as we passed a tiny two-room structure. I could hardly believe my eyes, it looked minute.

'Sure is,' Tony replied, 'mind you, the church is a bit of a clue!' He gazed at the dusty buildings as we passed. 'But most of the little houses gone now,' he added mournfully, 'everybody relative coming back from foreign and putting up some of those great big places we passed. More often than not, there's not a striking soul living in them.'

We continued for a few more minutes before leaving the road and turning on to a red dirt track.

'Dis is de track dat lead to the village, Erna,' Tony said.

He needn't have told me; I knew that track like the back of my hand. My heart raced with the realisation of how soon I would be seeing my beloved grandfather again. I felt like I should stop speaking, worried that I might somehow jinx everything. I even started wondering whether I was in the middle of a dream from which I'd wake at any moment, when we pulled up outside a new-looking three-bedroom property that my grandfather's children had built for him, right next to the spot where the old house had been. The property looked solid enough and was painted a dull yellow under a red slate roof. The neat verandah was smaller than the original one and there was no sign of my garden. Sitting on the verandah next to an empty rocking chair was Grandpa Sippa, in a huge brown armchair that had obviously been placed outside just for this occasion.

As I clambered out of the car and walked towards him, I realised that it wasn't that the chair was so big, it was Grandpa Sippa who had shrunk, shockingly so. Tony had underplayed his condition in his description of him. And I was sadly right about his eyes, because he didn't say a word until I was standing in front of him, holding his frail hand.

'Is yuh dis Erna?' he whispered, in a voice like dry leaves rustling. 'Lard almighty, is yuh dis fa true?'

'Yes, Grandpa Sippa, is me dis fa true!' I replied. I bent down and gave him as big a squeeze as his fragile frame would allow. My heart was still jumping around in my chest and my eyes welled with tears, but I was determined not to cry. I was here and I wanted to be as strong as I could be for my grandpa.

A young boy appeared carrying a chair.

'Evening, Miss Erna,' he said, as he placed the chair beside Grandpa Sippa.

'And who are you?' I asked him.

'Mi name Peter,' he said, 'mi Mass Sippa houseboy.'

Peter disappeared and returned with two tall glasses of freshly made lemonade. He handed one to me and the other one to Tony, who'd joined me on the verandah.

'Yuh want anything to eat, Miss Erna?' the boy asked.

'The lemonade is just fine, thank you, Peter. Mister Tony and I had a big fish lunch.'

'Tony, weh yuh deh? Is Erna yuh bring fi see mi fa true?' Grandpa said, peering at him.

'Yes, Uncle Sippa, same Erna,' Tony replied.

Grandpa Sippa blinked and his dull eyes released a trickle of tears.

'It's so good to see you again, Grandpa,' I said. 'I feel bad that I left it so long. But I am here now, and here you are.'

'Is yuh one come?' Grandpa asked.

'Yes, Grandpa. It's just me.'

'Soh weh Patricia and de bwoy pickney dem? Clifford... No, nuh Clifford. Mi memory nuh serve mi, Erna. Wah de older bwoy pickney name again?'

'Clifton, Grandpa. Clifton is the big one and Sonny is the little one. Except they're both enormous now. They're doing very well at school,' I added. It didn't seem right to even begin to explain anything about Patsy to him, so I just said, 'Patricia and the boys all send you their love.'

'But Violet, she nuh did have twin pickney dem?'

'She did, Grandpa, your memory is still good. Doretta and Barbette. They're eight years old now. Them and the boys went to live with Auntie Madge and Uncle Herbie when Miss Violet died.'

'Yes! Mi did memba sinting like dat. Mi did worry wen yuh mada birt more gal pickney, Erna, because she nuh fond a gal pickney after she loss har first bouy chile. She nuh get ova dat.'

My mouth almost hit the floor with this revelation. I had no idea my mother had given birth to a child before me. I didn't want to show my surprise, as Grandpa Sippa probably didn't realise that he was giving away a long-held secret, but I had to find out more. 'Who was the boy's father, Grandpa?' I asked gently.

'It was de same man who mash up de other little pickney gal,' he replied, his eyes coming alive with the memory. 'Mi nuh recall har name. Dat was de reason me and Melba sen Violet outta de village. But she still come back wit belly.'

347

Delphine! That was who he was talking about. Delphine whose little boy Leslie had died before his first birthday. But the only person I remembered being violent towards Delphine back then was her father, Mass Calvin, who had beaten her mother so bad she'd run away and never returned. Surely it wasn't him who'd got my mother pregnant? Or his own daughter? Ugh, maybe it was. I thought about what Monica had said, about the cycle of abuse. My mother. Delphine. Patsy. What horrors women have to endure.

I looked at Grandpa. I saw it would be too much to question him further about all this. The excitement of our meeting had clearly exhausted him and Peter, who seemed to have an almost psychic understanding of his needs, appeared from nowhere and offered to take him back into the house for a rest.

'You go and have a lie down, Grandpa,' I said, rising and kissing him on his head, 'I'm going to have a little walk around the village and then I'll come back and we'll talk some more.' I looked at Tony, who was sitting quietly sipping his lemonade. 'Would you mind if I went off on my own for a bit, Tony?' I said.

'Nah problem, Erna,' he replied. 'I'm just gonna sit here and wait fiyuh to return.'

I stared at him for a moment, thinking maybe he was being sarcastic, but he had stretched out his long legs and looked very relaxed after our drive.

'Mi could do with some more o' dat lemonade though!' he said, as Peter reappeared on the verandah.

'Yes, sarh, Mass Tony,' Peter said, and off he went again.

I wandered away from my grandfather's house, through the old fields towards the deep gully on the edge of our land. The vivid familiarity of everything was intense, and a torrent of thoughts and memories jostled for precedence in my head. It was so overwhelming that I left the path and sat down in the middle of a dusty cornfield and wept. I wept for my mother,

348

for my Grandma Melba, for everything that had happened, before and after I had left my island. Once again, I wished with all my heart that I had tried to get to know my mother better. It felt very strange to be back in the same place where she'd been born and where she'd given birth to me without her being around any more. Slowly, I became aware that the shadows were lengthening as the sun began to set behind the mountains in the west. I climbed to my feet and stretched and looked out across the eastern hills towards the rapidly darkening horizon. 'God bless you, Mother,' I said out loud.

When I returned to Grandpa Sippa's house I found a small crowd waiting for me. Tony was right, I hardly recognised any of the visitors, apart from Cousin Petra and Miss Blossom, whom I had forgotten to ask about in my excitement at seeing Grandpa. Cousin Petra's brown face had a few more wrinkles, but apart from that she looked good, her strong arms still youthful despite years of working a sewing machine and a machete. She was famous for her ability to cut an entire bunch of green bananas from a banana tree in one swipe. I was very pleased to see her, and I'd put away something in the bottom of my suitcase for her. I gave her a hug and when I told her I'd brought something for her, her eyes misted with tears. I had hoped to keep my arrival quiet, because I still remembered Mother's visit all those years ago and the avid expectation that went with it, along with horror stories I'd heard about how an entire village might appear in the hope that the returnee would have brought them all their wants and needs. Just in case, I'd bought a random selection of clothing and other knick-knacks from Brixton market in a last-minute panic, but these were intended merely as a gesture, as I had no idea who I would meet in the village. Clearly, I had underestimated the power of the bush telegraph, though, and the buzzing crowd seemed to swell around me as I made my way towards Grandpa's door.

But first I had to deal with Miss Blossom.

She must have been out and about getting provisions when we'd arrived, but now she sat in the rocking chair on the verandah, very much the queen of all she surveyed.

'Mi glad seh yuh come back fi see us old folks before de good Lard finish him business with us,' she said, eyeing me carefully as I climbed the steps towards her. 'And yuh ave such a strong resemblance to yuh Grandmada,' she added.

'Hello, Miss Blossom,' I smiled, once we were face to face, 'you're looking well.'

In truth, she looked all of her seventy-odd years, but she wasn't nearly as dipsy as I remembered her.

'Soh, a wah yuh bring fi mi?' she asked.

I was slightly blindsided by her bluntness. 'It was a rush trip, Miss Blossom,' I said, in quite a loud voice, as much for the benefit of the crowd, who were hanging on my every word, as for my step-grandmother. 'I only managed to bring a few bits and pieces for whoever can best use them. We can see how to work it all out tomorrow, if that's okay?'

There was an ominous rumble from the crowd.

'Well, if yuh kyan call coming back after seven years a rush, den a soh it goh,' Miss Blossom replied, 'but mi glad seh yuh come fine yuh Grandfada alive still.'

At that moment Tony walked out of the house, wiping his hands with a crushed handkerchief. 'I put your cases in the spare room, Erna,' he said, 'just as Miss Blossom instructed me.' He turned to her with a broad smile.

'Tank you, Tony,' Miss Blossom said, 'yuh is a good boy to yuh Uncle Sippa.'

'This is for you, Miss Blossom,' I said, taking an envelope containing fifty pounds from my backpack and pressing it into her hand. It disappeared unopened into her apron pocket at lightning speed.

'Tank yuh and God bless yuh, chile,' she said with a toothless grin.

I looked round at the crowd, wondering what I should do, but Miss Blossom solved that for me.

'Nah worry yuhself wit dem,' she said, patting her pocket, 'dem no better than crows looking for pickins.'

I gazed at their expectant faces. To say they looked disappointed would be an understatement. However, by now night had fallen, swift and dark, and they seemed to assume that the gift-giving was over and drifted away in different directions, leaving me alone with Tony on the verandah. Miss Blossom went back inside the house, but she returned moments later with Peter, who was carrying two lanterns which he hung on hooks either side of the wooden steps.

'Yuh Grandfada will sleep now till tomorrow,' Miss Blossom said. 'Peter will show yuh to yuh room.' And with that, she disappeared again.

Tony took this as his cue to leave as well. He stood up, stretching and yawning at the same time.

'Thank you so much for driving me, Tony,' I said. 'I really appreciate it.'

'Tis no bother, Erna,' he smiled. 'Me do it for me Uncle Sippa. But is good to see yuh, mi got to say.'

I fumbled around inside my handbag and pulled twenty pounds from my purse, which I handed to him. 'This is for the petrol and everything,' I said.

'There's no need fiyuh to pay me,' Tony replied, but the money slipped inside his pocket nevertheless. 'I'll see you in the morning,' he added.

I nodded and watched him walk towards his car, before turning and entering the house for the first time. I followed Peter along the dimly lit hall towards what I assumed was the spare room, because the door was open and light was spilling from it. As soon as he'd shown me in, Peter left me to settle myself.

# Chapter 47

I passed a restless first night in Grandpa's new house. It was baking hot inside the spare room and the bed, although it appeared fairly new and the sheets freshly laundered, sagged terribly in the middle, making sleep almost impossible. There was a rusty fan, but the noise it made was like the swarming of angry bees, which made it just as distracting as the heat. And then there was the usual tropical cacophony outside. In the end, I gave up my fight to get to sleep and settled on reading.

I awoke to the dull thud of the book as it fell on to the tiled floor. I yawned and opened my eyes. The different sounds coming from outside made me realise that day had broken, even though the dawn light hadn't made its way over the hills yet. I sat up and looked around the sparsely furnished room. I still couldn't quite believe I was back in my village, in my Grandpa's house. Rubbing my eyes, I grabbed the towel that lay folded on a chair, and my wash-bag from my open suitcase, and made my way to the bathroom, which to my amazement was a proper inside room at the end of a short corridor beyond the kitchen. It had a basic hand-held shower, the water pumped from a massive black plastic tank erected on a platform at the back of the house. I emerged feeling much refreshed, put my kimono back on and went outside. Peter was waiting on the verandah.

'Would you mind if I prepared breakfast for my grandfather this morning?' I asked him.

'Yuh nuh ave to do dat, Miss Erna,' he replied, 'mi will mek breakfast fa both of yuh.'

'Thank you, Peter, but I'd like to do it just this once.'

'Aright, Miss Erna,' he said, 'jus let mi know what tings yuh need.'

'Give me a moment then,' I said.

In my room I changed quickly, putting on a light linen dress and wrapped my hair in a clean towel. Then I followed Peter into the kitchen at the end of the hall, where he explained that Grandpa Sippa only took Ovaltine and a small bowl of thin cornmeal porridge in the mornings. He showed me where all the relevant things were and I set about making Grandpa his breakfast. I grated a small amount of fresh nutmeg into the Ovaltine and the porridge because it was something I remembered my grandmother doing. By the time I'd finished, Peter popped his head in and announced that Grandpa Sippa was waiting for me on the verandah, but that Miss Blossom was still in bed.

'She nuh like to get up till the sun move past her window,' he explained.

I followed him outside to find Grandpa sitting in the armchair, propped up with cushions, at a round metal table, which Peter must have placed there.

'Good morning, Grandpa!' I said, placing the porridge and the Ovaltine in front of him.

For a moment he stared at me questioningly, as if he didn't know who I was, then he dipped his spoon into the porridge and smiled as he recognised the taste.

'If mi nevah know soh yuh grandmada gone long time, mi would seh Melba cook dis wit har hand.' He sighed deeply, putting his spoon down.

'I remembered that's how Grandma Melba used to prepare your porridge. And yuh still know how to work your charm!'

Grandpa Sippa nodded his understanding.

Peter appeared from around the side of the house carrying a metal bucket and started a chorus of 'chick, chick, chick,' and dozens of hens gathered in the yard to peck at the handfuls of shelled corn he threw on to the compacted earth. Suddenly I found myself back in my village childhood. I could smell the pigs that were penned beyond the chicken coop. I saw Treasure Girl and Bugle Boy, my lovely donkeys, standing there swishing their tails. I saw Grandma trying to shoo an untethered goat from her flower garden. I saw myself, Patsy, Clifton and Sonny running around the yard playing and shouting with laughter in the dappled shade of the breadfruit tree.

'I just let de fowl dem wander,' Peter was saying, 'dem nevah leave de lot. But I put dem back in de coop at night, because dat is when mangoose dem visit.'

At that moment, Tony, who appeared to have given himself the job of looking after me for the rest of my stay, arrived at the house to discuss my schedule for the day. Although we were cousins, I understood how things worked well enough to know that he was not offering his services for free, and I wasn't expecting him to. It was, after all, a mutually beneficial arrangement. Peter had taken Grandpa Sippa back inside the house and Miss Blossom had yet to emerge.

'It would be good to take a stroll around the village,' I said, 'see who I buck up on and what I remember. But first I would like to pay a visit to Grandma Melba's grave.'

'That might be easier said than done, Erna,' Tony replied, 'but let's try anyway. Let me go get a machete.'

The heat was already oppressive as I followed Tony along a winding track that led through the tall guinea grass towards the hills on the northern side of the village.

As we neared the graveyard, twenty minutes later, I understood why Tony needed the machete: the path was completely overgrown.

'Nobody nuh look after graves, Erna,' Tony said, as he slashed his way through the dense thickets of cerasee, bitter bush and Spanish needle grass. 'Since yuh grandfada can't do it, it nuh get done.'

'That's really sad,' was all I could say, as mottled gravestones were revealed under Tony's flashing machete. Eventually a small tombstone emerged from the brush. Its edges had already crumbled away and couch grass grew from the central space where flowers were meant to grow, had the grave been properly tended. My lips moved as I read the inscription:

*Melba Florence James*
*Beloved wife, mother and grandmother*
*1902-1969*

Tony hung back at a respectful distance as I cleared away the weeds, and I discovered a glass vase in which I placed the wild flowers that I'd gathered on our way to the graveyard. Then I knelt down at the edge of her grave and took a deep breath.

'Oh, Grandma,' I whispered, 'I hope wherever you are, everything is alright with you. I went to England after you died and this is the first time I've come back to our island since. I hated it at first, because I had to live in the same house as the ugly Satan devil man. I know you would not have liked that at all. But it's okay, he's long dead now. Miss Violet died too, Grandma. I'm sorry to be the one to be telling you this. Her life was hard, but she's at peace now. She believed she would live on in heaven and, if such a place exists, I'm sure that's where you are, and perhaps Miss Violet is there with you, after all. But not him. The ugly Satan devil man treated Miss Violet very badly, Grandma, and he treated Patricia even worse. It caused her no end of trouble, but she seems to be through the worst of it now. At least, I hope so.' I felt tears starting to come and I wiped them away with the back of my hand. 'Clifton and Sonny are fine, though. They're both very clever, handsome young men. Oh, and I nearly forgot – Miss Violet's last children are twin girls. Doretta and Barbette. I thought you'd be really happy to hear that we have twins in the family.' I paused and looked at Grandma Melba's grave as if I could see through the weeds and earth into another realm, where she was listening to me. I imagined I could see her lovely gentle face, and how good it felt when she smiled. I was trying not to mention Miss Blossom, but I felt it had to be said. 'I'm sure you know that Grandpa Sippa married Miss Blossom,' I continued, 'he needed someone to look after him once you were gone. I hope you don't mind too much. I still miss you every day, Grandma. I don't really know how to stop missing you. I want to believe that you know all the things I've told you already. Maybe you do. I love you, Grandma Melba, I always will. And one day, when my time comes to leave this earth, it would be lovely to think I will be reunited with you somewhere.' I stood up and dusted my knees off and looked around for Tony, who was standing in the shade of a dogwood tree, watching me.

Seeing that I was finished, he walked over. 'Miss Melba was a sweet woman,' he said.

'She certainly was,' I agreed.

I started to walk back the way we came, following the path we'd made through the long grass. 'I was wondering if you could take me to see Dorcas?' I said. 'We were such good friends, but unfortunately, once I got to England, I didn't write to her as I'd promised.' I looked round at Tony. 'I'm embarrassed, now that I'm here, and worried that she won't want to see me.'

'I see her all de time, man, and mi kyan tell yuh now, Erna, Dorcas would dead fi see yuh.'

He walked past me and led the way. When we reached a fork in the path, we took a different track from the one we'd followed from Grandpa's house.

'I don't remember those!' I said with some astonishment as a low mountain range appeared over the tree line. The entire geography of the place seemed different.

'Well, they've always been there,' Tony laughed. 'Dem is the Porus Mountains.'

'I don't know what's the matter with my memory, so much about this place just doesn't look familiar any more. And look,' I cried suddenly, 'how did the parish tank get so small? Come on, that was a real big tank, Tony, really huge!'

'Same ting we talk about yesterday, man. When yuh little, every ting look big and when yuh big tings nuh look so big any more. The Porus Mountains dem was big doah and dem still big!' he laughed.

After about half an hour of trudging along the dirt track a small ramshackle house appeared in a clearing. As we got closer, I saw a woman, her hair in three old-fashioned plaits, seated on a large grey tarpaulin surrounded by a group of children. I counted six in all. The woman and the children were shelling dried corn. It was the children who spotted us first, and all but the smallest got up and started running towards us.

'Mama, Mama, is Uncle Tony, is Uncle Tony!' screeched a barefooted boy dressed in yard clothes.

Moments later I was standing in front of the woman, who was on her feet now, and we leant into each other and hugged for a long time.

'Dorcas, I don't know what to say,' I cried.

We stood for a while just holding each other's hands. When we parted we looked at each other. I didn't know what she made of me, but it was hard to see how worn down my friend looked.

'You look good,' I said.

She laughed out loud at this. 'Erna, dere's no need fa yuh to lie to me,' she said. 'But yuh sure is looking good yuhself mi see, yuh got big, girl!'

'Thanks!' I said, uncertain about the compliment. 'I have to say how sorry I am that I didn't write to you.'

'Erna, mi just glad to see yuh again,' Dorcas said, 'mi nevah tink seh de day would com. Some people come back often and some nevah come back. Dats ow life stay,' she added with a sigh.

'And who are all these little people?' I asked.

'Dem is all mine,' Dorcas said. 'God bless mi wit a big brood, but im figet to give mi one decent fada fi dem.'

I was trying to work out how she could have become a mother of six already, but there they all were. I wondered what miracle might need to occur to give Dorcas's children more of a chance in life than she had. Dorcas was clearly not given to self-pity, though, and there was something about her that had remained strong and undiminished. I looked over at Tony who was busy playing with the children. Dorcas followed my gaze.

'How many children yuh ave, Erna?' she asked.

'I'm afraid I have not been blessed in that way, Dorcas,' I said. 'At least not yet. But I haven't met that special someone, if such a person even exists, and anyway, I'm not sure I have the patience to be a mum. I think teaching kids might be enough for me.'

'Lard, Erna,' Dorcas cried, 'talkin bout coming a teacher, you doing good fa yuhself, sista!'

'Yes, I suppose I am,' I smiled. 'But I can see how good you are with your children, and how much you love them.'

Dorcas smiled a tired smile. 'Mi not saying it easy, Erna, but despite everyting mi can't imagine life without dem. But I don't mind telling yuh, Erna, after dat last little one born,' she said, pointing to the baby boy sitting on the tarpaulin, 'mi ask de doctor down a Black Hill Hospital to tie off mi tubes. And mi done wit man, Erna! Mi nuh lucky wit dem.'

'I think maybe I'm the same,' I laughed.

I gave my friend another hug and reached into my backpack and dug out an envelope, which I folded in half and tucked into Dorcas's hand.

'It's not much, Dorcas, and I hope you don't mind, but I hope it's a help.'

'Erna, yuh don't know how much it will help,' she said in a voice full of emotion.

Tony seemed to be happy to carry on playing with the kids, so we went inside her shack, where she offered me water mixed with cane sugar in a tin cup. I accepted it gratefully. Then we chatted at length about all the people who had left the village; who had moved to other parts of the island; who was living in America and who was living in Canada. Who was married, who had children, who did not. Who had become famous and who had died.

'Mi did sorry to hear seh Miss Violet dead,' Dorcas said. 'Both of mi parents dem dead, one after de other about three years ago.'

'Well, I'm sorry to hear of your loss too, Dorcas,' I said. 'I'm going to try and turn over a new leaf, though. I will keep in touch from now on, and, if it's okay with you, I will send you a little something when I can. Oh, by the way, I left a suitcase of children's clothing with Miss Blossom. It might be worth going to see what she's willing to part with, it's not like she has any grandchildren to give them to.'

With that we stood up and hugged again, before walking outside, where I bid Dorcas farewell. I couldn't promise to see her again, because I didn't know when, or even *if* I would be coming back.

I was still pondering this as Tony and I made our way back to the village. There was still one more person I wanted to see before I left the island. When we got back to Grandpa Sippa's house I found another small crowd had gathered and Miss Blossom was handing out the things I had brought with me to all and sundry. Thankfully, I managed to salvage the cotton pajamas I had bought for Grandpa and the three very nice shirts I'd bought for my father – for I still planned to visit him.

I mentioned this to Grandpa when Peter brought him out to the verandah. I also told him a little about life in England and some of my future plans. Grandpa Sippa mostly responded with a simple, 'Dat is good, Erna.' I was worried by how weak he seemed to be and how much difficulty talking caused him. When the sun began to set, Peter took him back inside. I wondered how long he had left before he would be joining Grandma Melba in that peaceful, overgrown graveyard.

# Chapter 48

I spent another uncomfortable night in the baking heat of the spare room and woke early again. After a makeshift breakfast on the verndah that Peter kindly prepared for me, Tony appeared. I was keen to get going, so after a cup of coffee, we left for my father's house before the rest of the household had emerged. Tony drove as fast as his truck would go, as if he was as eager to get there as I was. It was a hair-raising journey and by the time we pulled up outside my father's store I felt like I'd spent two and a half hours inside a tumble dryer. My father was sitting on the verandah nursing a soft drink. He stood up and peered through the truck windows, which we'd closed as we approached his village to keep the dust out. When I stepped from the cab, he looked like he was going to fall over.

'Lawd God, Erna, a how you come frighten mi soh!' he exclaimed. He removed his trademark baseball cap as if its removal would help him to be certain it was me he was seeing. 'Why yuh nuh tell mi seh yuh a come, man? As God a mi witness mi nevah expect to see you hereso again! A wen yuh come?'

'Morning,' I said. 'It's been a long time! I was in the mountains for a day and then I stopped in the village with my grandfather. And now, here I am.'

'Well, Lawd, mi glad to see yuh, man,' he said, giving me a great big bear hug.

My father was still tall and still handsome and little seemed to have changed about his appearance, apart from a small bald patch, which was revealed when he removed his baseball cap. He was dressed in linen trousers and a bold flower-print shirt.

'Tony, come and meet my father,' I said. He stepped away from the side of the truck where he'd been leaning and walked towards us. 'This is Tony, my cousin,' I said

'How yuh duh, sarh,' Tony said, as they shook hands.

'Come, come, sit down,' my father said, gesturing to a wooden table and three chairs at the front of the store. Smoke rose from behind the store and curled along its side, and the unmistakable smell of barbecuing chicken and fish permeated the air, along with the pungent scent of green island wood.

'That smells good!' I said, sitting down next to my father.

'De shop turn house now and a hereso Hazel she stay wit har bwoy pickney,' my father said, looking over his shoulder at the store. 'Is she round back a mek barbecue chicken and grill fish fa market. A little business she a do fi help harself and har pickney.'

A small boy appeared from round the back of the store and my father immediately dispatched him to get us some drinks.

'Nathan, run and ask yuh mada for soda for yuh auntie.' He looked at Tony. 'Driver, yuh want someting fi drink?'

'Soda good for mi too, sarh.'

'Two soda, and mek it quick, bwoy!'

Nathan ran off at speed towards the back of the store.

'So how is life down here?' I asked.

'Same as yuh find us, Erna. Wi nuh always get de rain when wi need it and dat can cause problems for de crop and de animals. But still wi kyaan complain down hereso too much, cause some part a de island ave problem worse dan us and mi still a supply de government with limestone, so wi better off dan most.'

As we drank our sodas, my father explained that, unlike my old village, his village was still a bustling place, although the majority of his children had left and just two of my half-sisters remained. Hazel was living in the shop with her son, and Adana was still living in the house with Miss Iris and my father – when he chose to be there. Alvita, who was the feistiest of the girls, had had the good fortune to meet a wanderlust Australian schoolteacher who had instantly fallen in love with her and whisked her off to his country. 'No, sarh, mi nevah hear one striking word from har again from de day she left dis place,' my father said, with a slow shake of his head.

All but one of his sons were now living in America, apparently, apart from Elsworth, the son my father had had at the age of fifteen, who was still living in the village. It seemed that Elsworth had never quite managed to do anything with his life. The little ganja farm that he'd started in the nearby bushlands had been discovered by the police after a tip-off and burnt to the ground. But my father seemed resigned to his eldest son's failures, given that the rest of his children were doing alright for themselves.

'Hinglan look like she a treat yuh good, Erna,' he said.

'I can't complain. It took me a few years to get used to the cold winters and their strange ways,' I laughed, 'but I'm settled now. That's not to say it doesn't have its problems, but I've made a life for myself there.'

'Mi did sorry fi hear seh Violet dead,' my father said out of the blue, resting a big hand on mine, 'she was young still.'

I gulped and shifted my hand out of my father's reach and looked directly ahead of me as I fought back tears of anger.

'But dat a how life go sometime,' he added, unperturbed.

I made no response. I had plenty to say to my father about my mother's death, but now didn't feel like the right time.

'Com an seh hello to Miss Iris,' my father said, standing up, 'she wi be shock fi see yuh!'

Tony and I followed him along the path towards his big house, the two men chatting about cars like they'd known each other for years. When we reached the front porch, the shock was all mine: Miss Iris's weight had ballooned so much that she appeared stuck to the same old wooden stool that I remembered, except now it could hardly be seen beneath her bulk.

'How are you, Miss Iris?' I asked, walking over to her.

'It's Erna dat?' she replied. 'Nathan tell mi seh yuh over shop, but mi did tink de bwoy talking foolishness. Come here, gal, let me look pon yuh good,' she added, grabbing my hand. She scrutinised me with what appeared to be her one good eye, the other being milky and blind. 'Yuh look good, Erna,' she said, 'but yuh fat eenh! A wah dem a feed yuh pon up in Hinglan?'

'Thank you, Miss Iris.' I smiled, even though the fat comments were starting to wear a little thin. 'Hinglan life is treating me okay!'

The door behind Miss Iris opened and a young woman nearly as fat as she was came out.

'Hello, Erna,' she said, 'nice to see yuh come back a yard.'

'Adana, get yuh sista one soda,' Miss Iris said, before I'd even had a chance to reply, 'and one for this striking fella here! Who dis?' she added.

'This is my cousin Tony,' I said.

'Lard, im is one good lookin fella,' Miss Iris chuckled.

Adana returned with the sodas, including one for my father

'How long yuh a plan to stay wit us, Erna?' he asked, as he joined Miss Iris sitting on the porch. 'We have plenty room we kyan put yuh up in.'

'Well, I was thinking of going to Santa Fe and booking myself into a hotel for the night,' I said. I was secretly looking forward to spending a day at Black Sands Beach and enjoying some hotel lifestyle before I left.

'Yuh nuh fi waste money like dat, Erna, when mi ave plenty room here! You too, Tony,' my father added.

'Oh, no, don't worry about me, sarh,'Tony said. 'I want to go and visit with my sister down the road. It's longtime I don't see har.' Then he turned to look at me. 'I will come back tomorrow to pick yuh up, Erna,' he said, standing up. 'Tank yuh for the soda, sarh,' he added, 'it nice to meet with yuh folks.' He smiled, and with a wave of his hand he strode off back down the road, leaving me alone with my father, Miss Iris and Adana.

'Oh, I almost forgot,' I said, dipping into my backpack, 'I brought you these.' I handed him the shirts I'd bought him. 'And here's something for you, Miss Iris,' I added, handing her the plain blue dress that I'd grabbed before Miss Blossom had given everything else away. Luckily it was an extra-large size, and she seemed very pleased with it.

My father handed the shirts to Miss Iris and stepped down from the porch. 'Mi have to go about some business now, but mi will see yuh later, Erna,' he said. And with a wave of his hand, he was gone.

I wasn't sure that I wanted to stay the night here at all, but now it looked like I had no choice. My main concern, apart from the discomfort I was feeling about revisiting this place of so many mixed memories, was Grandpa Sippa – he'd looked so frail the night before and I yearned to get back to him. But then I asked myself why I had even come here in the first place? Was it really just to see my father, or was it something else? Either way, it was too late for regrets and I reconciled myself to spending the night with him and his family. Miss Iris looked like she was going to sit on the porch forever, so I decided to go for a walk to kill some time before my father returned.

I wandered across my father's land towards the village, trying to enjoy the natural beauty of the place with its mountain backdrop and fast-flowing river glinting in the distance, but as I walked the words my mother had spoken to Auntie Madge about her encounter with my father jumped into my brain like an angry lyric: *him just throw me down*. I had spent years venting my anger at Patsy's father for abusing her, and all that time she had wished that she had a father like mine. Now, here I was in this most beautiful of settings having to accept that perhaps my father was no better than the ugly Satan devil man. In that moment, it occured to me that I didn't really know anything about my father. In the short time I'd spent with him, it was clear that everyone *saw* him as a kind and considerate man. All I really *knew* was that he had impregnated my mother, and that for the first thirteen years of my life I'd had no knowledge of his existence. I desperately wanted to ask him about the circumstances of my conception, but I was unsure whether I could be direct with my questions. What if he refused to answer, or worse, asked me to leave? After all, a part of me still wanted to know him, despite everything.

When I got back to the house, Miss Iris informed me that my father would not be back until later that evening, so I resigned myself to sitting on the porch with her and Adana and chewing the fat. But the talk waned as the sun set and the dusk deepened into night and still he didn't return, so with a yawning 'Good night' to Miss Iris and Adana, I took myself off to the bedroom that they had made ready for me and fell immediately into a deep sleep.

The following morning, I woke to the smell of frying food coming from the kitchen. I quickly dressed and found my father outside on the porch. He looked up from his breakfast and smiled at me.

'Papa, can we have a chat after breakfast?' I said.

'Sure ting, Erna,' he said, wiping the grease from his face with a red handkerchief. 'Mi have to go over to Frome, so we can talk while we walk.'

Once we had got going, I could hardly hold in the subject that had been weighing on my mind. 'This might sound strange,' I said, as we made our way towards the hill that marked the southern boundary of his land, 'but you know, I never really got to know my mother properly. I mean, who she really was. And I don't feel like I know who you are, either.'

My father looked at me curiously. Clearly no one, and most certainly no child of his, had ever spoken to him in this way before. But now I'd started I had to keep going in case the moment was lost.

'So, how did you meet my mother?' I asked, as casually as I could.

He stopped walking, tilted his baseball cap back and scratched his head. 'She was working for dis family, the Dees I tink dem name, helping dem wit dem children. I would see her every morning when I ride my horse out to the land. Man, she was young and pretty yuh see!'

'So, how did you come to have a baby with her?'

'Mi did beg har a few times, but she always run weh! Soh, one morning mi waylay har and mi catch har!'

His reply was so frank that I was taken aback. I hadn't expected him to be quite so candid about what was basically the rape of a child.

'Your mada was a pretty young gal,' he continued, smiling at the memory. Then his expression changed to one of sadness. 'Mi sorry to hear dat she gone, Erna, it must be hard for you,' he said.

'Yes, it was hard. It still is. Did you know she took her own life?'

He looked down at the dusty earth beneath his feet. 'Mi did hear someting fi dat effect,' he said. 'Lard, that is a terrible ting, Erna. De poor woman mussa been in some awful pain fi do such a ting.'

'I don't think she ever got over what happened to her,' I said. He looked up at this and I thought I saw a flicker of guilt in his eyes, but I pressed on. 'Did you know she had a baby before me?' I said angrily. He shook his head. 'By another man, who also chased her down?' My voice began to crack with the intensity of my emotions. 'She was only a child. Imagine if that happened to me, or one of your other daughters, at such a young age. Do you know, Papa, she was never able to show me one iota of love because I was a constant reminder, every striking day, of what you did to her.'

My father looked away, allowing his eyes to rest on the mountains in the distance. Then he turned back to me. 'Dat was de way tings was back then, Erna,' he said. 'Mi not proud of what mi did do, but it nuh someting me can change. Yuh can either accept it, or yuh can let it nyam you up, but you kyaan change it, girl.'

'But haven't you ever thought that what you did to Violet was wrong?' I asked.

He shook his head. 'I kyaan change how tings happen all dem years back, chile, and, God knows, mi glad seh yuh is me daughter still. Me kyaan be sorry for dat.'

I saw compassion in his eyes now and, even though anger was still boiling in my chest, I knew that my father had spoken the simple truth as he saw it. It may have been a crude and brutal truth, but in a sense he was right: whatever the circumstances were that had led to my birth, I was here, now, and I was grateful to be alive, and my anger would change nothing. And I had to accept that my father wasn't a sophisticated or educated man; he came from a very different world to the one I now inhabited. I took a deep breath and exhaled slowly, waiting until I felt I had enough control of my feelings to continue the conversation.

'This has been a hard thing to hear, Papa,' I said, finally. 'You have to know that I feel very angry about what happened to my mother, it literally ate up her entire life. I have never known anyone to be as unhappy as she was. But I don't want it to do the same to me, because I *cannot* regret my own existence. It's true that you can't change what you did, but I wish you'd found it in your heart to apologise to her. Who knows? It may have made the difference to her living a happier life. She may even have still been alive today.'

My father remained quiet for some time and then he too took a deep breath and pointed towards the top of the hill.

'Come, Erna,' he said, 'mi want fi show you someting.'

I scrambled after him as he climbed at speed through the stony scrub towards the summit. When I caught up with him, he was standing on a rocky outcrop, shading his eyes with his hand and gazing out across the flatlands that stretched towards the coast. He turned to look at me and smiled when he saw that I was panting with the exertion of climbing the steep hill.

'Hinglan life mek yuh soft, Erna,' he laughed.

I had to bend over, hands on my thighs, to catch my breath. After a moment, I stretched upright and looked at him, then I followed his gaze towards the misty horizon.

'Mi fada was a hard man,' he said, not looking at me, but staring towards the shrouded ocean. 'He use to beat me bad. Beat me for any damn ting I did wrong, and mi was always gettin tings wrong,' he added with a wry chuckle. 'But him did teach mi de rules, Erna, de basic rules of life. Wi run tings, tings nuh run wi, yuh understan what ahm saying?'

I nodded, still breathing hard. I did understand.

'An because of him teachin, mi run dis whole dyam place,' he said, encompassing the extent of his land with a sweep of his arm.

Apart from the gentle breeze and the thin cries of the swifts that swooped above us, the whole wide world was silent. I breathed deep of the clean island air and gazed about me: at the river curling far below and the smoke rising from behind my father's house in the distance. We are in control of our own destiny. It was a profound thought that stayed with me long after I had left my island and returned to England.

By the time we'd got back from Frome, it was late afternoon and Tony was sitting on the verandah chatting to Miss Iris and Adana, who were shelling peas into a large steel bowl. As soon as he saw me, he stood up and walked down the steps towards us.

'Are yuh ready to get going, Erna?' he said.

'Yes,' I replied, 'I'm really worried about Grandpa, he was in such a bad way when we left.'

Tony nodded, and with a wave to Miss Iris and a nod to my father, he climbed into his truck. I turned and looked at my father, conscious of the unsettled emotions inside me. He smiled.

'Mi proud to have such a strong daughter,' he said. 'You know how to say tings straight, an dat is a gift fa sure. Mi know mi don't need to worry bout yuh in de world, Erna.'

He held his hand out to me. For a second I hesitated, then I took it and he pulled me into his arms and hugged me.

'Thank you,' I said. 'I'm glad I came back to see you.'

'Me too, Erna,' he said.

He held the truck door open for me and I climbed in next to Tony and wound the window down.

'Bye, Papa,' I said.

'Walk good, Erna,' he replied.

Tony started the engine with a roar and I barely had time to wave to my father and Miss Iris before we disappeared down the track in a cloud of dust.

# Chapter 49

Miss Blossom was sitting in her rocking chair on the verandah when we arrived back at Grandpa's house in the early afternoon. She watched as we clambered from Tony's truck and walked towards her. There was an unnatural stillness in the air that seemed to permeate everything. Even the usually noisy sows and chickens were quiet. The only movement came from a doctor bird that hovered in the slanting light as it nosed into a red poinciana, its wings humming so fast they were just a shimmering blur.

'Mi glad yuh get back safe, Erna,' Miss Blossom said, as we climbed on to the verandah, 'but, chile, mi sarry fi tell yuh seh, yuh nuh come back fi good news. Yuh Grandfada nat in a good way at all. De doctor come out yesterday. Him give im a few days at most. Pneumonia, de doctor seh, an nutting kyan be done.'

I dropped my backpack and sat down next to her. Miss Blossom stretched out her hand, which I took in mine.

'Is it okay if I go and see him?' I asked.

She gave my hand a squeeze, then looked away, shaking her head as tears came to her eyes. 'Yes, chile,' she said, her head still turned away from me. 'He would like to see yuh, fa sure.'

371

I excused myself and found my way to the bedroom at the back of the house. The shutters were closed, but I could still make out Grandpa's form in the dim light. Peter had washed and shaved him and dressed him in the cotton pyjamas I'd brought. He was standing just inside the door when I entered the room.

'Mi wi do dat, Miss Erna,' Peter said, bringing over a chair, which he placed next to Grandpa's bedside. I thanked him and, when he left the room, I set about moving the chair as close to Grandpa Sippa as possible. I reached out and took his scrawny hand in my own. Grandpa's breathing was laboured and his eyes remained closed.

'Grandpa, it's me, Erna. I'm back again,' I whispered, 'but it looks like you're planning on leaving us already.' I had intended not to cry, but the tears rolled silently down my cheeks as I spoke and I couldn't keep the tremble out of my voice. I wasn't certain, but I thought I detected the tiniest squeeze of my hand from Grandpa. 'I am so glad you waited for me to come back home to see you, Grandpa,' I continued, 'thank you so much. Eighty-seven years, Grandpa, what a journey you've had! I can't tell you how happy I am to have been born with you and Melba as my grandparents. You've been the best grandfather I could have wished for, and I wish I could spend more time with you now, but I know you have unfinished business with Grandma Melba. You two have a lot of catching up to do and she is going to love having you around.'

Grandpa let out a deep, ragged sigh and I rested my other hand on his forehead.

'It's okay, Grandpa Sippa, I don't want you to go, but that's just me being selfish. I know it's time and it's fine, Grandpa. We'll all be okay. And you and Grandma Melba will live on in my heart for ever. Just you remember to give her a big hug for me when you finally catch up with her.'

. . .

Before I left my island again, I returned one last time to Grandma Melba's grave to let her know that her beloved Sippa had left to join her. As my return flight was only two days away, I was unable to stay with Miss Blossom and the rest of the villagers who had turned out to pay their respects to Grandpa Sippa during the nine-night ceremony. But I was able to say a proper goodbye to those I loved this time, and I especially thanked Tony for looking after me so well. He even took it upon himself to drive me all the way back to Monica's for my last night on the island, although I suspected that was as much to see Monica's housekeeper, Angela, as it was to help me out. Monica seemed delighted to see me again and welcomed me into her home as if I'd been away for a month, not a few days. It was lovely to spend one more night in her beautiful house and to enjoy the pleasures of my island without any stress.

In the morning, Conrad took me to the airport and, almost as soon as I'd arrived, I was gone again. But this time the journey back to London felt right. This time, there was no fear. I was returning to England with my heart sad, but full of good memories, especially of Grandpa Sippa and Grandma Melba, and all my huge extended family, and the beautiful paradise that is my island.

As soon as I'd cleared customs at Heathrow, I went in search of a phone box and, when I found one without a queue, I took a ten-pence coin from my purse and called Jennifer. After several rings she answered.

'It's me,' I said, 'I'm home.'

# Acknowledgements

My first debt of gratitude goes to Margaret Busby OBE. When I first mentioned to Margaret well over twenty years ago that I liked writing, she told me, 'Then, Yvonne, you must write.' Over the years, whenever we met up, she would gently ask, 'How's the writing going?' It mostly wasn't. However, without a hint of nagging, her gentle encouragement never wavered.

When Margaret suggested that I might like to submit a piece of writing for her *New Daughters of Africa* anthology, I was totally astonished and utterly delighted. I was more than a fan, having followed her wonderful career and having been gifted a copy of the first *Daughters of Africa* by my then-teenage daughter. Margaret Busby is, simply, one of the most generous women I know when it comes to encouraging budding writers to believe in themselves. I join my fellow contributors to *New Daughters of Africa* in saluting her.

In order to try and write this novel, I gave up full-time work and rewired myself. Heartfelt thanks goes to Hud Saunders, who appeared at the very time I made my decision. He knows how to teach and I thank him whole-heartedly for patiently mentoring me through this process. Like Margaret, Hud believed I had something. Twice he put me on the stage at the Queens Park Book Festival, and he called me a writer! He spent many hours working with me on developing my second, third and fourth drafts. He often knew what I wanted to say when I couldn't quite figure out how to say it, and he never failed to let me know what was working and what wasn't.

Big shout out to my first readers: my brother Andi McLean; my niece Zoe McLean; friends Penny Layne, Sally

375

Oldfield, Elizabeth Lowton, Becky Armstrong. All came back with the same constructive criticisms: 'The first few pages could work, but the rest reads like a travel guide.' When I returned to the manuscript, I decided to run with the idea of developing the story from those first few pages. Thank you to Verna Wilkins, who cast a writers' eye over the first page or two of my manuscript and reminded me of the importance of bringing my characters to life on the page. My sister Carly, friends Ruth and Wendy, thank you for believing I could do this. Every family member and friend who has supported me through the process, I appreciate you all.

Another big shout out goes to Mary Daly, my fellow writing mentee, who patiently listened and critically commented on every new section I wrote.

To the two halves of the Jamaican Massives – Sharon McLeggan and Sandra Williams, all the way from Harrow and Toronto, respectively – our daily patois talk made me laugh and cry. You kept it real and live as I attempted to use some of our lyrical language in my manuscript. And to Carolyn Cooper: your help with the patois spelling was invaluable. Nuff thanks.

Special thanks go to Candida Lacey, Publishing Director, and the team at Myriad Editions, for so boldly making the decision to publish my novel. Candida, thank you for that fateful email which has become my most precious thing. Thank you to Emma Dowson, publicist, and Vicki Heath Silk, editor, for your patience in working with a novice writer. Vicki, your eye for detail is much appreciated.

Finally, I must not forget all my fictional characters, who took over my head and propelled me to write this story. I hope that it captures the silent voices of many who have been impacted by a separation or transition for which they were ill-prepared. Immigrant children, whatever their journeys. Anyone who has experienced loss, whatever that might be. I celebrate every one of you, with your drive to exist and not be victims. You're all unsung heroines and heroes.

Sign up to our mailing list at
**www.myriadeditions.com**
Follow us on Facebook, Twitter and Instagram

# About the author

**Yvonne Bailey-Smith** was born in Jamaica and came to the UK as a teenager. She trained and worked first as a social worker before becoming a psychotherapist. She is also a Water Aid Supporter and passionate about providing clean water and sanitation in developing countries. She is the mother of three children: novelist Zadie Smith; actor, musician and children's book author Ben Bailey Smith; and lyricist and writer LucSkyz.